MAD SISTERS OF ESI

MAD SISTERS OF ESI

TASHAN MEHTA

DAW BOOKS
New York

Copyright © 2023 by Tashan Mehta

New material copyright © 2025 by Tashan Mehta

All rights reserved. Copying or digitizing this book for storage, display, or distribution in any other medium is strictly prohibited. For information about permission to reproduce selections from this book, please contact permissions@astrapublishinghouse.com.

This is a work of fiction. Names, characters, places, and incidents are products of the author's imagination or are used fictitiously. Any resemblance to actual events, locales, or persons, living or dead, is entirely coincidental.

Jacket illustration by Upamanyu Bhattacharyya

Jacket design by Adam Auerbach

DAW Book Collectors No. 1986

DAW Books
An imprint of Astra Publishing House
dawbooks.com
DAW Books and its logo are registered trademarks of Astra Publishing House.

Printed in the United States of America

Library of Congress Cataloging-in-Publication Data

Names: Mehta, Tashan, author.
Title: Mad sisters of Esi / Tashan Mehta.
Description: First edition. | New York : DAW Books, 2025. | Series: DAW Book Collectors ; no. 1986 | Summary: "Susanna Clarke's Piranesi meets Italo Calvino's If On a Winter's Night a Traveler in this stunning meta fantasy about the power of stories, belief, and sisterhood. Myung and her sister Laleh are the sole inhabitants of the whale of babel-until Myung flees, beginning an adventure that will spin her through dreams, memories, and myths"-- Provided by publisher.
Identifiers: LCCN 2025010205 (print) | LCCN 2025010206 (ebook) | ISBN 9780756420062 (hardcover) | ISBN 9780756420079 (ebook)
Subjects: LCGFT: Fantasy fiction. | Novels.
Classification: LCC PR9499.4.M45 M33 2025 (print) | LCC PR9499.4.M45 (ebook) | DDC 823.92--dc23/eng/20250311
LC record available at https://lccn.loc.gov/2025010205
LC ebook record available at https://lccn.loc.gov/2025010206

First edition: August 2025
10 9 8 7 6 5 4 3 2 1

*For those who kept my courage safe when I couldn't find it,
and who built me a raft when they learned I couldn't swim*

Contents

Myung's Diaries	1
WHALE OF BABEL	3
Finding What We Lost: Wandering the Museum of Collective Memory	31
OJDA	41
Mad Yet?: The Found Pages of Famous Explorer Myung Ting	139
ESI	149
What of Fairy Tales That Sing?	353
WHALE OF BABEL, AGAIN	359
Myung's Map	395
Acknowledgments	399
Ephemera	401

Myung's Diaries

No. CMXLII [Unpublished]

The problem with circular stories is that it is difficult to know where to begin. This story is circular, although no one told me this when I first entered it. A part of me wishes that they had; perhaps then I would have never traveled through it.

But as always, in moments of doubt, I find myself speaking to my sister. Laleh is not here—we have been separated for more than a century—but her memory does not fade. She answers as clearly as if we have never been apart, as if she is sitting beside me on this mad island, watching a painted sun shine in a blue sky. *Myung,* she says, *if you're the one telling this, then it must begin with us. Start with the whale, silly.*

So, imagine—close your eyes—another universe growing inside this one. A baby universe shaped like a giant whale, with asteroids and dwarf planets stuck to its skin. This universe is not filled with planets or stars or cosmic squids, but with interconnected chambers that Laleh and I call "worlds," some the size of a solar system, others as large as a galaxy. Academics call it the "whale of babel."

Now look at two specks living in this cosmic vastness. They float in a chamber near to the whale's heart. Peer closer and you'll find that these specks are two girls, their hands loosely clasped. Twins, you think, for they look almost—but not quite—identical.

They are the whale's only people. We begin with them.

WHALE OF BABEL

Laws of the Chambers

As recorded by Laleh and Myung, keepers of the whale of babel
In dedication to Great Wisa, Creator and First Friend

~

1. The whale of babel is a creature of boundless generosity. It is filled with many worlds, 780 of which have been recorded.
2. Every world has at least one door that leads you to a new chamber. The first door was discovered by Myung, ~~the second keeper~~ ~~the first keeper~~[*] one of the two keepers of the whale of babel.
3. The doors are varied in appearance. The first door was shaped like a crack in a rock; the second looked like the shadow of a tree.
4. Doors do not like to be found.
5. Doors do not like to be traveled through.
6. Door hunting is an art, and Myung has perfected it.
7. The splendors of each chamber are recorded by Laleh on heart-shaped leaves so that they may be witnessed.
8. New chambers appear all the time, for the whale's wonders are infinite.

---

[*] The first cancellation was made by Myung, who wanted to be called "first keeper"; the second cancellation was made by Laleh, who refused to be called "second keeper." The dispute was settled by agreeing upon equal status, as reflected in the phrase "one of the two keepers."

Fear

The first time I realize my sister wants to leave, we are in the White World.

I call it that because it is all you can see when you first fall out of the door—swathes of white. The ground's pull here is soft, bouncy almost, and we tumble gently into the milky mist. It covers our vision like a thin film, but I am unconcerned. The whale would never hurt us. As we bounce and tumble, I reach for my sister's hand. Only when we clasp does the white clear a little, and we see what this world is made of.

Below us is a landscape of ochre and purple red. When we touch the ground, we discover it is sometimes watery, sometimes made of brittle ice that easily cracks. But it doesn't matter; we are nearly weightless here. Myung's fingers slip from mine. She disappears into the mist and then reappears, thoughtful.

In most chambers, we cannot see the ceiling or the walls—the rooms are too large. Doors themselves do not stick to the walls. They position themselves wherever they like. (The door to enter this world, for instance, was in the sky.) But we have never seen a world as obscured as this one. I can smell its freshness.

I know, then, that we are in a chamber that is still forming. I can tell from the turn of her head that Myung has realized this too. I bounce into the mist, away from her, and stay with my awe. I am watching a world being born. For the first time in my life, I am witness to what Great Wisa, our creator and first friend, must have seen.

I listen for the whale's song. I hear only a hush, as if it is holding its breath.

When I look for Myung, I see her crouched on the purple-red plain, her head bent. I tumble toward her. She is staring at a pool of yellow water. When I peer over her shoulder, I find her reflection gazing at me: the wide eyes, the pointed chin, the small furrow between her eyebrows that means she is thinking. I feel a surge of love. My sister. My other half.

Myung touches our reflections, watching the water ripple out and our likeness disappear. She asks: *Do you think there are more of us?*

And I feel an emotion I have never felt before.

It strikes first in my heart, clenching it, and then sinks its fingers into my stomach. I cannot breathe. My skin is clammy. The name for it arrives a few seconds later, flowering in my mind's eye fully formed, carrying its meaning with it—as if I have always known this emotion and its name, but only forgotten it.

FEAR. One syllable.

I do not know why I am afraid. *There are only two keepers of the whale of babel*, I whisper. *You and I. Great Wisa made it so.* Instinctively, I touch the back of her neck for comfort.

Myung contemplates my answer. Still staring at the pool, she searches for my fingers and clasps them. Her reflection smiles—a kind smile, a loving one—and my fear grows.

Choosing Fabrics: Imagining the Whale of Babel

Zoya, Mina, University of Mirabilia Diachronism Press, 89019.
Retrieved from the Museum of Collective Memory,
Corridor -| | |•--, Object XIIIIV

Of all the man-made wonders of the universe, nothing has fascinated academia more than the whale of babel. When we still believed in the dominance of logic, it was assumed this whale was mythical and that its many chambers were fairy tales. But it is now widely accepted that the whale exists, although no one can find it. We are left, then, with more questions than answers. Who is Wisa and why did she make the whale of babel? What is its origin story? And what, indeed, is the whale made *of*?

Several academics have ventured to answer this last question. Early theories believed the whale was like any other, made of muscle, flesh and bone. But this conclusion is too simplistic: it doesn't explain the whale's chambers or how it keeps growing in infinite proportions. Tribes of the arboreal faith say it is made of wood and grows as a tree does: layers of rings accumulated as years pass. Common theory propounds that it is made of stardust, growing from the suns that birth and flake in its belly. This is why it swims so well in the black sea;* it is made of the stuff of universes.

---

* The size of the black sea is also why it is so difficult to find the whale: the black sea is more vast than we can map or understand. Academics and storytellers who speak of the "edge of the black sea" do so only metaphorically; we do not know where that edge lies or if we will ever find it. It is unsurprising, then, that we may lose a great big whale, even one that is expanding and growing into a universe of its own.

Forget those theories for a moment. Remember that the whale is man-made, that Wisa is likely its creator. Don't think in broad natural strokes but in the tools a person may use.

Imagine the whale is made of fabric.

Agreed, this is not a romantic notion. It is not sleek or aesthetic. If you are imagining it now, you'll probably see a flaccid creature and not the whale baby-universe of wonder you were hoping for.

But fabrics offer us a unique possibility: they can be woven together. They are plural and singular, complex and simple. And our whale of babel, if nothing else, has been a symbol of this duality: a children's fairy tale that remains the greatest mystery of our universe.

So, imagine the whale of babel as made of three materials. The first is a more traditional material, close to what we know as "matter." This is a dense fabric that retains the shape it is given and is the essence of the heft in the whale. The second is a more pliable material, capable of changing its form. Professor Uoe calls this fabric "wish-giving"* and it is likely responsible for the formation of the chambers within the whale.

The third material, of course, is the fabric of time.

---

* The term is derived from a story in *Fairy Tales of Wisa*.

Great Wisa

I handle my fear by fleeing from it. So I usher Myung out of the White World and into a chamber with a floating island. There, we settle into our usual routine: Myung explores (that is, plays with the mud prawns living among the roots of the mangroves) and I study (that is, speak to the teal monkeys about their family structures and systems of power). For a while, everything is normal.

But at storytime (STORYTIME, three syllables, meaning to speak tales of the whale and Great Wisa) Myung asks again. It is as if we never ended the first conversation, as if the thought has been running in a loop in her head.

How do you know there aren't others? she insists. *There are two of us.*

Why? I ask desperately. *Have you seen anyone?*

She can't have. We spend all our time together, so I would have seen them too. But she doesn't answer immediately, as if she must think about it. When she does answer, she says *No* slowly, as if she is not sure it is the right word she is looking for, as if a *Yes* lurks behind it.

It irritates me.

You're being stubborn, I say, relishing the word we learned only recently. *Laleh.*

I ignore her, tidying my pile of heart-shaped leaves.

Sister. She scoots closer, turns my face toward hers, places my palm on her heart. *I feel it. It's a certainty in my chest, a, a . . . need that's pushing* to get out. *Laleh, I see hundreds of us. Thousands. As many of us as there are chambers.*

There is no one else. You must forget it.

I cannot.

You must.

I cannot. It lives in me—she presses my palm to her—*it won't come out.*

I know I am meant to ask, either in earnestness or anger, *what would you have me do?* But I don't dare. The fear is pushing its fingers down my throat, traveling through my veins. *Do you want to hear the story of Great Wisa?* I say instead. *Maybe it will help.*

For a moment, she looks like she will argue. Then she drops her head, a peace offering, and I choose the most special story we have to call my sister back to herself:

> In the beginning of beginnings, there was Great Wisa. She was born of the whale's heart and she roamed through its belly, carving its insides into many marvels. The whale and Wisa were dear friends, but as the whale grew larger and larger, Wisa grew smaller and smaller.
>
> "My friend," she said one day, "as you grow bigger, I cannot roam through all your chambers. So I will make for you a pair of sisters, wise and kind and fearless, to watch over what I have created. Where I cannot see, they shall be my eyes. Where I cannot walk, they shall be my legs. Look to them, and see you have not one friend, but many. Love them as you would love me."
>
> And so Wisa created two sisters and named them keepers of the whale of babel. The sisters opened their eyes to a new world and have spent their time seeking their maker.

I know Myung loves this story. We take turns to say it, lingering on our favorite line—*love them as you would love me*. It gives us shivers. It doesn't matter that the words come from our tongues and our lips. It is as if Great Wisa speaks through us, telling us what we already know, filling it with a bright white light.

When I finish the story now, I let the last word linger. The whale, whose song grew agitated when Myung and I argued, is humming gently. Myung is at peace again, her face iridescent.

But later I see her staring into a puddle. She is gazing at it intently, trying to recognize her reflection. I hear her whisper:

But where did Wisa come from?

Choosing Fabrics: Imagining the Whale of Babel

Zoya, Mina, University of Mirabilia Diachronism Press, 89019. Retrieved from the Museum of Collective Memory, Corridor -| | |•--, Object XIIIIV

A whale made of three fabrics: a fixed fabric, a wish-giving material and the fabric of time.

The first fabric is obvious—without it, the whale would have no mass; it would not exist in the black sea. The second, a wish-giving fabric, is more startling but not unheard of. Sailors have long spoken of seaweed that, when plucked, can twist and transform into whatever you ask of it. It can grant only small wishes, but it shows that shapeshifting is not new in the black sea.

The third fabric, however . . . It is this fabric that has enthralled us for centuries.

Imagine it. Time as a fabric. Imagine silk gathered in your arms, satin slithering down them. Crêpe draped over your elbow. Long gossamer cloths of time hanging in the whale's chambers like the forgotten ornaments of an old era, like the curtains that tumble down the sides of enormous palaces to flutter against diamond chandeliers. Imagine gossamer cobwebs hung across vast spaces, swimming with the colors of a diffused rainbow. Imagine touching time.

Sister

Myung has not always been my sister. We first met in the World of Bird and Leaf.

How do I describe those early days, before Myung and I were whole? I had woken up in a chamber filled with plants, some enormous and others tiny, and with birds that screeched their song across the sky. I woke up with nothing in my mind except the feel of grass beneath my fingers and a smell I did not recognize. A moment later, a name for it appeared in my mind's eye: WATER. Two syllables. I went in search of it.

My days were peaceful. The whale would sing to me, teaching me how to weave the broadleaves into baskets (BASKET, two syllables) for berries and nuts. Each day, it would hide gifts and then trill when I found them. My beloved, darling whale. I tried not to have a favorite gift—it seemed ungracious to the rest—but I did, of course. It was the down feather from a simurgh, fallen from its nest. It became my first quill.

I knew everything and nothing about the whale and Great Wisa. The contradiction didn't bother me. I wrote down my observations of this world on heart-shaped leaves. I measured my time in SLEEPS, for my writing stopped when my eyes closed and began again when they opened. Sometimes, I did nothing except watch the simurghs fly overhead or marvel at the giant palm trees that poked their fronds into clouds. Every moment of beauty felt made for me. It was the voice of Great Wisa, saying: *My friend, my keeper.*

One day, a shadow fell over me. It was a simurgh—not flying, but standing only a few feet away. I saw its beak first, golden and hooked, so big I could have climbed it. Then its ruby feathers, catching and trapping the light. Eyes, turquoise and kind. And then—

—perched on the creature's head—

—someone who looked like me.

And then my life truly began.

Later, I learned that Myung tried to climb the great palm trees. She climbed and fell, and it hurt her for a long time, but when it stopped hurting, she climbed again. One day, she reached farther than she had before, but her foot slipped and she fell again. This was when a simurgh caught her in its talons and carried her to its nest. *To eat me,* Myung said, but I didn't believe her; terrible things do not happen in the whale. Anyway, Myung charmed it and instead of becoming a meal, she and the simurgh turned friends.

Since then, Myung has flown to the top of the palm trees. She has eaten the fruit of the clouds. She has even seen the chamber stretch out below her, a tangle of leaves that ends on a border of a river basking like a long, lazy serpent in the sun. This I did believe: from the moment I saw her, perched on the simurgh's head, I knew my sister was meant for the exceptional.

There are no words for the joy I felt upon finding Myung. We chose our names together. I picked Laleh because I liked the calm of the syllables, their weight and rolling depth. She decided on Myung; she liked the way the "y" sounded, like you are an instrument struck and still ringing. We chose our names because of each other, for what use is a name if there is no one to say it?

We shared everything: food, words, knowledge. We talked till our throats hurt, reveling in speech (CONVERSATION, four syllables). We learned that we both knew of Great Wisa, creator and first friend. And, of course, we knew the whale. These truths rang deep in us, and saying them to each other made them truer.

Have you ever been lonely and not realized it until your loneliness was sated? Do you remember seeing your reflection for the first time and the uncanny feeling that accompanied it—of standing both outside yourself and inside? That is what Myung was like to me. In the vastness of the whale, in a bounty of shapes and sizes, I had found someone shaped like me.

―

It was Myung who found the first door, and who coaxed me through it. It was I who looked for heart-shaped leaves in each chamber and recorded what we saw with my quill. It is Myung who charms the creatures to do her bidding, but it is I who can hear the whale's song. To Myung, the whale remains silent, no matter how much she presses her ears to the ground or sits in absolute stillness. I am pleased by that, a pleasure that is quiet and shameful. I want Myung to hear our whale, but I also feel useful because she cannot.

In our third chamber, a new word appeared to me. SISTER, two syllables. Meaning to belong to and love forever. When I told Myung this, she took my hand and forgot there was a time before this word. But I remember. And because I remember, I can imagine a time after it.

She will leave me. My fear tells me so, even as I try not to listen.

Stranger

After our conversation about the people, Myung begins to change.

We are still in the World of the Floating Island, but now there are whole sleeps where I cannot find her. She keeps disappearing and will not tell me where.

Usually, my Myung wants to leave a chamber as soon as possible. *There are so many worlds*, she would plead. *A glut, a surfeit! Who would not leave to see them? Run from chamber to chamber to gather the whale's riches?* But now she does not ask to find the next door. I am left free to record the chamber meticulously, without her gargling loudly or sighing or kicking stones. I am left alone.

The gap between the Myung I know and the Myung she is becoming is widening. Two images that were once superimposed slide apart. I feel like there are secret chambers within my sister, bubbling into existence. She is expanding into a whale of her own.

Then I skitter away from the thought and take my fear with me.

Myung

Sometimes, Myung closes her eyes and pretends she's not from the whale. Crawls away from Laleh and hides. Holds her own body close. Imagines she has new eyes and no memories. Opens them and sees the world anew.

But it's never what she sees that strikes her. It's the sound. The whale of babel has a strange kinship to sound—it holds it close and pushes it away, revels in it but masks it. Sea rocks rustle with the voice of the ocean. Crustaceans bloom into soundless nebulas. Twelve-headed beasts slither and howl as they lay suns, the feathers of a giant kestrel flutter and then still as they turn into silver. Sounds from vanished chambers still hang in the air, sounds from chambers that are still forming trickle into your ear.

But it is always muted sound: sound controlled by the space it must traverse, blanketed and muffled by the air it lives in.

In the moment before her sister finds her and she becomes herself once again, Myung feels like this sound. A speck, weighed down by the enormity of the whale she must traverse.

If she ever meets the silent and absent Great Wisa, creator and first friend, she would ask her only one question: *Why did you make us so small?*

Dream

I begin my leaving ritual for the World of the Floating Island. I organize my piles of leaves and read them, memorizing what I can. Then, for ten sleeps, I wander across the chamber and scatter these sheaves. It will be picked up by the monkeys or the prawns, even the trees, and they will make what they like of it. But they will know they have been seen with the gentle eye of someone who wanted to understand. That, in my own way, I have tried to love.

The writing in these leaves is sadder than usual. The monkeys braid my hair; one of them holds me as I cry. *I don't know why I'm crying*, I tell him softly. He only smooths my hair and pats my head, as if it is very obvious.

Myung finds the door far away from the island, hiding in a fluffy gray cloud. She holds it open for me. My sister is a stranger. I go through.

The next chamber is filled with water, stretching endlessly to the horizon. Below the surface are the sprawling ruins of a city. Farther away, also beneath the water, is a pitted moon, shining with an eerie light. Myung and I plunge into the gray-blue sea and float, listless.

Then Myung says, *What about the people you see?*

I strike out, away from her, to sink beneath the surface.

Everything calms. The water presses against my ears, changing the whale's song into a ghostlike melody. The moon shimmers beneath me. I spread my arms and shape the words with my lips: *Great Wisa!*

No one answers.

It is true. I dream of people. They live in a place outside the whale, where there is no song. In that place, there are no chambers: only nebulas, planets and ships that sail between them, their sails unfurled.

I see many people, but I see one person most. A woman, living on an island that changes shape—a place that wants to befriend and kill her. I've seen her young, running and playing, and I've seen her old, banging pots and yelling at the island in bitterness.

But these are only dreams. DREAM, one syllable, meaning that which is invented, imagined, untrue. Myung knows this!

I break the surface. My sister is lying in wait. The whale's song is jarring now, agitated; it is warning me, but I don't know about what.

What if they aren't dreams? Myung insists, holding me so I don't submerge again. *They could be here, in the whale, waiting for us to find them. Think, Laleh: more of us, lost or scared—*

But they aren't here!

An indiscernible expression flits across Myung's face, too quick for me to place. She releases me. Slowly, she says: *If the people are not in the whale, then . . . could they be outside?*

It is how she says it. Carefully. The emphasis on specific words. She has practiced it.

The moment I realize this, I recognize her expression as well. Triumph. She has played this conversation in her head and decided she must get me to say "but they aren't here," so she can pull the thread I offered and tie me up in my own logic. Perhaps she thought that if it was my own logic, I would have to say, *Yes! Of course, they are outside.*

And if I said that, then she would say, *Why don't we find them?*

For this—I feel sick at the thought—is what Myung has been planning when I believed she was simply running away from me. This is the careful, predatory sister I do not know, hidden in one of her cavernous chambers.

Myung isn't running from me. She's fleeing the whale.

I hug her without thinking, pressing her to me in panic, and she clutches me too, reacting to my fear, pouring her love into me.

Myung, no.

She goes still then. She says urgently, *Come with me. You'll come with me.*

But that is all I keep saying, over and over. *Myung, no.*

Fear

The whale is weeping. There is no other word to describe its song. My sweet, kind whale.

Quest

I plan carefully. If Myung can lay traps and wait patiently for them to bear fruit, then imagine how much better I am at it. I am Laleh, recorder of the whale's chambers, and I have taught myself to think in pieces such that I can assemble those pieces into a particular whole. I have heard the song of the whale. I have sung to it. And now I will sing to my sister, calling her back to herself.

Myung doesn't leave my side, watching me with eyes that are worried and calculating. I ignore her. In my mind, I revisit my records of the chambers, searching for anything useful. The whale's song is lower, deeper, giving me space to think.

We have never returned to a chamber once we left it; we don't know how. Each door leads us to a new place, so I'm lost on how to retrace our steps. I don't even know how to find the doors. Door hunting is Myung's specialty, and she always says it is a stealthy act. You have to hold your breath and move through the chamber like a shadow, eyes trained to look for even the slightest disruption to the scenery—a faint crack or a ripple of light. *Doors*, Myung always says, *don't want to be found. You have to surprise them, catch them, and only then will they yield their secrets.*

But when I put my mind to it, I find it is nothing like that. The doors want what you want. If you want to find them, they will come. If you want them to hide so that you can chase them, they will hide. They will do their best to be good at hiding, in fact, and disguise themselves as all sorts of things. I get the impression they have been playing this game in every chamber we have visited, waiting and giggling.

But I don't want to hunt. So I close my eyes and hum softly, calling them to me. After a moment, I hear Myung gasp, and I look around.

The doors are here. Some have opened above us, others are slithering their way across the water to gather at our feet, still others are bubbling into life in the pitted surface of the underwater moon. I cannot see them, but I know there are doors in the submerged city, hidden in ledges and windows and cracks in the wall where fish sleep.

I hold my hand out to Myung.

Today, I announce, *we are knights.*

Her shoulders straighten, her eyes slowly flaring to light. *Knights?* she whispers.

Knights, I confirm, my voice ringing out. *We run in search of adventure. And when we find it, no matter how big or terrifying, we will not balk. We will rush into it, headlong and fearless. But!* I hold up my finger and Myung leans in. *We are not only knights. We are also witches and magicians and alchemists. We are all the things we once were and all the things we will become. We are larger than the whale.*

Myung's fingers are hesitant in mine; she doesn't know what to make of this new Laleh. I tighten my grip. This will work. This will work or, so help me Great Wisa, I will remake everything in all of time so that it works.

I pull her close. *Ready?* I whisper.

She grins.

For two hundred and twelve sleeps, we adventure. I pull her through doors I know will lead us where we want to go, and we become different people. As knights, we wrestle giant ospreys and ride on their backs through floating statues. We dive into the depths of the ocean to find a single purple rock—which Myung insists I sketch—that we carry around as a trophy. As witches, we howl at animals a hundred times our size and dance around each other in a frenzy, pushing ourselves to the edge of something we cannot describe before collapsing. As magicians, we mix roots and stones and sand, and giggle as it blows up into little puffs of spark and smoke. As alchemists, we search for the great herd of yakuths that swim through doors, a silver sheet of animals with squashed dragon faces and eel tails. We learn their language of gesture and then we listen to the ancient stories they pass among themselves.

Each time Myung tires, I pull her up. Each time she says, *let us stay, let us be a medicine doctor or gardener,* I drag her on. Each time I do, she is joyful. These questions are tests. She wants to see if I mean this, if I will say, *yes indeed, let us rest. Let us record this new stone I found and while I am recording this stone, let me record this chamber and once I do that, let us never leave.* But I do not. My Myung needs "more," and so I give it to her. I search for the experiences I know will light her up in the right way, which will make her feel alive and living at the limits of herself. I show her that the whale is inexhaustible.

Everything we need, we will find here.

The World of Bird and Leaf

Finally, I take her home.

We climb into the World of Bird and Leaf and are surrounded again by our beloved broadleaves. We have come out near the river that snakes around the chamber, and I am filled with a sparkling love for what I call my own. I walk through the trees in a happy daze, Myung's hand in mine. The whale's song is jubilant. Far up in the clouds, a new song mixes with it—a cry that speaks of ruby feathers and old friends. I know it is coming before I see it, and then we are washed in a long shadow and the simurgh is here. It is as glorious as the day I first met it, and I reach out my hand in awe. But Myung is faster than me, running into the simurgh's claw, laughing and crying as the bird lifts her up and presses her to its chest. It trills with delight.

Later, after we meet the simurgh's babies and are thoroughly examined—they seem fascinated that we have no feathers—I take Myung to where we first met. Here, finally, I allow us to rest. We sit against a weathered rock I have leaned on many times, and we stare at the sky. Myung rests her head against my shoulder, half lulled into sleep. I am content.

But we are not done yet. There is one gift left. The best gift. I nudge my sister awake and tug her to her feet. Still holding her hand, I close my eyes.

What are we doing? Myung asks.

Shush, I say. *Listen.*

I concentrate and will my concentration to flow down my arms and into Myung. I focus on calming her different frequencies, on making space in her many thoughts so that there is a clear, pure gap of silence. And then I try and focus that silence on the most beautiful thing I know, the sweetest gift there is.

The whale's song.

Myung asks again. *What are we doing?*

She has to feel it. The whale's song moves *through* your body, speaking gently to all parts of you. You must live it with everything you have, and I want Myung to live it so badly.

My longing is so great, my focus so pure, that the song begins to change for me. It is asking me to dance.

It is a strange request but so simple to do. I can feel my body move with the melody. In a trance, I sway and it is like an old memory is surfacing, as if my body is a repository of lost experiences that . . .

But the hands I am holding do not move with me. They are not as harmonious as mine; they are hesitant, all angles and jerky movements. When I open my eyes, I see Myung's confusion.

Worse, I see that the good of two hundred and twelve sleeps has been undone. Myung is vulnerable again. She has retreated into herself, sensing there was someone she was meant to become and couldn't. It makes the whale alien to her.

And now, in this moment where I catch her raw, open and distant from me, I see it in its glory. The idea. I see its roots traveling through Myung, down to her core. I see her desire as a soft creature nestled in her heart, sleeping. My sister is changed from the inside out.

Two hundred and twelve sleeps have not brought Myung closer to the whale. They've brought her closer to *me*, and she has been dreaming of the people we will find together, the adventures we will go on outside the whale. She cannot wait to leave.

As I see her clearly, she sees me too. All this time, she thought we were traveling through chambers because I was saying goodbye to the whale. She didn't realize I meant to stay.

It is devasting, the knowledge. We are standing in two different worlds. We are no longer the same shape.

Then I am weeping, and she is too; we tangle together on the floor of this world, bereft. She whispers, *I am sorry.* She says, *I will never hurt you. Laleh, my sister, kestrel and knight and wisest of wise magicians, don't cry. Don't break. I don't know how to put you back together.* I keep crying because I don't know how to stop. She babbles, *I won't leave. I promise I won't. I will always be with you. I am always with you.* She says it like she means it.

Gradually, I stop crying. My mind has emptied. Myung is warm and soft beside me, her tears drying on my shoulder. Our breathing slows, in harmony with each other. I feel tiredness reach for me, asking me to fall into it. I must stay awake, stay here. But the whale's song moves in time with our breathing, and I am lulled. My eyelids flutter. Myung's eyelashes brush against my cheek and I hear her say something as if from a great distance, *Sister* maybe but I am not sure. I fall asleep.

When I wake up, she is gone.

Home

For eight thousand and sixty-two sleeps, I don't see my sister.

I know she has left the moment I open my eyes. The whale's song is broken, its pain vocalized. In it, I sense Myung's presence, moving as a dark shadow. She is a million chambers away, calling doors to her, leaping through them. Looking for a way out.

She will find it.

I stay in the World of Bird and Leaf. I hardly eat. I call *Great Wisa!* and then just *Wisa*, softly and to myself. But no one comes. The whale keeps singing. I cover my ears; I want to forget.

The simurgh saves me. It plucks me from the ground and douses me in the river, holding me under with its claw until I thrash and struggle, desperate for air. When it brings me out, dripping, I feel clean. I comb through my hair with my fingers and breathe out. *Enough*, I tell myself and tuck my pain away.

I leave the World of Bird and Leaf. The simurghs gather to see me go. The little ones have grown up now, and their ruby feathers are even brighter. Every moment of beauty is made for me. I call a door and step through, into a chamber of shifting, changing sand.

I call this chamber the World of Many Things. It heals me. Here, I make cities and ships like the ones I see in my dreams. I create cosmic squids and watch their tentacles shift as the sand flows in and out of position. I even try to shape the people I see in my visions, especially the woman on the mad island. The statue-making calms the whale. Its jangling, stuttering song soothes, and it watches me.

Once I finish four hundred statues, I feel better. I step back and survey my chamber of sand. Crumbling cities, ships, people. Then I let it go, blowing it into shapelessness.

I won't leave you, I tell the whale. *You are my home.*

Its song then is the sweetest I've heard.

And this is how it has been for eight thousand and sixty-two sleeps. I am no longer knight, magician or witch. I am simply Laleh, keeper of the whale of babel, and I move through rooms as I like. I know which doors to summon when I want to return to the World of Bird and Leaf, and I do most of my sleeping there. I disintegrate all the statues in the World of Many Things and build a lattice instead, one that stretches from one end of the chamber to the other. I bring my heart-shaped leaves here, records of the chambers I have seen, and I keep adding to them.

I look again at the gossamer fabrics that hang in every room. They are giant cobwebs that glimmer with the faint colors of the rainbow, present in every chamber. They don't seem to belong to what is in the chamber; they don't change substance or shape depending on the room's theme. They just seem to be.

Myung called them TIME COBWEBS, a phrase that came to her. Now they remind me of me. They flutter in an unseen breeze, and even though they look light and airy, they give off an atmosphere of ponderousness and depth. I feel an affinity to them, like we are old friends. For they are fixtures of the whale, unchanging in the face of ever-changing chambers. Like me, they keep witness.

I think of Myung. I wonder where she is. What she is doing. If she is happy. I long to see her in my dreams, to know she is safe. But each time I close my eyes, I dream of the same woman on a shape-shifting island, and my sister slips further away from me.

But on the eight thousand and sixty-third sleep, I enter the World of the One Tree. I climb to the top and crawl along its branches. I lay my cheek on the gnarled wood and let my hair fall toward the floor like Spanish moss. I sleep.

And I see her.

Finding What We Lost: Wandering the Museum of Collective Memory

by Roshni Kawia

Research Fellow at the Department of Museum Anthropology,
University of Cosmic Artefacts and Creatures (UCAC)
Currently visiting faculty at the University of Mirabilia Diachronism

First published in the Universal Journal of Collective Artefacts, Vol. 101, Issue 8. Retrieved from the Museum of Collective Memory, Corridor |•\|••, Object DCCCVI

Abstract

The role of the museum of collective memory in how we live, love and understand ourselves is undeniable. As an engineering feat, it is a marvel. But why was the museum built in the first place? This article argues that the museum was not constructed on a whim, but with a clear aim: to unite two estranged sisters. Using the methodology of mirabilia diachronism (i.e., the discipline of separating the wheat of the truth from the chaff of fairy tales), we connect the museum to the greatest mystery of our time: the whale of babel.

Keywords: memories, museum, Magali Kilta, whale, babel, fairy tale

INTRODUCTION

The term "black sea" is a strange one. We don't know for sure when we started calling our universe by this name—as if it were made of water instead of nothingness, and had tides, winds and waves. Robyn Janap suggests the phrase originated when the Vortex of Noma was discovered, a spinning whirlpool in space that only children can travel through. It was the first time we realized that the cosmos did not make "sense" and could not. It wasn't made only for us.

This is when "space" became the "black sea"—when we learned to see what we considered empty as full and unfathomable, similar to oceans. It is so long ago now, hardly any of us remember it. We call our universe the black sea as if it is the only name it has, as if planets have always been "islands" and we always saw ourselves as sailors.

But once in a while, it is valuable to think of where that name comes from. The wonder in those words, our terror and awe. The name marks a moment of recognition: when we realized that what seemed empty was simply not for our eyes, and what appeared story-less was only unknown.

This is the feeling I get when I think of the museum of collective memory. Of vastness and depth. Buried stories and hushed motivations. And at the center of it all, the mad, enigmatic figure of a woman who created one of the greatest man-made marvels we know: Magali Kilta.

OUR VAST AND SPRAWLING WEB

Every child knows how to enter the museum of collective memory. You tap your tragus, that triangular bump in your ear, and you say *khol*. We know this instinctively, without being told. No matter how young you are, if you tap your ear and you say the word right, the museum comes to you.

"Comes," of course, is the wrong word. The museum is always there, invisible and waiting. *Khol* is not so much a summoning as it is a door. Poets have described the transition as a melting—your reality is swept away and replaced with the museum. It doesn't matter if you're sitting, standing or perched in the belly of a ship sailing through the black sea—when you whisper *khol*, you will find your feet on sandstone floors and when you look up, you will see you are in a corridor made for giants.

To truly understand the significance of the museum of collective memory, you have to imagine it. Visualize a corridor a hundred times your height. Silver-green ivy spills down walls, whispering and snaking. Here and there, through the foliage, you glimpse the twinkle of jewels—mosaics, you realize, of stories you don't know and creatures you have never seen. They loom above you, watching.

Yet you are not afraid. There is something familiar and warm here, like sitting around a fire with your family on a crisp night or listening to your grandmother tell you a story she heard from her grandparents. It is not comforting; it doesn't have the same feeling of enclosure. But you are not vulnerable either. You're known.

Now imagine a thousand corridors like this. A hundred thousand. More. Each corridor has differently sized doors, and behind those doors are rooms so large you cannot see their end. These are packed with objects and records arranged in no discernible order. This is a museum that follows a pattern of its own making—one that is chaotic and, crucially, living.

So seamless is the transition from your location into the museum of collective memory and so bewitching is the experience that early visitors considered the museum an illusion, one of those hallucinations you get when you inhale too much pallé pollen. Most of these first visitors were sailors, who, when reminiscing of home, found themselves idly touching their tragus and whispering *khol*. They couldn't explain the impulse to do so. Nor could they explain the museum itself, a network of corridors that intersected with no map.[*]

But they found that if they simply walked, the museum would lead them toward where they needed to go.

One sailor discovered a mosaic of herself, crouching by a ship and hugging her mother; it was the moment she left for her first voyage. The vines parted to reveal it; now they settled gently on her shoulders. She saw the lines on her mother's face, felt the warmth of her arms. She saw the necklace her mother slipped into her sailor pocket, a family heirloom believed to ward off evil. The likeness was uncanny.

She wept for days afterward. "It was like finding yourself remembered," she said, "and knowing you always will be."

Another found a record of an ancestor he didn't know he had—a distant branch of a distant cousin, but the ears were unmistakable. He began studying this ancestor's life to learn they shared the same soul, just reincarnated into a new time. The knowledge exhilarated him. Life had given him what it gives so few people: a dress rehearsal. Here was his chance to learn from his ancestor's mistakes and shape a life that was perfect.[**]

---

[*] Indeed, academics believe the museum is almost maze-like and resists attempts to be charted. Corridors are occasionally named with an odd system of |, \ and •, but there are many corridors that remain unmarked.

[**] No one knows what happened after that. Romantic versions of the story speak of a man who became a saint, but seaside dhabas whisper maliciously of how he made all the same mistakes, simply because he knew them.

This is the magic of the museum. It ties you to a history that is vast and sprawling and tenderly you. It lets you wander through memories that have always been yours to keep, if only you remembered.

What you make of them is up to you. It has given back people reasons to live, helped others discover themselves, allowed still others to lose themselves.

Today, the museum is visited by everyone, although rarely do you cross paths with another person in its mammoth halls.* We cannot imagine our lives without it. What family argument would be settled if we couldn't tap our tragus and say *khol*? What homesickness would be cured if we couldn't wander through its corridors to find our great-grandmother's recipe? How would we grieve for the ones we lost if we couldn't spend time with the objects they touched and loved, if we didn't know we could find those objects always? The museum is our friend, our companion, and the quiet witness to the lives that came before us.

And yet we know almost nothing about its maker, Magali Kilta, or why she created it.

THE MUSEUM'S SONG

Here is what we do know.

When Magali Kilta decided to collect the universe's memories, she knew the museums of early humans would not be enough. Spatial museums were limited, both in what they could collect and how they could display. She needed something elastic, capable of worming into the fabric of the black sea when not needed and yet springing into life when called upon. Song was the answer.

Most of us will not be surprised by the spatial properties of sound. A *boom* seems to spread out and flatten, for example, like a ripple across a dry landscape, while a spike in frequency leaps up and down like an excitable rabbit. Connecting these properties to the mind's eye, so that you *see* the ripple instead of *hearing* the boom, is what makes the museum of collective memory unique. This is why when you walk down its

---

* Wandering the museum has always been a sacred and personal act; it opens for you in a particular way and very few will share your path.

hushed corridors, you can see sand trickling from cracks, singing as it falls. The whole thing is made of song.

The mechanics of it still baffle us. For one person to access memories stretching back eons, many of them small and forgettable except to the people involved; for the same person to find a way to transform these memories into sound such that you can wander through millions of corridors without ever leaving the seat you were in when you whispered *khol*—these answers are beyond us. We don't know how the museum knows your father died, how it builds a shelf for him in the haphazard room of your family and how you will always find on it anything you seek. The museum is so vast that researchers believe we have cataloged less than 15 percent of it. They suspect there are memories here of animal and plant species, and of objects we consider inanimate and so pay no attention to. We know so little of how to navigate the museum, we may never find these memories. We simply can't hear the music.

But there is one thing scholars agree on: the museum is alive. If its mechanism of action is song, then someone—or something—is singing it.

Thanks to Professor Pari Tujik's seminal work in the field of mirabilia diachronism, we now know this "something" is an island, made of bone-white crystals that transmit the museum across space. Sea stories confirm its existence: they speak of a small island bobbing at the edge of the black sea, with its own painted sun and madness in its soil. No one has been there. But sailors say the black sea knows of it. And sometimes when you pull in a cosmic fish and pry open its maws, you can hear the universe whisper of it.

Its name is Ojda.

TRACING ROOTS: THE FABLE OF OJDA

Mirabilia diachronism is an academic discipline that studies how fairy tales change through time. Sailors don't like it—it is bad luck to tell the sea her stories aren't true. But cartographers carry oil-skinned books on the subject that they tuck into hammocks below deck and read carefully by candlelight. Much of mapmaking imagery comes from this discipline. The serpents. The monster heads. Submerged islands.

Here's how it works. You start with the myth you have and move backward, peeling away layers added through time to get to the seed first spat out by the black sea. If you're lucky and you peel well, you'll find a bit of history the historians missed, the quiet pieces of time no one was looking at.

This is how Professor Tujik discovered the museum's island. She studied a fairy tale that is colloquially known as the "Creation of Ojda." It speaks about a woman cursed to vomit the universe's memories. By the end of the fable, these memories are bound into a single island (Ojda), which her family then makes their home.[*] By plotting the story against the scant records of Magali Kilta, Tujik's ground-breaking paper proves this fable was "a creative echo" (Tujik, 5) to Magali Kilta's construction of the museum and Ojda.

Tujik's hypothesis, while robust in its own right, was reinforced by the appearance of a stranger, two centuries after the museum was discovered. This stranger had no papers and a very rudimentary idea of cosmic rules of law. He was fascinated by the simplest implements and had all sorts of strange ideas about how islands should behave and what they should say or do. But sit with that stranger in a room, lamps lit and only the glow of flames on your faces, and he would tell you things you didn't know were yours. Memories you had forgotten. Ancestries you had lost. Beliefs you had once claimed for yourself and then given away. There was no mystery about him. He would say these things with familiarity and joviality, as if you were discussing the weather.

He called himself Rostum Kilta.

Since then, and across broad tracts of time, more Kiltas have emerged, although always only one at a time. Unlike the first stranger, they have been shy of public attention; they run away from travelers and have tried to erase themselves from history books. But they broadly corroborate what academics believed. Ojda exists and it is the heart of the museum, a small livable paradise in the far reaches of the black sea.

You can't find it, they say. *Only a Kilta can.*

---

[*] The fable itself is long, but well worth reading. It has been reproduced in the Ephemera of this book.

Nor will they take you there.

We've only just left, they tell you abashedly. *Besides, we swore an oath.*

And so, a strange picture of Magali Kilta emerged. A mad woman who trapped her children and their descendants on an island she created and forbade them to leave.

The question is: why?

SEARCHING FOR THE LOST PIECE

It is my contention that the "Creation of Ojda" shows us not only how the museum works, but also why it was built.

Common versions of the fairy tale include only three parts, and end with the famous lines: "Never again would a Kilta leave the shores of this island. They were home." Tujik herself remains content to analyze this version.

But there is a fourth part to the story, discovered by a fisherman who harvests lilta bones—the slender, moon-white bones used to play the popular game of lilta. These bones are plucked from dead chand fish, who crawl onto sandbars to rot when it is their time. This was where the paragraph was found, written out in bone carcasses that shone dully in the wet sand.

It says:

> At night, while her family slept, the woman crept onto Ojda's beach. She had a secret; she knew why the universe's memories had chosen her. She spoke this knowledge into a single nugget of gold and buried it, saying nothing to her family. This memory was meant for only one person, a sister she had lost long ago. Thus this nugget remains, waiting for the sister to claim it.

No record of Magali Kilta mentions a sister, nor do her descendants. But the fairy tale gives a clue as to who this person might be.

You will recall, in the story, that the woman's husband travels to a divine star to ask guidance on why the stories plague his wife, and what to do about it.

> When at last he arrived on the shores of the dying star, alas! He was struck dumb. The star was so majestic, his voice grew fearful of making an appearance; it leaped out of his throat and hid. In vain, he searched and searched. He began to despair.
>
> Then the sea shook. Above him, a dark shape moved among nebulas. He shielded his eyes and squinted, then clapped his hands over his ears. A high-pitched and mournful cry filled the air. It was the whale with a scar on its belly. It did nothing, only swam past, but its cries reminded him of an ancient and lonely creature. Of his wife, growing softly mad.
>
> And so he searched harder, scouring the bottom of the boat until, at last, he found his voice and spoke.

It is the second paragraph of this extract that is of interest here, the whale that swims past. It is "ancient and lonely creature," filling the air with "a high-pitched and mournful cry." It is alone, bereft, majestic and, as implied by the husband's deduction of his wife's state, possibly mad.

Who better fits that description than the whale of babel?

If the fairy tale refers to the whale of babel, then we have a priceless cipher to unlock who Magali's sister might be. For there is only one person associated with the whale: Wisa.

Indeed, if Magali and Wisa are related, then the fact that they created two of the greatest marvels of the universe cannot be a coincidence. I believe Magali built the museum of collective memory not as a whim, but to call Wisa back to her. What stronger beacon is there than a museum that sings to every corner of the cosmos? What better way to ensure your lost sister will hear your call?

But Wisa did not return, at least not in Magali's lifetime. Thus every Kilta is sworn to spend their lives on Ojda, waiting for the day that she does.

But here the trail ends. If there are records or fairy tales about the two sisters, those stories are now lost.* We don't know where Magali or Wisa came from or why they became estranged. We don't even know how Magali created the museum, forget how Wisa is associated with the whale. Mysteries curl into each other like serpents. As in a Gordian knot, we won't know what to unpick first, which part will yield just enough for the knot to come undone in our hands. All we can do is keep picking.

But look again toward the museum of collective memory, to that feeling of being watched and remembered. All over this museum, there are imprints of Magali. Her quest. Her wishes. Her longing. Her presence seeps into us the moment we step into the museum's halls.

So we wander down giant corridors in search of what we didn't know we were missing. We seek to become whole.

We long.

And around us, the museum sings gentle reminders. *That which seems empty is only invisible*, it sings. *What appears story-less is only unknown.*

---

* Strangely, there is nothing about Magali Kilta in the museum. Yet if you close your eyes and ask the museum who made it, the answer comes singing to you, your tongue forming the syllables of her name of its own accord. Magali is with you in this museum, always, an old friend who will never let you go adrift.

OJDA

The Long-Awaited Meeting

I

Centuries ago, two sisters lived on the island of Esi. In a story that is now lost, they were exiled into the black sea and separated by time and space. One sister, Magali Kilta, spent her life looking for the other.

Centuries later, her descendants are trapped on the mad island of Ojda, sworn to wait for a lost sister no one knows, because of a story no one can remember.

Also centuries later, Myung travels through the black sea, toward this same island. Eight thousand and sixty-two sleeps have passed since she left the whale—forty-nine years in black sea time. Forty-nine years since she's seen Laleh. Alone on a ship, Myung is following a map she made herself, from fragments of myths, fairy tales, history and rumors. She is hunting for the island they say cannot be found.

If you asked her, she would say she's trying to go home.

II

Dreams are strange creatures.

Laleh's dreams always follow standard laws. First, within its confines, a dream is vivid—none of that blurry, wispy nonsense that fairy tales describe. Second, each dream has its own specific rules it follows faithfully. The rules are not always sensible, but they are obeyed. And third, irrespective of what Laleh believes when she wakes up in the whale of babel, every dream is real.

This dream obeys all of these laws, but it is also different. Laleh realizes this the moment she opens her eyes.

It is the sound that hits her first—a wave of whispers and cries that builds until she must curl up under their onslaught and cover her ears. The sound crashes over her, then disappears.

Silence.

She sits up. She wriggles her toes experimentally. Pinches her nose and tugs her lower lip. Her other dreams were lifelike, but this dream is raw and more vivid than any other. It is like heartache compared to the gentleness of an afternoon sleep. It is tiptoeing across a beach of hot, jagged coral versus padding on soft soil in well-stitched shoes. In short, this dream is a gut punch. Laleh's nerves are raw and heightened. Coarse particles of soil shift between her toes, her skin tightening under the sun, her throat parched.

The sensations are so vivid, she wonders if she is awake. But no, she remembers falling asleep. She was in the World of the One Tree and she had climbed along a branch, where she had laid down her head and closed her eyes. Even now, if she concentrates, she can feel the wood faintly chaffing her cheek. She was definitely in the whale before this dream.

She stands. She is not in the whale of babel now. This place gives her the impression of expanse and edges, like if she wanders too far, she could fall off. This landscape stretches as far as the eye can see. In the distance, dry snow billows clouds into the sky. Below her, the ground changes color: from blood red to ochre to blue, a rainbow glaze extending to the horizon. She is surrounded by what look like small stones, multicolored and spongy.

This is Ojda. She has been here before; it is the island she visits in her dreams. But in those dreams Ojda was notional—a two-dimensional concept of an island that functioned as a backdrop. Now, Ojda is layered, with a depth that churns just beyond her awareness. She reaches for it but it evades her; this island is not ready to open up yet.

For a moment, Laleh considers pushing; Myung would. But then she reconsiders. The whale wouldn't like it if someone pushed it, so why would this island? Politely, she pulls her consciousness back to focus on what is accessible to her.

Three things become apparent at once.

They arrive with the same confused sharpness that accompanies knowledge in dreams—the simultaneous feeling of *oh, I didn't know that!* and *oh, but I've always known that.* They arrive so entwined that it takes Laleh a moment to sort them into their three distinct forms.

First: each time Laleh visited Ojda in her dreams, she saw a woman who banged pots and shouted at the island. This woman never spoke or met anyone else. She was alone. Now Laleh realizes she isn't; Ojda is filled with many people, each as shadowy as Laleh herself, a thousand cobwebs on the island's skin. A name for them pops into her mind's eye.

GHOST. One syllable.

Before she can fully explore that word and its many implications, she is pulled into the second realization, which is: the spongy, multicolored rocks covering the landscape are not rocks at all. They are plants. And the one closest to her is watching her.

Before she can fully absorb *that*, she is into the third realization, the most pressing of all—

Someone is coming.

This last one is not technically a realization conferred by the special power of dreams; Laleh can just see it. There, on the horizon, a black dot is moving. Laleh squints, trying to get a better look. The person is walking toward her, growing in size as they get closer. The sun is shining right in Laleh's face, so she can't discern their features. She shields her eyes and squints again. Then she cries out and falls to her knees.

It is Myung.

Laleh scrambles up enough to lurch forward, and space moves as it does in a dream, when you wish desperately to be near someone and you suddenly are. Her sister is so close—right *there*—and Laleh reaches out, Myung's name slipping through her lips as a hard bubble of confused joy rises to fill her, and all of language isn't vast enough to contain it.

Myung.

Myung walks past her.

Laleh's arms drop. *Myung!* she shouts, running after her sister. But Myung cannot see Laleh. Or hear her. Or feel her, it seems, for when Laleh pinches her viciously, Myung doesn't notice. This is all consistent with Laleh's past dreams but she is disappointed nonetheless. She sits down with a thump and watches Myung walk away.

She is suddenly furious.

Go! she shouts. *Why must I be the one chasing you? Go, you coward—leaving when I was asleep! Asleep, Myung! And you didn't even say goodbye. I hope you fall off the island. I hope you get everything you want and it makes you sick. And then, and then you'll say, "Laleh, I wish I'd listened to you," but it will be too late!*

Myung keeps walking. She is growing smaller.

Coward, Laleh shouts. *Coward! Coward in all the things that matter, always forever cowardly. You're no knight. You're no sister!*

This is a step too far. Laleh slaps her hand to her mouth, ashamed. Myung is gone now; she is once again a black dot moving across the landscape. *You make me so mad,* Laleh whispers, wiping her tears.

Then she runs after her.

Myung has stopped to observe a spongy stone that is actually a plant. She is on her knees, peering at the plant with distilled concentration, careful not to touch it. In the first flush of finding her sister, Laleh was too overwhelmed to truly see her. Now she does, and is startled by what she sees.

Myung has changed.

Eight thousand and sixty-two sleeps have passed since Myung left the whale, but it looks as if a thousand more have passed for Myung, for how else could you explain this transformation? Her sister is wearing robes similar to what Laleh has seen on sailors: knotted and heavy, stardust and antimatter encrusted in the seams. Her hair is cut short, close to her nape, and it brings out the sharpness of her features. Her face doesn't look different—it is the same face Laleh has always loved—but *she* is different.

In the whale, Myung had a guileless energy to her. Everything was full of wonder, each step a leap. Now that energy has been tempered into a shrewdness; there is cunning in her posture. This Myung has explored the black sea, stolen its secrets and poured them into diaries sailors use as their guides.

Laleh crouches, peering at Myung as Myung peers at the plant. Is her sister in there?

Myung stands abruptly. She stares at the plant in contemplation for a moment longer, as the plant fidgets nervously. Then she hisses at it, and *boom!* It bursts into a flower forty feet tall.

Myung's face opens in surprise, and she laughs. It has been so long since Laleh heard that laugh. Around them, more plants burst into flowers, the air filled with clouds of pollen. Myung is still laughing, her face tilted in delight as a flower maze erupts around the sisters and—of course she is Laleh's Myung. How could Laleh have believed otherwise? Here is her endless capacity for wonder. Her eagerness for novelty. And underneath that, the same tender and desperate core that drove her sister out of the whale thousands of sleeps ago:

A desire.

There is something on this island that Myung wants very, very badly.

Laleh has no time to ponder what it might be because Myung is moving. She weaves through the maze with a confidence that borders on arrogance—this is a woman who has tamed many islands. Laleh keeps close; she doesn't want to lose her sister among the flowers. So when Myung stops suddenly, Laleh almost runs into her.

Myung has realized something. She plucks at her breastbone. Drums on it. Then in one fluid movement, she sits.

Waits.

For a while, Laleh is not sure for what. The flowers sway gently in the breeze, pollen drifting like snow. Clouds move languidly across the sky.

And then Laleh senses it. The fog that keeps Ojda's depths hidden from her is lifting, until she has the barest glimpse of its rolling underbelly. Ojda is sentient. It has wants, likes, behaviors it is peevish about. And it pays *very* close attention to the people walking on it.

It has been studying Myung. Its ground has learned the shape of her feet; its wind has spent time caressing her hair. It recognizes the robes; they belong to sailors who have drifted past the island but never noticed it. In general, Ojda would have quite liked one of them to visit. It likes travelers—although it hasn't had one in centuries—and it sees no reason to distrust them.

Ordinarily, Ojda would have been delighted with Myung.

But Myung is different. She *feels* different, like someone not quite made of this universe. Displaced. Like salt in your sugar or stones in your black rice.

Laleh turns to her sister, startled. *Myung—*

This knowledge moves like an arrow to Ojda's core, where it sets off a seismic wave that rolls as a giant dust cloud around the island, shaking creatures from trees and uprooting plants. For a brief moment, Ojda is cacophony. Then the wave arrives in a perfect circle around the only built structure on the island, a cottage hanging precariously off the edge of a cliff, and subsides.

In the cottage's bedroom, on a rickety bed made from old fairy tales, Ojda's keeper opens her eyes.

Myung's Diaries

No. CMXXXVI

Rostum Kilta, when asked if he would show the sailors how to reach the famous island of Ojda, had reportedly laughed out loud. "My friends," he said, "do you know what you are asking? Only a member of the Kilta family can visit the island of Ojda."

When the sailors pressed him, he said: "I wouldn't take my enemies there, forget my friends. Do you know what Ojda means? Oh, you know it is the heart of the museum of collective memory, but do you know what the *name* means? My great-great-great-grandmother named it, once Mad Magali died. It means *oops*."

After that, people decided they'd rather not look for an island that even its creators thought was an accident.

Everybody except the academics, of course.

And me.

You can't ask sailors if they are willing to go on an expedition to find Ojda. Even those with salt-matted hair and faces ravaged by sea monsters—even they spit and push you off their boats. Others avert their eyes. "Don't ask us, Myung," they whisper. "Look elsewhere."

But the fishermen are happy to talk. They pull great fish from the black sea and widen their maws to listen to the whispers of the cosmos. Parchments will tell you Ojda is the heart of the museum, but the fish say otherwise. "It has changed, sister . . . into a land that doesn't know what it wants to become." The fisherman tugs his silver earring, squints at me. "They say whales are drawn to it, spend their lives seeking it, but don't be fooled by such innocent stories. It is a treacherous island. Some call it the goddess of change, a landscape of mist where anything can become anything else. Tree into animals, earth into air . . ."

". . . You're asking the wrong question." The woman licks her gold teeth, rubbing a fish bone down her thumb. "The question is not what it is or where it is, but what lives on it . . ."

"It's the mad family." Back to the fisherman with the silver earring, now pulling out the guts of a fish. "You know. The Kiltas. My mother used to say that Magali Kilta was so mad, the sea would sing to calm her. She was so mad, she made a museum as large as the black sea itself, and then she built an island as its heart and her family has lived there ever since. Who knows what time has done to them? How madness ripens?"

"Yeah, I've heard of the island." The old man is toothless; each time his lips part, I see his gums. "They say a demon lives there. That if you visit, she'll take your eyes. Clean her teeth with your bones. What do you want to go there for, sailor?" His gaze is unnerving. "What's so precious you'd risk your life for it?"

I don't answer him. Ojda is my only hope.

III

Ojda's keeper is not a demon but a woman, and she is sleeping when the seismic wave rattles her cottage. She turns to glance at the timepiece, a contraption of half-moons and suns, before going back to sleep.

Laleh kneels by her bed. One moment she is beside Myung with the island shaking because of an earthquake, and the next she is in the cottage, watching this keeper sleep. The abruptness of the move startles her, but this dream doesn't care much for logic or rules of perspective. It goes where its heart delights, and Laleh will be swept along. It will last for however long it likes, and Laleh will live it.

The woman shifts restlessly in bed. She is the same person whom Laleh sees in all her dreams, her face always fixed in a scowl. This is a woman who keeps one eye on the land of the waking and a bone knife under her pillow. Laleh touches the corners of her lips, filled with a sudden urge to wipe away her bitterness. *Blajine*, she says soundlessly, trying out the name. Then, without knowing why, she adds, *Sister*.

The half-moons move, night ends and Blajine awakes.

Time unfolds as a routine. Blajine pokes embers in a dip in the flagstone floor; she starts a fire. Hangs a kettle to boil. Eats a plant as she waits, ignoring the plants flinging themselves at her door to die. Makes tea. Drinks it. Puts the kettle on again, shakes off the plants that have found a way under the door and are crawling up her leg (a sharp jiggle and a stamp, so that the rest scurry away). Ojda's soil is growing up the sides of her cottage, trying to get her attention; her circular windows are covered with bone-white sand. She pours herself more tea. Drinks it. Sits on the floor watching the ground change into a giant sea lion, its face widening into a maw that grows crystal incisors. Listens to it roar. Ojda wants her attention. But Blajine is a Kilta, last of the keepers, direct ancestor of the mad Magali Kilta, and she will not be *told*.

When the sea lion rips off the roof of her cottage, Blajine sighs. She pulls the knife from under her pillow and walks out the door. The sea lion pauses, surprised; it doesn't see the knife slit its underbelly, dragged along its length as Blajine walks; it meows and turns into dust. Blajine turns toward the plants crowding her cottage; they huddle away from her.

A traveler, is it? she asks and they quiver. *Come on then.*

She marches on. The plants hop after her, keeping a safe distance. The farther Blajine gets from the cottage, the clearer Laleh can see it. It is tipped precariously on the edge of a cliff, a hair's breadth from falling in. Many times, Blajine has practiced what she would say to a stranger who asks her about the cottage. *Oh this!* She'd laugh. *We built it like this.* She would pause long enough for the stranger to grow uncomfortable, to wonder what strange mind would like to live so close to death. Then she'd lean in. *You don't believe that do you?* she'd whisper. *Not a smart traveler like you.* Their eyes would widen. Their palms would grow clammy and they'd think, *no, we don't believe that; there's something more here.* Then she'd lean back abruptly and laugh. *Is it crooked?* she'd say, suddenly surprised and innocent. *I never noticed.*

Blajine likes to imagine her travelers scared and confused. She likes to think they would run away. Of course, she has never been able to act out this scene. No one ever visits Ojda.

Blajine crosses the island swiftly, moving toward the snow fields, which is where Ojda says the traveler is. The shortest route, of course, would be past the thick, gushing river that runs along one end of Ojda, but Blajine doesn't want to cross that river. There are too many bad memories there. So she takes the long way around, marching through the nests of the mirre birds.

Once upon a time, she would have tread softly among those woven nests. Mirre birds have a unique ability to blend into their surroundings, even into the sky—honestly, their feathers just *disappear*—and they use this talent very effectively to capture and eat prey.

Once upon a time, Blajine was very scared of being eaten.

Now, of course, she could not care less. She strides effortlessly, never tiring, and the mirre birds stay humbly in their nests. When one pokes its beak out, she twitches her finger and it quickly retreats. The plants who follow her are not so lucky; seven of them don't make it out alive.

Finally, Blajine can see the snow fields, and beside it, the multicolored plain. She stops. The plain is dotted with flowers now slowly wilting back into their usual rock shapes.

The plants rarely burst into flowers. Something must have startled them.

Even then, it is a surprise to see the figure sitting cross-legged among the shrinking flowers. Blajine's upper lip grows sweaty, her heartbeat quickens. The plants stop behind her, bumping into each other in their haste to keep distance.

So, there is a traveler. She hadn't believed Ojda. She thought it was another one of its tricks. How did the traveler get here? Why is she here? The ghost of her mother flits at the edge of Blajine's consciousness. *Beware*, her mother says in an ominous voice. *No one walks here but us.*

But it is not wariness that is filling Blajine's heart. It is an emotion she has not felt in so long, it takes her a surprised moment to recognize it.

It is joy.

Oh God, she wants to keep the stranger.

She squashes the feeling before it takes root. It is a traitorous thought and unbecoming of a Kilta. They protect Ojda; they shoo away anyone who may land.

But no one has landed on the island's shores for over three centuries. Surely there must be something special about this one?

Kill her, her mother says.

Blajine turns the knife in her hand, thinking. The traveler is slumped forward, the back of her neck exposed. Her short hair is drenched with sweat. When Blajine traveled the black sea, sailors were built as taut as wet rope, their muscles never failing. This one is wilting under Ojda's sun. *Where did you anchor?* she would ask her. *Which are your favorite islands? Do they still sell crystallized honey from the mines of Peydra?* God, Blajine loved that honey.

She turns the knife a last time, and then tucks it into the back of her dhoti. She stretches her lips into a smile; it comes out cracked and unnatural. A brave plant has hopped up to her feet and is now nuzzling her toes. Blajine scoops it up and puts it in her jacket, where it nestles close to her heart. She will eat it later.

She sets off.

Myung doesn't see her approach as much as hears her. The plants are whispering. She turns and there she is, a stranger crossing the landscape. She moves effortlessly, as if . . . as if the ground makes itself shorter and tighter for her to cross. Myung's heart murmurs; she flushes with excitement. *Calm,* she tells herself. *Calm.*

She stumbles to her feet.

Friend, she shouts across the distance. *I am Myung—*

Blajine waves her words away. *We don't do greetings,* she says. *Dangerous place, traveler. You shouldn't be here.*

This is not the welcome Myung had hoped for. She tenses. There is danger here, real danger. Blajine approaches with the same stride that took her across Ojda, easy and confident—a woman sure of the ground beneath her feet. She appraises Myung as if looking at a piece of meat and deciding where best to stick the knife. Laleh shrinks slightly into herself; Myung is wary.

The women are a few feet away from each other now. Blajine is circling so Myung circles too, each keeping her eyes on the other. It is strange, but Myung can do strange. Myung thinks briefly of the whale of babel and smiles to herself. She *is* strange.

My ship crashed on the rocks, Myung says. *I don't know where I am.*

Blajine unties a waterskin from her waist and offers it. *Drink,* she says. *You must be thirsty.*

The words are an order, the smile not right. This is a test. How much trust exists between two strangers dancing the dance of greeting? How naïve is our traveler? Myung takes the flask. Shakes it. Doesn't drink.

Where am I? she asks.

Where were you headed?

The Vortex of Noma.

Blajine raises her eyebrows. *The famous Vortex of Noma that whispers the secrets of the black sea? It talks about the whale of babel now, I believe.*

You get news here?

Sometimes. What did you want with the vortex?

Myung shrugs. Her shoulders lift too high, the movement too sharp to be natural. She asks again: *Where am I?*

Blajine shrugs, an imitation of Myung's. *You're not drinking.*

Myung uncorks the flask, smells it. Doesn't drink. Blajine is watching her. Both women coil tighter. Laleh has a very desperate urge to insert herself between them and steer this conversation into calmer waters, but it is difficult to do this when no one can see you.

You don't trust me? Blajine says sweetly.

Myung thinks: you could try to be a little more trustworthy. But she doesn't say it; she has learned to measure the value of her words. She smells the flask again. Pungent. Poisoned? No way to tell.

Say no, Myung, Laleh whispers. *Make yourself bigger, scarier. Show her your strength.*

Instead, Myung drinks.

The dream shudders, liquefies. Laleh starts forward, arms out, lips opening in a cry. *Myung, no.* Then the dream finds form again. She lets out her breath.

Blajine relaxes. It matters to her that she is trusted. Her voice grows tender. *Sail back, traveler,* she says. *It is not safe here.*

She tries to put as much care into her words as possible, so that this silly visitor grasps the danger. Kiltas are good at surviving Ojda's moods because they are Kiltas. It is in their blood. A stranger doesn't stand a chance.

And Blajine likes the traveler. Or she *could*, if she got to know her. The traveler is dumb (Blajine would have never drunk that water), but she is not easily scared. Plus, from here, her arms look like they would be very good at whacking Ojda's many monsters. It would be a pity to find pieces of her strewn across the island.

But the traveler seems oblivious. *Why is it not safe?* she asks.

Blajine sighs. *Better not stay to find out.*

Wait! Don't go—I don't have a ship. It's wrecked.

Blajine turns and lifts the edge of Myung's robes. *There's sea dust all over your clothes, sailor*, she says. *You've been around. I'm sure you've built a hundred ships—*

But something has caught Blajine's eye. Behind the traveler, there are markings on the ground. No, not markings. Drawings, made by a finger. They are not elaborate sketches; it is *how* they're drawn that has caught her attention.

These are doodles, made to while away time.

The traveler was not slumped forward in exhaustion, Blajine realizes. She was drawing to *waste* time. She was waiting.

Blajine acts on instinct. In a flash, she grabs Myung's hair and presses the knife to her throat. Myung doesn't struggle.

You know what they do to trespassers this side of the black sea? Blajine hisses. *Boil them. Drink a soup made of their flesh. Use their skulls as cups.*

You got that from a fairy tale, Myung says.

Blajine did, but she doesn't appreciate it being said. She yanks Myung's hair harder. *Out.*

But something has changed in Myung. A calm settles over her. She presses her neck into the knife, as if testing it. Surprised, Blajine pulls it back. Nothing changes in Myung's face; she is still staring up at the sky impassively. But Blajine knows Myung is laughing at her.

Blajine releases her abruptly. Myung stumbles forward and straightens her robes.

At the edge of Blajine's consciousness, her mother tuts. *Now what?*

IV

All her life, Blajine has been told: Never let a stranger visit Ojda.

The details of why are not clear. The Kilta family doesn't like explanations; they find them boring. Blajine's mother, who was the most kind and patient Kilta ever known, so much so that they wondered if she *was* a Kilta, tried to explain the reasons to Blajine, but even she could not do a good job because she didn't know them herself. So it was all said in vague terms. Their ancestor, Mad Magali, had made the Kilta family vow to live on Ojda forever; they were to protect it. They were to wait for her long-lost sister to return.

And because Blajine was very concerned about being a good Kilta when she was younger, she accepted this explanation. She didn't ask questions.

Now she stares at the stranger standing on Ojda and her heart crimps painfully. Three hundred years and no one has come to Ojda—and then this one turns up while Blajine is keeper, the only living keeper as well, so there is no one else to blame. Just her luck. The last visitor to Kilta had been Xenia Urag, and that was only because dumb Hormuz Kilta left the island, fell in love with her and brought her back. Everyone still tuts every time they say Hormuz's name.

Blajine must buy time.

Your ship is wrecked, she says slowly.

Myung looks at her impassively, her hands clasped in front of her. *Yes*, she says.

Then we must find you a ship. Once you have a ship, you can be a traveler again. Away from here.

Blajine turns the knife in her hand so that the blade catches the light. Myung looks at it.

Where will we get a ship? she asks mildly.

Blajine has already thought of this. *Wait here for me*, she says. *Don't move. No matter what, don't move.*

Then she hurries away.

Myung sits. Of course, she has no intention of leaving once she has a ship, even if Blajine does manage to conjure one up out of thin air. But she decides it is wise to not say it.

Blajine is a strange one: prickly but tender-hearted. She is a twisted amalgamation of rage, loneliness and an unsquashable desire to be loved, which she nonetheless tries very hard to squash. Myung can see the battle play out on her features. She wonders if Blajine knows she is so transparent. She probably doesn't. You don't spend years with no one to talk to and still have a grounded understanding of yourself.

Now Myung watches her disappear over the horizon, noticing that Ojda once again changes its law of space to make sure Blajine covers more distance than a normal person would. Myung wonders how this works, then wonders how Ojda works in general, and then finds herself thinking of the one person who would find a way to know.

Laleh.

As with every time she thinks of her sister, Myung's heart grows heavy. Images crowd in on her. The horror on Laleh's face. Her crying in Myung's arms. Her curled on her side, sleeping deeply, as a voice in Myung's head whispered, *Leave now. You'll never get a chance again.*

And Myung had listened.

She rubs the heels of her palms on her eyes. The sun is still shining brightly, but when Myung checks her watch, adjusted to standardized black sea time, a whole day has passed. It should be night now. She's heard of this phenomenon; because Ojda's sun is painted, it never sets.

She sleeps. When she wakes, her watch tells her it is early morning. Blajine has still not returned. Myung's fingers have started to feel funny now, a cold tingling creeping up her wrist.

That would be the drink Blajine gave her.

It is slow-acting; Myung expected to see its effects much sooner. What is it? Poison? Unlikely, or Blajine wouldn't have pulled out the knife when she realized Myung had arrived on the island on purpose. Some sort of potion that affected the nerves? More likely.

Myung rummages in her satchel and pulls out a wad of rubiad, a thick purple moss you find on asteroids. Useful for combatting most potions. Myung pops some into her mouth and chews.

The tingling doesn't stop, but it doesn't spread. Myung scans the horizon for Blajine. No trace of her. She frowns. Maybe it *is* poison and Blajine has abandoned her so it can finish the job. She feels a thin spike of panic, but controls it. No point in worrying. If she is going to die, she will know soon enough.

But the longer she waits for Blajine, the more she thinks of Laleh.

How do you describe those initial moments when Myung left her sister? *Cleaving* is the only word Myung has for it, but it doesn't do it justice. At times, she pretends her decision was impulsive, that she fled in a sudden rush of emotion. But the truth is she had planned it. Not idle fantasies, actual planning. She knew that if Laleh wouldn't come with her, she would go alone. She even imagined the worst possible case: she would leave her sister, get lost in the whale's many chambers and then learn there was no way *out* of the whale. That was her most terrifying scenario, but she still knew she had to try.

It was more terrifying to stay.

To stay, Myung would have to cut out a part of herself. She would have to pretend she wasn't who she was: desperate for this larger life promised in Laleh's dreams. Desperate for people. Hungry, above all, for an answer to a question that Laleh never seemed to ask herself:

Where did they come from?

If she asked her sister this question, Laleh would answer without hesitation. *Wisa*, she would say. No, she would say *Great Wisa*. But if the answer was Wisa, then where did Wisa come from?

When Myung thinks about these questions now, on Ojda, they sound silly. It has been decades since she left the whale, and it is difficult to conjure up the urgency she felt then. *Who are we? Where do we come from?* They sound like the cold and dead questions you find in academic papers.

In the whale, though, these questions were anything but cold or dead. They were made of life itself, entwined inexplicably with her breath, with every choice she made.

She couldn't tear them out.

So she had left. It broke her, but she had to. Staying with Laleh was like staring at a glass of water when you are parched, but you are unable to pick it up and drink because your sister wants to keep holding your hands.

Is that fair to her sister? Even thinking this feels unfair. But it is unfair *and* true, and Myung still doesn't know how to reconcile that contradiction.

This was what she had thought as she had leaped through the whale's many chambers: unfair, and true, and that glass of water, because she couldn't think of Laleh. If she thought of Laleh, she would turn back. If she lingered on her sister, she would lose her courage. So she tried to forget her. She called doors to her as she had seen Laleh do, and even though the whale called out to her—she felt its cry reverberate in her bones—she kept leaping through each chamber, never stopping, until she found a small opening that didn't scurry away like a door but felt fixed and true, and she tumbled out.

Cold. That is what the black sea was. Cold and empty. The moment Myung left the whale, she felt scooped out, like someone was pulling her insides from her body, slowly and gently, and letting them drift into the midnight black of the sea. She was made of nothing but skin. If she pressed a finger to her chest, she would deflate.

The emotion was overwhelming. Her skin was stiffening, turning slowly numb, and Myung felt light-headed. The edges of her vision turned black. On the verge of passing out, Myung had only a moment to look at the whale.

It was a moment that lasted an infinity. She couldn't discern the shape of the whale; it was too large for her eyes. She saw skin, thick and deep blue. Saw craters where asteroids had sunk into it. She saw, as she drifted back—

An eye. Kind and loving.

And in the corner of the eye, as large as a lake, a tear.

Then Myung passed out.

When she awoke, she was on the smooth floorboards of a ship. She had been dressed in sailor robes; the cloth felt strange on her skin. When she walked, it hampered her movements and she wondered if she could take it off and be free, as she was in the whale.

Then the people came. They called themselves strange names. Captain. First Mate. Cartographer. Myung couldn't talk for the awe of it. People. Real people. Made in different shapes and sizes, with different voices. Different mannerisms too—one of them gestured high and grand when he spoke, another fiddled with her lip. Myung watched these gestures hungrily; she would imitate them when she was alone. *People.*

They said they had found her floating on the black sea. She must have been floating for weeks because her skin was almost blue when they pulled her out; she had felt so cold to the touch. But she had been breathing and had murmured a word. *La-leh?* Does she remember how she got here? Does she remember herself?

But Myung was backing away, shaking her head frantically. Laleh. The pain was sudden and deep, and she didn't want to remember. The people were murmuring. They were holding their hands up. *Calm*, they were saying. *Calm*. The man who called himself a Ship Doctor gave her a bright blue liquid, and she fell into a deep sleep.

They left her on the nearest dock. Myung could not wrap her head around the number of people. People pressing into her, people breathing down her neck, people saying, *do you mind, girl? Out of the way.* It smelt of fish and salt, stardust and sweat. Everything was hot, crowded, intimate. The sounds were overwhelming: shouting, frying, crying, laughter, fights. Myung wanted to scream with the elation of it.

People.

Thus began her journey of understanding the black sea. The island she was on catered to sailors; it processed the cargo they brought in. She apprenticed with a fisherman for a while, cutting through the bodies of cosmic fish to search for metals and treasure. Then she worked in a sea dhaba, pouring drinks and listening to sailor stories. The owner even let her cook; you couldn't get a more enthusiastic cook than Myung. She would work for days, nonstop, as long as you brought her ingredients that delighted her. And everything delighted her; the owner once saw her crooning over an onion. (He shrugged and didn't question it. You get all sorts in a port for sailors.) Her food wasn't *excellent*. Because she was so easily pleased, she was often delighted with her food even when it was half-cooked, sometimes raw. (The owner shrugged again. You take what you can get.)

For a while, Myung was busy with the business of living. She ate, swam, drank. Talked to anyone and everyone, for hours. She imitated people when she was alone. She tried different accents. She would spin to her left and say, *Laleh, you won't believe . . .*

She didn't mind that Laleh wasn't there. She pretended she was. It was the best way to cope.

But on some nights, she would dream of her sister, curled on her side and sleeping deeply. Of Laleh waking up, her hair tousled, still drowsy. Looking around and whispering, *Myung?* But Myung would be gone.

Myung left the sea dhaba soon after. She loved that island but the sailors talked of other places, better islands. She wanted to see those. There was so much left to see.

She bought passage on a ship with the pearls she had saved from her time with the fisherman. On impulse, she bought notebooks with her coins from the dhaba. She didn't know why she bought them, except that they reminded her of Laleh's heart-shaped leaves. They kept her sister close.

The sailors gave her strange looks when she carried five bundles of notebooks onto the deck. Myung didn't mind. She had got lots of strange looks since she came into the black sea; she rather liked it.

But once she had the notebooks, the temptation to write in them was too much. When the ship left port, she opened one in her cabin. She touched her quill to the beautiful paper, wondering what to write. Then she scribbled the first thing that came to mind, just letting her hand flow across the page. She wrote:

Forgive me, Laleh.

She stared at the words, then shut the book.

But after that, Myung was no longer living for herself. She lived for her sister too. She disembarked at every island and wrote down what she saw. She put all her feelings into it, so that if Laleh ever read the notebooks, she would be able to live the journey.

These were the first *Myung's Diaries*. They described common places but with such tenderness that people saw these places anew. Sailors used to ask Myung to read them passages on long nights. They would ask if they could copy pages to keep. An enterprising merchant promised her riches if she distributed her words; Myung never saw any riches, but her diaries were copied, stitched and sent off into the universe. Myung didn't care. Not really. They were only written for one person.

When Myung began visiting undiscovered islands, her diaries became invaluable. Sailors found that Myung Ting—she gave herself a last name because everyone kept asking for it, and she liked how *Ting* sounded—had a distinct knack for survival. Nothing fazed her. Nothing surprised her. She faced the largest sea monsters with glee. She wrote about the smallest plant with sensitivity and care. She spent years on the wildest islands, decades even, and she tamed them. *Myung's Diaries* became gospel. They taught you how to love the black sea, to understand its strange and erratic islands. Sailors read them for instructions; they acted them out for entertainment; they even read them in their spare time, because there really wasn't much to do on a ship when you had been sailing for ages. They called Myung by other names now. Holy Word. North Star. Albatross. They welcomed her onto their ships . . .

Myung clutches the back of her neck, startled. She was wrong—the tingling has not stopped. The drink Blajine gave her is now working on the nerves in her neck. Alarmed, Myung pinches the area to stop it, but the shivering sensation keeps climbing. It travels up, into her skull.

Myung's vision blurs. Ojda distorts and she feels herself falling into a hallucinatory state. She is calm; she has experienced this before. A lot of islands use hallucinogens as defense. As long as she stays level-headed and doesn't do anything stupid to herself, the delusions won't hurt her.

The trick is *remembering* not to do anything stupid.

Just before she passes out, Myung sees her sister. She is leaning over her. *Are you okay?* she asks. *Can you hear me?*

Laleh blurs and distorts. She disappears. She is replaced by three people: two men and one woman. They stare at Myung appraisingly as she lies on the ground, sweaty and blinking blurrily. She doesn't know any of them, but she knows they are Kiltas. They share the same facial pattern that Blajine has: strong jaw, distinctive nose.

The older man bends to peer at her face.

What do you think, Rostum? the woman asks. Her voice echoes. *Do you think she's the one Mad Magali keeps waiting for?*

Rostum squints at her as if appraising a rock to ascertain its age. *No,* he says. *Can't be. She doesn't have the Kilta nose.*

Or the jaw, says the other man.

Then Myung passes out.

V

Once Blajine is sure she has lost the traveler, she drops to her knees. She looks left, then right. She doesn't want her mother witnessing this. Then she takes a deep breath and picks up a handful of Ojda's soil.

On the ground, Ojda's soil shifts colors—blood red, ochre, blue. But in her hand, the particles drain of pigment, turning a distinct and unmistakable bone white. This is the true appearance of Ojda: a bone-white island made by Mad Magali, so that the Kiltas could paint it into anything they wanted.

Of course, now no one paints Ojda but itself.

Blajine stares at the particles in her hand. They look so small and simple, yet they achieve amazing feats. These particles sing endless memories across the black sea. It is beautiful, when you think about it like that.

It is less beautiful when you think about Ojda as, well, Ojda.

But Blajine steels herself. Irrespective of her problems with this island, she needs it to help her now.

Ojda, make a ship, she commands.

The particles rattle and then lie still. Blajine knows the request is not impossible. Ojda is a shape-shifting island; it makes things anew all the time and changes into whatever it likes. Blajine's grandfather used to ask Ojda to create statues of the Kiltas he didn't like; he would make these ugly, giving relatives bigger noses or larger bellies, then he would laugh every time he saw those statues (Blajine's grandfather was a bit strange). But the point is he could get Ojda to make those statues. Blajine's mother, Ayesha, used to sing to the island and Ojda would murmur happily under her song. It adored her. If *she* had asked for a ship, there would be twenty of them right now.

Blajine is the only one failing at being a keeper.

Logically, she knows this is not her fault. With all the other Kiltas, Ojda was only a docile island. Its consciousness hadn't fully developed until then; it was like a helpless baby. It did what anyone asked; it nurtured the family and it didn't change too much. In short, it was a good island. But now it has grown up, and Blajine is stuck with the tantrum-throwing toddler version.

Make a ship, she says again, infusing her voice with authority and wisdom. Then she resorts to cajoling. *You want the traveler gone too*, she reminds Ojda. *You're the one who woke me up in a panic, remember? Make a ship and I can get rid of her.*

It is true that Ojda woke Blajine up in a panic. It is true it didn't like how the visitor felt—displaced and wrong. But now, Ojda has changed its mind. Or it has forgotten why it was so upset in the first place and can't be bothered to remember. Or it is simply distracted and doesn't want to make a ship.

Exactly like a toddler.

Blajine yells in anger and fear. She is so very tired.

Blajine's yell travels across the island to a small patch of trees. These trees do not have leaves on them. Instead, they have tiny blue birds, each growing from the branch and chirping mournfully. Below these branches, the ghosts of the Kilta family are having an argument.

There are three ghosts right now. Laleh has seen all three; they were the ones peering at Myung as she fell into delirium. The older one with a rather large belly, the one they call Rostum, is clearly the leader. He stands with his feet apart and his hands on his hips. He is the sort of man you would imagine saying *well now!* a lot. Jilla, the thin woman who asked him the question about Myung, looks secretive by comparison. She is tall and thin to the point of spindly, and she hunches over, drumming her fingers together in thought. The third man is so insignificant Laleh almost misses him. He has a knack for blending into his surroundings, like he would rather not be noticed. But when you do notice him, you see a square jaw and a general stubbornness that Laleh is beginning to understand is a Kilta family trait.

Well then, Rostum says, *if she's not the one . . .*

No one is the one, Jilla says gloomily. *I bet Mad Magali made the whole thing up so she could chain us to this island forever. It is the kind of thing she'd find fun.*

Mad Magali loves us, Hormuz offers tentatively.

The other two look at him in disgust.

The others will be here soon, Jilla says. *Although I can't see what is taking them so long. They're ghosts—it is not like they get tired. They could just close their eyes and wish to be here and they would be here. They are delaying on purpose. I hate this family.*

But Rostum has just spotted Laleh. He frowns and says, *Hello*. Laleh, who has never spoken to anyone except Myung, almost runs away. But being the keeper of the whale of babel has taught her to approach petrifying things head on, so she steps forward boldly and says, *Hello*.

Jilla looks at her. *I haven't seen you before*, she says. *Have you just arrived?*

Laleh nods.

Ever heard of Ojda? Rostum asks.

Laleh shakes her head. She is about to add, *But I am learning more every moment I am here, in accordance with the laws of the dream*. But Jilla is talking.

Poor girl, she says. *Shall I give her the explanation or would someone else like to?* She looks at the other two, who shake their heads. *Welcome to Ojda*, she tells Laleh when she turns back to her. *Everyone belonging to the Kilta family is meant to spend their life on this island. Some of us*—she shoots a look at Rostum—*didn't. They left and traveled the black sea and had lots of children. Lots. Many of whom didn't know they had Kilta blood in them. Which would be fine, except—*

Except when you die, Hormuz says, *you learn that you are tied to Ojda. You come back here, as a ghost. Bit of a disconcerting experience if you have never been here before, but don't worry, you are already dead—nothing on the island actually harms you. Ojda mostly ignores you.*

Bit of a disconcerting experience even if you have *been here before*, Rostum grumbles. *Imagine thinking you have escaped this crazy island for good,* traveling the black sea, dying peacefully in some lush paradise, and then landing up here again. None of us know how to stop it.

We are working on a treatise, Hormuz says eagerly. "How to Escape the Shackles of Ghosthood: Understanding Mad Magali and the island of Ojda." That's its title.

It will never be published, says Jilla.

It could, says Hormuz.

Hormuz, Jilla says and, at the mention of the name, Rostum tuts obediently, *you're dead.*

Laleh listens to them bicker, fascinated. Perhaps it would have been confusing to her if this was not a dream, but dreams always bring their own knowledge with them. And so Laleh understands that the Kiltas are tied to Ojda. In life, they are made to take a vow that they will not leave. And in death, they live on the island as ghosts, wandering aimlessly. If you are a child or grandchild of a Kilta who broke their vow and left the island, which means you are born on some innocent land in the black sea, *even* then, even if you do not know you *are* a Kilta—your ghost still ends up on the island when you die. There is nothing you can do about it. It is a question of blood.

Laleh is not a Kilta; she has lived her life in the whale of babel and Myung is her only sister. She is also not dead. She can feel her body sleeping in the whale, and can still hear a faint echo of its song. But these three *think* she is a lost Kilta ghost, and it seems easier not to correct them.

Wrap it up, wrap it up, Rostum says hastily. *They're coming.*

A swarm of ghosts descends on the scene at once. There are so many of them, Laleh cannot count their number. Nor can she tell them apart. They are a blur of defined noses and scowls, most of their brows set in stubbornness. They jostle for space, talking over one another, grumbling about why they have been called here—

—*What else do you have to do, Guza?* Rostum roars. *Not much to do here but wander*—

—and generally making a ruckus for no other reason than to make a ruckus. Laleh gathers that they are enjoying themselves. Myung's arrival has given them something to talk about. There's some conversation about Myung being the one they have been waiting for. Jilla throws this suggestion out there, but the ghosts squash it immediately. She doesn't have the nose. Or the jaw. Or the scowl. No, Myung is just a plain old stranger. An infringer on Ojda. The first person to land here in centuries without being led.

At the mention of "led," everyone looks at Hormuz, who shrinks slightly. They tut.

It's settled then, Rostum says. *The only thing to do is to kill her.*

Laleh gasps in horror.

But the other Kiltas are also not a fan of this plan. Murmurs of discontent travel through the group. Kill her? The most exciting thing to happen to Ojda in centuries? Of course, no one wants to say out loud that they would rather disobey Mad Magali's instructions, so they hum and haw. Perhaps it would be more prudent to find out what the traveler wants first. Perhaps she *is* the one. Could anyone really know what Mad Magali meant by "Never let a visitor visit Ojda"? Was it "visit" or was it "stay"? It was very vague phrasing really.

―

In her cottage, Blajine lies awake in her fairy-tale bed and listens to the ghosts squabble. It drifts to her as a murmur. It sounds rather like the cries of Ojda's kiko rocks actually. Kiko rocks like to imitate sound, especially voices. They spent a lot of time last year trying to imitate Blajine, which was very disconcerting. But not as bad as when her mother died, and they spent their time imitating *her* so that Blajine heard her mother's voice everywhere. It made her grief a thousand times worse.

Blajine glances at her timepiece. According to this, it is the middle of the night. She has only a few hours before she must wake up and find the traveler. It is disorienting to live on an island with a painted sun that never sets, but Blajine has got used to it. In the early days, Ojda used to cover its sun with dark clouds so that the family got the impression of nighttime. Now it is more finnicky—it does this only when it feels in the mood. But Blajine has learned to cover her windows and watch her timepiece, and she has a firm grasp of time. She is glad for it. Time is the only sane thing she has to hold on to. She doesn't know what she would do without it.

She knows, therefore, that it has been fifty years since her mother died. Fifty years since Blajine has been alone on this island. She misses her mother like an ache. She is here, wandering Ojda as a ghost, but the living do not always see the ghosts. They cannot always hear them. Blajine doesn't understand how it works; perhaps it will be clearer to her once she is dead.

God, to die, to finally escape this island in death—only to be reborn on it as a ghost that can never leave . . .

But Blajine longs for even that. For at least then she will be able to see the other ghosts. She will have people to talk to.

Blajine's loneliness is a creature. It is shape-shifting and hungry. It appears first in small doses—as a tiny fluffy bird by her ear lobe, cooing and chirping. It looks at her life, its head cocked; it looks at her. Then it spends its time pecking by her feet, unpicking structures she has put into place, eating moments of joy and serenity, swallowing—whole—stories Blajine has told herself about herself. It eats; it grows. It diffuses at the edges, feathers fluttering into the sky to dissolve into smoke and then even the breath Blajine takes smells of loneliness. More birds grow in her stomach. They peck toward her heart.

Blajine turns in her bed. *Mama*, she whispers. She is so tired.

Sometimes, she imagines she is meeting Ojda—its spirit, its consciousness or whatever word they give it now in the black sea. She always sees this spirit in the shape of a woman. This woman would sit by Blajine's feet as Blajine threatens to leave.

There are islands with real sunrises, you know that? she'd say to this spirit-woman. *With real nights, not those created by clouds.*

This woman would smile, play with her bone necklace and flash blood-stained teeth.

Blajine would become threatening. *I could leave, you know*, she'd say. *In fact, I will leave. I will leave now. See how well you do without me.*

Then the spirit would grow contrite, holding her ankles and crying. Blajine likes to imagine Ojda like that. Needing her. Loving her. But there is no way to be sure.

She realizes, suddenly, that everything is quiet. The squabbling has died; her family has dispersed. It is unlike them to end a family meeting so quickly. They normally drag on for days; you don't have to stop proceedings to eat if you're a ghost.

It can mean only one thing. Mad Magali is about.

A metal moon moves on the timepiece; another hour of sleep lost. Blajine rolls over onto her back. She thinks of the traveler, sleeping in the plains. Her arms would be over her eyes, to block out the sun. Blajine remembers how Myung pressed her neck into the knife. This traveler is a crafty one. How do you get rid of the crafty ones?

It's not my fault if she stays a little longer, Blajine says to the ghost of her mother. *I am trying.*

Her mother flicks dirt from her nails. *How hard?*

The Confession

I

Blajine finds the traveler exactly where she had left her. The flowers have subsided, so Myung is curled against the cold, using her satchel as a pillow. She really is asleep. Blajine finds this careless, but the innocence of it is also touching. She imagines sitting her down and educating her, as her mother once educated her. *One eye always on the world of the waking,* she would say. *You never know what might happen.*

It takes three shakes to get Myung up. She looks clammier, dark circles under her eyes. *Is there a ship?* she murmurs as she sits up. *Are we making a ship?*

She sounds almost eager for it. Blajine smiles. The water she gave the traveler induces petrifying dreams; it is heartening to see it worked. Very hard to know if it will work if you haven't had a traveler on your island for three centuries or longer. Blajine had to test it on herself.

No, Blajine says. *We're going to find one.*

When Blajine was younger, she drew a map of Ojda. It was very pretty. Blue-green mountains, a steady buttercup-yellow sun, sparrows wheeling in the distance. Her trees were not very good, but trees are difficult to master—ask any artist. Her mother was very proud. When Blajine left the island and came back, she talked to her mother about the sketches she made for black sea expeditions. Birds. Flora. Reptiles. *We should make one for Ojda*, she said. *You can try*, her mother replied.

Ojda was already changing then. Mad Magali designed this island to be a paradise but as Ojda grew up, it began to change what Magali had made. It crumbled mountains and carved gorges. Shred up birds to make a river of feathers. Brought the clouds low to make mist and then snow, fiddled with its colors. At times, Blajine could feel it turn its vast consciousness on her.

It's mad, she whispered to her mother, frightened. *It's turning mad.*

Her mother tapped her nose and said, *Aren't we all?*

Now Blajine doesn't bother with maps. Ojda doesn't like being only one thing; it changes all the time, fast and slow. A magpie, she called it once. Collecting all the shiny bits it could imagine.

Somewhere on this shiny landscape, there will be parts to make a ship. If they are lucky, a whole ship.

Where are we going? Myung asks, slinging the satchel across her. Even thin and shivery, she looks prepared. Blajine is impressed.

I don't know, she says. *We walk.*

This is a dramatic statement that Blajine hopes lends her an air of mystery. In reality, she doesn't know *for sure*, but can guess where they might find a ship. Ojda has what Blajine calls "the sea of changing mists." It is not an actual sea, just a patch of land covered in dense fog. If you cross it, you will find all sorts of objects emerging into being. It can be quite beautiful, but also petrifying—Blajine once found herself hanging upside down with no idea of what had caught hold of her leg. But if they are looking for a ship, then it is a good place to start. They just have to hope Ojda hasn't changed the sea of changing mists into something else by now.

Where did you go, by the way? Myung asks. *You said you'll be back soon.*

Crafty. The traveler wants to know about the cottage, but Blajine is craftier—she won't be caught out.

She waves her hand airily. *I was only gone a night*, she says. *Don't get too attached, visitor. You'll be gone soon.*

But I thought—Then Myung shakes her head, dislodging a thought. There's a glimmer in her eye, a cut of slyness, but it's gone before Blajine can look closer.

Never mind, the traveler says. *My mistake.*

―

The quickest way to the sea of changing mists is, as always, past Ojda's river. For a while, Blajine cannot decide if she wants to cross it, just this once. After all, the faster they find a ship, the faster the traveler leaves. But she decides against it in the end. She cannot bear what the river makes her feel. She takes the long way around, through the jomin desert first and then into the jungle.

This also gives her more time with the traveler.

Blajine tells herself this is for official purposes. As keeper of Ojda, she should find out how the traveler discovered the island. She should question her about her practices. It is necessary to gather news from the black sea, and check if there have been any new stories that the traveler particularly liked . . . God, Blajine misses stories. She misses someone else's imagination doing all the work. She hopes the traveler is a good storyteller.

The traveler is. As they walk, they talk about new islands that have been discovered on the black sea, the latest ship trends and the best place in the universe to get roast rabbit with plum sauce. Myung talks rapidly and easily, as if she has known Blajine all her life. Blajine, who hasn't spoken to a living person in fifty years and is nervous about the fact that she may have forgotten how to do it, finds it remarkably easy to talk to the traveler. Maybe people who aren't Kiltas are just easy to talk to? Less arguing and more listening? Blajine cannot tell. She feels a little hop-skip-jump of joy in her chest to be speaking to anyone at all, but she crushes it before it can take root.

She is a Kilta. She knows her duty.

―

If you have read *Myung's Diaries* closely, you will know that islands have desires. Some islands like to be beautiful, others grand. Some like the patter of a thousand animals on their backs, others prefer the feel of their surfaces cracked into rocks and gorges. Ojda isn't an ordinary island. It doesn't care what it becomes. What it likes is the moment of change. That shift between one form and another, the in-between flow that's half and half. It also likes surprise.

Blajine and Myung are now walking across an arid landscape scarred by a network of brittle roots.

Did you not want to travel? Myung asks, picking her way through the many giant roots erupting from the ground.

Blajine shrugs. It is the same as Myung's shrug; she likes imitating it, getting it just right. *I imagine it would be more of the same,* she says.

Do you speak to many people?

Blajine stops, stung. Is her conversation that bad? *Why do you ask?*

Myung slings her leg over one particularly large root, stumbles as she lands on the other end. *There seems to be no one else around.*

An alarming thought has struck Blajine. What if the traveler has friends? What if those friends are on their way to Ojda right now? More travelers? The Kiltas would never forgive her.

She leans in, suddenly menacing. *Are you speaking to many people?* she whispers. *Speaking to them now perhaps, bringing them here?*

Myung's eyes widen in surprise. *No,* she says, raising her palms to show peace. *No.*

Blajine leans back, contemplating this. *I speak to people,* she says finally.

Okay.

Many people.

Myung nods.

They keep walking. Conversation has died, and Blajine feels bad for overreacting and then feels bad for feeling bad. You're a Kilta, she reminds herself. You must be ruthless.

But she doesn't feel ruthless, only curious about what the traveler was going to tell her about a recipe for iyu rice. And now she may never know.

You're like a rhinoceros, she says as Myung stumbles over another root. Myung smiles and Blajine feels a bit better.

After a while, Myung says: *It's not the same. Each island is different if you look carefully. You'll find that—*

The roots change from wood to silvery scales, the landscape becomes a mass of writhing coils and a many-headed jomin bursts out of the ground, hissing and spitting. Blajine saw this coming; a root had slithered twenty steps back and the wood on another had gleamed. She dives behind a rock she had scouted for this purpose, knife in hand, watching the ground churn, Myung flailing as she is dangled from her ankle, the jomin's fangs glistening. It *is* kind of beautiful, if you look carefully. At one point she thinks the traveler really will die. That would be sad. But there it is again, the change she saw on the first day. Hapless Myung becomes a shrewd and cunning Myung. After a close fight, the jomin collapses with a strange contraption sticking from its neck—a pair of compasses?—pulled from the depths of the traveler's satchel. Myung lies on the ground next to the dead creature, bleeding and breathing heavily.

You could do it now, the ghost of her mother whispers.

Instead, Blajine leaves her rock to crouch beside her guest.

The first thing I learned, she says, *is Ojda likes to change. The second thing I learned is that Ojda likes to change* you. *Use your eyeballs as stars, make your bones into a tree, pluck your teeth out to grow a new animal.* She feels a sudden swell of tenderness for the traveler and adds, *Be vigilant.*

II

Blajine dresses the traveler's wounds and carries her to the Rock of Respectability, which is named such because it is only a rock. Which on Ojda—where you cannot trust anything to *be* what it looks like—is very respectable of it. Blajine sets the traveler against it and makes her comfortable.

We made good progress today, she says. *Rest. I'll come back to find you.*

Myung's eyes widen. *You're not taking me with you?*

Blajine feels a stab of guilt. But the cottage is a sacred space; no visitor could possibly be allowed. She shrugs. *Sorry,* she says, and disappears.

The Kilta cottage is no more than a hundred steps away for Blajine, no matter where she is on Ojda. She doesn't worry about Myung following her; even if Myung could find the energy for stealth, only Kiltas can find this cottage.

Back home, Blajine cooks dinner. She repairs her roof with mud and plants. She sits outside the door and stares at the scenery. She taps her tragus and says *khol*.

The museum of collective memory unfolds around her, so that when Blajine stands, she is in a different place altogether.

Laleh has spent her whole life in the whale of babel, so she is no stranger to marvels. But the museum is unlike anything she's witnessed. Standing here, beside Blajine in this singing corridor, she can feel *people*.

Each of the museum's billion objects has a network of people attached to it: people whom the object symbolizes, the tribe or family those people belonged to and the people who have touched the object, searching for it. Laleh can sense these nets of intimacy criss-cross above each other in these corridors, a silvery web that ripples across the black sea.

It takes her breath away.

Blajine navigates the museum's corridors with an ease that is magnificent to watch. She moves as a dancer and the museum flows with her, corridors spinning and twisting around her like a puzzle box. There is awe in this spectacle. Has she seen herself like this—lithe and powerful? If Laleh could find a mirror, she would show her. She would whisper: *Blajine, look. There is wonder in you.*

But there is another feeling underneath this one. Fuller and sourer. Careful. Blajine's mastery is a trick; you could never possess it. The museum is made from song as sweet as a siren's. Listen for too long and you will drown. How many corpses has Blajine found? Travelers who let their bodies waste away as their mind drank from the museum's wisdom. Visitors who forgot how to leave. Only a Kilta knows how to dance through the museum, into its depths, and not be lost.

Now Blajine wanders down the corridors searching for Myung Ting. She finds articles on the traveler. She discovers the room where *Myung's Diaries* are stacked; she stares at them lining the walls. But she cannot find where Myung comes from. There is no Ting family.

She strolls through the museum, pondering this. As if by instinct, the corridors around her shift and whirl. They open into a long passageway covered with cobwebs and dust; the air smells musty and the plants along the walls are dead. Blajine walks down the corridor absent-mindedly, still lost in thought. She doesn't notice where she is until she comes across a door; it is made of simple teak, the same height as an ordinary cottage door. Then she sighs, realizing where her feet have taken her, and pushes it open.

The room she enters is circular. The high ceiling is domed, and covered with different floor plans, each marked with detailed annotations. These are the first floor plans of the museum of collective memory. Across the walls there are shelves crammed with notebooks, sketchpads and loose sheets of paper. These belong to the Kiltas; they are diaries, stories and drawings they have made during their lifetimes. These shelves are bursting; there isn't much to do on Ojda except write and draw.

The center of the room is filled with statues.

They are all caught in different moments, crowded together with no thought to aesthetics. Blajine wanders among them, squeezing through gaps between legs, occasionally brushing her fingers along a shoulder or a cheek.

The Kilta family.

No member gets to choose how the museum remembers them; it picks the age at which it likes them best and memorializes them. Blajine meanders until she comes to the statue she always visits: her mother.

Ayesha Kilta has been memorialized a few years before her death. She is old, crow's feet spilling from the edge of her eyes, but she is caught in laughter. Blajine's heart aches. She will never know anyone as good, truly good, as her mother. Ayesha Kilta could laugh at anything. She could sing Ojda into calm and silence. She could fix all your hurt with a touch and a few simple words.

Her mother was magic.

Normally, Blajine would leave the room, having seen what she came for. But today she moves on, into the heart of the crowd, toward the statue at the center of it all.

Mad Magali.

The museum has remembered her as middle aged. She's close to fifty, standing with her feet apart, hands on her hips. She glowers at Blajine. It is an accurate representation—all anyone in the family remembers of Mad Magali is her glower. She was said to be petrifying, with a voice that carried across Ojda. A few feet behind her is the statue of her husband, Jinn. He has been caught at around the same age: fifty, a beard sprouting, with large kind eyes. Even as a statue, he looks patient.

Blajine supposes he had to be, being married to Mad Magali.

She looks back at the family matriarch. Beyond the glower, there is determination and a fire. She feels suddenly close to her ancestor. Mad Magali did incredible things. Impossible things.

And if the Kilta myth was true, then she did it for one person.

When Blajine was thirteen, she asked her mother why they had to live on the island. Ojda was living—why couldn't it welcome the long-lost sister? Or, you know, why couldn't they *visit* Ojda once every five years and *check* if the sister had turned up? Why did they have to *stay*? *Forever*?

Memories can be corrupted, little leaf, her mother had said. *Look at sea stories or fairy tales or the secrets being spilled by the Vortex of Norma. The truth disappears if you don't keep it safe.*

This wasn't what the books had told Blajine; they said the truth always survives. But maybe it did survive; it just changed shape. And for the Blajine who was watching Ojda wake up and who was terrified . . . well, she could understand why Magali might have wanted to keep the truth looking the same.

Blajine scowls at the statue, trying to get the glower just right. Hands on hips. Wrinkle your nose a little. Glare. What was the name of the sister again? Something with W. Wey . . . No. Wel . . . No. Wi . . . Wisa!

The dream wobbles. In the World of the One Tree in the whale of babel, Laleh shifts in her sleep, agitated.

Blajine turns in surprise—she could swear she saw a person, right there—but there is no one behind her. When she reaches out, she finds only air.

Perhaps if Blajine were in a different frame of mind, she would have lingered on this moment. She would have pondered whom she saw and how she saw them. Ghosts can't enter the museum of collective memory; it is no place for the dead. The person she saw then must not have been a ghost. And if she had asked herself that question, then she would have stumbled down paths that would have taken her closer to the truth . . .

But she does none of this. She turns away from Laleh and stares at Mad Magali's statue thoughtfully. A plan is hatching in her mind. If *someone* is meant to come back to Ojda at *some* point . . .

Why can't it be Myung?

This has very little logic to support it, but Blajine is pleased. Mad Magali's sister is obviously dead; it has been God knows how many centuries since Magali herself died. But all the Kiltas are *also* dead. Look around. This room of statues is nothing more than a graveyard. Blajine is the only one left.

If Magali is dead, her sister is dead and everyone else is dead, then why can't Blajine do what she likes?

Why can't she keep the traveler?

Joy rises up in her, hop-skip-jump. Someone to talk to. To eat with. To take care of, chastise and love. To be loved, even if it is in that same shouty way Kiltas show love. (It is a Kilta trait to shout when you care a lot and then, when the other person gets upset, pretend like you hadn't raised your voice at all.)

Ojda will have to be convinced, of course. It is very picky about who gets to walk on its surface. But that is okay . . . All it would take is a bit of cajoling. And if Ojda didn't agree—well, so what? Blajine has been fighting with this stupid island for years; a bit more fighting won't hurt anyone. And, this time, she would have someone by her side.

Joy.

So much joy, Blajine doesn't notice the room is transforming.

Shadows gather at the ceiling's corners, spreading to the center. Laleh stumbles back—the air has grown thick and heavy. The statues darken. They grow. Their gaze turns to Blajine, who is still lost in her happy thoughts.

Should she teach Myung the Kilta family recipe for plant stew first or the recipe for fish cutlets? The stew is easier, so maybe the stew. Although so many of the ingredients have changed it is barely a stew anymore, but the traveler won't know that . . .

Then Blajine looks up, and the full force of her family's censor crashes down upon her.

Families are a collection of moorings, patterns of behavior that they swear to and unspoken promises they make. Some families swear a delight for meat. Others enjoy arguing. Still others contemplate morbidity on a frequent basis and are proud of it—who else but a Pohtra would be so blasé about death? *No one*, they say with pride.

For the Kiltas, this mooring is Ojda. Each Kilta grows up knowing two things. One: they must spend their lives on Ojda. And two: no one else may walk this island but them. No one else may belong.

Blajine cowers. She feels flayed, her skin split open and her inner self exposed. Centuries of Kiltas bear down on her, chastising her for her thoughts.

Never let a visitor stay on Ojda.

Kill her.

Blajine whimpers. She is an old woman now; she has lived through more terrifying things than most of these statues. But in this moment, she is a child again, wide-eyed and scared, and she cannot bear the disapproval.

She flees, spinning corridors this way and that, until she stumbles out in front of her cottage door, once again on Ojda.

Once again alone.

III

When Blajine leaves Myung at the Rock of Respectability, Myung waits to make sure she is really gone and then digs into her satchel. The jomin hurt her all right—who knew a three-headed eel-like creature would have such large fangs? But Myung has suffered worse. Her body is a tough one; she has always been able to endure what would kill other men. She checks her dressings quickly, wrinkling her nose at how foul the ointment smells, and sure enough: the skin is already healing. She will be fine.

So she plucks out her watch from her satchel and studies it. She was correct! Three days have passed since Blajine came to her to search for a ship and they trekked across this island . . . But Blajine believes only one day has gone by. By the time Blajine's "night" ends, two more days will have passed in black sea time.

Five days and five nights in black sea time, for one day and night on Ojda.

Myung glances up at the burned orange sun. It looks a bit like a toddler painted it—lopsided and oval.

Her instinct tells her there is more to the story here. It isn't just that Blajine measures time differently . . . her body acts as if it is different too. She ate only once in these three days (dried mushrooms she carried in her pocket) and barely drank. Myung's body has always needed little sustenance, but even then, her stomach rumbled at every one of the six lunches and dinners she has missed . . . but Blajine didn't even notice.

Could Kiltas be born with a different measurement of time?

But this made no sense. Magali Kilta was born and raised in the wider black sea; she traveled across it. She would have followed the standardized measurement of time, like everyone else.

Why change it on this island?

No, this isn't a person's doing. This has trickery written across it, the kind performed by shape-shifting islands.

Myung smiles. She *loves* an intelligent island.

Slowly, she stumbles to her feet, clutching her notebook and charcoal pencil. If Blajine isn't going to return for two days, then she has time and freedom to explore away from the eyes of a jealous keeper.

She will make it count.

For unless she is wrong—and Myung Ting is rarely wrong—the person she needs to win over to find what she is looking for is not Blajine, but Ojda.

Myung has befriended numerous islands—so many now, she cannot keep count. Ojda is a tough one, but she is certain it will yield to her eventually. Patience, as she writes in her one hundred and fifty-eighth *Myung's Diaries*, is key:

> Wait. Watch. Move as slowly as you can. Don't move at all. Islands don't like you being on them. They'd like to know why you're here. Human time is wrong: you walk too fast, speak too loudly, die too quickly. It is irksome. Islands like change as a slow curve, the build and break of a gentle wave. To befriend an island, sit still. If you must walk, tread as if on a butterfly. Ossify to become a part of them. Show them you can change your time, even if it brings you close to your death.

But after one day of wandering across Ojda, Myung is forced to face a few realities.

First, she is not as healthy as she believed. The wounds she suffered from the jomin keep opening, and her body is not happy with being dragged under Ojda's sun.

Second, the islands Myung usually visited were wild and unexplored. They didn't know what to do with Myung when she arrived. They certainly weren't *wary* of her. But someone must have warned Ojda's beasts and birds about her, because they inch away with definite suspicion. Even an even-tempered mammal that spent his time chewing thoughtfully on Ojda's soil hisses and scampers when she comes close.

Third, Ojda is watching her.

Myung can feel its consciousness press down on her shoulders. It is not the same as when she was in the plains—then, there was a definite sense of dislike in Ojda's gaze. Now, there is curiosity mingled with suspicion. Ojda doesn't know her. She doesn't look like a Kilta, and Kiltas are the only people Ojda tolerates.

Tired and hot, Myung tries to soothe it. She drops to her knees and presses her palm into the dirt. *Friend*, she says. *Friend*.

But either Ojda thinks this is a stupid thing to say—what actual friend says *friend*?—or it can hear the edge of desperation in her voice. Its opinion doesn't change.

By noon the next day, Myung knows there is no tricking this island.

A part of her is determined to deny this. She is Myung Ting! She was keeper of the whale of babel! Which island dare best her? She simply needs to find the knife to pry its heart open. She only needs time.

But Myung may not have time. She does not know if a ship is indeed growing in the sea of mists, and what Blajine will do when Myung refuses to board it. She has been a keeper too, and knows that keepers will go to any length to protect their charge.

But it isn't just time, is it? Laleh would say it straight: *You know Ojda cannot be fooled, silly. It sees you; it's smart. You won't get what you want by being witch, knight or explorer. You'll need to be a truth-teller, give it your honesty. That's what it wants.*

Honesty. One of the most potent ways to pry open an island: to metaphorically roll on to your back and expose your soft underbelly, and then hope it won't eat you alive. Myung hates honesty. Fools use it, explorers who are novices at their craft. Honesty can earn you the heart of an island, but it can also leave you dead.

Fine, not dead. But maimed. Or at an island's mercy. Or with the horrible feeling of having exposed the rawest parts of yourself. Which are all terrible things! Worse than death!

Overhead, Ojda's sun bores into her. She glares back, each waiting for the other to blink.

IV

Laleh walks through the snow plains—although it is not snow but salt and it clings to the bottom of her feet. Somewhere on Ojda, Myung drops to her knees and presses her hand into the ground, murmuring *friend*. In the cottage, Blajine curls up in her bed, crying silently. Laleh wants to be free of all of them, to be alone with the knowledge she has discovered.

Great Wisa has a sister.

It is baffling. Great Wisa is one of a kind. Yet here is a sister, and the sister has a family. It means Great Wisa has a family. In the black sea, outside the whale. Myung was right.

It feels too raw, and too much for Laleh to handle.

And yet . . . it also feels nice. The only person Laleh has been linked to is Myung. To now find she could be linked to many people is . . . strange. Wonderful. She can be part of those people-webs in the museum of collective memory. And she would not have only one mirror to reflect herself, but hundreds: each showing different sides of her, offering her different possibilities. She could trace her behaviors to an old uncle who lived two centuries before her; she could predict how a niece or nephew may get her eyes. She could make patterns.

Just arrived?

An old woman is looking at her appraisingly. She is sitting on a collection of stone-plants, all of them sighing under her weight; she taps her walking stick thoughtfully. Laleh knows this woman is a ghost. She also knows, without a doubt, that it is Mad Magali.

Magali sighs. *You must be new; the new ones never talk. Damn that Rostum and all his children.* She taps her stick again. *You'll get used to the island*, she says kindly. *You are made for this place; you're a Kilta.*[*]

---

[*] When little Kilta children say they'd rather live on a nicer island, like the island of Gultan, where birds bring you fruit and bears hug you, their parents tell them the

Laleh sits by the old woman's feet. She doesn't say anything; she simply wants to be near her. This is Great Wisa's sister. They shared the same life, at least for some time. That must make this woman goddess-like. There must be some of Great Wisa in her.

Magali looks down at her, amused. *I like you*, she says. *You are calm. None of the young ones are calm. Everything frazzles them. When I was your age...*

She pauses and looks at Laleh again. Something about Laleh's age has pushed her into sadness, and she stays quiet for a while. The two women stare out into Ojda.

I miss her, Magali says.

Laleh doesn't interrupt; she knows Magali is not talking to her. She stays still, making space for the old woman's memories.

She would have loved this place, Magali says. *She would have delighted in what Ojda became. All these little ones are so scared all the time. But Wisa—Wisa would have laughed. She would have danced with glee. She would have wandered across this landscape learning everything, and then she would have relearned it when Ojda changed it all. I didn't make it like this—I made the island nice and kind—but I'm proud of it. It has changed itself into something she would have admired.*

Laleh is filled with a light, white joy. She is content. To sit here, with Great Wisa's sister. To sit here and talk about Great Wisa. She could not have asked for more.

Why doesn't she come? Magali says.

Laleh hears her pain, and it strikes deep into her own heart. She holds Magali's foot in comfort; it is the only part of her she can reach. It is a question Laleh has asked herself so many times in the whale. She would call out *Great Wisa!* and no one would answer.

---

story of Dastur Uncle. Dastur Uncle left Ojda to settle on an island once, nothing but blue water and fat palm trees; he was cutting up the silent and peaceful island within a year, trying to goad it into a reaction; he was cutting himself up a year later, a lattice of lines across his skin that he would keep reopening just to remind himself he was alive. You see, asleep or awake, Ojda has always been more. And Kiltas cannot do without it. Kiltas like madness. This, at least, is what the parents tell their children. No one knows if Dastur Uncle is a lie.

Why didn't she come?

Magali!

Someone is shouting for her. Laleh doesn't recognize the voice, but Magali clearly does. She lurches to her feet, cursing.

Magali!

A man is striding across the landscape. He is older than his statue in the museum, but the features are the same: a beard, thick hair, a strong body. Although Laleh can't see from this far, she's sure he has the same kind eyes.

Don't tell him I was here, Magali whispers hurriedly. *Keep it to yourself.*

Then she disappears.

V

Blajine doesn't arrive on the second day (as measured by Myung's watch) that is meant to constitute her night (as measured by Blajine's sense of time). Myung waits by the Rock of Respectability for a few hours, then considers resuming her quest. But what difference will it make? Ojda has won. She can sense its shriveled heart pumping in stubbornness. It doesn't care how many islands she has bested—she won't best it.

If Myung wants to stay, she needs to give it all of herself. Ugly, good, true—everything. Ojda will accept no less. (In fact, it would be very appalled at the thought that anyone would accept less. After all, it has had a family chained to it since its birth, dedicating their lives to its care. That's the kind of dedication it knows. Not this useless dropping to your knees and saying *friend, friend*.)

So, Myung can explore as much as she likes, write notes and scheme; it won't make a lick of difference. There is only one option open to her: radical honesty.

Myung grimaces. Laleh would love this; she would see it as a sweet bonding; she would sing and coax Ojda out of its shell with the tenderest parts of herself. But Myung is awful at it. Being honest with yourself is hard enough. Being honest with someone else is agony.

But Ojda cannot be convinced any other way.

I suppose you want to know how I found you, she says. *Or why I found you. I am quite proud of it actually; I don't think anyone has done it in centuries. It did take a bit of hunting. I made a map from fragments. I went across the black sea and I asked about you. Your myths, your legends, any gossip. I wrote it all down, what anyone would tell me, and then I made a map of it.*

I don't know how I made it, nor do I think I could read the map again. It was a bizarre thing—a sketch of circles and triangles that just seemed to . . . make sense. Some part of me knew how to make it, and then some part of me knew how to sail with it. And then I landed up on you.

Ojda is listening but Myung can tell her speech hasn't impressed it so far. "I made a map of nonsense that I can only read once" isn't enthralling stuff.

I like you, she says. *I used to live in a place like you once. Bigger than you, much bigger. Kinder too. I think it was just older; you're a little baby planet. That one was a universe. I had a sister there. I left her behind. She used to say the whale—that place I was in—would sing to her, but I could never hear it. I always felt . . . punished, you know?* Myung's voice grows thicker. She clears her throat. *Punished a bit for being me. I know the whale loved me but I . . . I couldn't feel it. And its kindness made it worse.*

I like you, though. I like that you don't love me. That you are not easily impressed. I understand that. It feels more real, more equal this way.

Myung looks at her lap; she fiddles with her fingers. God, she hates this. She hasn't said these things to anyone—even to herself. It's all coming out as nonsense.

My sister and I, we knew of this one other person. Our maker, Wisa. Great Wisa, we called her. She made us and she loved us, but we never met her. I became obsessed with finding out who Wisa was. Where she came from. I began dreaming about people. So I left. I came to the black sea, and I became this. She gestures to herself. *Traveler. Explorer. I'm famous, you know. Written lots of diaries; many people call me smart.*

She smiles; she hopes it is endearing. Ojda's consciousness is still here. She feels a prickle of pride that she has kept its attention for so long. She takes a deep breath—this is the tough part.

But it wasn't enough, beyond a point. The diaries, the explorations. I missed Laleh, my sister. But I couldn't find the whale again, no matter how much I looked. I swear, on Laleh, I looked. I read all the literature they have on the whale of babel. I've researched everything they say about Wisa. There was nothing there. Nothing about how to find the whale or who Wisa may be. It was all a dead end.

And then one day, I was on a ship. We were about to face an electrical storm and a sailor was rocking back and forth. "Please, Alban," he said, "please don't let the mad sisters get me." And I remembered hearing that somewhere, when I first became an explorer. About the mad sisters of Esi who roam as spirits in the black sea, enticing sailors to jump in and join them.

It's just a sea story. I know that. "Don't let the mad sisters get me"—that's just a sea phrase. There are so many of them: sea phrases to pray for good food, safe passage, fat treasure. Maybe that's why when I heard it for the first time decades ago I didn't pay attention. But when I heard it this time . . .

Myung falls silent. The blue-bird tree above her is silent too; it has been listening intently. Now it nudges her with its root. Go on, it seems to say. Ojda is still here.

Have you ever felt an impulse so strong you know it is correct, but you cannot understand it? Have you ever chased something, a tail end of a feeling, always whipping out of sight? And you run and you run, hoping to catch it. That's what this was like. I heard the sailor say the words "mad sisters" and I knew Wisa was one of them. I knew as if I had heard her tell me herself. I can't explain it. Don't ask me to. But I didn't question it. I chased the impulse—I looked for the story.

Mirabilia diachronism is a branch of academia that says that every fairy tale, every sea phrase or myth has a seed of history in it. I looked for that seed. I read up on Esi and on all the famous people that came from its shores. I found out about Magali Kilta. And then I found a paper that said Magali and Wisa were sisters. That Magali made this museum for her.

So I came here. I read up on Magali Kilta, I found out about this place, I hunted for it and I came here. I came because somewhere on this island there is a story about who Wisa really was, about the mad sisters of Esi. And if I can learn that, then maybe . . . maybe I didn't leave my sister for nothing. Maybe I can better understand myself. And once I know it—

Myung tilts her face to the sky, her body trembling.

—*Once I know it, I'll understand her creation better. I'll understand the whale, I'll know how to find it and I can be with my sister again.*

The Cracking

I

Blajine wakes up from the nightmare of Kiltas chasing her and realizes she has overslept. When she reaches the Rock of Respectability, the traveler is gone. Panic swells in her, but she quells it with practice. Where can the traveler go? Her satchel is here and Blajine knows she would not leave without it.

This is simply a ripe opportunity.

She tips the satchel, watching its contents empty onto the ground. She rummages through them with her toe. Quills, charcoal pencils, some dried meat, medicines, a folded piece of paper that is a drawing of triangles and circles, a book and a nondescript orb, probably used for navigation.

Of these, the book is the most interesting. Blajine flips through it, noting the clear "MYUNG'S DIARIES, NO. CMXLI" on the front. She opens it to a random page:

> There is no smell. I close my eyes and expect to find it: the sharpness of vegetation, of brine or perhaps cold flatness of shell. Instead, I find sound. When the soil shifts, I can hear an island's worth of conversation. Then I find smell,

light but growing more pungent. Masked, always masked,
by whispers.

Blajine drops the book, startled. This is Ojda in the stranger's handwriting, caged on the page. She feels a giddy rush of protectiveness—Ojda should *never* be caged.

She picks up the book again and flips. She reads a passage to the end, then flips and reads more. She learns Myung has a sister, someone to miss and love, someone to call her own. Tears gather in the corners of her eyes. She keeps reading. Another page and another.

She cannot stop.

Her thirst frightens her. Nothing here is new to her; she has lived her life in the museum of collective memory, wandering its collections; she knows everything there is to know about most islands. It is not what is written, but *how*. She reads to quench something in herself.

When she sees "Vortex in Noma" she pauses, then reads the entry in full.

> There is a vortex in Noma that eats into the black sea. Peasants gather at its edge to shiver and peer at it in wonder. Among the cluster of boats, you can find the sleek canoes of the academics, their books bound in waterproof leather, quills rolling around at the bottom. They take notes with the frenzy of those who feel an idea will disappear if not set down in words. They catch, as desperately as they can, the maelstrom's wisdom.
>
> For here is the wonder of the Vortex of Noma. Those who travel through it say that, through the veil of the whirlpool's edge, you can see the secrets of the black sea. These are unlike anything seen—mysteries, fables, knowledge so far beyond our grasp that we did not know we do not know.
>
> And now the crust of boats has grown thicker, for the vortex is speaking of a beloved children's fairy tale, a story so old that its origin has been forgotten.

What prize will they earn, those who can find the whale of babel?

But the academics' notes are piecemeal, their information second-hand and scattered. No adult can travel through the vortex and come out alive. A few have tried. Julop Crace was the first, and other adventurers followed her. Their bodies were never found.

So the academics must rely on a more capricious source—children. They are the only ones who can travel through the vortex and return. They leap into the eye of the whirlpool and come back out of the cosmos, falling into their panicked parents' arms.

This, then, is Noma. A gathering of boats like a jigsaw puzzle, children whooping and yelling as they leap into the vortex. Professors in single boats, scribbling what they can hear. Parents with their faces turned heavenward and their arms out, panicked, waiting for their children to be returned.

I catch a child that does not belong to me. She squirms in my arms, giggling and trembling as she reaches for the vortex, eager to go again—so young, not yet three. I hold her until a worried mother picks her way across the boats and pulls her child to her chest. She forgets to thank me. I do not mind; the child is babbling to her; an academic three boats down is trying to inch closer to glean snatches. The mother keeps her eyes closed, cheek pressed to her child's temple, not really listening, and I find a new wonder: in the face of the sublime, it is our humanness we hold close.

Someone shuffles behind her, and Blajine turns, startled. Myung is staring at her. Blajine drops the diary. Her cheeks are wet; she wipes them hastily. Then she bends down to gather Myung's things and put them back into the satchel. Myung helps.

Blajine is still crying. She cannot stop. She doesn't know what it is in those passages that affects her. Hearing about the world maybe, from such a human voice? Or is it that Myung writes about everything she sees with such tenderness?

In fifty years, who has looked at Blajine like that?

When everything is back in the satchel, Blajine whispers, *You write well.* Myung nods. She places her hand briefly on Blajine's shoulder, the touch searing, and they never speak of it again.

II

The ghosts can tell something has changed.

Look at how they lean toward each other, Jilla says, *the way they choose their words carefully.*

Observe the footwork, Hormuz says excitedly. *You can tell a lot by footwork.*

Classic friendship forming, Rustom announces. *Two lonely people trying to figure out how not to be lonely together.*

Laleh doesn't know how she feels about this: both to hearing Myung described as "lonely" and that her sister might form a sisterhood with someone else. She observes them wandering across Ojda, still searching for that ship. Something *has* changed. Their bodies fall into rhythm as they walk, their legs keeping time. When they talk, they mirror each other—repeating words to signal their approval, echoing accents, imitating gestures to bring their two worlds of living closer. They don't seem aware they are doing it.

It's irritating.

She is ashamed of her irritation. She is glad of Rostum, Jilla and Hormuz's company as they follow the women; they distract her from her thoughts.

Why is it that Blajine never talks to you? she asks Hormuz.

Can't see us, Jilla answers. *Not many living people can.*

Too busy with the act of living, grunts Rostum.

Takes up a lot of brain power, Jilla agrees. *She sees her mother sometimes, though. Ayesha.*

Which is not a lot, Rostum says, *when you think of how often Ayesha follows her around.*

In the distance, Laleh can see another ghost walking behind Blajine and Myung. She walks in line with Blajine's footsteps, as if tied to her.

Love does that to you, Hormuz says.

Laleh wonders if there an invisible thread tying her to Myung. She wants her sister to turn around and see her. She wants her reunion.

Blajine and Myung have entered the forest now, which has the last vestiges of Mad Magali's paradise. Blajine loves the forest but it also scares her. Forests remember everything, her mother had once said, which unsettled Blajine. Does she want everything remembered?

Still, there is peace to the forest. Fresh air. Birds. Engorged flowers spitting pollen into the air to turn into dragonflies (this was still Ojda, after all). It is a good place for Myung to rest. Blajine chooses a tree she knows won't swallow Myung in the night, and settles the traveler in its roots. She hunts in the bushes for large purple flowers, which she lays carefully on the ground. Then she clicks thrice and blows on them. They blossom into a purple fire.

They will burn for most of the night, Blajine says shyly. *The fire won't spread. The light is nice, and it will keep you warm.*

Myung nods. Under the shade of the forest, it has already grown chillier. *Thank you.*

Blajine waves her hand in acceptance. She pauses. She doesn't know what to do with herself. Go back to the cottage? But she doesn't want to leave.

Will you stay? Myung whispers. *Just for a little while?*

Well, a traveler is a kind of guest. And when a guest asks you for something, how can you say no?

—

Blajine returns to the cottage hours later. She checks her timepiece and then begins putting up leaves to cover her windows for the night. The ghost of her mother watches her from the corner. Blajine doesn't look at her.

Blajine.

Blajine puts a leaf down. *Why can't I keep her?* she says, agitated. *Who's to know? There is no one left but me, Mama. No one will mind.*

You know why, her mother says. *You must protect Ojda.*

Ojda doesn't need protection—do you know how many times it has tried to kill me? Five. Five! Name one Kilta that's gone through what I have. They just lived in Mad Magali's paradise; they don't know the half of what I've lived through. I deserve her. Why can't she stay? Why can't I keep her?

Blajine buries her face in her hands. The ghost of her mother strokes her hair soothingly, her voice achingly sad. *I'm sorry, little leaf. I'm so sorry.*

You made me kill you, Blajine whispers.

Her mother closes her eyes in pain. She keeps stroking her daughter's hair. Blajine knows she should stop talking. That this will only hurt both of them. But she cannot. *You made me kill you. You said, "I can't do it any longer, little leaf. Free me." And so I carried you to the river and I held you down. I held you down even as you struggled.*

You did free me, her mother says.

Who will free me? Blajine cries. *I am the last one, Mama! I can't go to the river now. I can't even look at it. Each time I do, I see you. Every time I look at my reflection, I . . .*

Blajine sobs. When she thinks of that evening, a knife twists deeper into her gut. She knows it was the right thing to do. Her mother was desperate to die. She begged Blajine. But none of this makes the pain easier.

Her mother sits with her until Blajine's sobs subside.

I miss you, Blajine whispers.

Her mother presses her ghost cheek into her forehead. *I miss you too.*

III

That night, something in Blajine cracks. It is a slow crack, so slow it doesn't wake her. But beneath her sleeping eyelids, her thoughts are changing with an alchemy that will alter her forever.

When she wakes up, she is different.

The ghosts notice it first. They see her striding out the door with a knife in her hand and death in her eyes, and they whisper. Something is happening. They are sure of it. A crowd gathers outside her cottage, ghosts sliding into form from wherever they were on the island, already mid conversation. *Did you see the knife? And that stride?*

They trill.

That's how a Kilta should be! one of them shouts after her.

A few of the ghosts clap enthusiastically.

Don't kill the visitor, fool! another shouts. *What else is there to do on this damn island?*

Jilla watches the keeper with shrewd eyes. *Something is not right . . .*

The crowd follows Blajine. Someone says, *Does Mad Magali know?* And someone else says, *Let's not tell her.* Word spreads and more ghosts appear. *Blajine's going to threaten the traveler,* Rostum tells anyone who will listen, and they all titter and talk, offering their opinions. No one has seen Blajine threaten anything in years. Sure, there were some shouting matches with Ojda. But threatening a *person* is different. Plus, Blajine likes the traveler—they can tell. How will she handle it? What will she threaten her with?

Ayesha talked to her, Hormuz whispers to Jilla. *She told her she has to kill the traveler.*

Jilla is still squinting. She shakes her head slightly. *Something is not right . . .*

Blajine finds the traveler already awake. She helps her pack her satchel for the day. Blajine has brought rye cakes, and they sit together and eat them. Blajine certainly doesn't look like she is threatening the traveler. She looks positively friendly with her. They laugh. They chew. Myung is smiling happily. For the first time in years, she feels like she can be all of herself, even the strange parts she was in the whale of babel. She wishes Laleh were here. Her sister would like this.

Blajine is smiling too, but there is something else to her . . .

Is she going to stab the traveler in the back?

Push her off a cliff, more likely.

Someone snorts. *She won't do either. Couldn't kill a fly, Blajine.*

Rostum cocks his head. *Weellll. She did murder her mother.*

Ayesha asked her to! Hormuz says, appalled.

Tch, asked, begged, doesn't matter. Lots of people ask me to do things. Doesn't mean I did them.

The traveler and Blajine stand. They dust off the crumbs of their meal. They continue their journey through the forest, toward the sea of changing mists. The women talk as they always do—except, Blajine is talking more. Talking a lot, Jilla notices. She is talking about her childhood and her earliest memories. She is showing Myung what plants are safe to eat and how to talk to Ojda.

Jilla says slowly: *Rostum . . .*

But Rostum is stuck in an argument about whether or not a promise constitutes a binding contract to actually do what you promised, and he doesn't hear her.

Myung too has changed. The traveler who wandered around the island on the first day was gaunt, with dark circles under her eyes. She stumbled over every root. Now her body has filled out. Her feet find easy footing. Her gaze takes in the landscape in impressive sweeps; Ojda's strangeness doesn't faze her. *This way!* she says to Blajine and it is always the best way down a slope or across a pond.

And Blajine, who doesn't listen to anyone—she follows.

Is it normal for a Kilta to listen to a stranger? a ghost asks, frowning. *Ojda is ours, after all. No one knows it better than us.*

Something is not right, Hormuz says wisely. He is only copying Jilla, but he shivers when he says it.

Blajine's knife remains tucked in the back of her dhoti. Once in a while she brings it out and the crowd of ghosts gasps . . . But she only uses it to cut through a vine or hack into a fruit. Sometimes, when Myung is crouching, she looms over her ominously. The ghosts clutch their hearts and press their faces into their friends' shoulders. *I can't look*, they whisper. But Blajine does nothing.

Jilla, Rostum says, *does this remind you of anything?*

Theater, Jilla says grimly. *I don't think Myung is the one Blajine's threatening.*

And almost as if she heard her, Blajine glances over her shoulder. She grins. It is a furious grin—a reckless one. It says:

Damn you all.

—

Panic. Alarm. Whispers, furious and confused. Suddenly everyone notices just how much Blajine has told the stranger about Ojda. She has told her almost everything, really. Any question that Myung asks, Blajine answers in great detail. She is one step away from drawing out the Kilta family tree. She uses names, she references past events. She is even—Mad Magali help them—she is even telling the traveler how to find the island again. She is saying it casually, but they can hear the anger underneath her words. The threat.

For fifty years I have been the last one of you, she is saying. What power do you have over me now?

And truth be told, Blajine is enjoying herself. She cannot see the mob of ghosts that is definitely following them, but she can sense its agitation. She feels powerful. Better still—she feels powerful because she *took* the power. No one gave it to her. She plucked it for herself.

The only person she doesn't want to see is her mother. She doesn't want to see the disappointment in Ayesha's eyes. In fact, she doesn't want to think about that at all. She is the last of the Kiltas and she has upheld every single tradition for them. They owe *her*. Let them fret and agitate. They have no power in the world of the living. Besides, it is only small transgressions. The silly ones. The traveler will leave in a couple of days—what does it matter if she knows that the yellow berries kill you or this species of tree is friendly?

Blajine is having so much fun.

Get Mad Magali, someone whispers and the ghosts hum and haw. No one wants to be the one to tell Magali.

By now Myung has noticed the recklessness in Blajine's eyes. She has realized Blajine is not herself: she has been talking animatedly for hours, almost dominating the conversation. She is no longer wary. Myung feels a prickle of excitement.

She smells opportunity.

You said to me once that Ojda likes to change. Why?

It woke up, Blajine says.

You mean it wasn't awake before?

Blajine shrugs—the Myung shrug, perfected now. *The island is made of particles that sing the museum of collective memory. It wasn't supposed to be alive.*

But it grew alive?

For a moment, Blajine hesitates. Then she decides this will definitely annoy her family, so she tells Myung the truth.

Mad Magali knew, she says. *She said on her deathbed: "Put enough of the world's memories together and it becomes the imagination." And that's what happened: Ojda has become the black sea's imagination. What else could it be? It likes to change. It breaks apart and makes anew. It wants to kill you, but it doesn't understand that it can actually hurt you. Imaginations are curious. They believe that anything broken will reappear. It may be patched up and made of other things, but it will be here. How is Ojda to know we can only live in this body? How can it understand we cannot change?*

The moment she says it, Blajine feels lighter. She hadn't realized how much resentment she was carrying against Ojda for what it has put her through. Living through Ojda's awakening was terrifying. Blajine couldn't sleep at night because she was scared Ojda would come for body parts. It did, several times. She only survived because she learned how to fight, to toughen herself so that nothing could break through. Ojda made her *her*—shriveled, angry, alone.

She has never forgiven the island for it.

But now . . . describing it in these words, it looks different. Ojda didn't do it on purpose. It couldn't help it. It didn't want her to die; it just couldn't understand that she *couldn't* live in a different shape.

A rock-plant rolls up to her feet. It nuzzles her toes gently. Blajine stares at it impassively, then picks it up. *I forgive you*, she says and is surprised to find she means it. The rock-plant sighs in contentment.

Blajine's recklessness rises and then tips over.

We have a corridor, she says. *In the museum. It is reserved for only the Kilta family. Would you like to see it?*

Myung's eyes widen. She nods.

This, Blajine knows, is not a small transgression. This is truly reckless. Her heart is beating fast, her neck sweating. But oh, Blajine doesn't care. She doesn't; she refuses to.

Behind her, the ghosts' clamors have grown so loud, she can finally hear them. They wash over her, brittle and sharp. *She wouldn't. She can't. Get Mad Magali.*

And then a hush spreads through the crowd.

Blajine doesn't turn. She knows, from the chill climbing up her spine, that Mad Magali is here. Right behind her. Blajine closes her eyes. Then she takes Myung's hand, taps her tragus and says *khol*.

The ghosts fall away.

The museum spins into existence around them, and they are once again in enormous corridors, mosaics sparkling in the heavens. Myung keeps her hand in Blajine's, but doesn't look at her; she is focused ahead. Her shoulders are tense.

Myung? Blajine asks.

Myung looks at her and smiles.

It is a dazzling smile. It puts Blajine at ease. *Stay with me*, she tells Myung, and then Blajine is dancing through the corridors, moving them this way and that, until they arrive at the same darkened hallway, cobwebs hanging down the sides. Blajine leads the way, but only for a little bit. As soon as Myung sees the door, she strides forward and pushes it open.

It gives Blajine pause, that action. It worries her. But she swallows the worry and follows.

The chamber is bathed in a cold, blue light, the dome obscured in shadow. Blajine's palms are sweating; she wipes them on her dhoti. The statues haven't moved; they haven't leaped on Myung the moment she walked through the door and smashed her to pieces. Blajine half-expected them to skin her alive while they were at it. But the statues stay still, and Blajine decides this is worse, because it means that whatever will happen is still coming—and she has to live through this terrible period of *anticipating* it.

Myung is gazing at the statues in awe.

Awe and . . .

Blajine doesn't know what. But she doesn't like it.

Which one is she? Myung whispers. *Magali?*

She is in the center, Blajine says. *We should go. I only wanted to show—*

But Myung is striding into the statues, slipping through the cracks, disappearing among the crush of stone bodies.

Myung!

Blajine runs after her. The statues are too many. Myung is always one step ahead, too far out of reach. Blajine makes a grab for her, but she cannot catch Myung's robe. The traveler arrives at Magali's statue as Blajine is trying to squeeze through a gap between two legs. Myung glances at Magali's stone eyes for only a moment before moving on. She is running now.

Myung, wait!

But Myung is at the shelves—she is pulling down sheaves, sketches, books, hunting frantically. *Where is it?* she is murmuring. *It is here. It must be here.* She is possessed, her desire so strong, she is entranced. Blajine has reached her now. She grabs Myung's shoulder, but Myung shakes her off. Blajine tries again and this time Myung pushes her, hard, so that Blajine falls to the ground. *You don't understand!* Myung cries. *I need to know! I need to find my sister!* She throws herself back into the pages.

But Blajine draws herself up to full height. She has been coming to the museum of collective memory since she was two years old; she has imaginary friends in these corridors; she knows its rooms. Now she summons her knowledge, and it fills her.

She brought Myung here. She can take her out.

The room shakes and dissolves. Myung cries out. She tries to grab as many books as she can, but the museum disappears and Myung is spat out, her arms empty, to huddle on the forest floor.

She is sobbing.

Blajine stares at her. The traveler is shattered; her pain is so great, Blajine can *see* it running through her.

I'm sorry, Myung says, reaching for Blajine. *I am sorry.*

But Blajine takes a step back. Then she hurries away.

IV

Magali!

The old man that Laleh knows is Magali's husband is climbing over the horizon. He is no longer striding with energy; he looks exhausted. He takes a deep breath.

We can't have this fight forever Magali! he shouts at nothing. He takes another deep breath and then just lets it out, slowly. He says in a normal voice: *We live on the same island. At some point, we'll have to talk about it.*

He catches sight of Laleh then and smiles. It is such a kind smile to offer a stranger that Laleh warms to him. She doesn't want to speak to anyone right now. She wants to travel back to the whale and take her sister with her, then she wants to visit again when she has had time to think about everything she's learned. But this man . . . this man she could talk to. She doesn't know why, but she knows it will make her feel better.

Have you found Magali? she asks.

She is hiding, he says, sighing. *Help me sit, will you? Today has taken everything out of me.*

Laleh helps him to the ground and sits beside him. From the corner of her eye, she can see Myung stumble about. She tries not to look.

Magali hides when she doesn't want to look at something, Jinn says, massaging his knees. *I'm trying to make her look. Does she scare you?* He squints at Laleh. *Don't let her scare you. They call her Mad Magali and make up all these stories, but she is soft really. So soft and so large-hearted, I don't think you can find another heart like it in the black sea. No one loves like Magali Kilta.*

You love her very much, Laleh says.

Yes. And she loved her sister very much. He gestures at Ojda. *Love makes you do mad things.* He takes another breath and bellows, *Magali!*

The more you shout, the more she'll run, Laleh says. *All the shouting does is tell her where you are.*

Jinn scratches his beard. He hadn't considered this. He gives Laleh a sidelong glance. *Whose daughter are you? I can't keep track with all the people.*

Laleh shrugs.

Ah yes, he says wisely. Obviously, several new Kiltas were confused about their parentage. He pats her hand. *Don't worry—it is not important to know. I only asked because you remind me of someone. Wisa used to say things like this all the time; I often felt like a fool next to her.*

Great Wisa? Laleh asks.

Are we calling her great now? Great Wisa then. Yes, that one. Thank you for the tip. He taps his nose. *No more shouting.*

He stands up slowly, and Laleh offers him her shoulder for support. *Magali wasn't always like this*, he murmurs as he stands. He seems to be talking to himself. *I just have to remind her.*

V

Blajine paces in her cottage. She is unsure of how to deal with Myung. What she saw in the museum is proof that the traveler cannot be trusted; she came here for something that belongs to the Kiltas, and she will do anything to get it. It is exactly what Blajine has been warned against. It would be best to get rid of the traveler as soon as possible.

They need to find that ship.

But when she dreams that night, it is of Myung staying. Of both of them sitting outside the cottage eating stew. Of this wise and brave traveler making Ojda her home and playing lilta with Blajine at night.

She shakes off the dream the moment she wakes. Ojda is tense; she can sense it in the air. They are on the precipice, balancing on the knife-edge of change. *I'll make her leave*, she promises the island, but Ojda doesn't seem relieved. It is as confused as she is.

―

Myung has had days to think about the incident. She has had nights to imagine what she would have done differently, for if she had, maybe she would be clutching Wisa's story now. She has cycled through it in her head.

Be nicer.

No, kinder.

No, more assertive—make Blajine show you the island's secrets.

Stop waiting for her to show up—run away, hide. She's going to get rid of you and you will never find your sister.

Go back to the museum. Look for the room.

Beg Ojda.

Scour the island; do whatever it takes. This is your last chance—find your way home.

By the time Blajine walks over the horizon, Myung has already lived a dozen different versions of herself. She's played out multiple scenarios, over and over, each one leading to a dead end. She is tired.

And when Myung is tired, when she is frustrated, when the black sea tells her something is impossible . . .

VI

The traveler looks harrowed. She stares at Blajine in . . . wariness? There is a sharpness to her, like a cracked vase on the verge of splitting open and slicing you.

Blajine understands wariness. She knows that when someone looks at you like a wounded animal, it is because they need kindness.

She has been that animal.

So she offers her hand to the traveler, feeling suddenly old and very wise. Myung takes it and lets Blajine pull her up. There is something different about Myung, tangible in the set of her shoulders and how she moves her body. She's retreated into herself. It is like the first day again, a return to their roles: Blajine, keeper; Myung, unwelcome.

The traveler doesn't apologize for the museum. Good. Silence is best now; this camaraderie is at an end. They walk toward the sea of changing mists.

—

And there is their ship.

The sea of mists settles on their shoulders, lifting locks of their hair, poking their ears curiously, wondering what it can change them into. The fog is thick, so sky and ground are the same imperceptible white. But there is no mistaking the ship. Its sail is made from silver leaf, its prow a sea serpent. Four paws protrude from its hull, their claws gleaming. It is not complete as yet—bits of it are missing, and the deck has gaps. How long? Blajine estimates a day. Then they can push the ship out of the fog, and the traveler can leave.

Oh, she feels it. The past coming for her, her life pulling back into shape, squeezing her into the mold of what she was taught to expect and cherish: endless, empty time.

One last day.

The women stare at the boat.

Do you want to see my cottage? Blajine asks without looking at Myung.

Yes, says the traveler.

―

Myung doesn't mention the strange alignment of the cottage. She sits on the sloping floor and accepts tea, putting her feet against the bedpost to prevent herself from sliding.

You'll want to know then, Blajine says. *How it happened.*

Myung doesn't answer, only sips her tea. There is a lightness to her that Blajine likes; she never rushes you or expands to fill the silence. Blajine can say all the quiet thoughts she has had for years, alone, and not worry they will be too much.

Ojda did it, she says. *When it woke up, it didn't like something on its back. So it rose into a cliff and tried to shake the cottage into the abyss.*

Were you scared?

No. Yes. I crawled out and clung to the ground, waiting for the shaking to stop. I had lived my life in this cottage. If it went, so did all of me. Blajine rubs the rim of her shell cup. *It didn't fall, though,* she says. *Mad Magali built it with foundations so deep that Ojda would have to rip itself apart to destroy it. Mama used to say that to me, when I grew scared. Toward the end.*

How did she die?

In bed. Peacefully.

I am sorry.

Blajine doesn't like that. She doesn't like to think there is something to be sorry about. She drinks her tea and stands. Tomorrow, the traveler will leave. *Would you like a meal?* she asks and Myung nods.

Not here, Blajine says. *Come to the song bowl.*

―

What Blajine calls the "song bowl" is a glade. It is filled with sculptures made of entwining branches, each with the same face, their bodies curved in dance. Out of their hands and hair grow leaves covered with the softest gold fur, like a shade of sunset, and these grow into canopies with traceries of black and then only black. At the highest points of the canopy, Ojda has pressed hard diamonds that sparkle as stars. There is no sign of Ojda's sun.

It is a perfect night sky.

Myung helps Blajine pick the ingredients for dinner. She watches her cook. Myung has spent a lot of time observing how different cultures prepare their food. In Tuleman, they eat as they harvest—men swallowing berries straight from the branch, women gutting silver deer and smoking the meat over a makeshift fire. In Contrini, they eat alone and then return to the great fire with seeds and bones to tell the story of their meal. In Esop, they make their food into intricate rangolis and then devour these with frenzy, for they believe order always gives way to chaos. Each culture eats in the same way they understand the world, and it makes Myung feel so alone that she cannot tell Laleh this.

Blajine makes her food in rhythm. She boils plants and reptiles in a charcoal pot, sprinkling weeds she carries in hidden pockets, tasting as she goes. She uses fresh materials: scales from a river snake, crystals plucked from Ojda's soil, sap from a bulbous plant that swells as she whispers to it. But her North Star is song. She sings as she cooks, under her breath and absent-mindedly, and her actions change with her melody, growing fiercer as the song swells or more languid when it ebbs.

Blajine has a home. Blajine was taught to cook by someone who was taught by someone else, and a memory of those hands will always live in her.

Yet she is preventing Myung from going home.

The traveler's heart hardens further.

They eat in silence. Blajine uses a stone with a dipped center; Myung eats from the pot with an old shell she carries in her backpack, slurping noisily and picking fibers out of her teeth. The stew is salty and stodgy, textured with an odd mix of rooty sweetness. It's good.

Tomorrow, Blajine thinks, the traveler will leave. They will walk back to the sea of mists, where the ship will be waiting for them. Blajine will say, *Don't tell anyone what you saw here,* and Myung will promise. *Sail safe,* Blajine will say because it is polite. She will not cry. And then Myung will go on adventures and Blajine will go back to being a Kilta—tied to Ojda with a foundation so deep that the only way to uproot yourself is to die.

The stew is too salty. She is annoyed by the fibers tickling her tongue, by the crystal spices that have not melted even though she boiled the mixture for a good length of a song. She is annoyed by how much Myung is enjoying it, her whole concentration on the stew.

What do you see when you look at me? she asks.

Myung picks out a piece of root, considering. Blajine has wanted to ask this question since she read Myung's notebook, and Myung knows it.

If you could write me, Blajine says, when the silence stretches, *what would you write?*

Still Myung doesn't answer. A childish, perverse self has taken over. She is enjoying this: Blajine reaching to her for something, her withholding it. How does it feel now, keeper?

Blajine senses the resistance, and beneath it, the taunt. *You can't write about me,* she says. *I forbid it.*

You can't stop me.

I'll burn the diaries.

How will you find them after I leave?

Promise you won't write me.

I won't promise.

Myung's eyes in the firelight—hard and cold. Her jaw tense. It makes Blajine's hackles rise; she wants to fill out with her own power, match Myung's petulance with hers.

But what is the point? The traveler will be gone tomorrow. And she is right—how will Blajine know if she's written about her once she is out in the black sea? Maybe it will be good if the traveler records her. It will mean that someone—anyone—will remember she had lived.

Can I ask you a question? Myung says.

No.

Myung asks anyway. *Why did you read the diaries? I watched you—you were reading for a long time.*

Blajine looks for a lie, then gives up; she can't see the point in pretense. *You write warmly,* she murmurs. *Like a fire on a cold beach night. You see what others don't care to look at.* Then she empties the stew onto the ground, where it hisses and dissolves; collects leaves into a pillow; lies down.

Blajine? Myung's eyes are softer in the firelight, her voice gentle. *Can I stay?*

No.

That night, Blajine dreams again.

Blajine? Can I stay?

Dream Blajine considers it. She rolls the possibility in her mind like a loose tooth. *You can stay,* she says finally. Dream Myung cries.

Dream Blajine holds out her hand and Dream Myung climbs down from the ship. *You are Myung Kilta,* she says solemnly. *Sister of Blajine Kilta, daughter of Ayesha Kilta, granddaughter of*—and she recites the genealogy back to the name her ancestors used to wait to say, the diamond of their heritage that would elicit gasps of wonder when unwrapped from its velvet cloth. Magali Kilta. Creator of the museum of collective memory. Keeper of your stories.

Her mother claps furiously. The spirit that is Ojda cheers. Blajine's mother wraps Dream Blajine in a hug.

One eye on the world of the waking, she whispers into her daughter's ear. *What are you missing?*

And Dream Blajine knows. She never told the traveler her name.

Blajine? Can I stay?

When Blajine opens her eyes, she finds the traveler staring at her, playing with a cut fingernail. Blajine keeps still. Her heart is pounding, the dream still fresh behind her eyelids. In the soft light of the glade, Myung looks like a predator.

Do you know, Myung says, *about the two types of quests?*

Slowly, Blajine sits up. Her heartbeat is slowing; she is regaining control of herself. She is Blajine Kilta and she has survived the awakening of Ojda. No traveler can outwit her.

I don't, she says.

My sister used to say there were two types of knights. Knights who dressed in shiny armor and rode in search of princesses. And knights who were actually learned women, who sat under a tree in the forest until they became the tree.

I don't understand, Blajine says.

It is the quests. There are two type of quests—moving and waiting. The first kind of knight moves in search of what she wants. The second . . . she waits. Myung looks at her cut fingernail; she shakes her head imperceptibly. *I've spent my time being the first knight. But Laleh always said the wise ones were the ones who waited. Who sat under the tree until they became the tree. Until knowledge came to them. I want to wait. I want to stay.*

Any animal, when cornered, lashes out; Blajine knows this. Myung may be a predator, but her eyes have a hunted, haunted look, as if she exists on the edge of her own quiet madness. Can she be guided? Shown a path out of here that she follows with her own free will? She has a sister, an anchor to the black sea.

What about your sister? Blajine asks. *Won't she miss you?*

I don't know. I left her behind.

Blajine blinks. Left her behind? Blajine would kill for a sister. Bathe in Ojda's volcano. Give it her fingers, like it had once asked, to have another Kilta by her side. And to say, so easily, "I left her behind"—

Swiftly, Laleh kneels at Blajine's feet. *It isn't like that,* she whispers, placing a hand on Blajine's knee. *She loves me, I know it.*

For a moment, it is as if Blajine can see her. She is staring at Laleh intently, like she's trying to understand why the air feels both hot and cold, like two currents meeting, the same way it felt in the museum of collective memory when Blajine thought of Wisa.

Oh, Laleh is desperate to be seen. To reach out to this world of the living and actually participate, to be . . . She tightens her hand on Blajine's knee.

But Blajine is already looking up.

Sister is a careful word, she says.

What?

Sister is a careful word. That's what we say in the family. It is a special relationship. You have to love and hate each other. Want to drown them but also burn the world if it threatens them. She taps her head. *You have to be slightly mad to love like that.*

Blajine, when did your mother die?

I never told you my name.

I know a lot more than your name. How long since you've been alone?

But Blajine has had enough. She won't answer any more questions. She is keeper again, vested with the responsibility of a Kilta, and she will not betray her family. Ojda and she are better off alone.

I know your type, she says. *Mama warned me. She said, "The ones with the maps and diaries are the worst, little leaf. They're alchemists. To them, islands are only real once they've seen them, secrets only true once they've heard them. Many names they give themselves—pioneer, explorer, adventurer. Never let one stay." But I did. I let you stay and now you think Ojda is yours, after four days. It's not; it's not even mine. Sail away. Now, in this light. We won't wait for tomorrow. I won't ask again.*

What makes you think I'll leave?

Blajine laughs. *Traveler, you'll go. You'll go or Ojda will gnaw at your insides. You can't last a day without me.*

The traveler raises her eyebrows. Alchemist, is it? And so Myung the alchemist reaches into her robes and pulls out a piece of her alchemy. There is rage in the gesture, focus and cunning. She is holding in her hand the cold hard truth and she wants Blajine to see it.

———

Myung is holding a rock.

But Blajine knows it is not any rock. It is *Ojda's* rock, and it was sitting in Myung's pocket and now is in her hand as docile as a pet rabbit.

Suddenly Blajine knows that Myung's pockets are full of Ojda's flora, her ears filled with their secrets. The landscape is leaning toward her, as if Myung draws all of Ojda with her charisma. The soil is playing with the traveler's toes, plants reaching for her, clouds hovering as if they cannot bear to be far from their new love.

Myung is not a stranger any longer. Ojda is besotted with her.

There are very few beliefs in Blajine's life.

Protect Ojda.

Trust and love her family.

And: if mad and bloodthirsty Ojda were to tolerate a human, even love one, it would love only her.

She was wrong.

―

When Myung talks now, it sounds to Blajine like the sinuous hiss of a riverside snake, the soft opening of an hjui flower oozing poison. It carries a power Blajine could not imagine when she first saw her in the flower maze, the ancient pull of a spell.

When you were young, Myung says, *you tried to leave Ojda. You asked the land for ships, to make rafts from stones, and wished for a boat. Your mother said no, your place was here. But you left anyway. You cajoled an abaia to swim you out into the waves, stole onto the first ship you found. You left at night, without telling her. Years later, you came back. You told your mother it was because you missed her and it was true, but not the whole truth. The whole truth is that no island in the black sea felt right. You wandered, trying to find the wonders you hoped for, but they were pale. And when you came back and you held your mother, you learned a truth very few people are given: that home is a person.*

But this person had been changed by your leaving. Your mother was fragile; you could feel her bones when you held her. You took care of her. You carried her across the island on your back when she was too old to walk. You made her laugh as often as you could—and she did laugh; she adored you. Ojda hadn't woken up yet but it was murmuring at the edges of sleep. Your mother sang lullabies to it and you dozed at her feet. You cherish these memories. I think you imagine them sometimes, when you can't bear the loneliness.

When she asked you to kill her, you did—you took her to the water and held her under; she fought only a little; it was serene. She was in pain; she said it was her time. You wanted longer but you didn't argue. You burned her here, and Ojda grew these statues in her memory. Each of these has her face.

You don't leave, sister. Not when this island turned mad, not when it tried to kill you. You don't know where to go. You won't try to find out. You think you are unknowable but that is only because you don't know yourself. You have spent your centuries running away from your reflection, covering any mirror you find.

How long do you think it's been since I came here? Four days, you said. It has been twenty suns and twenty-one moons in black sea time. I've walked around this island over and over. I have made friends and they have told me stories about you. I have dreamed all the hideous dreams you wished on me, brought about by the water you offered and that I drank. I don't scare. It has not been more than fifty years since your mother died—it has been over two centuries. Two hundred and fifty years of you believing you are the keeper of Ojda when it has been keeping you. Thank you for the ship. I'm not leaving.

VII

Blajine kneels outside her cottage. It is still night; Ojda's sun is covered in clouds and fog. The traveler is gone, wandering somewhere on the island. Blajine doesn't care.

She digs a hole with her hands. Two hundred and fifty years. Time is the scale against which we measure our lives and now Blajine's valuations are off. All this while, Ojda was keeping her alive, doing its best to keep her.

I'm so tired, little leaf, her mother whispered as Blajine carried her to the water. *Shush, don't cry. I love you, I love you, I love you.*

Mama. Everything is quiet in Ojda's fog, eerily so. Through the mist, Ojda's ghosts have gathered to watch her. Blajine does not notice. She crouches until her face is close to the earth. She presses her lips to the edge of the hole and whispers to Ojda: *I will protect you. I promise.*

Then she covers the hole and leaves.

Tomorrow, she will kill the traveler.

The Murder

I

Myung sits with her knees curled to her chest, rocking slightly. She is out of the glade; the sun burns above her. Ojda has grown colder since her speech at the glade, since Blajine left, half running and stumbling, away from her words. Myung doesn't blame it. She behaved badly.

I'm sorry, she says miserably.

She is talking to Laleh, as she always does when she is upset. Laleh is lying beside her, staring at the clouds. This is nice, just the two of them. Even if Myung can't see her.

Blajine has to see the truth, Myung whispers now. *I was only trying to show her that the stories she tells herself are not . . . they don't have to be . . . I had to show her. Didn't I? If I didn't show her, she would have built this wall between her and the world, a wall that goes on forever and ever, into the clouds, above the clouds. She would have built it between me and her. And I had to break it to say . . .*

Her words are not convincing. Myung buries her face in her knees and screams soundlessly. She is angry with Blajine, with herself, but mostly with Magali Kilta, the woman who has a story that Myung wants, needs, but she hid it so well that Myung cannot find it.

I know you're ashamed of me, Myung whispers.

I am, Laleh says, even though Myung cannot hear her. She feels it must be said.

A movement to the left of the frame. Both girls look. Laleh sees her instantly—it is Mad Magali, appraising Myung.

You're not her, Magali says.

Myung is scrambling to her feet and running—*Wait!*—trying to get to the ghost before she disappears. It is too late. Magali Kilta is out of the frame, wandering elsewhere on Ojda. Laleh is scrambling to her feet as well, hope rushing to her head and making her giddy—Myung can see them, she can see her—and she reaches out, eagerly, desperately, *Myung*.

But Myung runs through her and is gone.

II

A murder has several moving parts. Even a simple one requires magic: a person must change into a killer; someone alive must become dead. The crafty killings—ah, they are intricate beasts. They say the black sea was made from murder, a knife plunged and dragged through a whale so that its insides spilled out into a flood, carrying the universe's islands on it. Who murdered the whale? Why, the islands themselves! The cut was from the inside; demons always try to get out.

The parts to Blajine's murder are simple. She lays them out in bird bones and covers them with sand, so the spirit of her mother can be witness. Then she goes to the traveler, who is lying in the rainbow plain where she first found her.

She says: *You are not as smart as you think you are.*

The traveler sits up. She knows Blajine is right; she is out of her depth. Blajine likes that—it is a small gesture of wisdom, too little, too late, but Blajine likes it.

Twenty suns and twenty-one moons you've been here and still you haven't found what you're looking for, Blajine says. *All that sneaking and nothing to show for it. Who can't see clearly now?*

The traveler blinks. She offers her hand to Blajine. Blajine slaps it away. The traveler is hurt and Blajine is pleased.

I can help you, Blajine says.

For what price?

That you leave once you have it.

The traveler says: *You don't know what I am looking for.*

But Blajine doesn't want to know. *You like her,* her mother said last night and Blajine covered her ears and babbled nonsense until her mother disappeared. So what if she did? Kiltas stay carefully aloof from the black sea because the black sea lies. It pretends friendship when it means deceit.

Collects precious islands like rubies to drop into its pockets. Her poor Ojda. The traveler has it in her clutches; who knows what she would do with it? *Protect it,* Mad Magali said to her family on her deathbed. *Promise me.* So Blajine doesn't want to know. It is best to see the traveler now as a body, a collection of bones with movement, empty of wants and needs. It is best to see the traveler as simply this: a threat.

And so she says: *I know you have been everywhere on Ojda looking for it and you haven't found it. But there is one place you have not been. Let me show you.*

I am sorry, the traveler says, suddenly and desperately. *I am. Forgive me?*

So different now from that witch at the fire. So loving, so earnest.

Blajine looks away. The dream trembles with the force of her emotion; it cracks at the edges. Then she looks back and says, *Yes.* She says it with a smile we know is false, for it is completely natural.

—

Ojda's consciousness is large, moving with the glint of water, pebbled in places, ribbed, layered, boned, leafed—too much. To step into Ojda's consciousness is not just to see its landscape, be minutely aware of each plant, rock and creature, among them two humans named Blajine and Myung now climbing down a ravine with a dead cottage overlooking it, the only dead structure on Ojda's landscape—oh, how it hates that structure—it is to see all of the museum's memories, feel its sand corridors crumbling and reforming, step into every piece of information it has, all mixing, changing, solidifying and flowing again; it is to look at all of the black sea at once even as you—the limits of you—are stretching, out and out, liquefying, dissipating. The dream cannot take it—it breaks, its parts swallowed by Ojda, and Laleh screams, panicked, *Myung!*

Everything quietens.

Laleh is standing on a bone-white landscape, particles rough between her toes. Magali Kilta is kneeling. She is flesh and blood here, younger than Laleh has seen her.

Make a tree, Magali says and the particles do, a white tree that looks like it is made out of snow. Ojda isn't alive as yet—the museum is just being made—but we can taste the resistance in the picture. What imagination likes being told?

The tree dissolves.

Then Magali changes into Myung, lying in the rainbow plain. This is the beginning of the dream; Blajine has left her for the first time. Stay here, she was told. Myung obeys, waiting for Blajine to come back. One day, two, three. Myung's lips crack; her stomach caves—she drinks more of the water Blajine left her even though her nightmares are now waking with her and staying during the day . . .

Myung re-forms into a child. The rainbow plain becomes a riot of flowers so tall, the child is hidden. The flowers jostle; the child runs to a table filled with people—all Kiltas, eating, laughing, talking. And our dreamer can feel the child's annoyance. Everyone is too loud, too bossy, always pushing into her space and giving her advice she did not ask for . . .

Re-forms—is it reforming or simply stepping to the side, into another moment happening simultaneously?—into Ayesha Kilta, who is burying her husband. She pushes the spade into the earth and showers bone-white crystals to the side. There are no vultures to eat Ayesha's husband, otherwise she would have left him out in the forest. That is the old Kilta way. But no vultures and so she must bury him, her arms hurting and sweat running down her forehead. Little Blajine watches somberly, thumb in her mouth. The flowers are gone, the noise, the laughter. Ojda is bare.

. . . The picture reforms into Myung, in this moment, now, peering over the edge of the ravine as Blajine clambers down. The cottage looks with her into its dark depths.

This way, Blajine says.

Myung hesitates and then follows.

―

Blajine is using her knife to help her descend. Myung uses only her hands and toes. Blajine imagines Ojda making footholds for the traveler, and her resentment deepens.

Together, like two monkeys, they clamber down the cliff face, toward a gash in the rock that Blajine has visited only once before. It was when Ojda rose to shake off the dead cottage on its back and a timepiece belonging to her mother clattered into the ravine. Blajine watched the timepiece fall and then move *sideways*, disappearing into the cliff face. When she traced its journey, she found this hole. She went in to retrieve it, and when she came out, she swore never to return.

Now she waits at the lip of the cut for the traveler. Together, they peer into the long gash. It smells of seaweed and wet rock; they can only see darkness. Fear wells up in Blajine; she squashes it. Myung is unperturbed, staring only in curiosity. How Blajine admires her. How she would kill for a sister.

Don't think of it, she tells herself.

Together, they disappear into the blackness.

The blackness reshapes. Ayesha Kilta is lying in the plain of wildflowers, except now the flowers are as big as a finger. You can see the shape of what Ojda will become; it has begun its decades-long process of waking up. Blajine is gone, left on an abaia and stole onto the first ship in the black sea. Every inch of this frame sings it: *Blajine is gone*.

Ayesha carries the pain with grace. Zoom out and you find the field full of ghosts. Dead Kiltas, lying in the flowers like Ayesha, gossiping.

Blajine is gone, they grumble. *Can you believe it?*

Leave her be, Ayesha says to the sky. She is both glad and heartbroken her daughter has left. *Let her learn to be someone else.*

She sings to Ojda as she once did to Blajine, keeping the island on the edge of sleep. As she sings, her song rises up and becomes . . .

. . . Blajine and Myung. They are crawling through the natural slit in the rock, the curved walls pressing into their necks and shoulders. The air is musty, hot. Then the tunnel ends. In front of them is a ripe strip of cerulean blue.

Now what? Myung asks.

Blajine maneuvers herself to crouch at the lip of the opening. She looks back. *Don't be afraid*, she says and falls.

Myung's eyes widen. Then she closes them and follows.

The women fall through a cerulean blue sky, plunging into black-blue water. They swim, spluttering and coughing, toward a beach. The space they are in is limitless *and* has boundaries, a feeling that is indescribable except to say that the edges of this space are mirrors—the space ripples endlessly through it, but you cannot.

Blajine wrings out her hair and tries to control her panic. You are a Kilta, she thinks. You have survived this before.

She looks around, but of course her mother cannot follow her here.

The traveler is also looking around, at the black cliff faces and the slit caves, at the seaweed clinging to rocks, at strange creatures gliding overhead—birds? But not quite—filling the space with a haunting song. Her toes curl around sand that glints blue-black; chunks of crystal wash onto the shore to disintegrate, shimmering in rainbow colors.

They are in Ojda's center. A space not made by any Kilta but carved out by the island.

It's here, Blajine says, *what you're looking for.*

Myung, Laleh says, realizing what is happening. *Myung, you must get out—*

—and Laleh is yanked to another time, where Myung is slinging her satchel on her back; this is the third time Blajine leaves her. Ever since Myung confessed to Ojda what she was looking for, the island has softened to her, but she knows she hasn't won it over entirely. She's been studying Blajine: there is a power to the way a Kilta moves through the landscape. It is almost as if Blajine becomes a different self for each aspect of Ojda, animals, plants, birds, soil. If Myung is to earn Ojda's respect, she must move, think, breathe like a Kilta. Only then will the island yield its secrets . . .

. . . Myung, sitting among a circle of plant-rocks, taking notes as they gossip about the Kilta family. When one jumps into her pocket, she doesn't object . . .

. . . Blajine stares at the stranger for long moments. At night, she cries, loud and gulping, although she doesn't know why. When she whispers to Ojda, *stranger*, Ojda knows she doesn't mean it.

. . . Myung, wandering across Ojda, looking for the story of Wisa. *Please*, she says to Ojda. *I promise I am the right person. Please.*

―

They are in Ojda's center. If Ojda is the black sea's imagination, then this is its frontier. The vast sea sloshes in and out of its shores, space hardening into crystal, melting into sand, particles that are simultaneously part of and other than Ojda. This is the center of Ojda's madness, a place of fluidity, where anything becomes anything else—where it *must*.

Blajine walks along the beach. She says: *This way.*

They move past sand toward the rocks, pools of black sea trapped within them. Blajine can feel her skin prickle. Stretch. Panic rises to her throat; she wrestles it down. The traveler hasn't noticed. They enter a cave, the air salty and thick. Dull crystals push out of the walls.

Deeper, Blajine says and the traveler obeys.

The cave opens into a cavern, the uneven rock lit in fluid ribbons of light. Every inch of it is covered in gemstones. Heaps of rubies and sapphires, pearls rolling under their feet, emeralds sliding down mounds. Gemstones like sand that you could sink your fingers into, your face, your body.

It'll be here, Blajine says. *You only have to find the right one.*

The traveler is enchanted. She moves as if in a spell. Laleh is pushing at her, screaming, but Myung—smart, wise Myung who turns childish and focused in the face of what she wants—cannot hear her.

They are not gems. They are crystals.

How will I know? she asks.

Blajine takes her hand. In the corner is a tall, burnished mirror, leaning against a wall. Myung's reflection has a mercurial dullness to it, eaten by splotches. She feels ethereal. Blajine removes a string of pearls and loops it gently around Myung's neck.

So beautiful, she says.

And Myung sees her reflection change. The pearls melt into her skin, sprouting feathers; her neck elongates; her lips change into a beak. Fascinated, Myung touches her chest. There is only skin. Here she is Myung, but in her mirror, she is a swan. She is unfolding her wings; they are vast, almost the size of the cave, and powerful. *She* is vast and powerful.

The mirror shows her the stories in the crystals. And somewhere here is a crystal with Wisa's story.

Blajine feels her spine prickle. Her jaw grows heavier, as if it is unhinging. She looks down. There is webbing between her fingers. *Stay calm,* she thinks. She creeps out of the cave.

Myung, Laleh says, reaching for her and passing through. *Myung!*

But Myung is enchanted with her hoard. She sifts through it delicately, searching for a gold nugget. If she finds it, she can hold it up to the mirror and it will show her Wisa's story. And then she can find her way back to the whale.

So obsessed is Myung that she doesn't feel the slow prickling of fur at the nape of her neck. Doesn't notice how her shoulders are bulging, muscle knotting underneath.

Blajine is running. A sliver on her stomach has turned to ash; it is slowly crumbling with each step. A shoulder and part of her chest have turned to wood; its weight means she is unbalanced, but her panic keeps her going. This place is Ojda's own. This is where it takes all things in the universe and scrambles them into hybrids. Nothing can resist the pull of this place; change is simply a physical law governing this beach. Anything that stays here long enough *has* to change. It has to become a hybrid of different things. *Out, out.* If you change here, you lose yourself.

Laleh is shouting and tearing at Myung, whose eyes have turned bloodshot. Myung sweeps through a pile of crystals and a gold rock tumbles free. Her heart constricts. This could be it. Doesn't the Creation of Ojda say it is gold? "And she spoke this knowledge into a single nugget and buried it, saying nothing to her family."

This could be *it*.

She goes to the mirror and it is Myung staring back at her, ordinary Myung, her hair not made of lizard tails, her shoulders not muscular and heavy as a lion's. She holds up the gold piece.

Slowly, her reflection lifts the piece even higher, opens her mouth. Places it below her tongue.

Myung knows she must copy her. Slowly, as if in a trance, she lifts the nugget, opens her mouth . . .

Laleh slams the dream with the full force of her desperation. It gives; she is in the mirror, staring at hybrid Myung, Myung's eyes are widening, Laleh screaming, *run! run now!* and Myung sees her lion's paw, feels her strange haunches and writhing hair; she drops the crystal and flees.

Blajine is climbing up a cliff face, a sapling now growing from her shoulder weighing her down. As she climbs, it elongates into a slender branch. She can see Myung sprinting down the beach but doesn't care. Her panic overwhelms her. *Let me live*, she whispers, *please*. But no Kiltas are around to hear her; their memories only live on the surface. Myung is climbing below her, her ascent much faster. *Come on*, Blajine whispers, sobbing. *Come on*. She is at the top of the cliff; her branch has sprouted twigs, now leaves; she drags herself over the edge.

Myung's palms are over the cliff face; she is pulling herself up. Blajine looks at her; Myung's face has turned into marble, her cheeks cracking. Blajine looks away, horrified. She doesn't care if the traveler escapes with her or not, she only wants to live. She can feel clamminess on her legs. Skin bursting as scales erupt. *No, no, no.*

Myung is some way behind her, crouched on the ground as a hunter. Blajine will not think about it. This cliff is the highest point in Ojda's space; from here, the gash in the sky is a leap away. One leap. All Blajine has to do is jump. Then she can hold the edges and pull herself up, like she did last time, the changes to her body falling away. She will be safe.

Blajine staggers to her feet, using her hand to support the shrub now sprawling from her shoulder and spreading above her. Cherry blossoms drift into her hair. Her legs quiver—*don't think about it*—and she runs to jump.

It happens in a blur. She can feel Myung run behind her, the thump of her paws on stone, hear her hot and labored breathing—and then, nothing. Myung has leaped, a second before Blajine. She has planted a foot in Blajine's tree and used it as a ledge to push herself higher. Blajine cries out; she's airborne now. She can see Myung hanging from the lip of the gash, her body changing back as she pulls herself into it, *let me live*, and then Blajine's legs melt into a fish tail and she falls.

III

There are moments you wish never happened, not for the moment itself but for what you learn about yourself that can never be unlearned.

Myung, scrambling in the cave, so desperate to find what she's looking for that she cannot see what is happening around her. Myung, planting a paw in Blajine's tree to push herself higher, pumped full of a wild and desperate desire to live, live as herself.

And Blajine, leading Myung to the space at the center of Ojda when she knows what will happen. Sentencing her to the worst death—a terrifying changing of self, a consciousness trapped in the creature she would become.

Blajine closes her eyes. Everything is quiet. It is quite peaceful, falling. Perhaps it is best that Myung made it out safely. Had that not happened, Blajine doesn't know if she could have lived with her reflection.

I love you, Mama, she says, even though her mother cannot say it back.

IV

Her shoulder jerks; she opens her eyes. She looks up, through the leaves. Myung has caught hold of her tallest branches and is hauling her to safety.

Transformations

Transformations are slow, even on an ever-changing island. Patterns of behavior harden over time and it is difficult to shape them into something new.

Yet, it is possible.

Blajine and Myung clamber over the cliff to collapse by the cottage. It takes them a while to climb out of the ravine. They climb slowly, scared of falling back into Ojda's mad center. Now on solid ground, the women tremble. Blajine curls onto her side. She holds her body close, focusing on the feel of it, grateful to be herself again.

Myung is pushing herself onto her hands; she is crawling toward Blajine. Blajine catches sight of her and whimpers. Myung is going to hit her, and Blajine deserves it.

But Myung isn't hitting her. Myung is holding her, desperately, as if Blajine is the last solid thing in the black sea and if she lets go, she will drown. The traveler is crying, her whole body shaking.

I saw-aw her, Myung says, and there is joy and despair in those words. *I saw-aw my sis-s-ter.*

They don't move for the rest of the day. They lie outside the cottage, arms entwined. We should eat, Blajine thinks, but she is too tired to move. Myung is not dead, and Blajine could weep with the relief of it. She looks at the traveler, her face covered in light and shadow. The last vestige of everything she has been taught rises up in Blajine and she thinks, once: You shouldn't be here.

But then it is done. The thought is swept away, and Blajine is left clean. Clean of everything she believed she must do and must be. Myung saved her life. Ojda loves Myung. Myung is as much a keeper of Ojda as any Kilta.

Myung belongs.

From the corner of her eye, Blajine catches sight of her mother, and the wispy outline of ghosts. They are arguing. She cannot hear them, but she sees the wild gesticulations and chest thumping. They are talking about Myung.

She doesn't care. *I can keep her*, she thinks happily.

The traveler is still crying. Tears slide slowly from her closed eyes and drop to the earth; she is struggling with her own memories.

In her mind, Blajine wipes away Myung's tears. *Thank you for saving me*, she says. *I now pronounce you Myung Kilta. Sister of Blajine Kilta, daughter of Ayesha Kilta, granddaughter of*—all the way back to the name her ancestors used to wait to say. *Magali Kilta, creator of a singing museum, keeper of your memories.*

In reality, Blajine sits up and says: *We should eat.*

She makes them charred plantain, stuffing them with the sweet petals of an iola flower. For twelve days, she cooks; she makes all the Kilta recipes she knows. Myung sleeps in the cottage now, in the same bed. She doesn't speak, only shakes her head or nods. Blajine wonders if she has lost her voice. She wonders how you go about getting something like that back.

For these twelve days, the ghosts of the Kilta family argue. Several are appalled by Blajine's decision—it is not up to one child to change the way things were done for centuries. These people, Rostum points out, are the Kiltas who never left Ojda even once. *Lack of imagination*, he says loudly at family discussions. *Ninny-minded, with no spirit*. It doesn't help discussions at all.

But most of the Kiltas are on Blajine's side. After all, spending eternity wandering an island with your family tends to change your perspective on things. Myung saved a Kilta's life. She survived everything Ojda threw at her. And even though she doesn't speak anymore, it is obvious she loves

Ojda. She treats it with gentleness, the way you would a child. What better keeper could the Kiltas ask for? *Besides*, Jilla points out, *it all ends after Blajine anyway. I don't see any children hanging about. Do you?*

Laleh sits among the ghosts and watches as a family changes their moorings. Slowly, gradually. Some drag their feet; others sprint over to the other side. Several pretend to still have objections so that they can prolong the discussion—these are the ghosts that come up to you and say, contemplatively: *So, I was thinking about the nature of Ojda's blood relationship with the Kilta family and how memories work. Do you know . . .*

They are the ghosts you do your best to avoid.

Rostum is having the time of his life. He shouts the loudest at family gatherings, threatening ghosts with death and other terrible things that can't hurt them. He gesticulates; he beats his chest. His passion disappears as soon as he leaves the group, and he is back to his even-tempered, happy self.

Haven't had this much fun in centuries, he confides to Laleh. *Feels a bit like living.*

Mad Magali is nowhere to be seen.

On the thirteenth day, unaware of how her presence is changing generations of a family, Myung says to Blajine: *I owe you a story.* And she tells her about the whale of babel. About Laleh, the chambers, her desire to leave, her time in the black sea and her quest for the story of Wisa. For four days, she speaks. Each night, she comes to the fire and tells Blajine a little bit more. Ghosts gather around to listen.

Laleh sits closest, her cheeks wet, listening to how Myung saw their life and the love in her words. She wishes she could bottle that love and keep it, to look at it on days when she is lonely. Most of all, though, she is proud of her sister. The black sea has made her stronger; she has grown into her vulnerability.

On the fifth day, when Myung finishes with Laleh's appearance in the cave, Blajine whispers: *I can't help you. I am so sorry. I don't know anything about Wisa except her name. I don't have the story.*

But someone does.

Mad Magali roams Ojda now, avoiding her husband and the ghosts of the Kiltas. Jinn has stopped shouting for her, which makes it harder to know where he is. Once, she nearly ran into him and had to hastily change direction.

Big things are happening on Ojda and to her family—she knows this. What she doesn't know is why she can't be there for it. Why she keeps running and hiding instead of being in the thick of things, making decisions and taking charge.

What is wrong with her?

Jinn finds her eventually. He lies in wait, that crafty man, and then when she is almost upon him, he jumps out from behind a rock and catches her. Sometimes it annoys her how well he understands even the most mysterious parts of her. Sometimes she loves him for it.

She considers if she wants to stamp on his foot and run away, but decides that this would be unbecoming of a centuries-old ghost.

Magali, he says, and she shrivels a little to hear the harshness in his voice; she hates his disappointment. She juts her chin out and stamps on his toe anyway, because she feels like it.

It's not her, she tells him defensively. *I would know Wisa anywhere and this is not Wisa.*

It's not her, he agrees. *But have you heard Myung's story? She knows Wisa. She knows the whale.*

But Magali is shaking her head. *I don't believe her. It's easy to make this up: all she had to do was read about* Fairy Tales of Wisa *or make notes from a few academic articles. Have you heard about her history with the black sea? Have you seen* Myung's Diaries? *She's crafty, Jinn. We know not to trust the crafty ones.*

Jinn sighs, exasperated. *Magali, you've been waiting so long you don't know how to do anything else. It scares you.*

Magali doesn't like hearing this. It's too close to the truth. *You tell them then*, she says. *You were there.*

No, Jinn says simply. *It's not my story to tell.*

Magali is agonized. She doesn't want to tell the story. It has been sitting in her for so long, pure and untarnished, she doesn't want to put it into words and see it fly out in the world. Watch it enter people's minds, and have them change it with their opinions or perspectives. It is *her* story. It is Wisa's. And it is the only thing of Wisa she has left.

Enough, Jinn whispers. *They deserve to hear it. They deserve to know why you have chained their spirits to Ojda. And you deserve to say it. Enough, Magali. It is time.*

And so, against her better judgment, Magali agrees. She walks with Jinn to the cottage, where the ghosts of the Kilta family wait for her, where Blajine and Myung are poking the embers of a fire, where Laleh is standing, heart in her mouth, to hear about Great Wisa. Already, images are flashing through Magali's mind—an ancient and lush island; a girl scampering along a tree, eyes wild; Grandpa painting the same picture over and over again, forehead creased in concentration, as he tries to find the shape of madness.

Softly, at the edges of the dream, the whale sings.

Mad Yet?: The Found Pages of Famous Explorer Myung Ting

Compiled by Olio Wagh

Department of Human Development, Tempest University

Published in 96003, Tola Publishers, Retrieved from the Museum of Collective Memory, Corridor |-| | | /•, Object (X)MLVI

Editor's Note

The following were discovered in Myung Ting's rooms on the last ship she boarded, bound in twine and hidden inside the figurine of a painted mermaid. Unlike Myung Ting's diaries, they are primarily the work of other scholars.

The contents are reproduced here faithfully, including any underlines or highlights that Myung Ting has added to mark out sections she found significant. The only task of this editor has been to trace the pieces to their original source, so that academics may situate them within their context.

The collection is unnamed, but this editor has taken the liberty of adding one for zest. "Mad Yet?" is Myung's only written note, scrawled on the last page.

The Tola Dictionary of the Inexplicable

15th Edition, Tola Publishers, 87459. Can be found in the Museum of Collective Memory, Corridor ---•|, Object XXID

"Madness" can mean a quest or an undertaking so foolish, it becomes a folly. It could be a white-hot rage that colors your perspective. It could be joy. It could be love (yes, love—for which person will not have claimed to have lost their heads at least once over a partner?). Or it could be a soured, dark madness, <u>the kind that cuts you if you look at it too long:</u> the madness of delusions, hallucinations, voices.

There is a wilderness in this word, a shifting color within it that encompasses more than we can grasp.

The earliest definition of "madness" was by Faraz Rili, an ancient explorer who set out to name everything in the universe that didn't have a word as yet. After he finished his list, the universe continued to not have names for all the things he named because he lost the list in a sea storm. But the list was washed ashore six decades later, giving us the earliest entry of the word "madness":

madness

(noun)
unknown
<u>*outside of understanding*</u>

And below Rili's entry, in handwriting that is not his:

Origin: undated. Believed to come from <u>"festival of madness,"</u> an obscure phenomenon that took place on the island of Esi every hundred years.

Chronicles of Cio Qual: Esi

Qual, Cio, first published in 970 and republished as part of the series "The Island Of," Leonin Library Press, 87702. Can be found in the Museum of Collective Memory, Corridor ••|//••, Object IV

Shifty people, all of them. If you read about the graciousness of Esites, of their kindness and charm, don't believe it—lies, all lies, multiplying like fleas on a rabid dog. If Esites are kind, it is the kindness with which you would approach a monkey; their politeness hides disdain. You won't believe me. You prefer to listen to the gilded nonsense of that sham traveler Juina. But if you've ever sailed to Esi and asked them about craft, you would have seen it too.

Craft. That famous specialty for which Esites are known, an ancient practice that keeps their island so hale and hearty and themselves so . . . well-fed. Esites have a nuanced and intricate bond with the land, Juina writes. It is a perfect culture of "living with," he prattles. Balance! Harmony! A secret that lives on Esi and will die on Esi as it should, he whispers. How he claims to know so much about it is a mystery, considering he has visited the island only once.

For I'll tell you this: <u>Esites lie</u>. Produce a peacock quill and you'll find a group of smiling Esites content to evade your questions and talk in riddles. May the Great Squid swallow me, but I promise you nothing real is known about Esi—only stories made up by idiot travelers like Juina. Esites don't answer your questions; I suspect they don't know the answers.

Hocus-Pocus: Summoning the Black Sea's Forgotten Magic

Losa, Priya, Leonin Library Press, 891117. Can be found in the Museum of Collective Memory, Corridor --- | • | /, Object III

Qual believed that Esi's festival of madness was not a festival at all, but a mistake—something powerful and uncontrollable that happened to the island once every hundred years.

There is no denying that Esites were secretive about the festival. They offered no details on what it was about, how it began or how they were to prepare. And when the time of the festival came, they pushed all travelers into boats and exiled them out into the black sea to wait until the festival was over. Interstellar clouds were summoned to hide the island from view, and for seven days Esi disappeared into this ancient ritual. On the seventh day, the clouds parted and sailors were allowed to return. Dagil, the prolific merchant, writes:

> It is as if the island never disappeared for seven days. Nothing is different in the harbor—not the land nor the smiles of Esites. But I have stood out on the black sea, watching Esi's clouds flash black with lightning. I have sailed into the storm only to find myself back in the same position as where I started. No Esite will speak of their festival, yet the unspoken lies as heavy as words. This is some strange magic.

If an Esite ever spoke or wrote about the festival, then no record of it now remains. We are still in the dark about a ceremony that may have birthed our universe's idea of madness. But, exactly like those trick pictures where if you stare long enough, the white space forms a picture of its own, we can learn from what we *do* know. If we stare hard enough at the black silhouettes, the festival may reveal its shape to us.

We know that Esites <u>abhorred madness</u>. More than one account has been written of Esites turning hostile when asked about the festival. Sailors of Esite origin are said to have picked fights in seaside dhabas over slights about their island and implications of madness. "There's no better way to make an enemy of an Esite," a pamphlet on ship-faring manners writes, "than to call them mad."

Yet we also know that Esites were not "ordinary," not in the normal sense of the term. They knew more about the black sea than they let on. "Craft," for instance, was a well-known talent across the black sea. Esites could do wondrous things with the land, it was said; they could shape it according to their will. Most of these claims are probably exaggerated, but stories do tally across records. Living spaces that grew and changed with the land. The ability to summon interstellar clouds. Double sight. The gift of fortune-telling, or "time-visions" as it was first called.

<u>And, of course, a strange magic that is captured by Esi's many maps—the island's ability to rearrange itself.</u>

Myung's Diaries

[Editor's note: Unpublished, and untraceable to its origin, as these pages were torn from a previous diary]

You can't draw a map of Esi, the cartographer tells me, annoyed. *I don't know what they've sold you, but it's a bunch of lies.*

We are surrounded by ink bottles. In the center of the room is a table, a circular cut of an oulbom tree, one of the largest in the black sea.[*] It's cluttered with parchments and sketches, only a small corner clean. This is where the cartographer works.

Think of mirabilia diachronism, I remind her, and it sounds silly even to my ears, as if I am evoking ancient magic. *If you look at a fairy tale, you can peel back the layers to the seed of history . . .*

Yes, but the mad sisters have no fairy tale. It's a sea phrase, "Don't let the mad sisters get me"—no one knows how it came about. There is no story.

There must be something in my eyes because the cartographer sighs. She flits to the side irritably, searching through drawers to pull out a thick stack of sheaves, which she thumps in front of me.

The top sheaf is a map. It shows a black-blue sea around an emerald island, the waters becoming bluer toward the shore until finally shimmering into clear white in the island's lakes, their glass surfaces revealing a world of rainbow fish and seaweed. Along the north, there are the whalebone mountains like a spine, flaking bone dust into the wind. Rain hits these mountains to carve holes in them and then sculpts their

---

[*] Editor's note: The strongest wood in the black sea, got from the oulbom tree. The oulbom tree is so large, it covers an entire island. The trunk is never cut; its fallen twigs are big enough to make trunks, tables and chairs. Oulbum wood cannot be used to make ships, though; it doesn't like swimming in space.

insides, so that water travels through filigreed bone channels to sprout from the base of the mountains and into rivers.

At the bottom of the whalebone mountains are the purple-emerald forests. These trees are so large, their leaves brush the clouds. The map records snapshot sketches of their wonders: Ruby flowers. Pearls embedded in leaves. Mounds of gold between roots.

Fringing the forests in the east are the red sands, the brittle roots of the forest's trees plowing in and out of its soil like giant water snakes making their way to the sea. Along the coast, there are the white sands. And lastly, in the south, there is a small patch of black ice, made cold by strange winds.

Esi. A map of the fabled island.

Look—the cartographer lowers her spectacles, taps her nose with her quill—*Yunal Gua tried. He found a chronicle by Cio Qual and drew a map of the island like he described it. Whalebone hills to the north, the jade forests at their feet, red sands to the east, the coast in white, and to the south, black ice. The whole lot, very detailed. Some call this beautiful, but I'm not that keen on Gua's style myself. Anyway*—she pulls out the first sheet, revealing another map underneath—*Gua found another chronicle dated several centuries after Qual's account—except the whalebone hills ran diagonally across the island, forest to one side and the red sands to the other.*

And a description centuries before Qual—another sheaf, a new map—*talks about the hills running zigzag through the island, the red sand inside the jade forests and the black ice covering most of the island.*

There are thousands of these. You see what I'm saying? You can't draw Esi, even if it were real—the island won't stay still.

"You may shiver from the word, but you long for madness.

"Oh, you cannot lie to me. I see you, reaching for what lies beyond your understanding. I see. Losing your heads, jumping off cliffs, swallowing hallucinogens and screaming to the blood moon, changing your personalities yearly so you can be born anew—you are desperate for the sublime. You don't just fear me, sailor. You envy me."

—Magali Kilta, as recorded at the Ruma seaside dhaba, after a brawl started by a drunken patron who insulted Magali's heritage as an Esite.

MAD YET?

ESI

The Night of Climbing

I

Laleh sits between Rostum and Hormuz, their shoulders pressing into hers. The family is huddled as close to Mad Magali as possible, although Magali had demanded a circle of space so she can pace and gesture. Jinn told the protesting family members to just let her have it.

And so that is how Laleh finds herself on one side of the fire, with a sea of ghosts, and Magali on the other. Myung is up front somewhere, sitting next to Blajine; as the only officially living people, they get pride of place. Jinn is next to them, and so is Ayesha, Blajine's mother.

Once in a while, when the woman with the top knot moves her head, Laleh catches a glimpse of Myung. Laleh wishes she could touch her, but otherwise she doesn't mind her position. There is something comforting about being pressed together with all the other ghosts. It rubs away some of the boundaries of herself; it eases her loneliness. Here, at last, is what Myung craved. A family, large, disparate and loud. People. Laleh never understood her sister's desire for more people, but now she feels their allure.

I, she says wonderingly, touching her lips. Rostum looks at her in puzzlement, but she shakes her head. She hadn't meant to say it aloud. She had always thought of herself as a singular "I." But now, sitting in this crush of people, "I" doesn't seem to matter as much. A new identity is forming, strange and too large to glimpse at once. A "we." The Kilta family, collected across centuries—they formed a "we."

Laleh shivers, and the girl next to her peers at her. *One of the new ones?* she asks and Laleh nods, because she has learned to by now. The girl leans forward, so she can look at Rostum. *One of yours?* she asks and Rostum shrugs.

Shhh, says Hormuz. *Mad Magali is beginning.*

And so she is. Magali is sitting with her eyes closed and her hands clasped in front of her, her head bowed. She is breathing deeply, as if accessing a sacred space. The fire casts shadows on her cheeks, as if she is being eaten by otherworldly spirits. Laleh stares in awe but Rostum snorts.

Always the one for theatrics, our Magali.

Shhhh.

For all of Rostum's skepticism, even he cannot help but feel a little thrill when Magali begins humming. The delight is spreading now, traveling through the sea of ghosts, solidifying Laleh's impression of this collective "we." This is it. This is the story they have been waiting centuries for, the story they were sworn to protect, the one thing that shaped their lives as Kiltas.

Magali begins to speak.

But it isn't only words. Laleh feels her boundaries melt, feels herself merge with the listeners as a single drop in the ocean, joining into this large "we"—

And then we drop, *thump*, into the middle of a story.

II

We are looking at a girl.

She is small and waif-like, arms sinewy and collarbones noticeable. Her head is tilted up, eyes wide, her mouth slightly pursed as she listens and then speaks. She is talking to a jackfruit tree.

We know it is a conversation although we cannot hear it. It is a quiet picture. If you want sound, you will have to imagine it. Leaves brushing against clouds. An engorged moon, heavy in the sky. The smallness of a girl sitting before a tree, so small that she is no more than a dot at the bottom of a picture, and we have to sweep our eyes across the forest floor to find her.

She is familiar.

We have never met her before, but we feel as if we have known her all our lives—for longer than our lives. This, we realize, is Wisa. The lost sister. The hidden story. Laleh feels her insides twist; she wants to drop to her knees and touch her forehead to the ground. She wants to shout *Great Wisa!* and have her creator look at her, hold her, bless her.

But this Wisa is only a girl. No more than eleven, maybe twelve. She has a mischievous energy to her that sits alongside an eerie stillness. This is a girl of contradictions; she is uninterested in coherence. She is smiling as she talks, and although this is still a silent picture, we realize she has done this before. Talking to trees is an everyday activity for Wisa. The trees talk back.

And so Laleh does neither of these things: fall to her knees or call out Wisa's name. She drinks in the girl who knows more about the whale of babel than anyone else, the person who has given Laleh and Myung comfort in impossible times. She revels in the joy of finally seeing her, even if Wisa cannot see her. She focuses on Wisa's features, making mental notes so that she may draw her when she wakes up. *Wisa*, she murmurs—and then she laughs with the joy of it, of having found someone you didn't know you have spent your whole life looking for.

Wisa turns slightly, as if she can hear Laleh, but then focuses on the tree again.

Sound, when it does arrive, comes all at once. Wisa and the tree are speaking of different landscapes. We hear places that are not this twilight forest. The rush and gurgle of waves. The clamor of a family piled into a cottage. Singing as hands work the fields, the bubble and hiss of metal as it melts in a shallow pan—and then the quiet pours back in, broken only by the rustling of the forest's leaves.

Wisa moves.

She flows to her feet and runs toward a cluster of houses we glimpse between the trees. A colony. The houses are simple; they are built from abandoned rocks and wood, each with an overrun garden, piled high with vegetables and fruit trees. The colony was not made with any sort of design; houses spring up like a patch of wild mushrooms, clustering together. Some houses are connected to each other while others stand alone. Short trees grow into these structures, roots digging into walls and doors. The occupants of these houses seem to like this. They have hung colored cloth from these branches and decorated them with stone chimes and shells.

It is so rudimentary that it is hard to believe we are in Esi.

But we are.

There is a flavor to this island—a tang in the air that speaks of more than what meets the eye. Even here, even among these simple houses, you sense an invisible power. This is the magical allure that travelers speak of when they write about Esi. This undeniable feeling that you are in a place not quite docile and with more history than your mind can comprehend.

But the houses here are not the wonders of craft described in the travelogues. This is a luddite colony. These are the only people on Esi who do not practice craft, having shunned it as unnatural and against the laws of nature. They *build* their houses instead of growing them and they do everything the hard way. Hunt, eat, live. *The craftless luddites*, the drifters call them. These luddites wake up and toil in their fields to the rhythm of song; they let their houses disintegrate with glee so that they may rebuild them, over and over. *This is how it should be*, they murmur; *we are small enough to be engulfed*. The zealous luddites, the crazy ones. The people who say to Esi, *oh, we want no part of your craft* and so suffer, quietly, in the limits of their humanness.

Wisa runs through these houses with the surety of a mapmaker—someone who has swept these same alleyways onto the page with smooth ink, and so knows them inside out. She sticks to the shadows. She doesn't want to be seen. She runs so fast, we are losing her. As she grows smaller, we see more. The whalebone mountains in the distance. A thorny, tangled forest reaching for the heavens. Giant roots that snake among the grass and curl between cottages.

Someone else is running behind us.

Another girl. Taller than Wisa and better built too. This one is used to working in the fields; she has muscle to her. She is not as good at sticking to the shadows, but she does not want to be seen either, so she is trying. Up ahead, beyond the crooked cottages, Wisa pauses and so the other girl stops. She presses herself into the shadow of a tree, aiming for stealth.

When she pushes the hair off her face, we get a good look at her.

It is Magali.

But it is Magali so much younger and so different, it is difficult to recognize her. There is no sourness at the corner of her lips, no bitterness in her eyes. She is young, curious, and with an edge of self-righteousness she will carry into her old age. She is still staring at Wisa and so we stare too, swooping in until Wisa grows larger.

Wisa is crouching, her ear pressed to the ground. Crawling forward a little, Wisa parts the weeds to reveal a long gash in the ground. She looks up, left, then right, and drops in.

Magali waits for a few seconds, then sprints forward, finds the crack and jumps in too.

We follow.

We are in a cave. Wisa clambers down the sides, once again an ant in the enormity of the cavern. She moves with deftness, like she is part monkey, part girl, part bird, although you cannot see her wings. She drops lightly to the floor and we look up with her.

Instantly, we see what she has noticed. Along the walls of the cave, high on the ceiling, down stalagmites and up stalactites, someone has etched a delicate pattern, a tracery that runs one inch into the stone. These are not like the straight lines of a floor plan. These are irregular and interwoven, more roots than lines, growing into a pattern we cannot see as a whole—we are too small—but that feels entangled and sprawling. The pattern glints. It has been filled with gold.

Wisa glances behind her, into the shadows. Directly at Magali.

Magali Kilta knocks her sister in the stomach; Wisa kicks at her, and they both fall to the floor. They tussle as siblings do, using their nails and teeth, pulling hair. Magali is older, about fourteen, and she pins her sister to the uneven floor, triumphant.

I knew, she says. *I knew there was something strange about you.*

But Wisa isn't struggling. She is smiling, that wide and gleeful smile she gets when she cannot contain her joy. She winks at her sister.

You've been lying, she says.

Magali is startled. She says: *About what—*

But Wisa has already wrapped her legs around her and tipped into a back roll. We fall forward, into a memory.

Chronicles of Cio Qual: Esi

Qual, Cio, first published in 970 and republished as part of the series "The Island Of," Leonin Library Press, 87702. Retrieved from the Museum of Collective Memory, Corridor ••|//••, Object IV

The sanest of Esites are those they call luddites. They live in crumbling cottages, grow their own plants and talk to the land like it is a pet, a lost family member, a dear lover—strange, I agree, but real. Luddites don't believe in craft; they don't practice it. They're not enchanted by Esites' show of gild and smoke. They'll never feature in Juina's *Many Wonders of Esi*. They drink too much and they like their dinner fat and juicy, but they are honest and when they speak about the island, it is with a familiarity that warms you. Like a sailor talks about the black sea or a merchant their coin purse. I suspect, under all their foolishness and blathering about the island, they are a shrewd lot.

They know more about Esi than most.

III

The memory

The luddite children are playing a game. It is forbidden, which makes it sweeter. You must climb out of your bed on a full moon night, on the day the parents have been drinking and so sleep as deep as the cold sleep, when they cannot hear the soft tread of your soles as you gather at the colony's edge with candles under your scarves and lamps swinging from your fingers. You must keep your whispers low and your excitement naked, and if you shiver with the thin lace of madness in the air, the scent of Esi's approaching century, you must hide it.

Don't let anyone think you are scared.

This memory is only a few weeks old. Wisa is here, standing quietly in the middle of the crowd. The children are shuffling from foot to foot, nervous, whispering. Magali is here as well—up front, at the very fringe of the forest. The children are looking at her; they are waiting. She lights her lamp and lifts it, her face an orange emblem in the silver night. Then a cloud of lamps lights up around her, and hushed and thrumming, we melt into the forest.

Across Esi, there is a collection of broken stone structures.

No one knows where these structures came from. No one builds in stone anymore and no one can remember a time when they did. The ruins remain a mystery, long and square and oblong shapes now eaten over by nature. The children don't know the stories. To the children of the luddite colony, the stone structure in their jungle is special for different reasons. It transforms at night. Clashing leafage dissolves into shadow; dark things scuttle with sudden yellow eyes. Sound presses into you: the *brrrrr* of an insect's wings, the soft squelch of an animal's paw. There is ripeness to the night; we shiver with the taste of the forbidden.

And then we are here. Before a mango tree erupting from a stone wall, roots dripping to the ground, branches silver in moonlight. Children swarming into the ruins. Lamps going off, only a few left lit to create a soft glow. Breathing. Animal sounds, melting and breaking into recognition. We spot Magali, lifting her lamp, looking for Wisa—although she does not want to be *seen* looking. Wisa moves in the corner of the frame, pushing to the center; Magali looks away before they catch eyes.

We are confused. This sisterhood is strange and half-formed. It is almost . . . absent.

A boy walks to the wall, bony as a hatchling. There is magic in him; it pulls at the frame, centers it. Beyond our vision, we can taste Wisa's eagerness; she hasn't played this game before. The boy is rolling his shoulders, eyeing the wall and mango tree. A wineskin bounces at his hip. A few children call out—whoops, goads, incomprehensible sounds. The boy grins.

It is Jinn.

He leaps and climbs.

It is like watching water. He flows up, up, up, quick ascent, flawless grip, disappearing into clusters of taro vines and emerging again. No one cheers now. They are holding hands, holding their breath, and still Jinn climbs higher. He's at the roots now and his ascent is slower; the mango tree is a tricky goddess; she is not to be trusted. Still, he climbs. Higher and higher, up the last cluster of roots and to the sweeping bark. Here he hangs, swinging as a monkey from the trunk, and the children go wild.

We are breathless, caught in a spell. The world has shrunk to us and Jinn.

He makes it a bit farther, then finds a good perch to paint a branch with color from his wineskin. When he holds his hands up, he is different—cheeky, triumphant, bathing in the whistles and whoops from the pack.

Lazy. He could have gone farther.

Then Magali's hand is on our shoulder and she is turning Wisa away from the spectacle, whispering, and it is clear now—these women are strangers.

The memory still

The memory opens wider; we lose footing, tumble deeper.

Grandpa brings Wisa home one evening. He leaves in the morning for the bazaar and returns with this, a lost and hungry thing. This is what he claims; Wisa seems neither. She seems unwavering, sitting on the kitchen table wrapped in a blanket, consuming everything with her large eyes. When Grandpa is not looking, she pulls Magali's hair and Magali pinches her viciously.

Magali hates her.

After that, Wisa's strangeness only becomes more apparent. Ask her what she did for the first eleven years of her life, and Wisa says she was a "skywalker," a person who walks on sticks and dances on threads in the sky. Then she'll follow you around and keep talking, even after you have stopped talking, even after you have tried to get away. Magali cannot get rid of her.

I was good, Wisa says to Magali in the kitchen, *a lot better than they thought a child could be. Of course, some of the travelers wanted me to fall to my death, at least break a limb, you know, for a show—so I had to pretend to wobble but I never did really because I am very good with my feet. I was light too*, she says outside the fields as Magali tries to lose her in the tall grass, *and you couldn't see me; sometimes I was here, then there, like a red lizard, and so the merchants could never catch me. Sometimes they caught me*, she says during a game of hide-and-seek when she is meant to be counting, *but I always ran away and anyway I only took what I needed as one person to eat and that's not wrong, not when people can't see you or know you're there, so I was saying hello!*—Magali jumps from behind the door—*I'm here, look at me.*

News of Wisa's arrival spreads quickly through the colony. At first, neighbors bring food, herbal tea, fermented beer, even an oddly shaped rock—*reminds me of the child*, Haza says gruffly, trying to elbow his way through the door—anything to get into Kua's house and see the girl. Wisa says nothing to these visitors. She watches them with large eyes until they look away. She's unnerving, the colony decides. Strange. Voiceless as well, most likely. But they bring gifts and wonder about where Kua will take her.

Give her to drifters, Lira says. *That's what he'll do. They'll find a home for her.*

No one has heard of drifters carrying a child with them, so they look forward to the possibilities. Drifters travel alone; how would they feel about a strange little one towing along? And where would they settle her? So many delicious questions. For weeks the colony hums with anticipation, waiting for the first drifter to arrive.

But the first drifter comes and goes, and Wisa is still here. Then the second one comes, and the third, and still people can see Wisa sitting on the steps of Kua's cottage, staring listlessly at the plants or dancing by herself. She still won't speak, not to anyone who is not a Kilta.

He's planning on keeping her, they whisper. *She's going to stay.*

The colony doesn't know what to do with this information. Keep her? Kua is the most respected member of the colony; he is their memory keeper and their conscience. They cannot dream of criticizing him. How can you criticize Kua with the life he has had? Lost both his son and his daughter-in-law to an illness no one could cure. Oh, the *craftsmen* could have cured them, but Kua refused to betray his principles like that. His son didn't want to be saved like that. And little Magali, left behind in his care, raised to be such a wonderful girl.

The colony adores Magali Kilta. They adore how she smiles at them, moon-faced and cheeky, promising you the world. They adore how she laughs despite the sorrows she has been dealt, how she is growing up to be a beautiful woman with her own reserves of conviction and strength. *She is a smart one*, they say and tap their noses.

But most importantly, she is a good one. Good in the way only Kiltas can be: inside out, with no questions or agonizing. Her father was like that, Kua is like that too, and Magali will continue this tradition. More than one mother has wished their child was like Magali Kilta.

But keep Wisa? Wisa who is definitely not a Kilta, and who doesn't look like she will become one anytime soon. What is Kua thinking? He is kind-hearted, of course, and he is known for the animals he has saved and his intricate understanding of the land. But this is the first time he has brought a child home. And keeping her? What does Magali think of it?

Forced to have a sister, Caqn says to his neighbor while harvesting purple yams in his garden. *And that too a strange one. Not cheerful, no smiles. Just dances and stares all day. Follows Magali around too. I wouldn't like it if I were Magali. Not one bit.*

But no one knows what Magali thinks. If you catch her alone for a moment, without Kua or Wisa—who has taken to following her like a shadow—if you lean conspiratorially over bread baskets and collections of wax candles, and whisper to her that you are on her side, always, and that she can come over anytime if she wants food or tea or if she needs a place to escape, Magali will only smile. It is a reserved smile. Kind, but not forthcoming. You lean back, feeling your duty done but unsure if Magali heard you. Or if she will ever take you up on your offer.

Then Wisa will appear, right at Magali's shoulder, and stare at you until you hasten away.

Strange child.

The children also agree that Wisa is strange. They gather beneath the old jackfruit tree, their favorite meeting place, and discuss her with relish. Where did Kua find her? Do you see how she stares?

Maybe she's mad, Ava says and feels brave saying it.

Mad. The children consider it.

You should make notes, Jinn tells Magali. *See if you can spot the signs.*

The children nod. You can't have madness—not in a luddite colony, not with the festival approaching.

Look for chanting, Ava tells Magali.

And animal baying, Jinn adds.

Magali doesn't take notes but only because she is fighting with idiot Jinn, not because she does not think Wisa is mad. Oh, Wisa is unhinged. Just look at the time she spends looking intensely at trees. Patting flowers. Talking—talking!—to a lizard.

She's my friend, Wisa says when Magali mentions the lizard. She looks surprised, as if it is obvious. *I've called her Gul.*

Carefully, Magali considers her way forward. Grandpa is large-hearted, stubborn when it comes to his bad judgments. Still, Magali has righteousness on her side. You cannot let a mad person into the colony. What's next, craft?

Maybe give her back, Magali suggests to her grandfather one day, when Wisa is wandering somewhere. *We won't abandon her*, she says hurriedly. *We can give her food, enough to survive many seasons. I can give her all the ripe mangoes Lira has been saving for me. And a blanket. It is only*, she continues, *some people—not me—have been saying that she's . . . you know . . . strange.*

Grandpa says nothing. He simply stares at her, disappointed. Magali shrinks into herself. She adds miserably: *Jinn said it, not me.*

Grandpa stands and tucks a strand of Magali's hair behind her ear. He says kindly, *Magali*, and the word goes straight through his granddaughter, making her feel small and twisted. He says: *Wisa has no one to go back to.*

Next time she sees Wisa in the garden, balancing on one leg to show her lizard a pose, Magali buries her face in her hands. When she parts her fingers and peeks through, Wisa has not disappeared like she hoped. Magali puts her hands down, leaves the window, makes it all the way to the kitchen door. Turns back.

Don't do it, she tells herself as she steps out into the garden. *It's a bad idea*, she says as she walks across the flowers toward Wisa. *Turn back now*, she thinks as her shadow drapes over Wisa, who looks up with eyes wide and curious.

Can you climb as well as you talk? Magali says.

Wisa nods.

Tonight, Magali says. *After they put the candles out in the great hall. Don't tell Grandpa.*

The memory again

We are back in the stone structure. Magali is whispering to Wisa in a low, urgent murmur. Only go as far as you can. Don't show off. Most children don't get beyond the first third of the wall, so if you go higher you will earn their respect. You have to come down, don't forget that. No tricks, this isn't a skywalker performance. Be—

Ah, Wisa is not listening. She is looking over Magali's shoulder, at the children staring at her. One of them sticks out her tongue. Wisa hisses; the girl scampers.

Wisa, Magali says, furious. *Listen to me!*

She won't but she nods anyway. She is occupied with something, something we have not yet seen. And now Magali is uneasy; we sense it. Is Wisa nervous? Surely not. She has performed more daring feats at the market; she's walked across threads fifty people high, jumped from trapezes at the top of thin bamboo poles . . .

The other children are not as good as Jinn. Some reach the main root cluster but give up soon after. Others fumble in the beginning itself, mistaking shadows for crevices, placing their weight in unreliable holds. Only one falls—from not too high but his ankle is beneath him and you can hear the crunch in the hush. He cries into his friend's shoulder as they carry him out.

Then it is Wisa's turn, and she walks to the wall in a collective hush. She looks up but doesn't climb. One second. Two. The children don't say anything; you give the climber their space. Ten seconds, eleven. A murmur. Thirteen seconds, fourteen, and Wisa glances back toward Magali, quickly, involuntarily, and then it is so obvious Magali cannot believe her stupidity.

Wisa has been lying. No one has actually seen her perform skywalker tricks in the colony, not even by accident. Grandpa never speaks about Wisa's skywalker life; the only witness is Wisa herself. Crazy, strange, talkative Wisa. And now she is looking at Magali panicked, who jolts forward, without thinking, to get between Wisa and the wall. She is filled with a protectiveness she cannot understand; it is a desperate urge to keep this ridiculous girl safe.

But Wisa is already climbing.

She is terrible. Her feet don't synchronize with her hands and she places her toes in all the wrong places. Thrice she falls, saving herself by scrambling for a protruding weed or raking her fingers along the stone until she finds a hold. In the beginning, the children murmur but as she keeps climbing, the murmurs change to jeers. By the time she is one third up the wall, the children are laughing among themselves. So this is the famous Wisa, skywalker extraordinaire. Magali shrinks into herself.

Wisa keeps going. Up, past the one-third point, slowly, carefully, now touching the cluster of roots. The children have quietened. The game has changed. Jinn is whispering in Magali's ear—*get her down; she'll kill herself*—but Magali is poised with tension, terrified anything she says will disrupt Wisa's concentration and cause her to fall. When Wisa grips a wet root and transfers her weight to that hand, the crowd inhales as one. When that grip begins to slip—Wisa's legs still swimming in the air, trying to find purchase—some children look away; others bury their nails into skin. Magali doesn't look away. Wisa's toes find a crevice just as her hand slips off the root, and she is saved but barely.

She keeps going.

No one is laughing now. Madness scents the air, and the children are drunk on it. She is high, higher than most of the others now, this awkward, fumbling child. In fact, she is only a few feet away from Jinn's colored mark—it is there, in front of her, so close.

Wisa pauses at the start of the branch, wiping the sweat from her eyes. She is shaking, the involuntary shudders of a fearful body.

Just a bit farther, Wisa!

It is only a voice at first, but it becomes a crescendo—each child is suddenly Wisa, staring at something impossible that is now within reach, and they shout for her to seize it. *Come on, Wisa, almost there, reach!* Wisa is inching slowly along the branch, reaching out her fingers and she has done it; she is at Jinn's mark on her first try, this mad girl with golden courage. Jinn looks like he has swallowed lemons. And in the whooping and the hysteria and Magali's crumbling relief—she's alive, sing to Esi!—they don't notice something.

Wisa is still going.

She is crawling past the mark, toward the end of the branch, following offshoots slowly, so slowly, to get to other branches and climb higher.

Wisa! Magali says, her voice firm and urgent. *That's far enough. Come down!*

Wisa ignores her. Up, up, beyond what any child would sensibly reach for, and no one is cheering now; the madness has fermented and danger is all anyone can taste. Fall now and she dies.

Wisa stops. She is at a branch with no offshoots—the only way to climb higher is to jump from this one to another branch. It is ridiculous. She would need to stand, balance, cover the gap. *She won't dare*, Magali tells herself. *She won't dare.* But Wisa is putting her feet on the branch and trying to stand, wobbling as she does so.

Wisa Kilta! Magali shouts.

Wisa looks down. Magali has lifted the lamp to her face so that Wisa can see her clearly. She is furious and utterly, utterly terrified. Wisa smiles.

Magali says, *Don't you dare*—

Wisa jumps.

She falls, of course. Doesn't die, lucky girl. Catches another branch with the tips of her fingers, pulls herself up and clambers farther along another branch, lip bleeding, the children silent as the cold sleep now, and she wants to touch the leaves that cut into the night sky but she won't make it that far, not tonight, she's not that good, so she stops astride an offshoot, legs swinging, and marks a soft line with her dye as a gentle afterthought.

She looks down, and we see it—what Magali's been lying about.

Wisa is caught in the branches of her moonlit tree as the leaves open into whispers. They are speaking of a soft desire she hasn't told anyone, a want they know how to fulfill. She reaches for it, eager, but it eludes her.

When she looks down, it is into Magali's startled eyes. For a moment, we see Magali as the world does: orphan, granddaughter of Kua, beloved of the luddite colony, the girl with a half-smile that says she can do anything. Then we fall into her perspective and the ruins transform.

Chaos. The whispers are now an ocean, drowning us. Blajine is here, Myung, Laleh, Magali as a ghost on Ojda, behind her Wisa but a different one that is dressed strangely—all of them staring at young luddite Magali. Trees move between them, stretching, walking, talking. We smell smoke, hear the bubble and hiss of metal as it melts, feel the tightening as it forms into gold.

Then the world goes still.

Wisa is gleeful. Magali Kilta, the good luddite girl who is craftless and pure, has the first sign of madness: double sight.

Magali-Wisa-Jinn

I

If you come to Esi with what they call "stone eyes"—eyes that notice as little as stones—you will see the craft that Esites show you, but nothing else. You will leave talking of the simplest glamours; for years afterward, you will remain amazed.

If you come with a traveler's eye, sharp like that of a bird of prey, then you will see the stone structures. If you are very good, maybe you will even spot the gold-patterned caves. You will think: *Isn't it surprising that an island that possesses secret knowledge cannot remember these stone structures? That the people have forgotten their own history?*

So you will ask an Esite and they will say:

These?! They will slap their bellies and laugh. *These ruins? They're just stones, geometrical formations of rock. You can write about them if you like, traveler. But consider—who wants to read about rocks?*

It is a good question, so good it fills you with doubt. Who does want to read about rocks? No one, you decide. You cancel out your pages of structural theories. Fill them with tales of craft. Wander back to your ship pleased by the coin you will make once these pages are stitched into chronicles. You fail to hear the soft murmur on the wind, of how these stones may be connected to Esi's greatest festival.

For once every hundred years, Esites pile their visitors, travelers and old guests onto boats; they row them out to the black sea, leave them bobbing there for days and days; they make sure their island is clear, filled with only natives.

Then they go mad.

II

After the climbing incident, the children are suspicious of Wisa.

Not *all* the children—only some. But even this surprises Magali, for what Wisa did that night was magnificent. Still, she should have expected it. The festival of madness is ten years away, and the children are on the lookout for signs of madness. That's what luddite children do. Luddites don't participate in the festival—they have found ways to protect themselves from it—but they are wary nonetheless. *Madness finds you,* Kua used to tell her, *whether you are looking for it or not.*

And now Wisa is here, and she is different. The children suspected it before, but now they know it.

What she did isn't natural, Ava whispers loudly, so that Magali overhears. *No normal child could have climbed that high. They have stories about it—about people doing things they can't do, finding sudden abilities, seeing things. It's a sign*—she drops her voice—*of, you know, the festival. The drifters will tell you; you can ask them if you like. I'm not lying. That feeling that night—slithering and shivery and . . . alive. It is what they warn us against. It is what those seven days . . . feel like.*

Magali feels a prickle of irritation for Ava and her paranoia. Magali may not like Wisa, but you cannot help but admire what she did on that tree. It was brave and wild, and Magali finds herself . . .

Longing for it.

She shakes her head, trying to get the thought out.

Some children believe Ava and skitter away every time they see Wisa. But others don't care. Wisa has earned their respect. Magali is cornered in random places in the colony and bombarded with questions she doesn't have the answers to. Where does Wisa come from? Why did she keep climbing that night? Is she going to stay?

Freyn finds her in Lira's elderflower shop and asks her, in a voice that is too loud for what they are discussing: *Will Wisa show me how?*

He means climbing. What an idiot to mention it here in a shop full of parents, where anyone could overhear. If people found out what the children did, they would be stopped. She glances around and catches sight of Jinn.

It is not surprising to see him here; Lira is his mother. Jinn is rummaging in the earthen pots next to them, trying to pretend he hasn't overheard. Magali waits for him to say something. She has been watching him closely since that night; she knows how much it rankles him that Wisa climbed as far as he did—and then farther. Jinn is proud of his status as the best climber. So she waits for him to say what she knows he has been dying to say since that night. Any moment now, he'll lean forward and look Freyn in the eye. His voice low and urgent, he'll say: *I wouldn't ask that if I were you, Freyn. Wisa's clearly mad.*

For a moment, their eyes meet. Magali knows there is a challenge in hers. Go on. Say it. She doesn't know why she wants him to, but she does. She wants to know if there is any of her old friend left in this boy.

But he doesn't say it. He breaks eye contact and wraps a fistful of dried elderflower in a leaf.

Magali says to Freyn: *Ask her yourself.*

Four nights later, Jinn finds her.

Magali is by the river, the quiet place where she can be by herself. It is nice to be the golden child in the colony, but it is also exhausting. There is always someone who wants to talk to you, feed you or be loving. It is selfish to think like this, of course; she is lucky to have so many people love her. But she thinks it nonetheless.

So she comes to the river, to this tree whose branches skim the surface, where she can lie with her feet in the water and let the fish nibble her toes. The river is not as clear as the glass lakes, but you can still see almost to the bottom: weeds, fish, crabs, and there, buried in the loose mud, the familiar glint of gold. There is gold everywhere on Esi; if you dig even lightly with your fingers, you will find it.

When she looks up, Jinn is staring at her.

It has been a long time since they were alone, not since their fight. Seven years, Magali recalls. No one can carry a grudge like her. She waits for him to speak first, and enjoys watching him search for the words. What will he say? Sorry? Or *You're so wise, Magali; I miss you?* Perhaps, *Isn't Ava weird; I wish I didn't spend so much time with her?*

Jinn says: *What do you think?*

It is not what she is expecting, but she knows what he means. She and Jinn are no longer friends, but they haven't lost the ability to pick up in the middle of a conversation that never started. Magali is delighted to find she still knows him. Knows he has been bursting to find her alone, that that night put the same questions in his head as it did in hers. Who is Wisa? And is she "mad"? In fact, Magali senses that if she says what she really thinks, perhaps Jinn and she could be friends again.

But Magali is older now. She knows time only flows one way. So she says: *No*, and feels smug at his disappointment.

Jinn leaves, and she doesn't stop him.

Two nights later, though, Magali is still thinking about the meeting.

Not because of Jinn—she gave up on that fool long ago. But his question makes her look at Wisa in a new light. It makes her want to *act* on her thinking.

When Jinn and she were still friends, he described the two types of visitors to Esi. Those with stone eyes and those with eyes like birds of prey. He heard it from a drifter and it delighted him. He did the actions for her, putting pebbles on his eyelids for the stone-eyed, and curving his fingers into claws as a bird of prey. She was unimpressed. She had heard the same story, from the same drifter, which annoyed Jinn because he traded a whole silta pearl for it.

But now, she is curious. What if she looked at Wisa with eyes better than her own, with eyes like a bird of prey? What would she see?

It is thrilling to contemplate it.

For a while, that is all Magali does: contemplate. She thinks, and thinks, but slowly she begins to act. She observes Wisa at home, and writes down her behaviors. She notices Grandpa is oblivious to Wisa's strangeness; he is more concerned with teaching her to read. Wisa herself doesn't pretend to be better around Grandpa; she is as listless and endlessly talkative, her mind forming startling connections. In her notebook, Magali notes: *Is this madness??* She doesn't think it is, but how would she know? How would anyone? What happens during the festival is a mystery, and no one talks about it.

If Jinn and she were still friends, he would say: *You're changing.* For she is. Observing Wisa gives her purpose, the closest she has come to the giddy excitement of her adventures with Jinn. When they stopped talking, this part of her died; now, she is finding it again, by herself, which is more exciting. She catches a glimpse of her reflection sometimes, in pieces of glass or in still water, and she grins. She likes the way her cheeks are flushed. When she walks, there is lightness in her step.

Wisa disappears a lot.

Magali didn't notice before because she was avoiding her. But now she realizes Wisa likes her own company. She leaves each afternoon, when people are napping and won't miss her. Sometimes at night as well. She is not in the house or in the colony; she vanishes into the forest, and Magali is filled with an irresistible urge to follow her.

So she does.

She follows her for weeks. Wisa stays in the shadows; she has an uncanny ability to melt into her surroundings. Magali tries to follow her lead, but is not very good at it. No matter how hard she tries, people discover her crouching behind the earthen pots or nestled in thickets. They exclaim, chastise and then feed her. Much to her frustration, Magali cannot be invisible.

Nor does she really have eyes like a bird of prey. For if she did, she would notice that Wisa has been wandering around a patch of forest in elaborate loops. That she leans against trees and sighs dramatically, as if they hide special secrets. That when Magali is held up by someone in the colony describing in detail how much their elbows hurt, Wisa waits patiently until Magali extricates herself and only then does she continue her journey. And if Magali was really observant, then she would catch those odd moments when Wisa stares at her in the house, delighted. Followed by Magali Kilta! How thrilling. Wisa is determined to make this a good performance—stupendous, magnificent! Her *best*. She is careful to sit under different species of trees, so Magali cannot discern a pattern. When Magali is particularly close, hiding inefficiently behind a house or a bush, Wisa bends to talk to earthworms. What a show! She will make sure Magali remembers her.

But Magali notices none of this. She writes in her notebook, looks happily for patterns and follows her sister.

That is how we find both sisters on a full moon night, Wisa moving soundlessly through the colony and Magali trying to keep up. We watch Wisa find the crack to the cave and fall through it, Magali following. And here they are now, both sisters, Magali pinning Wisa to the floor of the cave. Magali saying: *I knew there was something strange about you.*

Above them, the gold pattern of the cave shimmers in an unseen light.

Wisa grins at her sister. She says: *You've been lying.*

III

Magali knows Wisa is talking about double sight.

Wisa doesn't say it, but the knowledge now hangs between them. For a moment, Magali is too surprised to act. Then she releases her sister. She clambers off her and sits down, careful to keep distance between them. *Look calm*, she thinks. She knew something happened that night. When she looked up at Wisa in the mango tree and the landscape around her transformed—far more chaotic than anything she had experienced before—she *felt* Wisa's eyes on her. And Magali doesn't know how, but she knew Wisa had guessed.

The first time Magali experienced double sight, she was nine. She was waist-deep in a pond catching milows, bright purple-and-white fish that are a little dumb, when she saw a woman staring at her from between the wild grass. The woman said her name was Ayesha Kilta, which Magali took to mean *I-am-a-long-lost-cousin-eleven-times-removed-from-your-father*. It was not uncommon. Ayesha waded into the water and they caught and released milows in silence, letting Esi hum and whistle over them.

Do you know any songs? Ayesha asked after a while.

Magali didn't like singing but Ayesha seemed nice and a little lost, so Magali sang "Huff Away Arugay," a children's song her mother used to sing all the time before she died. It is about a cloud that gets tangled in the branches of a tree. Ayesha didn't seem to be listening very carefully. She was marveling at the sky, at Esi's towering forest, even at the fish like she had discovered rare and delicious blue oysters. When Magali stopped singing, Ayesha said with a touch of awe: *You'll make a museum of song one day.*

Well, Ayesha was clearly crazy. Still, Magali liked the sound of "a museum of song" and so when she went home, wet and a little muddy, she told Grandpa.

She hadn't learned as yet what "madness" meant to an Esite but, in that moment, she saw it. Grandpa went silent. For the first time in her life, Magali felt her grandfather wander away from her, moving down paths she could not follow. She wasn't scared; she was too confused to be scared. When he returned, it wasn't with an overt gesture; she simply felt him back in the room with her. He continued tearing spinach for dinner.

Don't tell anyone, he said without looking at her, and so Magali didn't.

She didn't, even when the visitors became more frequent. They were eccentric people who called her "Mad Magali" and accused her of locking them away on an island for the rest of their lives. Magali didn't understand what they meant. She tried to shut her ears and ignore them. Ayesha turned up a few more times, and she was always gentle. She didn't try to talk to Magali, only joined her in whatever activity Magali was doing, which Magali was grateful for.

Once, she saw Jinn.

He was older, but it was definitely Jinn. He had the same smile, although there were a few wrinkles around his eyes now and he looked . . . calmer. Like the fight had leaked out of him. Not that he had had much fight in him to begin with. Coward. But when he smiled at her, Magali didn't feel angry. She just felt at peace. This was Jinn. Her Jinn. She was safe.

Then he asked, *are we still fighting?* in a soft and condescending tone, and she wanted to kick him in the shins, hard, and stamp on his toes for good measure. *Of course* they were still fighting; they would be fighting until the end of time; how did he have the *gall* to ask?

He disappeared before she could do any of those things.

There was a time, at about twelve years old, when the visitors became frequent, two or three at once. They began appearing when she was buying tools or helping Kua with his drawings. They talked to her so loudly, she *couldn't* ignore them. People in the colony began to ask her if she was unwell. If she needed to rest. They had asked her four times now if she could spare them some candles for the night, and she had not heard them.

Only then did she crawl into Grandpa's bed and cry. She held his big hand and said the words that had been choking her for years. *I am mad.* She didn't look at him, afraid of the horror and repulsion in his eyes.

But he only laughed. A soft laugh, the way Grandpa laughed when you told him you were scared of the dark, and there were definitely spirit-eating creatures under your bed. He held her and rocked her gently, and told her, *You're not mad my little one, not at all. You are only gifted.*

Double sight meant that Magali's ancestors and descendants visited her, but only she could see them. No one understood how it worked, how long they stayed, why they came. It had the mysteriousness of a gift. *Think of it as a muddle of personal time,* Grandpa said, *the yarn of your life all tangled up. But they cannot do anything to you, little one, nor do they want to. They just like attention. Nod to them when they arrive; show them that you are busy and can't talk. If they are very loud, go somewhere you can be alone and talk to them. Go to the forest. Anything can be said in the forest—trees understand. Don't be afraid of these people. They're your family—speak to them, enjoy your gift.*

He tucked a strand of her hair behind her ear, considering something. Then he said:

When you are home, you don't have to hide it. You can speak as freely as you like around me; I won't mind. I won't be able to see your visitors, but they are always welcome. But no one else can know, Magali. We live in difficult times.

Magali understood. Twelve years old was old enough to know she had been born in a time that would witness the festival of madness—the great, petrifying festival no one can remember. And that required special decisions.

But the visitors got easier to manage after that. They were quite amiable to being silent once they knew she wasn't ignoring them. They still passed loud comments, rather like a running commentary on her life, but Magali enjoyed these. At least her family was innovative.

And once in a while, Magali saw her parents. Sometimes together, sometimes only one of them. When this happened, Magali would rush to the forest, bursting with things to tell them. It was her mum who was the first person to hear about the fight with Jinn. It was her father who listened to how she had grown a batch of waterapples—shelled fruit with tart, pink-blue insides—and cooked them, and how Grandpa had said it was the best meal he had ever tasted. They both heard about how she was the best silta pearl hunter in the colony, how she felt alienated from the children—*they are so childish, Mum*—and how she wanted to be a memory keeper like Grandpa when she grew up.

Double sight was indeed a gift.

But now Wisa knows—*don't tell anyone*, Grandpa had said—and Magali's heart is pumping wildly. What should she do? Deny it? No, Wisa would never believe her. She *knows*, and you couldn't shake her from that certainty. Threaten her? Tell her that if she told anyone in the colony, it would be Magali's word against hers and everyone would believe Magali? It is her only option, but it isn't a good one. Even the suspicion of double sight is bad when the festival is so close. Magali has heard drifters talk about it. They say it is the first sign of madness.

You can't be mad and still live in a luddite colony.

Breathe, Magali tells herself, as her heartbeat spikes. It will be okay.

Don't be scared, Wisa whispers.

She's looking at Magali with concern, as if she cannot understand what she is thinking. She holds out her hand, the way you do with a wild animal when you are trying to soothe it. The idea almost makes Magali laugh; Wisa, treating *her* as wild? But it is comforting too. There is no guile in that gesture, nothing but goodwill.

Magali is suspicious.

How do you know? she asks, because it is pointless not to.

I saw, Wisa says. *In the stone structure.*

But Wisa knew before that as well; the jackfruit trees had told her. Or rather, they told each other, and she'd overheard. Tree speech is slow, elongated, so you can never be sure you have heard right.

No one will believe you, Magali whispers.

Wisa is puzzled. *Why would I tell anyone?*

Magali doesn't know what to make of that. Wisa is looking at her in triumph again, but it is not . . . the triumph of a game won. It is not the smile Ava has when she is more popular than you, so you *have* to be nice to her. It is . . . outside of them. Like Wisa made a bet with unknown forces, with herself, and she is pleased she is right.

What's double sight like? Wisa asks.

Magali is startled. *What?*

What's it like?

Wisa is leaning forward now, eager. She really wants to know. No one has asked Magali this question, not even Grandpa, and suddenly, Magali wants to cry.

She is horrified by the impulse. She tries quickly to blink back the tears springing up and swallow the lump in her throat. What is wrong with her? It is just a question. But the urge to cry doesn't fade. The more she thinks about it, the tighter her chest becomes. Her lips wobble. It is as if she is pressing some secret knot in her and it is releasing an emotion she cannot control. *Don't think about it*, she tells herself and as soon as she thinks that, she focuses on the other impulse that is unfurling slowly.

She wants to tell Wisa.

The rational part of her tries desperately to back away from this thought as well, but now she is tangled in it. Despite her better judgment, Magali is suddenly desperate to answer Wisa's question. She wants to explain the craziness of talking to people from different times and places and not knowing how you know them. She wants to say: *Do you know that sometime in the future there will be a whale of babel? A whole whale, growing in space and becoming another black sea. Can you imagine?*

If anyone could, it would be Wisa.

But she fights the impulse and wins.

You do that a lot, Wisa says mildly.

Magali frowns. *Do what?*

What you did just now. Change yourself. Or swallow yourself, actually. I see you around people. But when you are alone—

You've been watching me when I'm alone?

Wisa looks sheepish. *When you were following me. I watched you then. When you were following me, you became different. Like there was . . . more to you. You liked it. You were happy.*

How did you watch me when I was following you? You weren't meant to know I was following you!

Wisa says solemnly: *You are very bad at it.*

Magali is annoyed, which is comforting. Here is the irritating Wisa she remembers, and things are back to normal. The urge to spill her secrets has died. But not quite back to normal . . . for Magali is suddenly curious. Wisa has lived eleven years of her life outside of the luddite colony, among those who have practiced craft. She must know much more than Magali could learn in the colony. She even found one of the famous gilded caves, as beautiful and mysterious as the stone structure in their forest. No one else Magali knows has ever found a cave.

How did you get so good at being stealthy? Magali asks.

I taught myself.

How?

Wisa shrugs. *You have to seek the shadows. Listen to where they are going to fall and make sure you are there when they do.*

Magali can make no sense of this, so she asks another question: *How do you know about this cave?*

Wisa chews a nail, spits it out. *I found it.*

Do you know what the gold pattern means?

But Wisa is bored. She wanted to find out if she was right and now that she knows it, she has lost interest. She crawls toward the wall.

Wait!

Magali doesn't want Wisa to leave. She wants to stay in this cave and talk about whether Wisa really listens to flowers and if she thinks trees can walk. Does she know what the shape of madness looks like? Because Magali has been asking that question for years, quietly, to herself, to the strange people who visit her when she is alone, and she has no answers. She wants to say: Do you think the parents know what will happen during the festival? What madness is? Because I think they're only pretending; I think they are as scared as us because they don't know, because they can only guess, because the one thing you wish for—and Old Silu told me this; she always tells you the good stuff—the one thing you wish for is that you won't be alive during the festival. But no one can tell me why. Can you? Do they say something at harbors? Do other places remember? What do you know?

And even though Magali is sure she said none of this aloud, Wisa smiles, wide, gleeful, delighted. She is staring at Magali like she is finally seeing her real self. Magali wants to wrap her arms around her body—she feels exposed.

In a move that is uncharacteristic of her because it is too human, too normal, Wisa winks. She says: *You're a terrible luddite.*

And then she scampers up the wall, still grinning, before Magali can grab her ankle and wrestle her again.

By the time Magali climbs out of the cave and makes her way home, Wisa is asleep on the ghodra, a thin mattress large enough for only one person. Magali unrolls hers, and watches the rise and fall of her sister's chest. Wisa sleeps like the dead; Magali knows, because she once spent the night trying to wake her through various innovative means, including poking her in the ribs.

Magali cannot sleep. She lies awake and stares at the roof, filled with a strange buzzing underneath her skin. She cannot forget the last moment in the cave, when Wisa looked at her as if she was seeing a new person.

Magali *felt* like one.

Being around Wisa is like being under a waterfall—washed away by the sheer torrent of personality around you, no pretense left. Magali feels stripped to her bones, naked and bare. Animalistic almost and made up of only her essential components. It is thrilling, the rawness of what she could be. The wilderness of herself.

And Wisa had seen it and not balked. *Because Wisa is like that herself,* Magali thinks, but it doesn't seem to matter anymore. Wisa knows about the double sight and didn't run away. She understood.

Sleep does come, in the end. It comes on the heels of a simple thought, strange but no longer dangerous to think, or perhaps Magali is too sleepy to police herself—

Is this what madness feels like?

IV

After the night in the cave, Magali and Wisa are inseparable.

The colony is surprised. Parents are careful not to whisper about it in front of the children—no need to put ideas into their heads—but they discuss it among themselves. Magali and Wisa? They're "sisters" now, of course, but . . . they are so dissimilar. What do they talk about?

Kua must have asked the little one to do it, Old Silu says wisely, forgetting that Magali is fourteen and, therefore, not little anymore.

The answer to their first question—*what do they talk about?*—is actually very simple. Every time they are alone together, Magali asks Wisa questions. She frames these questions as simply as she can; she keeps them short, so there is no room for misinterpretation. But no matter how she frames them, it is difficult for Wisa to stay on point. Or answer. It is as if the format of questions and answers is not how Wisa understands the world; it doesn't get through to her.

Q: Who are your parents?

A: Wisa shrugs.

Q: How did you survive?

A: I taught myself.

Q: Do you have family somewhere? Are you a drifter?

A: Another shrug.

If Magali asks about Gul (the pet lizard) or the trees, Wisa talks in animated streams of conversation, words tripping over each other and with meanings so far from what Magali can grasp, it is gibberish. Wisa talks about giant turtles, tree conversations, being friends with as many fish as she can, although fish tend to be more mean-spirited than you would imagine. Magali listens to all of it, fascinated and baffled.

The only question Wisa answers properly is about Kua. Ask Wisa how she came to the colony, and this is what she says.

I'm hungry and I'm thinking of these julmas, yes? The merchant, he's squint-eyed and his cart is groaning under the weight of how many he's got. He's greedy. So I was going to take a couple—one or two, small ones. But Kua is a magician, silent and shadowy, he melts out of the shadows, like this . . . She makes a hissing sound. *He sees me eyeing the julmas and he thinks it is wrong because—bam!—he is in front of me, all tall and strange and smiling. I think, he's here to catch you; quick, Wisa, run! But no! He's offering me a meal and buying me a blanket. How do you say no to that? A meal? And so that's how I came here. End of story.*

But it isn't the whole story, although she doesn't tell Magali this. The whole story is that Kua offers to buy Wisa a julma and she says yes and so they eat one together under a bright orange awning. She likes him; he's square and comforting; he gives you the same feeling as a good cloth, the kind that doesn't tear easily and always does its best by you. So she's happy to sit in silence, eating, until Kua asks: *How do you survive?*

It's a silly question, the kind only the well-fed can ask, and usually Wisa would sniffle and mumble and take every last coin they could spare but she doesn't this time because it's asked truthfully, with no pity, not the way the merchants sometimes talk to you with their chin up and their eyes down. So she too answers truthfully. She shrugs.

But that question is important. For Wisa says yes to dinner at Kua's house, then to breakfast, then to lunch and chores and some of Magali's old clothes and the spare ghodra being unrolled in Magali's room for her to sleep on instead of a blanket, which is very important because a ghodra means staying and Wisa doesn't like to stay—she's a bird, you see, with the wind slipping off her wings. But Kua asked a question that created a feeling and that feeling grew roots and the roots liked this place and so Wisa stays. She doesn't know that home grows over you sometimes, like an igloo closing.

When that happens, it can be hard to remember if you belonged anywhere else.

But she doesn't say all this to Magali. She only waits for the next question, and when it is boring or unimportant or cannot be explained, she shrugs.

Magali grows used to Wisa's way of thinking. She likes it. It is broken but with enough space between sentences for new connections to arise. No one else she knows thinks like that. It is easier to be herself around Wisa, although she didn't know this *was* herself; she certainly didn't feel like she had been pretending for fourteen years of her life. But she is freer now. There *is* a difference, even if she can't explain it.

Wisa makes her feel like anything is possible.

Magali does tell her what double sight is like. She tells her at night, after Grandpa has gone to sleep. She only means to tell her a little bit but then talks till the sky lightens but the moon is still bright, and even then, she could have talked for longer. Wisa listens as if being given a rare gift. She will treasure it forever.

Several days later, when they are stripping the leaves off a fishtail palm for thatching, Wisa says: *I really won't tell anyone.*

She means about the double sight.

You can tell anyone you like, Magali says lightly. *I don't care.*

Wisa is hanging from the palms' long fronds, the berries stinging her flesh. *Liar*, she says. *They say it is the first sign of madness. I heard a merchant talk about it.*

Magali is unperturbed. *Do you think I'm mad?*

No.

Are you mad?

No, Wisa says but she sounds wistful this time.

Magali looks up from the leaves she is tying. For someone who couldn't climb a few weeks ago, Wisa is doing remarkably well. She remembers what Wisa told her when she first came to the colony. "Some of the travelers wanted me to fall to my death, at least break a limb, you know, for a show—so I had to pretend to wobble but I never did really because I'm very good with my feet." Was Wisa pretending that night in the stone ruins?

Magali watches Wisa disentangle a dead frond from the bark. There is no way to tell with Wisa, honestly. Not as yet anyway—maybe after five or six years, Magali will be able to read her better. Magali squints. No, twenty years is safer.

Then she blinks. She doesn't know when she made the switch into imagining the rest of her life with Wisa but . . . she has. Twenty years seems little now. Only a drop in the sixty or so years to come.

It is strange.

You couldn't be mad here anyway, Magali says, to distract herself. *If you stay with us, you will have to forget all about being mad or even seeing the festival. It is not the luddite way. We pretend the festival isn't happening. We go inside, shut the doors and stuff raw cotton in our ears. Then we sit, in silence, until the seven days have passed.*

I know, Wisa says. *Grandpa told me.*

And if you stay here, Magali says, *it means you cannot talk for seven days. Not a word. Grandpa says they cut off the tongue of anyone who does.*

Grandpa said nothing of the sort but Magali likes the drama.

I know, Wisa says. She is climbing down the bark.

I don't think you could be silent for seven days.

Wisa shrugs. She leaps down the last few feet and lands lightly on her toes. She settles near Magali and helps her tie the bundles.

Oh, Magali doesn't like what is growing between them. This companionship began as a curiosity but now . . . Wisa is her friend. Maybe even her sister. If her mother were here, she would smile and say, *One tree has become two; a forest is growing.* Magali is not sure she wants a forest between them. That feels large and scary. Forests, she knows, never die.

But as Grandpa would tell you, you don't get much choice in where forests spring up. You never know where you find family.

As they walk back to the colony, bundles on their shoulders, Magali finds herself accepting this. She meets so many weird visitors as part of her double sight, claiming to be her family—why not add one more? Wisa could be family.

She *is* family.

And despite herself, Magali feels a small thrill. She has never had a sister before.

Do you really talk to your lizard? she asks. *Or do you just pretend?*

Wisa frowns. *Why would I pretend?*

V

Monsoon comes, and Wisa learns what it means to be a luddite.

The rain comes in a sweep—one moment it is not there, the next you cannot see in front of you for all the water. It slams against doors, pours through roofs, hammers into the ground until it is a muddy lake. Plants open their leaves and drink. Insects that stay hidden now crawl into the open, bathing in delight. Dogs howl at the moon, remembering a life they could have lived.

Wisa has seen monsoons before, but always in the crafted world of Esi, where houses seal against the onslaught, where the harsh sound of rain is turned into a musical rhythm and where light is manufactured from the simplest sources: flowers reflecting the dim light of stars, roofs shining with the hidden glow of the moon.

But here, the monsoon arrives as itself, untouched and sublime. It moves with an unstoppable force. Night after night, Wisa sits on the steps of the house in pitch darkness, discerning cascades of rain by the pattern they drum on the ground. Magali sits with her, and they don't do anything—don't talk, read or light a candle. They just sit, witnessing something beautiful.

When daylight comes, they explore.

Wisa has never seen the island from a luddite's eyes and now she throws herself into their reverential awe for an ecosystem so much larger than them. Magali teaches her which snakes are venomous, shows her the greedy hulja leaves that turn vertical to the ground to soak up the light and the water that drops on the silta leaf to harden, over days, into pearls. The colony goes pearl hunting, and Magali teaches her how to identify which pearls will be ready soon and how to pluck them before Jinn can find them. Nature is relentless. Ferns sprout from their mud wall—*putuk*—spilling like lace; creepers claim their roof to grow fecund fruit.

Grandpa leaves their bamboo windows open, so beetles blur around candles at night and then lie mournfully on their backs during the day, awaiting death. Plants erupt—toward the sky, across the ground, into houses. Grandpa shows her the climbing root that is suspended in mid-air, seeking to outlive its brothers and sisters; Magali finds a purple pinguis flower and the sisters crouch over it for days to watch it swallow a frog.

Mad yet? Magali asks, poking her sister in the ribs.

Wisa shakes her head and rattles the tooth she broke while climbing.

The colony has its own rhythm during the monsoon. They make a sour juice from the pois fruit, a pale green-and-amber fruit that gives a tart golden liquid when crushed. Wisa links hands with Ava and Jinn (Magali is here somewhere in this crowd) and they stamp on the fruit together, laughing as they try and keep their balance. The juice stains stay for days afterward, so that it looks like Wisa has toes of gold. Grandpa teaches her the family recipe for pija aachar, a thick preservative that smells like rotting flowers and tastes deliciously spicy, chili seeds searing into her tongue with each bite. Magali and she eat a bowl full of it, crying and wiping their noses.

Through it all, Grandpa makes records. He draws slowly on paper made from crushed leaves; Wisa helps him hang the pieces to dry. He lets her mix the paints as well, and she sits beside him as he touches brush to page and captures a little piece of the land. It could be a fruit, or a new way of making an old luddite dish, or an abandoned nest filled again with bird eggs. Grandpa is the memory keeper, and he chooses what is worth seeing.

Always look for the small things, little Wisa, he says, never lifting his brush from the paper. *They are what matter.*

Wisa has never lived like this before—as part of a network of seeing and doing, linked so intimately with the land. In some ways it corrodes how well she can speak to the trees. For now when she approaches them, she comes with other people in her head: what Zia said about the ancient mango and what Pina thinks about the sturdy teak. But in other ways, she feels linked to a forest of her own, roots entwining with other people like her, and she cannot get enough of it.

Monsoon melts into summer, and the girls are caught in the clutches of hard labor, repairing what the monsoon broke. Wisa is sent to the forest to forage dead branches and bring them back to where the rest of the colony is gathered, patching up houses that have suffered more than others. Roofs are being fixed with shaved pieces of bark and dried palms. Walls are reinforced with mud. The small trees growing out of the crooked cottages have kept the structures together, their roots acting as binds. Now Wisa spends her spare moments whispering to the spiders that scurry up and down branches, disrupted by the bustle. Ava gives her strange looks.

When left to themselves, the sisters lie in puddles and make languorous shapes in the mud, complaining about the oppressive heat. They fight; Wisa pinches, Magali kicks. Grandpa teaches Wisa how to read. The colony comes to know them by one name—"Magaliwisa"—for the sisters are never seen apart. Children cross wayfares to say, *Wisa, will you share this fruit with me?* The children still remember the Wisa of the mango tree, and they love her for it. She is the girl with the golden courage.

Wisa is delighted. She stays awake at night and thinks about belonging, this strange bottle of sunshine she has been given. Can she swallow it? Whole? How else can she keep it?

Over months, Jinn begins to slink closer.

Wisa notices it slowly. At first, she sees him at the edge of groups, listening to her conversations. Then she begins to notice him in the same places she is in, always out of the corner of her eye. When she looks at him openly, he doesn't look away; a lot of people do; they are shy about these things. Instead, he smiles sheepishly. The first two times Wisa cannot understand what he wants. Then she does, simply, suddenly, and she is thrilled.

After that, she spends more time by herself, wandering among the giant trees of the forest and whispering to them. She is careful to choose the routes he knows and she is careful to not be with Magali, for she knows Magali will spoil any chance of Jinn approaching her. She doesn't do any of this with forward-thinking guile. She acts on impulse, believing the impulse is true and wanting to see if it can be.

Finally, after weeks, Jinn finds her nestled in the roots of a giant flame tree, its flowers tangled in her hair. He wants to be friends. On the ground, he is nothing like the boy who climbed that mango tree. That boy was certain, full of plump confidence. Here, he is unsure of everything. Wisa and he throw stones into the river when Magali is not around, and Wisa enjoys how he always looks for her sister, as if hopeful she will suddenly appear.

You climbed well that day, he tells her.

Thanks.

Actually, you were terrible but you kept going, which is great but also mad. You could have died.

Wisa wonders what madness would look like on him. Whether he remembers the stories his great-grandmother told him—*forbidden stories,* Magali says and then purses her lips and won't say more—and if they had anything to do with the cave or stone buildings.

Why'd you do it? he asks.

She doesn't know how to answer. She just wanted to touch the topmost leaves, that is all. She picks up a stone and throws it into the lake. People have a curious interest in the beginning of things. Magali keeps asking about her parents. And now Jinn, asking why she climbed so high. It is silly. It doesn't matter; things simply are.

Why did you stop? she asks him.

He is taken aback. *I couldn't go farther,* he says.

Liar.

He doesn't know how to answer that. He fingers a stone in his hand and stares out at the water, not throwing it in.

People do that a lot here, Wisa says. *Don't reach.*

Look, everyone knows Wisa is strange, even if no one says it out loud anymore. So Jinn knows he should just forget what she said. He certainly shouldn't brood about it on his way home from the river. Or think about it for days. Or wonder what it says about him, and if Wisa thinks he is Esi's biggest coward.

If Magali does.

And he certainly shouldn't let it influence his actions. That would be weird, and Jinn is not weird. He is a nice, normal boy. His mother spends a lot of time telling him so and he spends a lot of time making sure he is, for her sake; so he shouldn't let Wisa get under his skin.

Still, Jinn finds himself . . . not listening to himself. He will go for a walk in the forest and suddenly be near Magali and Wisa. He will lie by the river—to look at the fish, he tells himself—and feel a small leap of joy when he spots the sisters down the bank. And if he sees them, well, it is only normal to go talk to them. To spend an evening with them. To make plans for other such evenings, or afternoons, or any time he can get his hands on.

Magali is always cold toward these suggestions, but Wisa treats them like she would want nothing more in the world, so Jinn clutches at this and doesn't let go. As long as Wisa is enthusiastic, Magali won't shoo him away. It is not . . . ideal, but it will do.

Jinn tries to be his nicest self around the sisters. He cracks jokes, hoping to make Magali laugh. Summer is gone now, and it is deliciously cool, the way only Esi can be—light breezes that are fresh and crisp. The three of them dip their toes in the water; they go swimming. Wisa tells him his jokes are terrible, so he must stop. There are even times Magali forgets she doesn't like him. She talks with abandon, and Jinn is pleased she can be herself around him (although he feels stupid for feeling pleased).

The best times are when they climb the eucalyptus tree, as high as they can, and sit among the clouds. Magali is different then. She is not so guarded; her prickliness melts. He likes the way she lies along a branch, eyes half closed, clouds playing with her hair.

This is nice, he says once, without thinking.

But at the mention of how nice this is, Magali stiffens. She remembers she is mad at him and so looks like she would rather drop off her branch and die on the ground than be near him.

He is careful to never say it again.

But the time has come to ask for help. He goes to Wisa. Magali and he were best friends but now she hates him. He doesn't understand why.

You're fighting, Wisa tells him, surprised. *You've been fighting for years. Did you not know?*

The fight

Blajine knows this fight. It is a family heirloom, a story with pride of place in the family history and told to anybody and everybody, whether or not they want to listen.

Once upon a time, Magali Kilta had a friend. He was a small boy, not much to look at (the males in the Kilta family have a different version of this story), but he had what few children possessed in bright, sparkling quantity: wonder and curiosity. Ah, we know you think all children have it, but that's a lie. It is the few good fruits like Jinn who give the others their reputation.

Anyway, this story starts out happy, like these stories do. Jinn and Magali were inseparable, fellow explorers, and they spent all their time on expeditions across Esi (by which we mean the wilderness inside and near the colony). Magali was granddaughter of the greatest memory keeper the colony had ever known, so she was the smarter of the two. She showed Jinn how to spot the slime trail of the prickly biu snail and how to make necklaces out of saltgrass. She invented all the games.

But Jinn brought presents too. He knew stories, told to him by his great-grandmother. These were secrets, gathered from the belly of time. They whispered of alchemists and gold, of greed and mistakes, of forests both real and imagined, stories the children didn't fully understand but that they knew—they *knew*—were special.

Then his great-grandmother died. Jinn changed. He laughed more, but in that floaty and false way people laugh when the laughter is not attached to anything. He moved more deliberately, spoke slower. It was like a new spirit had taken hold of Jinn's body.

Magali tried to play with him. She said, *do you want to tell me a story?* She even told *him* his stories, to bring her old friend back.

But he only twisted his mouth so that it looked withered and said, *aren't we too old for fairy tales?* And when Magali said, *but you used to love these!*, he did his laugh. He said, *I've never heard these stories in my life.*

Little Magali didn't see the pain in her friend's eyes. She didn't notice the fear. All she could see was her best friend pretending their friendship wasn't so special after all. He wouldn't meet her in the wilderness or go on expeditions. In fact, he wouldn't meet her alone at all, even when she asked. He spent his time now with the other children, playing their silly games and talking about "normal" things.

It broke Magali's heart so completely, it would take her eight years to forgive him.

The Kiltas know there is no moral to this story. They just love it. They forget the sad and scared Jinn, for they didn't know why he was scared. They forget the hurt and weeping Magali, for it is difficult to imagine Mad Magali as a child, forget as a child who cries. They focus, instead, on the cleaving, on Magali striding away from a boy who chose to be ordinary. *This*, they tell each other with glee, *is the price you pay for being uninteresting.*

Jinn asks Wisa for help.

She doesn't try to hide her excitement. This is *incredible*—she's never been asked for help before. She has always existed on the fringes of groups, invisible and superfluous. She doesn't mind that, not at all. But this! This is *glorious*. Is there a greater gift than brokering peace between two people? Can there be anything more important than mending a friendship? *This* is her most crucial task; it will be her crowning glory.

Jinn is beginning to regret he asked her for help.

He is skittish, she must remember that. She soothes him by looking suitably contemplative about the task. She hems and haws, and wonders how she'll do it. People like that. Magali always does a great job of it—looking eager to help but also baffled by the sheer weight of what is being asked. It makes people feel better about not being able to do it themselves.

But when Jinn is gone, pleased that Wisa seems contemplative about his request, she lets her joy fly uncontained. A re-joining! A union! She will do such a good job that they will be inseparable for the rest of their lives—beyond that even!

She asks Jinn to meet her by the bulb jackfruit tree.

The bulb jackfruit tree is called such because its trunk has grown fat with knots, each of which protrudes out like a bulb. Its fruit is always large, sometimes the size of a small child, and you have to walk around their split and fermented carcasses as you navigate the tree's roots. It always smells fecund and tart around the bulb jackfruit tree.

When Jinn arrives, Wisa is sitting in its branches and talking to Gul, her pet lizard. He climbs up beside her. He is too nervous to ask what she has planned, but he hopes she will tell him soon. Preparation, his mother always said, is key to successful endeavors.

When time passes and she doesn't volunteer the information, he plucks up the courage to ask. She looks at him as if she doesn't really see him. Then, after a moment, she points to the ground.

Magali is approaching. Jinn is not one to be sentimental about things; life is best lived lightly, with little attachment to people or to outcomes and certainly not to looks. But he cannot help thinking how beautiful she is. She carries herself in a way that is uniquely Magali. As if she is striding somewhere incredible and you can't follow. As if she will punch you if you deter her from her path.

It is very strange that Jinn finds this appealing.

But he doesn't have time to wrap himself up in his thoughts because Wisa is climbing down the tree. He follows, and he can tell from a swift look at Magali's face that she didn't know he would be here.

She looks even more annoyed when she figures out where they are going. Wisa is leading them out of the forest, around the outskirts of the colony and toward a patch of wild grass just beyond. *Wisa*, Magali says once, and it is a warning, but Wisa ignores her, just skips through the grass as if they aren't there. Despite his growing awareness that it was a terrible idea to ask Wisa for help, Jinn is excited.

Then Wisa drops to her knees and parts the long weeds, looking for something. Jinn peers closer. It is a gash in the ground, traveling deep into the rock. It looks naturally formed. Wisa beckons to him, and then drops through, disappearing into the blackness.

Jinn is startled, but not as startled as Magali, who looks like she is now, finally, about to say something. She has the expression she gets when she is about to *stop the nonsense*. So he hurries after Wisa before she can. He doesn't look to see if she is behind him.

Jinn follows Wisa down the wall of an enormous cavern. The rock is undulated, so it is easy to find footholds. When he looks around, still clutching the wall, he forgets about Magali.

It is the most incredible thing he has seen. A gold pattern etched along the walls of the cave and high into the ceiling, intricate and natural and yet . . . human. Jinn feels as if he has tumbled into a pile of gold and for once, it sings of things travelers describe—promise, wonder and riches beyond one's dreams.

The gold carries and strikes the light, so that the pattern multiplies on motes of dust floating in the cave, on the water of a rock pool, on their skin. How delicate it is, how precise. The stone structures have the same elegance. Most of their stone is crumbling, plants springing between the cracks, but the structures themselves have not given way. Who would build like that—with permanence, with stillness? Even the crafted homes of the purple-jade forests or the whalebone hills change in the seasons.

He doesn't notice Magali climb down the wall and reach the cave floor. He never makes it there himself. Instead, he clambers over the cavern, flowing with the same energy he has when he climbs. This is astonishing. Better than any story, better than the stone structures. This is . . .

He doesn't have the words.

Have you drawn this? he shouts down to Magali. *You must get some of Kua's supplies and just draw this! Have you been coming here every day? Do you know how the pattern was made? What it means? It is incredible work! I've heard of these caves but I never . . .*

Wisa and Magali watch him clamber across rock, trying to glimpse parts of the pattern hidden by stalactites.

You shouldn't have brought him here, Magali whispers. *It's dangerous for people to know we come here.*

Kua's voice is ringing in her ears: *You're living in difficult times.*

Wisa is surprised. *It's Jinn*, she says.

People are changeable. You don't know because you don't pay attention.

Wisa wants to say that if Jinn changes, it is only as a barnacle cone, growing thicker and more entrenched to the rock on which it lies. He is a boy built to stay, clinging to what he finds most valuable around him. But she doesn't know how to explain this without explaining that she is a bird, made to feel the wind on her wings, so she doesn't say anything.

When Jinn finally joins the sisters, he is a new person. He's filled with a purpose he hasn't felt in years. He has forgotten why they are in the cave in the first place. So he is surprised when Wisa says to Magali, firmly: *Jinn and you will be friends now. He will make up for his mistake.*

This is definitely not the subtle meeting of souls Jinn was hoping for, and he dies a little inside. But really, he doesn't know how he can be surprised: you don't go to Wisa for subtlety. Magali is too astonished to be upset, and Wisa—wisely, Jinn notes—continues talking before Magali gets her presence of mind back.

This cave was made by the same people who made the stone structures. The trees told me. Jinn is sorry about his great-grandmother's stories, but you always say being sorry is not enough. Or saying it anyway. So he is going to show it. He is going to help us find out what the pattern means.

Wisa beams at them. This is a beautiful plan, and she doesn't know why they aren't clapping. They are not the clapping type, she reminds herself, and she loves them more for this. Then she worries that maybe they haven't understood the full beauty of what she is saying, so she adds: *This was made by the people who started the festival.* She adds: *Of madness,* because they are still staring at her like they can't quite hear. People are so strange sometimes. She loves them even more.

Magali finds her voice first. *Wisa, it is forbidden to talk about the festival of madness. It is forbidden to even think about it, forget examining secret patterns to learn more of a lost history that tells us about how it started. Don't ever,* ever say this to anyone—

But Jinn, who has definitely turned into someone who is distinctly not Jinn, is pointing at Magali. He is saying, with a sense of glee that surprises, terrifies and delights him: *Aha! Who is the coward now?*

Magali shakes with rage. Jinn's joy is absolute; it bubbles up in him, triumphant, his terror gone. For the first time in a long time, he is on an equal footing with Magali. He is speaking not from a place of apology or contrition—and contrition about what, he also didn't know—but from equality. There is a chance, finally, of becoming friends again.

Wisa watches Magali and Jinn shout at each other with mild interest. Magali is accusing him of being spineless and a betrayer of friendships. Jinn is yelling that she is closed-hearted and petty, nurturing her resentments until they become poison. Magali says she would never, ever have pretended not to know stories that were so important to both of them. Jinn says, *Aha, so you admit they're important!* Wisa notes that this was a very silly point, but he saves himself by saying how Magali doesn't know everything. She doesn't know pressures in his life or why he did what he did.

They love each other, Wisa thinks happily, for although there is a lot of yelling, both of them seem very committed to it. Magali accuses Jinn of leading Wisa down corrupted paths—*how could you encourage her?!*—and Jinn accuses her of not knowing the people she pretends to care about—*as if I could lead her anywhere! Wisa!*

Wisa lets this go on for a few more minutes, and then gently interjects. *We don't have to go mad,* she says. *I only want to know.*

The way she says it makes it seem so simple, so distilled to its essence that Jinn and Magali don't know what to say. When you put it like that . . . Well, it doesn't seem so horrifying, does it? What could be wrong with knowing? Magali is the granddaughter of a memory keeper and will take on the role one day. Surely it is her duty to know? And Jinn . . . He has spent his life trying to forget his great-grandmother's stories. But she told him about these caves. And, well, if he was going to truly become brave and a new person, he *owed* it to her to find out. It is in the interest of Magali and his friendship, right? Everyone agrees you should do anything for friendship.

Jinn sneaks a sidelong glance at Magali. She is still staring at Wisa—who is smiling peacefully—her forehead scrunched with the effort of thinking this through properly. Finally, she says in a vaguely defeated voice: *Madness is a sly enemy. They say even thinking about madness means it will worm and fester in your brain. Merely contemplating madness makes you mad.*

He can't help it. He mumbles: *Then Ava would be batshit crazy.*

Magali laughs. A real laugh, from her belly. At something he said! He laughs too, and Wisa joins in—not because she got the joke but because she likes laughing. It breaks the tension in the cave, and by the time they clamber up to the grassy field, their endeavor no longer seems so foolhardy.

What can be wrong with knowing?

Magali makes them promise that they will do the rituals of sanity. Keep their nails short and bury the clippings by the roots of a tree. Cut their hair and knot it into ropes they keep under their pillow. No pois juice after dark.* Only then does she agree to find out what the pattern means. Jinn doesn't agree outright. Memories of when his mother found out about his great-grandmother's stories still linger. But he knows he will do it. There is a recklessness in him that longs for expression.

And Wisa—well, it was Wisa's idea in the first place.

They are careful not to be caught sneaking out of the colony. If they want to arrange times to meet at the cave, they scribble it in code in the forest. (Wisa wants to teach Gul to convey spoken messages to the other two but Magali squashes this plan.) The sisters make copies of Grandpa's paper and take it to the cave with them; they trace the pattern section by section, Jinn climbing up and shouting descriptions. They are not luddites now. They are mapmakers, searching for truth in the mysterious symbols of people long gone. Looking for treasure.

And although they don't notice it, they are changing. Old friends fall away; old structures become irrelevant. They coalesce without knowing they are doing it, until one day the colony stops saying Magaliwisa, and begins saying Magali-Wisa-Jinn.

---

* Aliya Nihal wrote a chapter on the luddite rituals of sanity and their significance. Nails were clipped because they were believed to grow due to unnatural forces in the air. They were buried near the roots of trees so that they may be purged of evil tension and brought back into the network of the forest. Hair was seen as similarly evil, but a braid of your hair beneath your pillow was believed to be a rope back to yourself should your dreams become those of madness. Pois juice after dark was meant to attract evil spirits, specifically the *bhavla*, which sought to either occupy your body or take your shape.

Worldbuilders

I

Across Esi, people are beginning to write their dreams.

No one tells them to do it, but the action comes to them automatically. Wake up, reach over and scribble whatever you just saw. Later in the day, when they are awake and their conscious mind has taken hold, they study these notes. People who remember their dreams with clarity then write them down in detail. Those who don't, clutch at wisps and record those instead.

They don't know why they do this.

Some part of them guesses that it is for the festival of madness. Old wisdom says dreams are the pathway to the truth. Perhaps their subconscious mind remembers that now and is looking at their dreams in search of clues. What is the festival of madness like? It happens every hundred years on the island, and yet no one can remember it. No one knows what to expect.

Why can't we remember? people ask the drifters, agitated. *How have we forgotten?*

Here is what the drifters say. They roam across Esi with stories and they will tell you some of them, only the parts they like or the ones they have made up; no two drifter stories are alike. Ask them a direct question, like this one, and they will feed you veiled truth and opaque meanings. But any drifter will tell you that the luddites know more than they are letting on.

Those fools, they say. *They are as mad as us. No one knows better than a luddite, how to remember.*

II

Summer again.

Fronds grow yellow at their edges, plants shrink into themselves and birds look for puddles and then collapse into them, relieved. We hunt for shadows, lolling in any shade we can find. We watch Kua plod into the fields, working with a careful rhythm that is untouched by the heat. He blisters, he sweats, but still he works; he enjoys it, our Grandpa; he knows nothing else. When he comes home, a basket of vegetables on his shoulders, his granddaughters are waiting for him. By candlelight, they cook, they argue and they make a home.

When the sisters lie down on their ghodras and blow out the candle, he goes into the wilderness and sits by the trunk of a dead banyan tree. It has been cut low to the ground, its surface sealed with lacquer. Pale nightshades drop pollen on the wood, sprinkling it with gentle light.

Kua closes his eyes and listens to Esi—to the low drifting hum of a cicada, the croaking of surprised frogs, and there, in the distance, the faint cries of monkeys who are still awake and watching a stranger make her way through the colony to his cottage. He keeps his eyes closed, enjoying the fresh scent of crushed grass and the lightest trace of jasmine—Pio's flowers must be in bloom. It is only when he hears Old Silu's cat let out a soft and curious meow that he opens his eyes.

You can tell a drifter by their coat. Even in the night, it is unmistakable: long and thick, woven with the colors of the rainbow. They don't like to take their coats off, the drifters, not unless they are among themselves. They are Esi's wind, always moving, always alone, scattering bits of the island where it may be useful.

Like the wind, they come in many varieties. Good, bad, benevolent. Vicious. People fear them, out of superstition mostly. They are as changeable as any person. *Treat them with kindness,* Kua always tells the colony, *and they will treat you the same.*

This drifter is Ishita, her long hair wound into a knot. She smiles when she sees him and shrugs off her coat. She has arrived late this year—only by a few days, but Ishita is not usually late. Nothing deters her. This time, she does not know what happened.

I lost a few days, she says. *Woke up one morning and they were gone. Don't know where they went.*

Kua has heard of this. People usually lose an hour; on rare occasions, a day. Losing a few days is surprising. Still, it isn't impossible, not if you understand Esi. Time on the island isn't straight. You can hold on to the seasons and track days by how the plants change, but in these times even the land is uncertain. There is a . . . ripening. Kua senses it, especially in the forest. He doesn't know how else to describe it. He knows what it signifies (the festival is approaching) but he doesn't know what it means.

Do you have stories? he asks.

Ishita does. *They're chiseling in the black plains,* she says. *Four or five people for now, but more may have joined them since I left. They're trying to break through the ice; they say a creature lurks in there.*

Real or imagined?

Ishita shrugs. *We'll have to find out.*

Kua unrolls a page and places it on the wood. He draws a picture of a dragon curled in a glacier, his brush moving swiftly across the paper.

Would you like to keep it? he asks Ishita, when she leans forward admiringly. *I can make another.*

She shakes her head and pats her coat; he knows she means that she doesn't keep what she cannot give away.

I'll bring you more stories soon, she says as she leaves. *It's early yet.*

Seven years until the festival of madness.

III

Kua learned memory-keeping from his mother, who trained him and his brother from a young age. The components of memory-keeping are always the same: a dead trunk cut close to the ground, so you are anchored to the earth and sitting in the bowels of the forest when you draw. Paper, made from leaves. Paint, mixed from Esi's mud and colored rocks. The art of storing: rolling these pages up and preserving them for as long as possible. And the art of cleansing: burning what is no longer needed.

Papermaking was always Kua's favorite part of the process, but Isom, his brother, loved mixing paint. No one could extract color as well as Isom. Their mother said he had an eye for hidden things. But Kua was the more patient one. He would sit in front of a fallen vegetable for as long as it took to capture how its skin split. Yet no matter how careful he was, he was never satisfied. *I want to draw the feeling*, he would tell his mother in exasperation, and she never had an answer for how.

After Isom ran away, Kua left the colony. Luddites don't leave their homes; traveling is a drifter's business. But grief meant Kua could not stay still. He left in search of his brother but also in search of something more. Ask him what, and he could not tell you. Not then, not today. But he searched for it in each drawing he made, hoping that one day he would look at the page and see it.

Kua made a thousand and one drawings during his travels. He made his own paper, borrowing any tools he needed from the drifters. He mixed his paints from the new rocks he encountered, and the colors were surprising—soft purple, mango yellow, lizard green. Communities would come to watch him draw, whispering about the softness of his lines and the realism of his memory. Once a craftsman offered six times to enchant the drawings for him so they would never decay. Kua refused.

Things must end, his mother used to say. *Even memories. Only then can they become something new.*

So Kua kept his drawings the old-fashioned way, in tubes made of wood and sealed with tree sap. He strung these around his neck, and they clattered as he walked. He carried so many on him at one point that he formed his own musical instrument; *clack, clack, clack* went the tubes. You could hear him from miles away.

The drifters called him "the Fool." But they said it affectionately, with respect.

Across the white sands, into the purple plains and the mountains. Everywhere Kua went, he would draw memories from the communities he encountered. Some drawings he gave to them. Others—the ones he felt were important but couldn't tell you why—he kept. Everywhere he went, he asked: *Have you seen a man? Younger than me, but taller. His features are similar to mine. His name is Isom.* The answer was always no.

After a while, drifters began to offer to carry his drawings for him. *Let me keep that for you*, they would say. Or: *I can drop these by the colony when I pass.* That is how Kua knew his drawings were valuable. He knew if the drifters took them, he would never see them again; they had that look in their eye.

Why they wanted them was a mystery, but Kua could guess. The festival of madness was still far away, too far for any normal Esite to be thinking about it. But the drifters were *always* thinking about it. Memory, after all, speaks of history. Perhaps in some of Kua's drawings, there was a clue to what awaited them at the turn of the century.

Kua finally found Isom in the red sands, and brought him home. He did not throw away his drawings. Instead, he kept them in his workshop, and went on with the business of living. But when Isom died, he looked at them again. He pulled them out of their casings one by one and laid them on the floor of his workshop. His mother was dead by then, his father, his wife. Only his son remained. He drew these sketches when he was a young man, wild and purposeless. Now he looked at them with eyes that had seen much more, and he noticed it.

The drawings toward the end of his journey were different from the ones made earlier. His style had evolved, but it wasn't just the brushstrokes—it was the memories. The ones at the start of the journey were more sedate. People talked about the small moments they cherished, such as a bowl of hot soup at night or a particular shade of sunrise. A lot of people talked about food, the meals they ate that made them feel nourished and loved.

Toward the end of the journey though, they were reaching for . . . wilder things. Fights that sat deep within them and that they could not forget. Their great-grandmother who had wandered into a cave in the mountain and never returned. A secret desire niggling at them from a young age.

It is a small difference, but standing above the drawings and looking at them as a whole, Kua felt its enormity. Here, gliding through the pages like a watersnake under the surface of a lake, was the shape of madness.

Ever since that day, he has been chasing that shape. He gets his stories now from the drifters. They come directly to him. Who knows why they do it? Drifters are secretive people; they don't trust outside of their community—they don't even trust their community. But Kua is an exception. If anyone can find what is coming, it will be the Fool.

And so during the months that drifters visit the colony, Kua can be found by his banyan table, page and brush ready. Some drifters come to the colony to trade, and he meets them in the evenings or by early light. He talks to them over a cup of warm elderflower tea in the cottage, collects a few of their plant spores if they seem interesting. Then he leads them to the banyan and draws what they describe. Not all drifters come to the cottage, though. Some are only passing through the colony; they linger for only moments. These he waits for at night, for this is when a drifter does most of their walking.

A few years ago, there were barely any stories. Now, with only seven years to the festival, the sketches pile up. Ishita was wrong when she said it is early yet—not for the festival, for what is seven years in a stretch of a hundred?

Some of the stories he hears are difficult to believe. The drifter Eik—yellow teeth, a wide smile that is not pleasant—tells him of a girl in the purple-jade forests who thinks she is a leomir. She woke up one day and couldn't recognize her parents. She snarled and snapped. Tried to tear her father's neck out.

Seen her myself, Eik says. *She walks like a leomir too, prowling in her room with an animal grace.*

She has gone now. Escaped through a window she smashed and then melted into the forest. Locals say she is following the golden pack across the forest floor, eating the carcasses they leave behind. Kua draws a girl with features like Wisa's. In the painting, she is caught in the middle of becoming a leomir, her small paws wet with blood.

He makes sketches of the people the drifters report missing. An old man from the red sands who went to pick some water cacti for breakfast and never returned. The boy in the coasts who went fishing and never came back. He draws stories of the Puidra craftsmen. They are growing restless, carving more channels into the whalebone hills and luring strangers into them—mostly travelers, mostly the chroniclers who are terrible at writing. Still, it is no less gruesome. They say skeletons wash out into the rivers when it rains. Kua draws the victims caught in lattices of bones. He draws them faceless but imagines them screaming.

More drawings—from the glass lakes, the black plains, the emerald forests. Kua draws in fluid lines. He does not think about structure or coherence. He is not trying to capture the story. He is chasing the feeling underneath it, the nebulous spirit that gives it shape.

Through all of this, there is Wisa.

Kua sees her listening to his conversations, crouched at the door when he gives the drifters tea. He knows she is with him at the banyan tree, for although she is silent and swift, she has not yet learned that plants like to talk about creatures walking through them, especially to him. It makes him smile. He notices her looking at his workshop when the door is shut. She never goes in, but he can tell she wants to. So many times she says, *Grandpa* and then never finishes her sentence. She is waiting, he thinks, for him to ask.

But he doesn't. Wisa is a girl who needs space. She will come to it in her own time. He draws the drifters' stories and continues his work in the colony, listening to people's grievances and giving them tinctures to soothe their aches and pains, physical and mental. When they need a memory painted or a moment captured, he draws it for them. He likes these moments. He loves watching their joy and the tenderness with which they touch the painting.

He visits the cave.

It is a difficult journey for him to make. Isom and he have walked these paths together so often that he sees his brother's ghost everywhere. Leaning against giant roots. Peering among leaves. Walking beside Kua in his loping stride, grinning. Kua smiles back. He has learned to; it makes the pain easier.

And even though this Isom is only a figment of his imagination, a hallucination, he talks to him.

Do you remember the drifter who told us about the stone eyes and the eyes like birds of prey? he says. *The drifters tell all the children that story. Even my little Magali heard it. You were obsessed with it. You kept trying to hunt things, to become a bird of prey. "The eyes," you said, "I want the eyes." I think a lot about what you told me later, in the . . .* Kua wants to say "difficult years" but he doesn't. After a moment, he goes on. *You said, "They lied, Kua. If you look at the island with the eyes of a true Esite, you will look past craft and stone. Those are only man-made. They don't matter. The real thing you must look at is the island itself."*

Kua stops. He doesn't look down immediately; does his body remember the path so easily? He finds it does—here is a crack in the ground, right at his feet, visible between the tips of grass. He slips in.

This was the place where it all started. Isom and he came here together at first, then Isom on his own, even when Kua begged him not to. The festival was so far away then, no one was even thinking of it. When his parents asked him where Isom went, Kua lied for his brother.

Now he wishes he hadn't. He wishes he had betrayed him. Maybe it would have saved him.

Kua doesn't know how long he spends in the cave. Time is heavy here. So much of the present has been pushed and set into motion by the past—by forces you cannot go back and influence, and that are now barreling their effects through your life. Kua is shaped by Isom, and this shapes how he treats Magali. It shapes how he looks at Wisa. You cannot escape that knock-on effect, not entirely. Even Esi is caught in a force exerted long before they can remember, a festival that began who knows when and that shapes their beliefs, behaviors and fears. So much of how you live is molded before you are born.

The luddites have a saying for it—well, in a sense. They say: *A tree is found in the forest but the forest is also found in the tree.* Thinking of the phrase now makes Kua smile. He always feels warmly toward luddite sayings because no one can agree on what they mean. Old Silu will tell you it means the dead are always with us, but this could be because Silu is close to dying and wants to scare you into placing fruits on her memory stone. Rulni, the honeyfinder, believes that each tree has an instinctive sense of the forest just as each bee knows its place in the hive. Inu will tell you that luddites need to stop making metaphors about forests. Forests this, forests that, you'd think we would have moved on as a community by now.

But if you ask Kua—and they always do, in the end; he is the one person they come back to—he will lift you up with his big hands and say: *You are both one and many. Yourself and your community. Your present moment and your past and future. And if you squint on a moonless night and look out of the corner of your eye, you will see them: everything you were and everything you will be, a sea of ghosts stretching out behind you, even as you live in your skin.*

Then he will set you down and it is up to you whether you believe him.

He is thinking of this when he climbs out of the cave, and so he does not notice her immediately. But Wisa, for once, is not quiet. She has broken a dead branch and when he turns toward the sound, they lock eyes. Wisa doesn't move; she is too surprised.

Then she flees.

Kua walks home slowly. He should be worried, but he cannot bring himself to be. So much is different from when this happened with Isom. *He* is different.

For a while now, he has wondered if he is doing right by Wisa. He suspects there is drifter blood in her. If there is, then staying still would be torment for her; it is natural she would be curious about the festival, about change and largesse. He thinks of how she looked at him on the quay, half-starved, and his heart tugs for the life she lived.

When he enters the cottage, Wisa is crouched by the table. She looks up when he comes in, and she is changed—no longer the child from the forest, but the same solemn girl who looked at him on the quay.

Grandpa, she says, *what do you draw?*

It is the question she has been waiting to ask, the one she abandoned many times. He does not answer. Instead, he goes to his workshop. She follows. He pulls out wooden tubes from his collection. Not the old drawings, but ones made this year. He is careful not to choose anything too violent or scary. After the first few, Wisa shuffles forward to help, and he hands cases to her. They fall into rhythm.

The colony believes you should not talk to the children about the festival. *Puts ideas into their head*, Old Silu says. Kua does not argue with her—he rarely argues—but it is silly, of course, to imagine a mind will not think of something just because you don't talk about it. And so when the drawings are laid out on the floor, Wisa and he walk through them, looking for the shape of madness.

Hours later, they are still there. Kua has got them bowls of root ginger soup. They sit at the edge of the drawings, sipping it. Wisa has not said much. She sits with her knees to her chest, looking at Kua's work.

Why? she asks.

Why the drawings?

She nods.

He thinks. There are no books on the festival of madness, no memories. Only a feeling and later, maybe, stories of what happened before, although those only arrive when the festival is much closer. After what happened to Isom, Kua has thought about it a lot. About the shapelessness of what they know as "madness." Vast. Ubiquitous. Uncontainable.

I'm trying to find what it looks like, he says. *Things are less scary when you can look at them.*

Wisa doesn't answer but he suspects, from the way that she touches the drawings, that she doesn't find them scary. Is this the naïveté of youth—or something else?

Grandpa, she says, as if deciding something. *What about the ones they call worldbuilders?*

No. Kua stands abruptly and Wisa hurries to her feet. He begins putting drawings away, and she helps him. He doesn't look at her.

By the time most of the drawings are rolled up, he has calmed. For the last few tubes, his movements are again relaxed. He caps the last tube and pulls a blank sheet of paper from a pile near him. His brush is dry, but he dips it into the inkpot within reach and draws swiftly. Three trees, their roots and branches entwined. Then he crouches so that he is at Wisa's level.

"A tree is found in the forest but the forest is also found in the tree." Can you remember that?

Wisa nods.

Say it. So that I know you remember it.

Wisa repeats the phrase. She gets every word right, which pleases her. He presses the sheet of paper into her hand.

There are three trees there, he says. *Magali, you and me. Anytime you feel afraid or you feel . . . anytime you don't feel like yourself, remember this. Look at the drawing. Say the phrase I taught you. You are linked now; you have a family. We will keep you safe.*

Wisa doesn't understand. But she knows it is important to him, so she nods. She will love the drawing anyway. It comes from Grandpa.

Jaan, Kua says, *don't go near the cave again.*

Myung's Diaries
No. DCCLXXII

Gold, you quickly realize, is an uninteresting material. The closest it comes to splendor is by association: it looks like a sun. Glints like it too. But why would that interest islanders with two suns or three? Why would it fascinate those ecosystems nestled on the surface of a star?

"What we remember and what is true are very different things." This is what Olung tells me as we walk through his shop. Pans of boiling metal bubble around us; occasionally, clouds of sulfur rise up and obscure him. "Just because we don't understand the art of alchemy doesn't mean it can't make magic."

The origins of alchemists are not as clear as folklore would have us believe. There are, of course, those who boil metals to make gold and have used the myth of alchemy to give weight to their endeavors. You think (or at least I did): if alchemy has existed for thousands of years at the very fringes of our history and if, for all that time, they tried to make *one* element—well then, that element must be important. You twist and turn this obscure yellow metal in your hand, trying to see what is so fabulous. You are unaware, as I was, that you have been misled. Generations of alchemists have been misled.

For the origins of alchemy go back even further.

Old memories, pulled from your great-great-grandparents' stories, from letters, from a memory of a memory of an anecdote embedded in a dream, speak about alchemists on an island with concerns far wider than gold. This is before civilizations built boats or established trade networks, before travelogues or fairy tales designed as bottles to carry truth across time. This is before our collective memory. These alchemists were studying the workings of their island and their black sea, mixing philosophy, sunology, astrology, elementalism and architecture. Building, even, what some will later call "craft."

(Here, Olung pauses in his speech. "Go on," he says and I ask what is on every sailor's mind: "Do you mean Esi?" Esites are the only ones known to do craft. When their island died, craft died with them. "Other alchemists would say there is no connection between our art and the mythical island." He squints at me sideways. "But yes. I mean Esi.")

But some say the origins of craft go even further back. Back to before it is possible to remember or to dream. From this time, one word drifts to us. *Sona*. Linguists believe, through careful connection and comparison with twelve thousand black sea languages, that this means "gold." But the old alchemists, the ones with bent bones and long white hair, the ones you never hear of—they say it means "to sleep."

"We can play with gold," Olung tells me. "Maybe we can even go back and find a way to recreate craft. Esi's famed craft—imagine that, it would be something. But the real alchemists, the ones even Esites couldn't remember now"—he coughs and when he looks up his eyes have hardened, glinting like gems—"they made time."

IV

No matter how expansive you believe you are, no matter the context you account for or what you fortify yourself against, there will always be something you missed.

It is human nature to look at your life and only your life; you see yourself as the center and everyone else as the periphery. Or perhaps it is not human nature, and simply cultural conditioning. But even for a luddite girl like Magali, who has spent her life thinking of her community, even she cannot resist the simple fallacy of imagining Magali-Wisa-Jinn is the trio at the heart of the narrative.

Because for her, it is. Her life is now these two people; she spends her days with them; at night, she ponders their conversations. Wisa is teaching them how to talk to the land, and Magali lies awake practicing the ways of looking Wisa shows them. She tries out new sounds on her tongue.

But to someone else, you are the periphery of their life. And this makes it easier for them to pull you into narratives they find convenient. Narratives fueled by fear or influenced by a sense of self. Narratives that make them more aware of your every action, and teach them what to look for.

If Kua hopes to prevent disaster by his talk with Wisa in the workshop, if he hopes to halt whatever he sensed this could become, then he is already too late.

The colony is forming its own narrative.

Jinn is the first to sense it. He hears it from his mother. He is smashing duri shells with a rock—thick red shells like a boiled crab's, with a soft flesh and milk in them that is excellent for making duri tea—when his mother sits beside him.

Those girls, she says. *Magali and . . . the other one.*

It has been three years since Wisa came to the colony, so his mother knows her name. That is how Jinn senses what is coming next; his mother never likes to name what she is scared of.

Have you . . . she says and then pauses. She starts again: *Do you know much about her?*

About?

Where she was before she came to the colony. What she did.

Thu-cruck. A duri shell splinters and warm white milk pools onto the leaf. Jinn picks out shell pieces slowly, considering his next words.

She was a skywalker, he says.

His mother grunts at that old lie. *I mean it. You have been spending a lot of time with those girls.*

Sisters, he says.

Girls. I want to know what you do.

For a wild moment, Jinn considers telling her. He has an irresistible urge to see the look on her face. *Wisa is teaching us to talk to the land,* he would say. *Yesterday, she told us to press our ear to the ground—not like this, but like this—and then asked if we could hear it. I could hear nothing. But she claimed what we didn't hear was oia, which means "to wait but pleasurably and languidly," like you are swimming or holding a fish that is about to slip away but you don't mind because you know it will swim back. Then she told us seven other meanings I don't remember, all of which were as crazy as the last.*

He smiles at the memory and then busies himself by pouring the liquid into an earthen pot, hoping his mother didn't notice. She is still sitting beside him, waiting. He can feel the tightness in her shoulders as if it were a tightness in his, and it is dawning on him slowly that this is bad. Not as bad as when she found out about his great-grandmother's stories, but . . . it could be?

He tackles it the best way he knows. He says, *Ma,* in a voice that conveys tiredness and a strained *I-can't-do-this-anymore,* a voice that he knows makes her feel guilty. It works like craft. She drops her head in sudden shame and then spends the day brewing his favorite broth and telling him what a good son he is.

But he knows she has not forgotten.

Jinn tells Magali. He does it when Wisa is wandering through the forest's canopy; he does not want her to overhear. Magali listens with a strange expression, and it takes him a moment to realize it is skepticism. At first, he is offended but then even he has to admit how silly he sounds. *My mother asked me what Wisa did before she came to the colony, so now I'm convinced she thinks bad things of her, things that can hurt her later.* Maybe he is turning more into his mother than he realizes, paranoid at every shadow.

But because it is Magali, she considers it.

Why Wisa, you think?

Jinn is incredulous. *Because it is Wisa. She talks to animals. You think we are the only ones who have noticed?*

That is just Wisa, Magali says defensively. *She's loving.*

I know that, Jinn says. *Tell my mother.* Then, because Magali looks like this is a great idea and she is about to march over to his cottage, he adds hastily: *Don't actually tell her. Look, it is not my mother's fault. It is just her and me; she is bound to be worried.*

Magali is sure it is his mother's fault, but she doesn't say it. Families are careful subjects.

What is she worried about? she asks.

Jinn smiles and shrugs; Magali squints. Smile-and-shrug means it is bad.

Only the festival, he says quickly. *And you and Wisa can be . . . you know.*

Magali does not know.

Look at it like this, Jinn says, warming up to his speech. *Wisa's been here only three years, yes? But it feels like forever, like she was born here. And between you two, there is a . . .* He gestures vaguely, forming circular shapes with his hands.

Potato? Magali suggests.

A thicket, a growth, a thorny and entangling thing that can never be untangled, and it drags people in. She thinks I'm dragged in.

Now in the fields, Magali thinks of this thicket, resplendent with thorns that will not let you go. She called to Wisa in the forest, but her sister didn't answer so she is making her way home alone. A thicket. Magali didn't know that this is how people saw them—a force that dragged others into their center.

She likes it.

It is only early evening, so she doesn't need to be home immediately. She settles down under a golden iris tree, and tries to listen to what it is saying. She cannot hear a word, but she takes comfort in the fact that Jinn is worse at Wisa's lessons than she is. Not that Wisa is a great teacher. She talks in a torrent, unaware of her pupils. Sometimes she will forget Magali and Jinn even exist, and just teach Gul, although her best-friend-lizard is notoriously lazy as a learner.

Do you think she is making it up? Jinn asked once. They were sitting together by the riverside, trying to recollect what Wisa had said about the *twup-twit* of a rojk bird, and the explanation was so detailed, Magali couldn't blame Jinn for asking the question. It did seem far-fetched sometimes. Maybe Wisa was just pulling a fast one on them and giggling to herself each night as she fell asleep. It would be a Wisa thing to do.

But you couldn't make this up. The island responds to Wisa. She finds the crunchiest roots. She knows where the flock of hopoes—pale peach birds the size of a human—will be roosting in the evening so you can pick their eggs. When she whistles, fish swim into her hands, although she looks guilty at this (Grandpa would not approve). If you ask her where she learned it, she will say: *Learn what?*

But this is Wisa for you. Thinking the simplest things are strange and the strangest things are simple. They have been sisters for three years, and she has changed Magali. Magali feels herself growing, shifting, moving into larger skins like those lizards they sometimes watch. It delights her. It is petrifying.

Idly, she draws a box in the dirt. One line is her mother, another her father, then Kua and herself. Family. She rubs out her father and her mother, because they will not be coming back from the dead, and then it is two lines, perpendicular to each other, open and exposed. She stares at it for a while. Swiftly, giddy on a feeling she has had for these three years, when Wisa climbed a mango tree and Magali's world swelled and a stitch broke, when new ways of living suddenly seemed possible, giddy on it all, she connects the two lines with a third line, diagonal, sharp and straight. Wisa.

Her sister.

She knows then it doesn't matter what Jinn's mother thinks. What anyone does. Wisa has the one thing she needs to stay safe.

She has Magali.

But even this does not prepare Magali for what happens that night.

It happens when the moon is high in the sky. It is not a full moon, contrary to what they tell you to expect in these moments. It is only the barest sliver, a cut in an otherwise purple-black sky. If you stare closely, as we do, you can imagine the ripples of the black sea undulating in the distance.

Magali wakes up. It is a sudden awakening—she has been jolted out of bed. By what? Wisa is curled up next to her, sleeping deeply. The room is otherwise empty. She gets up and wanders into the hall, wondering if Grandpa is all right. But his candle is out as well, and he is asleep on his ghodra. She covers him, for he is shivering slightly, and goes into the garden.

It is a quiet night. The island is alive with a chorus she doesn't usually hear—night creatures crawling out of their holes, trees whispering in a different tone from the one they use in daylight. Magali tilts her face to the cool sky. The air is sweet, as it is after the monsoon. Soon it will be hot, then cool and then hot again. You cannot escape the sun.

She is about to go back in when she sees Wisa.

Her sister is at the bottom of the stairs, crouched among the weeds. No, not crouched. Fallen. Surprised, both at her position and at how she got here, Magali moves to help her. Then she stumbles back, aghast.

It is Wisa, but she is in bad shape. She is gaunt, dark circles pressed beneath her eyes. She looks like someone who hasn't seen a person in years, someone who is half-wild with loneliness. She is breathing heavily, as if trying to hold her panic at bay; she cannot seem to understand how she got here, why she is touching flowers and smelling wet earth instead of—instead of *what?* Where is this Wisa? For Magali knows in her bones that this is her sister from the future. Wherever she is, she is petrified.

When she sees Magali, she stares as if she doesn't believe it is her. And then her face changes—hope, spreading sweetly across her cheeks—and she cries out, a howl more than a word, *Magali*—

Then she is gone.

Magali is alone in the garden. The flowers shift gently in the breeze. Esi's night chorus continues to sing. The only evidence of Wisa, this glimpse offered by Magali's double sight, is the howl still echoing in the air.

Magali.

Magali sits down on the steps and holds herself; she tries to stop her trembling. Then she bows her head and weeps, although she doesn't know for what.

V

Two days later, Magali sets off into the forest.

She carries a small pouch filled with silta pearls, her entire haul from the past six years. She tells Grandpa she is spending the day with Jinn. She tells Jinn she is going on a hunt for a rare root Grandpa showed her. She tells Wisa nothing. You don't have to explain yourself to Wisa.

Magali makes sure she keeps to the quieter paths of the forest; she doesn't want to encounter anyone. It is also why she didn't go to the port for this. She would probably find a sailor who could answer her questions, but there would be too many luddites who would recognize her.

Her destination now is at the other end of the forest. It is a small patch on the fringes that was burned in a lightning storm. It is filled with split carcasses of dead trees, ash thick on the ground. This is a drifter meeting spot. She has seen them, their coats hanging off the dead trunks, exchanging stories about the island.

When she reaches the spot, she finds it has regrown since she saw it last. The tree carcasses are still there, but taro vines have grown over them, and flowers bloom between leaves. The ground has sprouted a soft fuzz of weed and grass. Instead of charred wood, it smells of forest now—leafy, and heady with the scent of petrichor.

There is only one drifter here. Her coat is off, and she is whittling a branch into a shape Magali cannot identify. Her hands are spotted and wrinkled, ink drawings etched into her skin. She is old, but not frail. No drifter is frail.

Magali hesitates. The drifter hasn't seen her yet; she is still hidden by the trees. Drifters are unreliable. You cannot trust them. Very few have their respect, like Grandpa does. What if this drifter lies to her? Takes her silta pearls and then takes her for a fool?

Come out, come out, the drifter sings.

Magali steps back, deeper into the shadows, then stops. This is ridiculous. She is Magali Kilta. She squares her shoulders and walks into the clearing.

The trade is quickly done. A pouch of silta pearls for two questions. Magali asked for three, but the drifter laughs. *Silta pearls aren't as valuable as you think*, the drifter says. *You can make ones with craft now.* So Magali settles on two questions. She places the pouch on the ground and backs away, so that the pearls are equidistant from both of them. *To show trust*, she tells the drifter.

The drifter is amused. *You're a luddite*, she says, and then nods at her own statement. *Only a luddite would be so old-fashioned. What is your question?*

Magali takes a deep breath. *How did the festival of madness start?*

If the drifter is surprised, she doesn't show it. *Wasted question*, she says, continuing to wilt her branch. *No one knows.*

There must be theories. Stories. Something.

The drifter looks up. *Is that your second question?*

No, Magali says quickly. *No. I . . .* She casts about for what to ask, what will make this exchange worth it. She does not have another pouch full of silta pearls. Nor can she get any more; the season is over.

Tell me about the gilded caves, she whispers. *And the stone structures.*

The drifter puts her branch down. *How do you know about the caves?*

I get two questions, Magali says. *You get none.*

Now the drifter is interested. She takes Magali in, from the top of her head to her toes, and Magali wishes she had not been so recklessly plucky. It was a very Jinn thing to do. Now the drifter will remember her, and the next time she talks to another drifter, she will mention Magali. How long will it take then for word to get back to Grandpa?

The caves and the stone structures are made by the same people, the drifter says finally. *The alchemists. They are our ancestors, but no one knows just how far back they lived. No one knows how old Esi is—not even your grandfather.* The drifter grins then, at her surprise. *Did you think I wouldn't recognize you? It is a pleasure meeting Kua's granddaughter asking about madness and caves. You are not the first family member to ask, of course. I won't tell him, don't worry. Where is the fun in that? The alchemists of Esi didn't make gold. Well, they made gold—that is why we keep tripping over it on this island—but they made something far more valuable. Time.*

You can't make time, Magali whispers.

And whole islands don't go mad for seven days every hundred years. You can make anything, luddite, if you spend enough time searching for it. And our ancestors spent eons. They dedicated their whole civilization to it. Craft is just a watered-down version of what they were capable of. Those stone structures—the one in this forest? You cannot imagine how old it is. It should have gone by now, claimed by the island, erased into oblivion. Whole islands do not last as long as it has. It is still here because it is held together by the strands of time.

The drifter leans back and appraises Magali. She says: *You don't believe me.*

Magali doesn't know what she believes. *Thank you,* she says. *I asked my two questions, so here is your—*

It is why Esites have double sight.

Magali freezes. She is not scared; she is too surprised to be scared. But an old wariness is creeping over her, the caution of prey who has met a predator who may or may not show their claws. This conversation is going down paths she didn't expect, and she is not sure how to stop it.

The drifter picks up her stick again and starts whittling. *Something about the island affects certain children. It messes with their sense of time. They are able to draw family to them across time and space. No one else can do it but an Esite. That is why they say it is the first sign of madness—it is uniquely Esi. Do you want to know the second sign?*

But Magali has found her feet. She kicks the pearls toward the drifter and says, *thank you, I must go, thank you.*

The drifter laughs as she runs away. *Ask Kua,* she shouts after Magali. *Ask him about the worldbuilders!*

VI

After Jinn, Kua is the second to learn about it. He hears it from Old Silu.

He is in the forest, in a patch where the foliage is not so thick and sunlight reaches the forest floor. He is observing the agamids—reptiles around three-feet long, their skulls similar to a lizard's. They have started coming out of the canopy and lying in the sun. They sit in the heat, their long bodies attracting insects and lemmings. Their thick skin protects them for a while, but it cannot hold the sun at bay. They begin to boil and cook.

Still, they do not move. They blink their eyes rapidly, as if surprised by what is happening, as if this patch was meant to be full of shade. There are bushes near them; all they need to do is take cover. But they do not move. Kua tries shifting the smaller ones. They wiggle their lizard bodies and snap at his hands. If he manages to push one into the leaves, it stays there for a while, until it is sure he is gone, and then it crawls back into the sun. It is as if the agamids are seeing a different island from Kua.

He sketches them, although he does not know what he's trying to catch. He wishes he could step into their minds, see what they see. Above him, the trees brush against the clouds. They watch him. Isom used to say the trees whisper. He said the whispers drove him mad, in the end.

When he comes home, he finds Old Silu sitting on the steps. She has a cloth folded with dates, her usual gift when she wants tea and to create a bit of mischief. But he is glad to see her; she is a welcome distraction after his day. He leads her in and makes her a brew of clove, ginger and fennel, which he knows will be good for her knees. She makes a face when he pours it, but she sips it valiantly. He smiles. Old Silu will rail against anything that tastes bitter and is good for her, but she drinks it all in the end—she is determined to live forever.

They talk idly. Old Silu complains about her joint pain, how hot the summers are getting, the terrible state of a fig tree she lovingly nurtured in her garden.

In fact, Old Silu is biding her time. She has come here with very specific information, but she wants to introduce it delicately. She wants to be *asked*. You cannot go around simply saying what she needs to say . . . It takes tact.

For Old Silu has been talking to the drifters. Well, if we want to be accurate, we would say she has been waiting for them. Lying in wait, really. But anyone her age would do the same. When you are the oldest in the colony, you have a responsibility to the children, to protect them— and everyone is a child at her age.

You cannot tell her that a luddite colony is a safe place. Why, after what happened to Isom (she puts her hand on her heart and bows her head in sorrow), after what happened to him, you *could* say it is the most dangerous place on Esi. You have to remember, the festival was decades away when Isom fell ill. No one was even thinking of it. But the spirit of madness comes from anywhere, and some are more sensitive to it. Isom was, and it tore him apart.

But this time, Old Silu would be prepared. She would look for the ones to root out. She has a theory, of course, about who is more susceptible to madness. She is convinced it is in the nose: the more straight the bend of the nose, the more sensitive to madness they are. But she keeps this theory to herself. Better to ask the drifters what they think, whom they suspect. The colony will be more amenable to it.

If the drifters were suspicious of the water she offered them when they wandered past her cottage, they did not say it. They took the water. The ruder ones asked for food. Silu kept them talking, although it was not easy. Drifters are not social; they spend too much time by themselves. But she made conversation, even if it hurt her brain, because it was for the colony's good.

It was Ishita who had told her. She said it with a smile, like she had known it would worm into Old Silu's mind. Like she had hoped it would give her nightmares.

I worry about granddaughters, she had said. *Kua's little ones.*

It had kept Old Silu up for nights. Her first instinct had been to tell Lira, maybe even Zia. What would they have thought? From the house of Isom, no less! But the more she had thought about it, the more she had decided it could not be Magali. Not brave, capable Magali, orphaned at such a young age with a tragedy that broke everyone's hearts.

It must be the other girl.

So she had made a small package of overripe dates and hurried to Kua's cottage. But now that she is here, sipping this disgusting tea, she does not know how to broach it.

How are the children? she asks finally.

But she must have said it in a certain way, because Kua says: *Silu. You and I know you haven't come for tea.*

She raises her eyebrows and takes a contemplative sip. She is aiming for wisdom and hidden depths. *Children need looking after—that's all I'm saying. Remember Isom.*

She waits for him to ask what she means. He doesn't. They sit in silence, as Old Silu wrestles with herself about whether to speak without invitation. He watches her struggle. When she finishes her tea, he takes her cup and tells her he will be over to look at that fig tree.

But then Lira comes in, a few days later. She is looking for a dream potion; she hasn't been sleeping well, not with the festival so close. He boils her a mixture of calamus, jasmine and snakeroot. She watches it bubble on the fire.

What will happen to us, Kua? she asks. *What will we become?*

He soothes her. Lira's fears are deep-rooted and octopus-like; they cling on to anything and grow tentacles that operate on their own.

Remember, he says. *We go inside. We lock the doors. We cover our ears. There is nothing to be scared of. Seven days and then it is done.*

He makes her drink some of the mixture here, so that she relaxes. By the end she is laughing and touching his wrist. Her gratefulness is so bright, it hurts. As she is leaving, she glances at Wisa's rolled-up ghodra. She says: *My son has been spending a lot of time with your granddaughters.*

He knows little Jinn; he likes him. But the worry underneath Lira's words floods the house, transforming it into a black and choppy sea.

Then he hears it everywhere.

All I mean, Zia says as she wraps up his meat, *is that you don't know where people come from. How madness may sit in them. I love Wisa, don't get me wrong. She is a nice child. But you don't know, do you? Plucked from the quay— her parents could have been drifters or leomir hunters, maybe even craftsmen, Esi forbid. You're too trusting, Kua . . .*

It is not my place, Pio says when he brings him a cutting of jasmine. He stares at the ground, miserable. *Kua, you know that—I mean, you are the best person we know; we're lucky to have you. I said to them, "If Kua has brought her here, he must have a reason." You have a reason, right? Don't tell me; it is not my place. But you just don't know in these times. I trust you, and Magali is a lovely child—bright, smart, eager . . . And I like Wisa, I really do. She is kind. A bit wonky, but which tree grows perfectly? But you never know—madness comes in many shapes.*

Kua is alarmed by how many of them there are; this narrative has taken root without him. He handles these concerns with care. He soothes, he chastises, he refocuses their attention on what matters: community, sticking together, trusting in the old luddite ways to protect them. He checks that they have all been doing the rituals of sanity. He gives them pouches of dried blue oyster, to help them sleep.

But he knows in his bones it is only a matter of time before the rumors grow out of control. Maybe not this year, maybe not the next. But three years later, four—at the cusp of the festival?

How does he stop it then?

It has never happened before, he reminds himself. *Luddites have never turned on one of their own.* But a small voice tells him they won't see Wisa as one of their own, and that none of them have lived through an actual festival of madness.

The agamids have died. Kua finds them where he left them, now dehydrated and sunburned, their flesh split open. He doesn't understand it. What illusion could be so persistent that it overwhelms your need to survive?

He buries them. It's silly; he knows the forest will claim them in a neater, less disruptive manner. But he does it anyway, for him, for the ghost of Isom now leaning against a tree and watching him.

"Madness comes in many shapes," Poi had said.

Kua knows, better than most. Luddites can only imagine the small madnesses: trying to fly, tearing out your hair, stripping your clothes and talking to rocks. He knows the large madness. When the whispers get under your skin and become an itch. When a thought hatches in your mind and the larvae grow fatter and fatter. When one day you wake up and this island is not enough. Nor is this sky, this sun, this black sea. You want to make a world.

And so he makes a decision. He goes to the kitchen, where his granddaughters are making dinner.

Magali?

She looks up from the pot she has been stirring, filled with a green pod curry. Wisa is lying on the floor, talking to her lizard. Kua feels a tug for her, and then an even deeper tug for what Magali will have to bear.

Magali, will you come with me, please?

She doesn't ask why. She just lifts the pot off the flames and sets it aside. Wisa stands too, but Kua shakes his head. Slowly, she sits down. Magali follows him out of the house and into the forest.

For a week now, Kua has been thinking about the agamids. He has thought about Old Silu and the narrative he didn't catch in time. He has thought, of course, about Isom. Six years until the festival of madness. How do you prepare your children for that? What do you do to keep them safe?

The best you can.

They come to the dead banyan tree; he gestures for Magali to sit and settles opposite her. Magali looks for the paper and paintbrush, but there is nothing. It is just a dead tree and the two of them.

Do you remember Granduncle Isom? Kua asks.

Magali shakes a no. She has heard of him; her father used to mention him. She assumed he was one of many luddites who died of illness in his childhood.

He didn't die as a child, Kua says. *I think your mother told you that to keep you safe, and I never corrected her. Isom was alive when she married your father, actually, but he was barely Isom then. Your uncle was mad.*

He feels pride at how she takes it. Steady, no hint of shock. What a strong woman she is, with grace as gentle as her father's and strength as unbending as her mother's.

I want to tell you the story, he says. *It is not long, but I haven't said it in a long time. So let me finish. Let me say it all and then I will answer your questions.*

Magali nods.

Kua finds that, in the end, there is not much to say. Isom was a bright child; he had an enthusiasm that was difficult to contain but he also loved deeply. If he couldn't concentrate on the drawings, he made up for it in his innovation for color. He liked color. He said it hid stories within its depth.

Kua and he were not close. They loved each other as brothers do, but there was no special bond. The one secret they shared was the cave. They had stumbled upon it together, and it became their hideout. They wondered about the pattern on the walls. Isom even tried to draw it. But Kua could never make sense of the pattern. Neither did Isom, in the end.

But it sparked something in him. He began talking to drifters more and more—trading silta pearls, his food, even rare paints his mother kept for any information about the festival of madness. *Don't you want to know* he would cry to Kua eagerly. *We're memory keepers. How can you be content without this memory?* He began living more and more in the cave. Kua told him to stop, but Isom wouldn't listen.

And although Kua didn't approve, he covered for his brother. This is what siblings do: you protect your other half. He thought it was just Isom being annoying: fixating on the one thing he could never get, and avoiding growing up in the pursuit of it.

Then Isom ran away, and Kua left home to find him. It took years, but he finally found his brother and brought him back. But by then his brother was already mad. Kua tried to keep him in the house for a while, but the colony grew skittish. Kua had a wife and son by then; he couldn't put them in danger. So he let Isom go, let him live in the forest where Isom wanted to be anyway. He always left him food; he didn't know if Isom ate it or if Isom even remembered him, but the food was always gone when Kua returned with more. For a decade, it went on like that. Then Kua stumbled across his brother's dead body, already half claimed by a taro vine climbing over it. Isom was gone.

This is what he tells Magali. He leaves out the details. He doesn't tell her how every morning he would visit his brother's corpse, covering his nose against the smell, to watch the forest eat him whole. He doesn't mention the relief. Nor does he talk about the time that Isom, gaunt and shaking, tried to strangle him—and almost managed it—while whispering, *it's not your fault.*

Then there was the time that Isom, lying on the floor of a stone ruin, whispered to Kua: *Your daughter is here.*

Except Kua didn't have a daughter. He had a son, who married a kind woman, and they had Magali, a girl born with the sun in her chest and Esi's will in her fist. And for a long time, years and years even, Kua forgot Isom. He never erased him, but he didn't think of him every time he woke up, of his brother's bony fingers and his *it's not your fault.*

He only thought of him on that terrible night when his son died and his daughter-in-law followed hours after. The specter of Isom watching Kua cry. Saying, *you could have saved them.*

Kua could have saved them, yes. He could have taken them to Boba, found the closest craftsman, and the craftsman would have healed them with his magic. But at what price? Why is the goal of something only to have more of it? More comfort, more food, more life? Did that matter more than the quality of the life lived?

But he tells Magali none of this.

Am I mad? Magali asks softly. *Double sight is the first sign.*

It is the first time she sounds scared. *No,* he says. *Your grandmother had double sight, and your great-grandmother. It runs in the Kilta family, and all of them lived to ripe old ages as excellent memory keepers. It is only superstition that double sight is a form of madness. You shouldn't listen to it.*

But Isom . . .

Isom didn't have double sight. Isom was what we call a "worldbuilder." It is the name for those who go mad first, long before the festival arrives. They call them that because their madness takes a particular form. They want to make worlds.

Worlds?

Isom couldn't explain it either. I don't think it is meant to be expressed in our language. All I know is Isom found this island and this universe . . . not enough anymore. He wanted more. He wanted it so badly, he would have died for it. He did die for it.

He remembers finding Isom in a stone structure in the red sands, mumbling to himself. He remembers fighting him to return home, Isom clawing at his face and screaming to be released. In the end, Kua hit him with a rock, kept hitting him until he was unconscious and then carried him.

Magali puts her hand on her grandpa's knee. He looks so old suddenly, as if the years have descended on him in one fell swoop. *Why tell me now, Grandpa?* she whispers.

This is it. This is when he says what he brought her here for. *The colony will turn against your sister,* he wants to say. *You must protect her. The closer the festival comes, the more scared they will be. And they will want someone to rally against. They will choose her because she came here later, because she has her own ways and because Isom was my brother. Be prepared.*

But he cannot say it. Saying it makes it real; it gives it power it would not have otherwise. As long as he does not say it, it is just the quiet fears of an old man. But once he does, it will become Magali's story as well; she will carry it. Maybe she'll tell Wisa, even Jinn, and they will feed it too. It will grow into reality.

He cannot bear that.

So he says, *I thought you deserved to know.*

Magali doesn't ask him any more questions. They walk back to the cottage, where Wisa has served out the curry into bowls. When Magali looks at her, she sees a flash of the future Wisa, gaunt and terrified. But then she blinks, and it is her Wisa again, well-fed and content. They eat in silence. After dinner, Magali and Wisa play a game of lilta. Kua sits beside them, lost in his own thoughts.

For years after Magali's parents died, Kua did not think of his brother at all. He thought sometimes of what the ghost of Isom had said on that terrible night—*you could have saved them*—but even those words faded after a while. The first time he thought of his brother in decades was when he was walking along Boba market and saw Wisa.

She was dancing absent-mindedly in one spot, for herself, the *la, la, la* of children going about their day. Except her clothes were filthy and her body emaciated, so there was no real "day" to speak of really, only the question of when she would eat next, if at all. Isom came back to him then. He remembered his brother lying on the floor of the stone structure and saying to him: *Your daughter is here.*

Isom was talking about this child.

Kua felt the certainty wash over him, and for a moment, it was so powerful it was true. This child belonged with him and Magali; it was always where she was meant to be. Isom *knew*. But Kua shook himself free of the thought. It was just his brother's madness talking.

When he caught her stealing, he told himself he would buy her a julma and that would be it. When he asked her how she survived and she shrugged, he told himself he would take her home for a good meal and restful sleep. But there is a quality to Wisa that reminds you of a lotus leaf; everything runs off her. She is part of the world but not *of* it. She accepts kindness but doesn't expect it. It is like she believes the world has only a finite amount of luck and wealth and love, and she wasn't made for a share.

When he was wrapping the blanket around her, she looked at him solemnly and stayed still, her trust given without question. When he asked her if she remembered her parents, she shook her head and said: *I've always been alone.* And he knew he would do anything to change that.

Now he watches Wisa doing a celebratory dance for stealing three of Magali's lilta bones and Magali trying to argue the move. Kua feels a fierce love. He cannot see what the colony is talking about. He has lived with madness. He knows what it looks like. His Wisa is not mad.

But, of course, she is.

Wisa was mad before she came to the luddite colony. She has been mad since the age of five.

Miqhai, the Seaspider Drifter

I

Four years until the festival of madness.

Esites now feel change creeping up on them. It is not in individuals as yet and you cannot see it in the land, but it exists at the level of the community. Across Esi, communities are deciding what is "not mad."

It is not a conscious decision. Rather, it is a drifting one, as when you are lost in thought and don't realize where your feet have taken you. Conversations circle around finding this new equilibrium, a standard against which people can be measured. It is sought in the quiet chatter after meals, in the surprise run-in with a neighbor, in the soft conversations you have with yourself.

No one knows what "mad" looks like. But "not mad"... that feels easier to define.

And so communities across the island begin to draw their own lines about what constitutes familiar behavior. Some tribes are more finicky than others: too much pois juice, for instance, can tell you a lot about a person and their *inclinations*. Other communities gather around their craftsmen. They seek their blessing on what is normal and what is not. Overnight, ordinary men are turned into gods; they are given the power to decide people's fate. Drifters move across the island and watch as the power-starved abuse what they have been given.

All this happens quietly, unnoticeable to anyone but an Esite. The travelers still come by ship. They still write of the island's marvels and Esites' exceptional ability with craft, and Esites feed them well—they make them fat with the gristle of old stories. This is why no travelogue speaks of the change Esites undergo years before the festival actually arrives; the travelers simply weren't looking. As they eat and write and talk about how glitteringly perfect Esi is, Esites have begun to root out their own.

They are hunting for the worldbuilders.

It is not easy to identify a worldbuilder but it is not impossible. Look for the ones who dream too big, who ask questions about the way things are, who obsess over the festival. Look for the glint in their eye, for long moments spent by themselves, thinking. Ask the drifters. The drifters can sniff out a worldbuilder the way a pig can sniff out a delicate truffle. They are attuned to it. Ask them, and maybe they will tell you. Or maybe they won't, and then once they have left your colony and months have passed, you will find your wife crouched in a corner of your cottage, whispering about the worlds she could make. You will see madness in her eyes.

Throw her out then, quickly, before the madness spreads. Before the community finds out and they burn your house down to keep the madness contained. Before they hang her from a tree until she stops moving and then throw her body to the animals.

Above all, don't plead with them to spare her. Don't tell them, *We all go mad in the festival, we must; for seven days, this is all of us. Does it matter that her time came earlier?*

Above all, don't trust yourself.

II

A blue-tailed stork is picking insects out of a hippo's ear when it spies a girl floating on the river. It settles on her forehead and stabs at her diffused hair, searching for grub. Wisa pulls out of the water and gathers the stork into her arms. It flaps and pecks at her shoulders until she releases it, laughing. It flies off, irate, an old lady tricked into a hug.

When Grandpa had asked Wisa if she had any parents and she had said, *I have always been alone*, she was both lying and telling the truth. Wisa doesn't know the people who gave birth to her; she has always been a small girl alone in Esi; she's always had to figure out how to survive. But it is also a lie. For Wisa has a family. She made one.

It is Esi: the birds, beasts, animals, trees. From an early age, Wisa talked to anything and everything. She spoke in a rush, not caring if the other creature understood her, but slowly she found she could understand *them*. It was only about forming patterns—once you realized rojk birds *twup-twit* in a certain way at a certain time, you could tell what it meant. The birds always understood her; they seemed to have been trained better than humans to make sense of languages that weren't theirs.

And so Wisa made a community with Esi. She scampered up trees and whispered to squirrels. She lay beside the agamids and hit them admonishingly over the head when they tried to eat her. A merchant saw her do this once, and ran to save her; she was only four years old then. Wisa found the intervention foolish: the agamids really would have eaten him; they like merchant flesh. But when he gave her a hot stew of long-stemmed mushrooms and sea molluscs, she decided foolishness had its merits. She drank it straight, tipping it hot down her throat.

Careful now, the merchant said, watching her lick the bowl. *Don't go talking to animals, okay? Or birds.*

Wisa was puzzled. *Why?*

They'll think you're mad.

Mad?

The merchant shook his head. *Don't do it, child. It is for your own good.*

And so the first time Wisa heard the word "mad," she associated it with love, warmth and belonging. She associated it with power. For although she didn't consciously know it, Esi had saved her. It taught her that there are as many forms of consciousness as there are hearts—to find them and understand them, you only had to listen. Wisa listened. And the more she listened, the more she felt free. To Esi, you are another soft animal, an element in a biodiverse landscape capable of flowing into another soft animal; there is no perspective of "apart" or "alone" or "distinct." There is no concept of "orphan." Wisa wasn't a hungry child lost on the harbors. She was simply Wisa, a bird in a human body, and if she opened herself to the island, it would teach her how to fly.

She never considered it was impossible.

Wisa has been mad, then, from one year old, from her first words, from the moment she learned to participate in the world. There are no boundaries for her. Anything she wants, she finds a way to get—she reaches, eager and fearless, to tug it into reality.

She became a worldbuilder at the age of the five.

You want to know how it began? With a word. Wisa was creeping around the edges of a sailor's camp when she heard two burly women talking. Wisa was looking for dried fish or millet balls, anything to help with her hunger, but she paused to eavesdrop, attracted by the timber of the woman's voice. It was as rich and deep as loamy soil.

. . . they'll be looking for worldbuilders soon. Not now, but in the next few years . . .

This is all she heard. The sailors moved away, still talking, but she couldn't follow them without being caught. By the end of the night, she had collected only two small dried fish, each no bigger than her little finger. She ate both slowly, thinking of what she had overheard.

Worldbuilder.

She liked it. The word had merged with that loamy voice, and it sounded rich and promising to her. It reminded her of a house so large, you could wander its rooms forever. She rolled it around her tongue.

Worldbuilder, she said, trying it out in different voices. *Wooorldbuilder.*

But no one else said the word. At that time, Wisa lived in the wilderness, creeping out to the market to steal. At each forage, she listened carefully for someone else to say it. She looked for explanations. When she didn't hear it in the market, she began to eavesdrop on conversations between drifters. She lay belly down on branches and tried desperately to hear the word again. She even snuck under the windows of seaside dhabas. But it was as if only one sailor knew the word and the rest of Esi had never heard of it. Wisa wondered if "worldbuilder" was a secret of the sea, but it didn't sound like it. It didn't belong with salt, spray and the see-saw of a boat. It sounded of Esi.

So Wisa asked the island.

More specifically, she asked the turtles. Huwas were a small tribe of giant turtles that swam into a sweet-water lagoon near Boba to rest from their journey across the black sea. They were cosmic turtles and they made their homes in many islands, but they were familiar with Esi. They had been visiting this lagoon for half a million years. Wisa becomes friends with them in the same way she did most things—without any awareness that a friendship may not be possible. She simply appeared in the lagoon and swam with them.

What did a seven-year-old human girl have in a common with a tribe more than two million years old? But two-million-year-old tribes tend to be kind and very patient, and the turtles were no exception. If the human animal wanted to be their friend, well—why not?

And so that was how Wisa found herself floating on Kin's shell, listening to gray seagulls screech above them. Kin was a baby, only five centuries old, and her shell was still blue and silver, instead of the pure silver it would become. She swam slowly, in gentle strokes, not really feeling the human on her back.

Kin, Wisa said, *do you know what a worldbuilder is?*

Kin had never heard of a "worldbuilder." But she had heard of "worlds." A century ago, she spoke to a swarm of ants that came from an anthill in a stone structure. The ants themselves had never seen a festival of madness, but the anthill had lived through one, and knowledge had been passed down from ant parent to child.

So Kin knew about the worlds that appeared during Esi's festival of madness. But she didn't know how to explain it. She could repeat it in ant language and she could describe it to her brothers and sisters, but how to say it to a human girl? She flapped her fins slowly, thinking.

Think of it as if other islands appeared in the stone structures, she told Wisa. Glimpses of them. Pieces. The other islands were not really there, but they could be visited. She described it like two ocean currents meeting—one hot and one cold. You feel strange when you are in it, but in the end, it is all water.

Wisa pondered over that. She didn't grasp what Kin meant about the currents, but she could see what she was trying to say. It was like cottages, she decided. Each of the stone structures was a different cottage, but they remained closed for a hundred years. When the festival happened, their doors opened and you could look inside, at their different rooms. Except they weren't rooms, but glimpses of other islands.

For a while, Wisa fantasized about it. She had never lived in a cottage. They must be places of wonder. She decided a cottage mirrored its owner's personality, and if you lived in a cottage long enough, it would talk back to you in your own voice. Or in a voice of what you loved. Wisa's cottage would speak to her in the language of the trees, and the shrill, jumping song of the blue-tailed stork. And if her cottage was a piece of another world—well then. She could live quite happily with that.

But over time, the dream lost its allure. Cottages were *small*. Even the stone structures, although impressive, were not as large as where Wisa currently lived. She lived on *Esi*. A whole island. She didn't want to wander into a piece of someone's cottage and sit in a tiny space. She wanted to *make* one, as large as an island. Larger. She wanted one as plural and teeming as the landscape she had come to love.

It is commonly assumed that people shape their dreams in their own likeness. They understand themselves and what they want, and so they make a dream that reflects these desires. But dreams have a life of their own. They choose you, slipping into your mind when you least expect it, and suddenly you find yourself changing for them. This is what Wisa's world was like. The more she imagined her dream world, the more she became herself. It *made* her. She didn't want logic. She didn't want tameness. She wanted surprise and danger—wilderness, curling up the sides of her world, imbibing it with delicious unpredictability. She wanted the opposites of the black sea crammed, arguing and bickering, into a singular space.

But she didn't know how to say this to herself. It was only a feeling, skittering at the edge of understanding, waiting for her to grow up and articulate it. Wisa turned eight years old, then nine. She got better at stealing; almost no one noticed her now. Some evenings, she climbed onto the branches of an old magnolia to listen to a merchant tell a story. It was a story in five parts, each about a genie that grew and grew and grew out of a shell, ready to grant anyone's wishes. Wisa was so enthralled, she forgot she was meant to be hiding; when the fifth part ended, she clapped harder than anyone else. Then she fled, jumping from branch to branch, as the merchant chased her, demanding his coins.

That night she dreamed of the genie.

It was large, so large the sky was too small. It had to hunch, and the pale blue dome pressed into its shoulders. It cooked her a feast. Fruits bursting out of their skin. Thick, lazy squids wrapped around a stick and smoking with the scent of spiced charcoal. Plump crustaceans, their shells yawning open in invitation, rainbow fish, ruby berries, silta pearls crushed and powdered onto engorged roots, golden honey hardened on fried insects . . .

When Wisa approached the feast, the genie bent down. Its torso curved with the sound of an island crumbling, and it brought its face to Wisa's level. Her heart closed in panic and delight. Its eyes were black and bottomless; they looked as deep as the black sea.

Wisa woke before she could eat.

But she knew she had seen her world. It would be a genie, as large as the largest island. It would be wish-giving.

She never considered it was impossible.

She turned ten, then eleven. Grandpa brought her to the colony, and she made it her home. *I'm still a bird*, she told the jackfruit tree, *but even birds have nests*. Wisa liked having a nest. She liked how Magali woke her up in the morning, and how they cleaned the cottage—so small— before spilling out into Esi to see what the day held for them. She liked watching the slow slide of Grandpa's brush along the paper as he made his memories. She liked using the same brush to make maps. When she introduced Magali and Jinn to her community on Esi and taught them how to speak to it, she felt a thrill that could only come from uniting two things that would not have known each other without you. Her universe was expanding, filling itself with contradictions and plurality, and she was happy.

But still she listened at doors when drifters came home. It was like listening to a gale, their conversation twisting through all topics; it made her feel airborne. *I'm a bird*, she told herself, *with the wind slipping off my wings*. She felt like a bird the night she climbed the mango tree. (She was faking the fear, of course; it was fun seeing the unflappable Magali Kilta trembling in her sandals.)

But up there on the higher branches, still not as high as she was desperate to go, in the moment before she looked down at Magali and saw her double sight, she heard whispers, flitting out of reach.

On how to make a world.

She reached for them, but they eluded her.

Months later, before Jinn came to her for help with Magali and his friendship, she went back to the stone structure. Looked up at the mango tree, now warm and majestic in daylight. Climbed again to the same place. *Tell me how*, she asked the tree. The leaves whispered; they rustled. *Please*, she said.

Again it told her, but she couldn't understand. The explanation was too long, too difficult to guess. It would take decades for her to grasp it in their language. But the mango tree felt pity for this strange, clawless person clutching its branches. It remembered people like her, from an older time. People who did mad things in these very stone structures. So it whispered an answer she could hold in her tiny hands.

Ask the alchemists.

That's how we find ourselves in the cave, Wisa, Jinn and Magali with us, drawing sketch after sketch of the gold pattern. If we tilt our gaze and peer into Wisa's face, we will see a glint of what we missed. An idea. An obsession. She knew the same alchemists who made the stone structures also made the cave. Somewhere in this gold pattern, there were instructions on how to make her world.

But there is none of that obsession now as Wisa wades out of the river, still laughing at the irate stork. She is sixteen, so different from the child who first came to the colony. But she radiates the same unpredictability nestled alongside an unnerving stillness. She is carefree today. She shakes her hair, scattering droplets onto the grass. Gul is perched at the end of a stalk. Wisa picks her up and she nestles in her hair, gulping slowly.

It has taken years, but they have almost completed a sketch of the cave's pattern. They have been methodological about it, which is not Wisa's nature, but she likes watching Magali number each drawing and write detailed notes on the side. *Like a map*, Wisa thinks but this pattern is different, not as distinct as the many elements of a map. There is no island here, no sea, no stars. Everything in this pattern flows into one, so that it is impossible to draw distinctions or mark a break. *Like a story*, Wisa thinks and this fits better; it feels right. There is no understanding the different parts of this pattern. Either you understood it all at once, or not at all.

Ask the alchemists, the trees had told her. Wisa knew the alchemists had made the pattern in the cave. If there was an answer on how to make her world, it was here. She hadn't understood it yet, but she didn't feel any desperation to know. It would come. All important things did, and Wisa knew her world was important. Magali called this the "Wisa certainty": a belief that things would always go her way and, even when it seemed like they wouldn't, everything would turn out all right in the end. Wisa likes it when Magali makes up names for the things she does; she tucks these names close to her heart. They are her treasures.

Today, she wanders through the forest with a lightness in her step. The festival is four years away, but Wisa longs for it. She is grateful for the life she has. When she goes home, she will show Magali how to call to the storks so that they gather at her feet. Then they will summon them into the garden and hug them together, laughing at their grumpiness.

III

Magali also no longer fears the festival of madness.

She realizes this in Boba.

At the same time as Wisa is pulling herself out of the river, Magali is in Boba market, looking for a particular colored kew, a deep red fruit with small spikes that you have to peel, but then zings and tickles when it touches your tongue. Wisa has never tasted one, and Magali wants to see her face when she does. She won't tell her what it tastes like as well, so that her sister is properly astonished. It is delightful to surprise Wisa.

The market is more crowded than before with sailors, merchants and travelers thronging along narrow alleyways and vegetable owners shouting their wares. Here and there, bazaar alchemists bubble gold in shallow metal pans as travelers peer and marvel. It is all a trick, of course. The alchemists merely forage gold in Esi's soil, use craft to make it look like metal and then boil it in a pan on upturned crates, so that visitors can see it change back into gold. The coin they get isn't from the gold itself, but from the books they sell on alchemy. It is a thriving business. Esites know it is a scam, but they love it—nothing makes them happier than fooling strangers.

As she watches the gold boil and spit, the noise of the market changes. It shapes into a melody, the disparate sounds coming together not in harmony, but to complement each other. Magali doesn't notice it until she hears herself humming; it is a swift tune, the same bar over and over. She has never heard it before, but she feels like she has sung it forever.

Then she sees it.

It is brief, a moment that pounces on her and then flees. The market speckles into particles. It dissolves. Around her is another place. A palace. Magali has never seen one, but she knows this is the right word: she has heard about them from sailors. This is a palace built for giants, and it is composed entirely of corridors. Large corridors with jeweled mosaics, one of which shows a towering figure. She gasps. It is her, standing in Boba market. The mosaic is singing the same song Magali was humming a moment before.

On the corridor walls, there are doors.

Then, less in images and more in impressions, Magali sees the Kilta family drawings, every memory, stacked into rooms behind the doors. Except they are not drawings anymore but . . . items. Representations of the feelings in those drawings. Each of them is singing. And for one breathless, giddy moment, Magali is flying and she sees this palace in all its entirety. It is not a palace but a museum, and it is as large as the black sea.

Then the image is gone, and Magali is once again in Boba market.

She stumbles to the nearest wall and leans against it. Her heart is beating wildly. She doesn't know what she saw . . .

But she wants it.

Oh, she *wants* it. The sheer magnificence of it shakes her. It rattles her bones and hurts her teeth; her heart has swelled to an impossible size and it is pushing at her, urging her forward. She wants to laugh. She wants to—oh, this is ridiculous—she wants to cry. Imagine it: the Kilta family tradition of memory-keeping, expanded into a museum you could visit anywhere, anytime. A museum of song. It feels to her like double sight: wild but ordered, vast yet intimate.

Magali stays against the wall until her trembling subsides. When she walks back toward the colony, she is still elated, her fingertips tingling. Part of her cannot wait to tell Wisa, but another part wants to keep this to herself. This vision felt uniquely hers and she doesn't want to spoil it by spilling it into words. She will spend more time studying Grandpa's methods of memory-keeping, she decides. She will visit her great-great-grandfather's stories in the *Principles of Memorizing*. There may be something in there that could help her.

Magali has just entered the forest when she hears people talking. Sailors come to this part sometimes, drinking heavily under the shade of Esi's giant trees, kissing the ground in gratefulness. The bazaar alchemists come here too, to dig up gold or settle disputes with other tricksters in the shelter of the trees.

Magali lingers. She stays just out of sight so that their voices drift to her. They are talking about a malevolent spirit, a *bhavla*, which can take the form of anything it touches. Those from the red sands believe *bhavla*s usually live in trees, which is why they prefer the wide, open desert to Esi's forests. Grandpa always said this was nonsense. He said nature is scary to anyone who doesn't understand it simply because it inspires awe, and awe reminds you that you are a lot smaller than you think you are. *Some people have made peace with that*, he had said to little Magali. *Others have not.*

The people in the trees are whispering about the festival. It is close now; you can tell by the *bhavla*s. *Bhavla*s are leaving the trees. They are coming out into the open in droves. Can't you see them? Thick, invisible spirits that look like ripples of light and smell like rust. They travel in whispers, on the wind, looking for things to become. There are so many *bhavla*s now that they cannot help bumping into each other. When two *bhavla*s collide, they ripple into memories of their previous shapes. This is why you can see strange visions on Esi. Why you see ghosts and hear voices . . .

Magali has heard most of this before, usually from drifters. They're fairy tales. She wants to creep up and tell those sailors: *Did you know you can catch a bhavla by luring it into the heart of a bougainvillea? The sap gives the spirit a rash and by the time they have finished scratching, the plant has grown so big and the spirit is now stretched so thin, they can never leave.*

This makes her smile, then giggle. She imagines it, strutting out among a crop of burly sailors, announcing her wisdom. She creeps closer, wanting to get a good look at them. She is still filled with a giddy power; nothing can touch her.

But when she looks through the leaves, she finds it is not sailors speaking, but children from the colony. There are Ava and Freyn. There are two or three more, but she cannot see them clearly. They are huddled in a tight ring. They are unaware that they are being overheard.

Magali's elation vanishes. She feels cold and clammy. Her heart has suddenly sped up and her muscles coil, ready for a fight.

Bhavla can turn into girls, Ava says. *It is the shape they like most. They can live as girls for years and years, decades even. They grow, eat, laugh. They like it; it makes them feel human.*

Why? Freyn asks, entranced.

To spread, Ava says. *Think about it. You come to a new place, small and fully formed. No one asks who your parents are or where you came from. You slip in. And then slowly, over years, you learn the people you are among. You grow stronger and put bits of yourself into these people. You sour their minds and stretch their thinking until they don't know which way is up or down. You make mischief. You bring madness.*

Ava stops. A feeling has overtaken the group. It is crawling up Magali's spine, forming itself into an impulse to run, to fight, to claw the next words from Ava's throat so they are never said. For she can sense what is coming. It is written on Ava's face.

I don't want to believe it either, Ava says softly. *But look at what she's done to Magali. To Jinn. She's made them mad. Who else can you blame but Wisa?*

IV

Magali sprints back home.

She doesn't know what she is running for; running won't change Ava's words. It won't take away how Freyn looked when she said it: like he had known it in his bones. She just knows she has to get to Wisa. She remembers Jinn telling her years ago about his mother's concerns. The suspicion in her voice. How did Magali not think the story would grow? Why hadn't she curbed it?

And she had taken them to the cave. She had drawn pictures of the pattern. Those pictures were there, in fact, hidden in a crack in an old tree trunk. Anyone could find them.

She runs faster.

Across the forest from Magali, right at the fringe before we move into the colony, Wisa is encountering her own form of fear.

Wisa doesn't know fear. Or rather, she knows it, but she has made easy friends with it. When her body trembles high in the boughs of a tree, she keeps going. When her lungs burn from being underwater too long and her limbs twitch in panic, she looks at it dispassionately. When Old Silu talks about burning and death and the terrible things that happen in the years before the festival of madness, about the horror of being insane, Wisa can tilt her head and notice how strange Old Silu's lips look when she talks. Rather like a shriveled fruit. Then she will imagine shriveled fruit with a whole host of things to say, eulogizing mournfully on a bough and in the mud, and will miss most of what Old Silu said.

But this time, at the edge of the forest, Wisa feels real fear.

She meets Miqhai.

She runs into the drifter by accident. She is still wet from the lake, Gul sleeping in her hair, when she notices a yellow-spotted frog. She chases it, bellowing softly in her most frog-like voice, hoping to trick it into believing she is a female frog. But the yellow-spotted frog is smart. It hops as far away from her as it can. Wisa crouches, hoping to pounce on it, and a shadow drapes over her. She looks up and there he is.

Miqhai.

She has heard of him. He is not the most popular drifter, but he is different. There is an intensity to his gaze, an intelligence that could sharpen itself into cruelty. He is charming. Words fall from his tongue like jewels. When he tells you about the octopus they made into a settlement or the living fossil the seafarers carved to watch over them, you hold your breath. He is dangerous, his perception sharp as cut glass. She knows she must avoid him.

Now the yellow-spotted frog jumps onto his coat and he is staring at Wisa like she is a new secret, smuggled into plain sight, and he is delighted by the trick.

Hello, he says.

Wisa's heart clenches. The word is an invitation and a challenge. Miqhai isn't smiling but he might as well be. He might as well have said: *Oh, you have them fooled, have you? Try and fool me.*

You stare down a drifter as you would a predator. Look straight into their eyes, keep your back straight, shoulders thrown back.

And who are you? Miqhai asks.

Wisa.

Miqhai whistles and the yellow-spotted frog jumps into his palm. Sits there, docile, throat moving up, down, up, down. Wisa is this frog. He is looking at her like her heart is large and juicy, like he knows the thought that has been dripping like fat through her mind for all these years.

Were you following this one?

It was speaking, Wisa says. *I wanted to hear what it was saying.*

Miqhai tilts his head appraisingly. *You're not from here.*

I am a Kilta.

It is the first time she's said it. It comes out big and bold, bursting forward in its bombast. It is trying too hard. Miqhai laughs, without humor. It strikes ice in Wisa's heart.

This man is bad, she thinks. She knows he will upturn everything. Then he is gone, coat whipping behind him.

This is how the sisters find each other a few feet away from their cottage: shaking and scared, suddenly aware of dire things to come. All Magali could think of as she ran home is her vision of Wisa howling that night in the garden. She is desperate to protect her but doesn't know how. And all Wisa sees is Miqhai. His laugh when she said she was a Kilta, as if no one could believe that, not even Wisa herself. For years, Wisa has not thought her madness at odds with her life in the colony. She has not seen it as endangering what she has come to love. But Miqhai looked at her as if he saw what she was—*all* of what she was—and he knew a luddite colony was no place for her.

Little Wisa was made to be alone.

And so she clings to her sister, and Magali clings back. In this way, wordless, they make their way to the cottage. The lamps are lit; they can hear Grandpa moving around in the kitchen. The sound is comforting.

Once they are home, the world will fall away for a while; it will be the three of them, and everything will be more manageable.

But when the sisters reach the cottage, they find the table is set for four people, not three. It is spread with vegetables and fruits not from this side of the world. Giant woodnuts, fried green stalks, steamed jii beans. Miqhai lounges in the corner, his rainbow coat draped on the floor. He smiles at the girls, wide and wolfish. Wisa shrinks closer to her sister.

Then Grandpa is here, carrying a bowl of sugarplums. *Girls, this is Miqhai*, he says. *He's an old friend. He'll be with us for a few days.*

Magali can sense her sister's fear but she doesn't understand it. Wisa is quiet throughout dinner; Miqhai is rambunctious. He is full of stories of how he met Kua.

Did you know your grandpa traveled around Esi once? All the women loved him; they used to line up for one of his paintings. A thump on Grandpa's back. *We drifters used to call him the Fool, but we liked him really.*

And Grandpa laughs, lighter than Magali has seen him. Miqhai reminds her grandfather of a certain time, perhaps when things were easier. Or maybe Grandpa just likes him because Miqhai is shrewd and because he can see so clearly. Grandpa likes people who are light and quicksilver, Magali realizes. He has an affinity for what moves too fast or cannot be contained.

Later, Miqhai goes into the garden to sleep. He says the grass will do, but Grandpa pulls out the spare ghodra and Magali beats it down on the steps, dust floating around her. Wisa is hiding. Magali gives Miqhai the ghodra without meeting his eyes.

When she comes into the cottage, she finds Wisa crouching at the window, spying on Miqhai. Her eyes are wide and intense; they remind Magali of the first evening when Grandpa brought her home. How she had stared.

What happened? Magali whispers urgently. *What's wrong?*

But Wisa won't look at her sister. *Nothing,* she mumbles. She crawls to her ghodra and lies down.

Magali stands there for a moment. Then she unrolls her own ghodra and curls into it.

Wisa?

Mmm?

I don't like him.

Magali hopes Wisa can read between the words and hear what Magali is really saying, which is: You can tell me anything. But her sister only shuffles position until her back is to Magali. She begins breathing deeply. Magali knows she is faking it.

Wisa?

Silence. Then after a moment, Wisa says, *mmm?*

But Magali doesn't know how to say it. *I heard Ava talking in the forest today; she believes you made me mad.* She couldn't say that; the words sound wrong. So she reaches out until the tips of her fingers are touching Wisa's back. Like this, they fall asleep.

V

Miqhai stays in the colony for nine days. In the mornings, he wears his rainbow coat and wanders into Boba. In the evenings, he is back at the cottage. We see him in every scene now. Eating at the kitchen table. Bellowing as he loses in a game of lilta. Watching Wisa.

Wisa stays away from him. If Miqhai and her are in the room alone, she leaves. If he is in the garden in the early afternoons, she runs to the forest. She cannot bear how he looks at her. For Miqhai reminds her of what she doesn't like to look at. She wasn't always of this colony. This wasn't always a home.

Who is little Wisa? he croons when he catches her alone. *What is she hiding?*

Magali is nineteen now. She watches her sister flee each time the drifter approaches, and her anger builds. What is he doing? As often as she can, she steps in front of Wisa, shielding her. In that step, we see the Magali she will become, the one wandering the plains of Ojda. She is protector, the keeper of your memories.

But now, no matter how much she shields her sister, Wisa's unease doesn't abate. Magali cannot make it better. And Miqhai—he only smiles each time Magali picks a fight with him or gives him burned food. It is a smile that promises secrets Magali cannot guess. She wants to punch him.

If Kua notices how his two granddaughters are acting, he doesn't say anything. He continues to play lilta with Miqhai in the evenings and welcome him to the kitchen table. At night, both of them go to Kua's workshop and look at his drawings. Miqhai also doesn't know what will come in the festival of madness, but he radiates capability. Together, Kua believes they can come closer to finding an answer.

Miqhai was the first drifter Kua befriended when he went on his journey; he was the one who gave Kua the title of the Fool.

No one seeks a worldbuilder once they have left, luddite, Miqhai had told him. *Let your brother go. You'd be a fool not to.*

But Kua had not listened. And in the end, years later, it was Miqhai who led him to Isom. *They're saying a worldbuilder is in Jika, on the edge of the red sands,* he had told him. *It is a one-day journey if you travel through the night. Go, fast, before they kill him.*

Kua never forgets a favor.

But if you imagine Kua's love for Miqhai blinds him to his qualities, then you have underestimated our Grandpa. He knows how dangerous drifters are; they operate according to their own principles. They often act in curiosity, with no thought to the consequences of their actions. Tread carefully around a drifter.

So Kua plays lilta with Miqhai and welcomes him to the dinner table. He never tells him to leave. He pretends there is no reason for him to go.

The colony begins to talk. Nine days is a long time for a drifter to stay in one place. Kua and he may be friends, but there is something else keeping him here. *Refuge?* Pio suggests, tending to Old Silu's fig tree. Old Silu leans on her walking stick and shakes her head.

Something sinister, she says. *I can smell it.*

How Old Silu could smell it—or what it smells like—is never clear, but the colony catches on to the general idea. They begin to wonder. It is interesting, they murmur, that it is *Miqhai* who is staying. Shrewd Miqhai. The other drifters call him a seaspider, because his fingers are long and bony like a seaspider's legs. Miqhai, they say, is a drifter who can spin you a mirror—not an ordinary mirror, but one that shows you the blackness of your heart. He's a drifter who can pluck the truth out of anything, the slimmest crevice, the slenderest crack. Don't you know? He has the fingers for it.

VI

Jinn sees less and less of the sisters. When he comes to their cottage, the drifter Miqhai is always there, watching him with that unnerving gaze. It creeps Jinn out. So he avoids their cottage and hopes the sisters will visit the riverside. But each time he goes there, the riverbank is deserted. He tries the forest, wandering among the roots of their favorite trees. No one. He grows so desperate he even tries the cave, although it is dangerous to visit it with a drifter in town. But the sisters are not in the cave either. The last time he spoke to Magali was eight days ago, when she sent him a frantic message tied to Gul's leg.

Burn the drawings.

Jinn didn't burn them (they had worked hard on them!), but he changed their hiding place. He took them out of the crack in the old tree stump and instead tucked them into a high branch of the eucalyptus tree. No one climbed this tree but them. He was sure of it.

But now he is growing antsy. It is not like the sisters to disappear. To stare at the ground during the day and barely talk. Wisa is gone so often from the colony, he has barely seen her.

Desperate times call for desperate measures. He takes a chance and stops by their cottage. Miqhai is out—praise Esi!—and Magali is in! Praise Esi forever and ever. She looks glad to see him, which makes him smile more foolishly than he would have liked to. But he is not smiling when they sneak out into the forest, and Magali tells him what she had overheard.

She is trembling when she says it. If he didn't think what Ava said was so bad (who believes Ava?) then her reaction convinces him that they should take this seriously. Narratives are dangerous in the time of the festival of madness. Lira once told him of a traveler who got his eyeballs pulled out in Boba because people thought he was carrying madness with him. Only after they went through his satchel did they realize he wasn't even an Esite. What does it matter if Wisa isn't a *bhavla*? Truth is not important.

Impulsively, he puts his arms around Magali and she leans into the hug. They stay like this for a moment, their chests rising and falling in rhythm. Jinn tries not to think about how warm she is or how soft her skin feels. These are very silly things to love so much that your heart squeezes tight. But he doesn't let her go, even after Magali's trembling subsides.

Nor does Magali pull away.

The truth is Magali has been having dreams. She dreams of a shadow figure. It is always turned away from her, its features difficult to discern. But Magali feels irresistibly pulled to it. When she wakes, she contemplates this shadow. She cannot stop thinking about it. And the more she thinks of it, the more it takes on the shape of Jinn. His hard, sinewy shoulders. The slight bump on his nose. The elegance and precision of his fingers, capable of great strength but also delicacy when they gesture in the time and shape of words. She begins to imagine, in sharp and startled glimpses, those fingers on the soft underside of her breast, the flatness of his palm on her stomach, of—

Jinn pulls away.

Magali settles back and ignores her sudden sense of loss.

We'll stop her, Jinn says, determined. *Before she can spread these rumors further.*

How?

Jinn shrugs. *I'll think of something. Meet me at the jacaranda tree tomorrow after dinner? There is a pond at its roots; I know Ava goes there every night to collect white lilies for her father.*

Magali squints suspiciously. *How do you know that?*

I used to go with her. Not anymore, he adds hastily because Magali doesn't look happy about this. *A long time back. Her father thinks a brew of white lilies keeps madness away; they drink one every night. Just meet me there. We'll fix this.*

Magali spends the night and the next day in a state of nervous anticipation. A lot of things could go wrong with their decision to scare Ava. It may not work, and she may become more zealous about her story of Wisa as a *bhavla*. It might work, and she may become more zealous anyway, as a consequence of her fear. Perhaps she would guess Magali has double sight; Magali would not put it past Ava to guess it. The girl is shrewd, even if she is paranoid.

How would Jinn react if he heard she had the first sign of madness? She imagines him turning pale and backing away from her. No. Not her Jinn. She thinks of the older Jinn she saw during double sight. The kindness of his features and his soothing voice as he said: *are we still fighting?* Her stomach tightens. What does it mean, the fact that she saw him?

But she doesn't have time to contemplate it; the plan occupies all of her thoughts. She doesn't tell Wisa about it; she doesn't want to worry her. Already her sister has become a ghost. She is barely at home, desperate to avoid the drifter. Magali had asked Grandpa when Miqhai will leave, but Grandpa had only said *whenever he wants* in a tone that suggested Magali shouldn't ask again. So she doesn't. But she hopes it is soon.

Dinner is fried kikars (purple-and-green pods that, when you shell, reveal a yellow flesh). Grandpa fries them with chilies, onion and garlic, and the juicy sweetness of the kikars pops against the spiciness of the mixture. It is Magali's favorite dish, but she cannot enjoy it. She keeps glancing at the sky.

After dinner, Grandpa goes to his workshop but Miqhai doesn't join him. He stays out in the garden, lounging on his ghodra and chewing discarded kikar shells. Wisa sits in the branches of a nearby tree, staying out of sight. Although Miqhai never glances in her direction, you get the impression that if she moved, he would know.

Magali lets out a small growl of frustration. She was counting on the drifter disappearing with Grandpa after dinner. Now she will have to walk past him in the garden. She could try sneaking past, but Wisa has already assured her many times that she is terrible at stealth, so she doesn't think that plan has a good chance of success.

There is nothing for it but to stride past.

She almost makes it out of the garden when Miqhai says, *Do you girls want to hear a story?*

Magali curses to herself. She says, *I have somewhere I need to be.*

Miqhai glances at her. *Does Kua know you're in love with a boy? What's his name, Lira's son's?*

Magali turns. The drifter has a way of seeing into you, at parts you have not yet seen yourself. He smiles. *You could be with him, you know. It would be the regular way of things. Of course, the festival is coming soon, so nothing is regular.*

Magali glances at the sky.

So, a story?

No, Wisa whispers from her tree.

Miqhai smiles at the canopy. Magali suspects Wisa is the one he has been talking to all along, Magali just a welcome pawn.

No? he says. *Let me give you news then. They say a girl in the black ice plains has gone mad. She can't stop talking about making a world.*

We don't discuss worldbuilders in a luddite colony, Magali says savagely.

You don't, eh? Then how do you know the name?

Grandpa told me.

Miqhai looks surprised, then delighted. *Of course, he did. Good old Kua. Always trying to make sure the mistakes of the past don't repeat themselves. Did he tell you what happens during the festival?*

No one knows, Wisa says, poking her head out. She sounds upset. *No one knows what happens, not even the drifters.*

Ah, but we can guess. Collective knowledge is a powerful thing. You can store it in drawings, like Kua does. Or you can make them into stories. Little nuggets of wisdom you can keep safe—Miqhai taps his chest—*right here. How do you think we know so much about double sight? Double sight, worldbuilders.* He checks them off his fingers. *Do you want to know what the third sign of madness is?*

No—

It is when you see Esi from different times.

Magali makes a sound.

Is that—Miqhai turns on his stomach to look at her, amused—*disdain?* He laughs. *You don't believe me*, he says. *Understandable: you are a luddite, so you wouldn't know. As we get closer to a festival of madness, the air around the island . . . peels. No, not peels. Like a ripe fruit bursting, showing you its flesh. And you see visions of Esi throughout the ages. Strange visions. Dangerous ones. It is not like double sight, oh no. Double sight belongs to a single person. It is a muddle of their own time. Think of your lifetime like a long thin thread. When you have double sight, you spin the thread around you like a spool. You call to family members across your lifetime and they stick to you, caught in your web. But this—this is different. This is* all *of time, large and fat. This is the island going mad.*

The sky is darker now; Jinn will be waiting for her, wondering where she is. Magali shuffles impatiently. How to get away?

You still doubt, Miqhai says. *Let me see. Perhaps you are confused about how you can see these visions. Anyone can, but it is the worldbuilders who start seeing them first. And the mad ones. Think of the strongest fenni, burning down your throat. Imagine losing your senses so completely that you are not sure you are yourself or human or alive. Imagine not getting them back.*

Wisa shrinks farther into the foliage.

The drifter peers at the tree. *You there, little Wisa?*

But Wisa is gone, clambering from branch to branch to escape Miqhai's scrutiny. And Magali takes advantage of the drifter's distraction to flee the garden.

Magali runs into the forest full pelt. She is late. Ava must already be by the pond—maybe she has even left by now. Why had she been so stupid to stay and listen to the drifter? She should have kept walking when he asked his question.

But when Magali comes close to the jacaranda tree, she sees Ava bending by the small pool. It is a full moon tonight and the silver light filters through the black leaves. It falls on Ava's hair, lighting her in an eerie glow. Magali hides behind an ancient night-flowering jasmine, her hand on her chest to try and slow her breathing. Jinn is nowhere to be seen.

Ava is plucking three white lilies, her long hair skimming the surface of the pond. Ava loves her hair; it is her pride and joy. She oils it every night with walnut oil and brushes it often outside her cottage. Old Silu calls it vanity, but even she cannot resist touching Ava's tresses when the girl is nearby.

Now Ava slips off her shoes and sinks her feet into the water. Her parents think the pond is farther into the forest, and so they are never suspicious when Ava takes a while to come home. She likes it here. It is quiet. And easy. There is no one to worry about when she is alone. Nothing to be afraid of.

Behind her, the bushes rustle.

Ava turns in a panic. Nothing. All there is is an old teak tree, its roots curled and content. Ava peers suspiciously at it for a while, but nothing shows itself, not even a small lizard, so she turns back. But she is on edge now. The moonlight is changing the forest. It is filled with cold, hard secrets, like the sky has lit a lamp for a very particular performance and is shining it on her. The back of her neck crawls. Maybe she should put on her shoes and just go home tonight. The festival is so close . . .

Avvvvaaaaaaa.

Ava jumps. She almost screams. She claps her hand over her mouth and tries to slow her heart rate. There was no voice. She imagined it. She imagined—

Avvvvvaaaa. I hear you're talking about ussssss . . .

Ava wheels around. The voice is coming from the canopy, from the forest itself.

Magali crouches behind the oak tree; she is trying to calm her own panic. This is not her. What is happening?

Do you know how to call bhavlas to you, pretty Ava? You talk about themmmmm. You thinkkkk about themmmm. We liiiikkke it. It makes your body soft and warm for usssssssss.

Ava is putting on her shoes as fast as she can. She is stumbling to her feet.

Don't leave so sooooooonnn, my Avvvaaaaaa. Won't you be mine?

Slowly, out of the forest, animals are creeping toward Ava. They are small: frogs, rabbits, little boars. They stare at Ava in curiosity; they make their way toward her. And Magali realizes what is going on.

It is Jinn. That is his voice. It is high-pitched and eerie—he is distorting it somehow—but she can recognize the way in which he pronounces certain words. And he is layering everything he is saying with what Wisa taught them about the language of the forest. He is using the language of trees, of small animals . . . It is working. Branches are reaching toward Ava, animals are closing in on her.

Be miiiine, Ava. We'll be happy togetherrrrr.

Ava flees. She leaves the lilies by the pond and tears through the forest, not caring what animals she may encounter on the way. The small creatures watch her in puzzlement. They begin to disperse. After a while, Jinn climbs down the jacaranda.

Magali is both elated and guilty. It is mean of them to scare Ava, but then again, Ava implied Wisa was mad and that could get her sister killed—so not that guilty. She walks out from behind the teak tree, and Jinn smiles widely when he sees her.

Did it go okay? he asks as she walks up to him. *I tried to use the words of the trees, like Wisa taught us. Added in the animals. I'm glad Wisa wasn't here, though; she would probably be appalled at what a bad job I did. Ava looked rattled, though—Magali?*

Magali has stopped abruptly. She is close to Jinn, so close she can feel his breath on her lips. How did this happen? She thinks and then realizes it was her—*she* made it happen. She was walking forward to kiss him. She hadn't made a conscious decision to do this, but her body had made it for her, and she was just going to cross the forest floor and walk *into* him, until their lips met. She is aghast.

How did you distort your voice? she asks.

What? Jinn is staring at her lips.

Your voice, Magali says. Her whole body is tingling from his gaze.

Oh. He holds up a shell. *From the yku snail. Wisa did it once, as a joke.*

You were wonderful, Magali whispers.

Jinn swallows.

The truth is, Jinn has been going mad for a while. He has been going mad since he was thirteen, so that is six years he has been thinking about Magali Kilta, even when he tried not to think about her. Every morning, he tries to drown it out of himself by swimming in the river. He allows the mist of a day not-yet-born to obscure his thoughts. But Magali cannot be drowned out. She turns into the water he slides through, into the cold rivulets flowing across his back.

He holds the madness in place with logic. He has loved Magali for years now. If she saw him in that way, she would have told him. Magali, his Magali, who reaches for the moon, the heart of Esi itself, who takes what she wants without knowing that others may have found the same endeavor impossible. If she wants him, he would know.

But madness has no use for logic, for the spider webs we weave to hold in place the gush of life. Magali of the water calls him a coward. Magali of the water presses her soft lips against his, just to see what they taste like, and Jinn is undone.

So if you asked Jinn, he would tell you he is not a particularly brave person. But in this moment, he feels mad enough to be.

She called him wonderful.

Do you want to stay? he asks. Magali can hear the hesitancy in his voice. *For a little while?*

Magali nods.

They stay for more than half the night.

Magali tells him about her double sight; it comes out of her in a rush. He isn't surprised. He says, *I always knew you were special.* Magali blushes. He tells her about his mother and her many fears. About how being around her and Wisa these past years have changed him. *Maybe it is madness,* he says softly. *It is certainly nothing I have felt before. But it feels right, you know? I feel . . . not more myself. But more like the person I am meant to be.*

At some point, their fingers touch, and then they hold hands. Two hours in, Magali kisses him, because she is sure now he wants her and she is tired of waiting for him to make the move. Then they don't talk any more.

When Magali sneaks back into her room, Wisa is fast asleep on her ghodra. Magali crawls into her own bed and, on impulse, takes her sister's hand. Smiling, she falls asleep.

But Wisa isn't asleep. She has had a night of her own.

VII

When the drifter talks about madness in the garden, Wisa flees. She doesn't know where she is going, only that she must get away. She cannot understand this new fear, cannot make friends with it. It presses into her, telling her she needs to make a choice.

Between what?

Wisa goes to the stone structure. Begins climbing the mango tree.

Why am I disturbed? she asks a half-asleep squirrel. *What is this feeling?*

She climbs to the top of the tree. Breaks out of the canopy, tilts her face to the sky. Still not far enough. The moon is hidden behind a sea of clouds. Unreachable.

When Wisa first came to the colony, Magali was fourteen. She was moon-faced and bold, with a half-smile that said she could do anything. Make water out of air? Sure. Pull the moon closer? You got it. Wisa believed it. This is curious because Wisa doesn't believe much, not when it comes to people. But for Grandpa and Magali, her belief sprouted and then climbed higher than she could imagine. Kiltas have a strain of robust morals running through them, a miracle strain that makes them good, inside and out. Wisa used to wonder who planted the strain. If they could plant it in her.

What do you think? she asks the bulbul preening itself by her ear.

You have to plant it yourself, the bulbul says, bobbing its head wisely.

And so Wisa lays her cheek against a branch and breathes in, deep. The fear breathes with her. Make a choice, it says. *Between what?* she wants to scream.

But she knows the answer. Between the Wisa she was before she came to the colony and the Wisa she is now. Between orphan Wisa and Wisa Kilta. For Wisa Kilta can have a family, love and belonging.

But the other Wisa—she can have her world.

I can make it here, Wisa whispers to herself. *I know I can*.

But all she can see is the drifter Miqhai, his head tilted to the side. *Be honest, little Wisa*, he croons. *Be honest with yourself.*

Go away!

Wisa shouts this last sentence. It startles the birds; they fly from their nests, screeching. The monkeys wake up as well, chattering and howling, shaking branches in a frenzy. Leaves rain on the ground; fruit are shaken loose to splatter on rocks. Wisa welcomes the cacophony. It feels like the inside of her head.

When Wisa looks down, there is a man crouched in the corner of the ruins.

―

The man's back is to Wisa; he is murmuring as he grips the air and reaches for a wineskin at his waist. His gestures are tender.

Quietly, Wisa climbs lower. She moves stealthily through the branches, searching for an angle to see him best. Who is he? He wears a satchel similar to what luddites wear for traveling, but it is obvious he isn't from the colony. This man has come from far. His clothes are torn in patches, deep with grime and stuck to his back with sweat. It is a pleasant night, breezy. Wisa herself is not sweating.

The man uncorks the wineskin with his teeth and positions it against nothing. He tips, the water pours out and the vision transforms.

Around the bottle, lips form. Then a neck. Then shoulders, filling out into a torso, and then legs that are obscured by the undergrowth. This is the piece of the picture we have been missing: another man, propped against the wall. He is thinner than the traveler, his skin sickly. He drinks with his eyes closed, in great, greedy gulps. Wisa suspects that if the traveler removed his hand from his shoulder, he would collapse.

We're going to get you home, the traveler whispers. *I promise, we'll get you home.*

The man coughs, spluttering water, pushing the wineskin away, rivulets running down his chin. He is laughing. It sounds deranged, like someone has twisted the essence of laughter into a dagger. His friend keeps talking. *Isom*, he says, *Isom, listen*. But Isom does not stop laughing. Instead, he places a hand on his friend's cheek with a tenderness that is lethal.

He says: *Your daughter is here.*

Then he looks up, at Wisa.

Those eyes. You can tell instantly that they have lived more lives than should be allowed to a body. They are mercurial with personalities, all dangerous, even the kind ones, simply because they belong to a man who no longer operates as a man, who does not believe in the logic followed by civilizations, and so is the one thing most terrifying to the order we place on the chaos around us: unpredictable.

Let me take you home, his friend whispers. *I'm going to carry you—don't fight me. Isom—Isom, don't fight me!*

But Isom is struggling. He finds a rock and hits the traveler over the head; the traveler crumbles and so does Isom, no longer supported.

On his belly now, Isom crawls toward the mango tree. Toward Wisa.

Come down, he says urgently. *Come here and I'll explain.*

Wisa doesn't move, paralyzed by what she is witnessing. Isom reaches out to her, savage. *Come here!*

Slowly, the friend sits up. Wisa can see him clearly now, and she gives a little cry of surprise. It is Grandpa. But it is not Grandpa as she knows him. He is younger, none of the wisdom in his eyes. Blood trickles from his wound, making his hair sticky.

There's no one there, Grandpa says, watching Isom splutter in agitation. He wipes his tears briskly, as he does the blood.

Wisa is transfixed. She didn't know Grandpa had a brother—for they are brothers, the similarities are unmistakable. Even though Isom is ravaged by flaccid skin and wrinkles, she knows he is young. Possibly only a few years older than Kua. Those eyes.

Grandpa shuffles to his brother, propping him against the wall. Isom is exhausted; he falls asleep. Gently, Kua positions him across his shoulders and then they are blown away, both of them, disintegrating into ash that dissolves on a changed wind.

Wisa is alone.

She walks back to the cottage, unsure of what she has just seen. Was it a piece of Esi's past, the way the drifter described? Wisa cannot recall anything different about the moment. Nothing had burst, like an overripe fruit. But now that she thinks about it, the air had smelt different. Cloying and strange, with sounds and scents that didn't belong to a forest. She had glimpsed red sands in the vision, the rock made of a stone not found here.

Grandpa had a brother? And he was mad?

Wisa wonders if Magali knows. If it is a Kilta family secret not shared with her, or if no one but Grandpa knows what happened to his brother. Miqhai knows. She is sure of it; the drifter is in on the secret.

She sneaks into the cottage the way she had fled, via the trees. It is an easy way to steal onto a part of the porch hidden from the windows, and to slip into her room. But when Wisa is still crawling along a branch, she hears voices.

Grandpa—her Grandpa—and Miqhai are awake. They are sitting on Miqhai's ghodra and playing a game of lilta.

She knows she shouldn't. She knows she should go into the cottage and lie down. Nothing good will come of this.

But Wisa stays to listen.

Myung's Diaries

No. CCLXXXVI

Lilta is a game played with fish bones. It has to be the bones of a chand fish, a big-lipped sea creature that gleams silver, and the bones have to be more than a hundred years old.

"How can you tell how old they are?" I ask my lilta guide, a slender girl who has sharpened her teeth into points.

She holds up a bone. "Moon white," she says. "Not snow white or shell white or that shiny, shiny white of pearls. Old bones are like the moon."

Lilta is a game of the ancients. It was played by Esi's drifters, people belonging to the wind, and the rules are ambiguous, often based on the fragile movement of instinct. Winds turn. They change direction, grow stronger, fade. That's how you play lilta—like the wind. The only rules are these: a fistful of chand fish bones and six bird eggs.

"If you play it right," my guide says, "magic happens."

"What kind of magic?"

But this she won't answer, and I follow for game after game, for one year, two, three, waiting for lilta to show me its secrets.

Those who play lilta believe themselves to be descendants of Esi's drifters. They claim to touch something raw and primordial about the black sea each time they play. When they meet, the scent of belonging is overpowering and I am witness to people who have traveled across the black sea to find others like them. Games are played in caves or out by the sea. I am never allowed to participate. But one evening, as I watch a game, my guide glances at me and her eyes widen in wonder. To say she is looking at me is untrue; she is looking above me. And so I look too.

Two ghosts float above my head, playing a game of lilta with smoke-blue eggs and pale bones. The light has bent to offer us a glimpse into another world and we see a different place—wilderness, a cottage in the corner of the frame. Colors sharpen, the picture crystallizes. One ghost wears a coat that is dyed in rainbow colors. The other is older, and strangely familiar. The men look content, the strange pleasure we derive from rituals that make sense only to ourselves. The old man is studying the game. The drifter is studying him.

"Did I tell you about the first time I met Wisa?" the drifter asks.

The mood turns. The old man spins a bird egg; it careens, knocking bones out of alignment.

"I met her in the forest," the drifter says. "She was following a frog. Listening to it speak."

"Did she tell you that?" the man asks.

The drifter nods.

"Don't listen to her," the old man says. "She's fanciful."

The drifter doesn't reply. He's silent so long I imagine the vision has stopped, that the magic is over. I reach up to touch them, but my guide grabs my wrist. "This is the game," she says urgently. "If you play correctly, if you play on true instinct, the wind changes direction for you. You see?"

I do. Are these ghosts a piece of the past or the future? Which way is the wind blowing?

"Kua," the drifter says. He waits for the man to look up. "Friend, she's mad. She's going to make a world."

The man doesn't reply. Then he says softly. "Do you know what could happen to her if you said this to anyone else?"

The drifter looks amused. "I do. Do you know what could happen to you?"

The man spins a bird egg, and it topples four lilta bones. "I want you gone tonight. Don't ever come back."

VIII

Now Wisa lies awake, Magali's hand slipped into hers. She cannot sleep. The events of the night play behind her eyelids. Isom's eyes. Miqhai saying, *Friend, she's mad. She's going to make a world.* And Grandpa's rage. This stays with her most clearly. She has never seen Grandpa angry before. Not like this. He was white with anger, incoherent with it. He looked like he would change the whole island before he let Wisa become mad.

But she is mad.

She knows it. She likes it. She wants her world.

Her unease writhes in her. She turns, and watches Magali sleep. The night is almost over, but the moon has not hidden yet. It is a bright night, and Magali is colored in shades of blue and black, her shoulder rising and falling. Wisa places her fingertip on Magali's nose. She presses, gently at first and then harder, until Magali opens her eyes, groggy and unfocused.

What if I were mad? Wisa says softly.

Magali is awake now. She is taken aback but only for a moment. *Wisa,* she says, *you are mad.*

The sisters stare at each other quietly. This conversation is pivotal; they both sense it.

What if I said Miqhai was right? Wisa whispers. *That I want to make a world.*

Now Magali is terrified. She doesn't know if that is because Wisa admitted to being a worldbuilder or because she has known this conversation was coming for years, ever since Wisa sat on that kitchen table wrapped in a blanket, and she has always wondered how she would react. But the moment doesn't feel so big now that it is here and the answer is easy.

Then I'll help you, Magali says. *I'll help.*

Wisa is silent. Magali waits and waits, trying to understand what her sister is thinking, until the gentle rhythm of the night works its way into her and she falls asleep.

Wisa pokes Magali with her toe. Once. Twice. Thrice—Magali smacks it away.

What? she says, sitting up. This time, she is annoyed. She was dreaming of her parents; they were explaining double sight to her, telling her something about museums and collective memory. And now it is gone.

You don't have to, Wisa says softly.

What?

You don't have to help me. I wouldn't ask you to.

Magali rubs her eyes. *Give me your hand.*

Wisa squints at her.

Wisa, just give me your hand. I won't break it.

Gingerly, Wisa offers it to her.

I choose you, Magali says. *As my sister. Do you choose me?*

It surprises them both, Wisa's reaction. She stares at Magali and then weeps. Suddenly, swiftly—raw and animal-like, her body crumbling into the feeling. Magali stares at her in astonishment. Then she tugs on her hand until Wisa has to crawl across the gap in the beds and onto Magali's ghodra. She crawls straight into Magali's arms.

I choose you, Magali whispers gently to Wisa's neck, stroking her hair. Wisa is sobbing into her shoulder. *Do you choose me?*

Wisa cries for a long time. When she quietens, she says, *yes.*

The night Miqhai leaves, Kua visits the forest.

He travels deep into its heart. Our Grandpa is wise; he knows this is dangerous, that a forest is not a sweet, gentle creature but a beast deadlier than you can comprehend, yet he cannot help himself. He is possessed by an urge that seems logical—he can think it, twist it, break it down into its parts—and yet lives beyond his grasp.

Luddites know you cannot read a forest, not like you read a piece of parchment. A forest is not flat or fixed; it cannot be conveyed through dead words. You live in it and hope that, in time, its patterns become recognizable to you, its ways of working no longer a mystery. Then if you are good, if you are Kua, you wake up one day and the forest maps itself out for you, a multitude and singularity, chaos and order, and you are both observer and part.

Kua imagines it is the same with madness. For years, he has chased it, and for years, it has slipped from him. Yet he reaches over and over, desperate and urgent, furious, to stab it into shape on the page—to hold it in his fingers in its true form, so he may go to little Wisa and pluck it out of her.

In their cottage, Wisa slips off her ghodra. Magali sleeps spreadeagle, her breath slow and even. Wisa kisses her cheek lightly.

I'm sorry, she whispers. *You'll be sad, I know. But I'll come back. And then we can live in my world together.*

Then she melts out of the house and out of the colony. She doesn't look back.

Only four years until the festival of madness.

Jinn's Great-Grandmother's Story: The Real One

Look, imp, these stories are complicated. They're river snakes, eh? Coming to choke you at night. Tree roots that only want to eat your heart. You're scared? No, I thought not. Don't tell your mother, though; she can get very angry. Our little secret.

She taps her nose. Jinn doesn't know what the gesture means but he taps his too.

Complicated stories tell you this: you can't trust anything. You listening? Everything is a lie and the truth, at the same time, and you have to walk with your arms out and your breath sucked in—go on, show me. Deeper breath. That's it. You have to be careful not to fall.

Fall where? Fall where? Look, who is telling the stories? You or me? I thought so. You don't interrupt a story. You listen and swallow it whole, where it will grow birds in your stomach that will slowly peck out your heart. You scared now? No nightmares? No, I thought not. You're an old soul, wise beyond your years. No river snake is going to catch you—I've seen you climb.

So I'll tell you a good story today. The real story. The one you'll wake up longing for in a while, although not now; you're too young. But in a while. Your mother told you craftsmen have wolf teeth and blood eyes, yes? But that's nothing compared to what *we* once were. Not the craftsmen—us. You, me, Esites. Once upon a time, we were alchemists.

Ul-che-me.

No, alchemists. Al-che-mist. You've met one; they're all over the bazaars, selling gold like common thieves. These are not the alchemists I'm talking about. These are frauds, pale imitations of history. A bazaar alchemist tells you he knows magic, you run, eh? Run as far as you can. A craftsman knows more than these tricksters. The alchemists of this story are different. They're great. Here's the secret, little one—they're the ones we've forgotten.

Ul-che-*mit*.

All right, let's start again. Once upon a time, there is a story no one can remember. It is impossible to remember it because this story is like a river: the water never stays still. But still we try to remember—drifters can't help themselves. You know who a drifter is?

Friend.

That's right—they're Great-grandma's friends. You've seen Loilc and Piy with their coats, eh? You've hidden in them. Great-grandma had a coat just like that once. She gave it away to come here so she could have your grandma and your grandma could have your mother and your mother could have you.

Drifters are like the luddites; they're good people. But here's the truth, imp: we're haunted by a story. It's an old one and no one can remember it. Most people don't care. But drifters—we can't help ourselves. We need to know. It's hunger, eh? Where do you get hungry? In your stomach, that's right. Our hunger is all over. We don't just carry bits of the island; we don't just move over land. We *hear* bits of time. Listen closely, boy—hold this tightly in your fist. You're a drifter too; you get that from me. And one day this story is going to come for you like it comes for all of us. It's going to haunt you.

His great-grandmother pauses, squints. Scared now? Jinn shakes his head. Want to hear more? Jinn nods. Won't tell your mother? Jinn nods again.

Good boy. When you're older I'll tell you about the first time I heard a snippet of time. Scared the coat off me. But for now, all you need to know is this. Drifters hear bits from the past, but we don't hear them *in order.* They don't make sense. And that's what eats at us. We need to know how it all fits—these bits Loilc, Piy and I have. The bits that are with other drifters.

We tried for a while, as a community. Collected them, tried to form a whole. But it doesn't work. The bits are too many, the drifters living and dying too quickly, their minds remembering the pieces wrong so that by the time the snippet of the past ended, they had already recorded it differently from how they heard it. It's like trying to make a song from babel.

It drove us mad, imp. Drifters were throwing themselves off cliffs. Tying stones to their feet and dropping into rivers. Hanging from trees.

Don't be scared now—it's just a story. Don't be scared. Look at it. Look at the hard truth; you've got to. We stopped collecting the pieces after a while. Decided that it wasn't for the part to know the whole. But it haunts us.

She leans forward, rubs her knees slowly.

Then I came here and found it.

Jinn claps his hands to his mouth.

Once upon a time—this is where it begins—once upon a time, there lived an island of alchemists. Real alchemists, not fraudsters interested in making gold. These alchemists were fascinated by an element more elusive: understanding. They wanted to know their island, really know, the same way their island knew them. They spent their days studying the black sea, piecing together knowledge in great stone structures that reached for the sky. Hunger ate into them. Your mother will tell you hunger is bad. Don't listen to her. Hunger makes large things possible; it changes the black sea. And that's what these alchemists did. They studied and practiced until they found the strangest element of all—a thread of time.

Then the alchemists disappeared. Poof! All they left behind were crumbling stone structures. And what they learned changed into . . . craft. Craft is not as powerful as alchemy, but it allows us to shape our island to make life easier. Drifters ask themselves, where did the alchemists go?

I'll tell you. Nowhere. They stayed on Esi; they became us. And we don't remember because it was a long time ago.

She smiles and taps Jinn's nose.

Very long. Almost as long ago as the beginning of the black sea.

Jinn doesn't understand. His great-grandmother's story has grown too many branches. He rubs his eyes. But his great-grandmother is not done. She's carried away on an urge that's primal, that's larger than her listener.

I met a traveler once—his name was Cio Qual. He said he was famous, but they all say that. He was sad when I met him, so I cheered him up. I gave him one of Esi's famous rocks, what drifters call the "stone eggs." You know—the ones that glint with hidden depths. No? I'll get a drifter to show you one someday. Cio was so happy with this stone, he told me a secret. He said he'd been studying all the maps of Esi to try and understand how to draw the island. You know what he found? He found that there were hundreds of maps of our island. And you know what else he found?

She is leaning forward, peering at Jinn expectantly. I'm very small, Jinn wants to say but instead he shakes his head obligingly.

He found that each map was *different*. Some slightly different, but others—it was almost like it was a different island. A different island, imp! Imagine that. He said Esi's trees were so tall because they were special trees. They couldn't die. Instead, they lifted their great roots and walked all over the island, moving mountains out of the way and shifting lakes. Slowly, so slowly, you could not see it in one lifetime, or two or three. But over centuries . . . you'd make a different topography.

She claps her hands, delighted.

But I'm not done yet, imp. Once he told me this, I began to wonder: if there are hundreds of maps of Esi, and each of them is different, then how *old* is this island? And once I asked that . . . I saw it. I saw it so clearly that I couldn't believe I hadn't seen it before.

You know what I think? I think the alchemists changed the island's time. They meddled with the elements until they put the island's time to sleep, until they created a land that couldn't die. Esi's been alive for a lot longer than any island should be. And the longer it lives, the more memories it collects. A growing, sprawling forest of time. This is why they say luddites are the best at remembering; no one understands a forest like a luddite. You want to know why we go mad every hundred years? Because once every hundred years, we glimpse a piece of this forest; we shed reality and glimpse, quickly, furtively, the enormity of plural, instant time, everything all at once. And we lose ourselves.

Grandma!

Jinn is scooped up in his mother's arms; her hands cover his ears. He can hear his mother arguing, a furious hiss and tremor. He can hear his great-grandmother shout. And this—a line that he doesn't know now if he heard or imagined.

Look at the maps, Lira. Look at them!

Two Sisters, Two Paths

I

This is how it happens.

Magali wakes up to find Wisa's ghodra empty and her blankets folded. Wisa is not a neat person.

At breakfast, she asks Grandpa if he has seen Wisa. He tells her no, but she often sketches at the river by morning light. He is preoccupied. The drifter is gone, Magali notices, and the story behind his leaving sits heavy on Grandpa's shoulders. She doesn't ask; the less said about Miqhai the better.

After her chores, she goes to the river. There is no Wisa there, but a fisherman says he saw a girl walk past at dawn. She must be back in the colony by now—perhaps with Jinn?

So Magali visits Jinn. Then the butcher's, the bazaar, Grandpa again, the fields, the river once more, the forest, back to the colony. At each stop, Magali feels as if she has just missed her sister, that if she were only two steps faster, she would stumble upon Wisa crouched by a flower, admonishing it. But at every new place, there is no Wisa, until Magali learns she was only ever chasing a ghost.

Why, I saw her leave the colony at night, Old Silu says. *I woke up and there she was, a shadow in the mist. I'm sorry, dear, I thought you knew.*

Magali did not know. This is when it dawns on her: she has been abandoned.

Old Silu's seeing things, Jinn says, half-walking and half-jogging to keep up with her. He's been by her side all day, ever since she came to him and asked if he'd seen Wisa. *Wisa has got lost listening to something; she'll be home by night, you'll see.*

Magali only walks faster, trying to leave him behind. This is his fault. If she hadn't been so taken with him and his silly charm, if she had looked—truly looked—at her sister last night, if she had stayed in the garden and kept an eye on Miqhai . . .

If she had only done what siblings do and protected her.

She decides, then and there, to stop speaking to him. And once she decides that, she stops speaking to everyone.

It is an easy decision to make, for there isn't much to say with Wisa gone. Wisa doesn't come back the next day or the day after, and then not the next month or the next three. Grandpa goes to the market for the first six weeks, hoping to find her wandering among sailors or making a living among merchants. But each evening he comes back alone. Magali can tell by the slump of his shoulders that there is no trace of her. No one has even *seen* her.

This is how she knows Wisa left of her own choosing. No one can find Wisa if she doesn't want to be found.

The colony is shaken. A few of them help Grandpa by going to Boba and making inquires. But after the fourth day, this stops. A change has come over them; a new narrative ferments. Wisa's disappearance transforms from a tragedy into a blessing. In the street, people glance away from Magali and then glance back, as if daring her to ask what they are thinking.

In the year that follows, Grandpa and she eat in silence. They never take Wisa's name. At times, she can feel Grandpa watching her and the weight of his pain. How does she tell him this is her fault? So she takes his hand and kisses his knuckles; she smiles; she tries to tell him, with no words, that she is all right.

The older luddites avoid her now. Not overtly; they couldn't do that to Magali, the child they once loved. But they keep their distance. When she brings them fruit from her garden, they stay inside their doorway. *Just leave it by the steps*, they say, refusing to meet her eyes. Do they think madness is contagious? And if they do, how do they believe they haven't caught it by now?

The colony gossips about Wisa; they examine her every action in a cold and cruel light. Didn't Wisa remind you of Isom? You could tell the similarity immediately. Everyone seems able to believe Wisa was and was not a Kilta: they are able to say in the same breath *she did not belong* and *what can you expect? It runs in the family.*

Be glad they haven't burned your house down, Lira calls after Magali once, vicious, and Magali considers marching up to her and baring her teeth. Considers saying: Like they didn't burn your house down when they learned about your grandmother's stories? I know what you dream, Lira. How deep your rot goes.

But she doesn't.

And still luddites gather at Grandpa's doorstep. They ask for medicines for the upcoming festival; they tell him about their dreams. Grandpa still goes out to draw memories, although the drawings he brings back are less vibrant now. Magali cannot understand it. How can the colony whisper about them, and still call Grandpa their memory keeper? How could they have loved her so much—still love her, they claim—and not want to touch her?

There was always a circle of behavior you could dance within. Anything outside of it, and the colony as a collective cannot accept it. She turns to tell her sister this, and finds her still not there.

—

When she is at home alone, she lets the sun sink beneath the horizon without lighting any lamps. Then she ties a blindfold around her eyes, and walks from the kitchen through the hall, into the sisters' bedroom. The first time she does this, she trips over the chair and goes sprawling. The second time, she misses the door to smack into the wall. Again and again, she does it. By the twentieth time, when she can navigate past the kitchen table, around the low seating into the hall, and into the bedroom with her hands by her sides, she pulls off the blindfold in triumph. But the moment it is off, her triumph dies.

The house is quiet. Wisa is gone, and Magali didn't see it coming. No amount of blindfolding now, of learning her surroundings so intimately she can dream them, makes up for that.

She goes to the mango tree, because it was there that Wisa and her sisterhood started. She stands at its roots, where young Magali felt that blind urge to get between young Wisa and the wall.

Why did Wisa leave? If she was scared, she could have come to Magali. Magali would have helped.

Did Wisa not believe her?

Magali climbs. The years with Wisa have made her better and she is able to reach Jinn's faded mark, and then climb beyond that. She doesn't know what she is searching for, but she doesn't care. *Make me mad*, she asks the tree. *Make me mad so that I can find her, and then kill her for leaving.*

The structure obliges.

It is like the night Magali's double sight grew out of control. Again, the ruins transform. This time, there are Myung, Laleh, Blajine and all the Kilta ghosts—and ancient Mad Magali herself, staring up at her thin, twenty-year-old figure. But there are also the alchemists. Thousands of them, crowded into the structure, pulling from their pans a silver, web-like material, murmuring. And there, around it all, its corridors dissolving and reforming as they spin and twist, is the museum of collective memory.

Over them, the trees are walking.

Giant trees are lifting their old roots and clambering along the island. They are bending their great canopies to look at her. Lakes flow into the stone structure and then out. Fish flap on the dry ground and then melt into bones that press into the soil before disappearing. Boulders shrink into tiny stones. The mango tree is both a sapling and the majestic beauty Magali sits on now, its branches reaching for the moon. Magali is viewing the entire history of the island sped up, from this one vantage point. She is a witness to its secrets.

Then she is buried under a landslide of sound. Voices, song, memory. She clutches the bough of the mango tree, desperate not to fall off. She's elated, caught in the vortex in front of her, invincible, alive!

But then it grows stronger.

It drags her forward, into its epicenter. She can feel her grip on the tree loosening. She can see the outlines of the stone structure of her present fading. She wants to go—she wants to fall, be larger than the limits of her body. She wants to touch these wonders across all of time. She wants it so badly, it scares her.

It is this fear that saves her. It drags her back into herself; her hands tighten around the branch; she presses her body against the tree and clings on. *No*, she thinks, panicked. She doesn't want to be anyone else but Magali.

Then the pull is gone, and everything is quiet.

Magali doesn't open her eyes. She is crying, silent tears she cannot control. She doesn't know whether it is from sorrow or gratefulness.

When she looks down, there is Jinn.

Her Jinn.

Jinn has lived through his own kind of madness.

For a year now, he's tried to talk to Magali Kilta. But she runs at the sight of him; if he corners her, she pretends she cannot hear. What has he done wrong? Does she regret that night? He imagines her curled in shame at the memories—memories that give him so much joy—and it cleaves him. Is he so unlovable? But even this he could bear, if she would only speak to him.

His mother's fears have grown into giants; they sit with them at the dinner table. *She was a bhavla*, Lira tells him as Jinn mashes his rice with his fingers. *Zia says it is obvious now that she's left. She did her mischief and she went. Are you listening to me? You spent your time with a bhavla—you have to be cautious now. Do the rituals of sanity twice a day. No, thrice. If you feel anything strange, come to me. You must come instantly to me. Jinn? Are you listening?*

Jinn eats mouthful after mouthful and doesn't answer. It is his great-grandmother's stories all over again. The panic in his mother's voice, her desperation. She had begged him to forget them and never repeat them to anyone else. *I can't lose you*, she had said. Overcome with guilt, he had listened.

This time, he feels no guilt. The tightness in his chest is loss, and it has nothing to do with her. He can feel his mother's eyes boring into him, but he doesn't care. Just goes on eating. She reaches out then and stills his hand with hers.

I know it's hard, she says. Some of her fear is gone; she sounds like the mother he remembers when he was younger. Full of love and care. *But the Kiltas are corrupted. No one else may say it, but I know it. You can't go there anymore.*

Jinn pulls his hand away. He keeps eating.

Jinn!

He goes to the Kilta cottage. He knows this is silly: it only strengthens the story that Wisa has turned both him and Magali mad. What he should do is stay away and be as normal as possible, so that all hint of suspicion lifts. But it is not physically possible—his feet lead him back to her.

When Magali is inside the house, he sits at the garden wall. When Magali is out, he has tea with Kua.

Once, Kua says gently: *You shouldn't come.*

Jinn's throat closes; he wants to weep. Is this what Kua thinks of him? That coming here is a burden for Jinn, and he needs to be released?

How do you tell the grandfather of the woman you love that if you stopped coming to their cottage just to be in the same space as the people who once loved you for all that you were, you would crumble? Jinn doesn't have the words. So he holds his emotion in his throat and shakes his head—a small shake, which is all he can manage.

Kua understands. In that moment, Jinn imagines Kua's estimation of him changes, although he cannot tell for sure; maybe he is just desperate for Kua to like him because Magali no longer does. But in truth, he wants Kua to like him because he likes Kua. Because this is the house of Wisa and Magali, and it has their qualities: a kind of burnished honesty, a lack of guile and a willingness to love with everything one has. And Jinn knows that comes from Kua.

The colony still looks up to you, Jinn whispers. *They don't blame you for Wisa; they know you have a big heart.*

It is the only time Kua smiles, as if to say "I appreciate it" and "I wasn't worried about their opinions." It makes Jinn feel better, like the Kua they remembered is there somewhere, underneath the sadness.

For a year, Jinn climbs the eucalyptus tree alone. Ava invites him to the dances; Ori calls him on the evenings they drink fenni. He goes sometimes, but not always. What he wants is the sisters. To climb a tree and touch the clouds, but still look farther. To be all of yourself with friends so completely you don't know you're doing it. He thinks about his great-grandmother. She was a giant of a woman, big-boned and resilient, always looking at life like she could squeeze a bit more juice out of it. He imagines her watching him in the tree, brows furrowed.

What are you doing up there? she'd shout. *What you want is on the ground. Go get it!*

Esi is turning into water. This is the only way Jinn knows how to describe it—like they are all floating on a lake that was once a pond and that will grow into a sea. Like nothing knows how to be solid anymore. Sometimes he dreams of the future, but then he catches himself. Who knows how the festival will change them? What the future looks like? There will be a fault line in time, a crack that means the present no longer flows from the past and the future no longer comes from the present. He is sure of it. It takes great imagination to look at the other side of the fault line. He doesn't have it.

But if everything is turning into water, then he wants a raft with the people he cares about on it. He knows this. He is sure of it.

His great-grandmother barks: *Come down, boy! Go get it!*

―

And so here he is, standing under the mango tree, staring at Magali as she clings to a branch. For a moment he thinks she is Wisa, and then he realizes why that is—Magali is so gaunt, she looks like Wisa when she first came to the colony.

His rage comes from everywhere, at once. Magali is climbing down from the tree slowly, as if she doesn't trust her limbs. Stubborn, frustrating, ridiculous Magali—punishing herself and him and the whole damn world, always. Slicing him out, carving his heart into pieces—and for what?

Are we going to talk about it? he shouts.

Magali's foot has barely touched the ground. She stumbles, taken aback by his anger, deeper than anything she thought him capable of. Good. He steps closer. *Wisa leaves and then you disappear too—poof!, not a word, no explanation. What? Her name stings you? It hurts to say it out loud? It must because no one says it anymore. It's like she never lived. I didn't dream her, you know. Her paint mark is on that mango tree. She's your sister.*

Her face opens in shock. *How dare you—*

He cuts her off. *It's not right to slice her out! Burn her from conversations. When my great-grandmother died, my mother wouldn't talk about the stories she told me. If I mentioned them, she pretended she didn't hear. So I stopped talking about them but it made my great-grandmother smaller, trapped in some corner of my head. You can forget things, Magali, if you don't talk about them. They can disappear. Do you* want *her to disappear?*

How could he even ask that? Magali wants to hit him, to cry. She wants to say he doesn't know what she has been through, but then she realizes he probably does. If there is one person, apart from Grandpa, who knows what she has been through, it is Jinn.

Jinn is still shouting. *So she went away!* he says. *So what? She'll come back or we'll go find her. You don't just . . . You're Magali Kilta! You don't just fade.*

It's our fault, she yells back, wanting this conversation to be over. *My fault. That night, in the forest; if we hadn't got caught up, if I had paid more attention . . .*

She expects this to cut him to the bone. But he only looks incredulous.

You're joking, right? You have to be joking. Because if this is why you've been ignoring me for one year, Magali, I swear—

—I had a responsibility—

—*You're mad! You think if you were there that night, she would have stayed? This is Wisa! She does what she wants. And if you had only talked to me, I could have told you that. Told you how incredibly stupid this is. I am here, Magali! I've been here all this time. I knew her too. I was friends with her too. But you won't see that because you're obsessed with suffering alone. Needing someone isn't a weakness, and I don't know how to make you see that.*

Magali closes her eyes. He is right, and she doesn't know what to do with it. God, what she put him through this year: running away from him, pretending to see through him. Her shame is hot and deep.

I am sorry, she whispers.

It's not enough, he says. *This is the second time you've done this. Promise me you won't keep burning us to the ground. I can't keep . . . coming back.*

She reaches for his hand, then stops herself. *I promise.*

In the stories, mended friendships are bright and eager; each friend unburdens secrets they have been yearning to share in their time apart. But this mending is only awkward. The hurt lingers, as do the uglier and angrier echoes of themselves.

I should go back, Magali says when the silence stretches. *I promised I'd pluck the brinjals before dinner.*

Wait! Jinn doesn't want her to leave. He rummages around in his pockets and with a soft *aha!* pulls out a stone egg. *I found it in the river*, he says, *while listening to the fish. You know, like Wisa taught us? They're a strange lot, let me tell you—not very nice at all. Anyway, I got it for you. Ishita, the drifter, not the weird fruit lady at Boba market, she says there are probably more like this along the island. They're just . . . I thought you'd like it.*

Jinn is lying. He didn't just find the stone egg on the riverbed; he spent weeks hunting for it. It is the rock his great-grandmother described to him once: the Esi stone egg. He remembers her saying she gave it to a traveler to cheer him up, and the traveler told her about the changing Esi maps. She called it her good luck charm. Jinn hopes it can be his good luck charm too.

Magali holds the stone egg on her palm. It is blue-green, smooth to the touch. She lifts it up, into the sunlight, and it . . . moves. Light runs off it, flaring on flecks of gold. Inside the stone, there's a sea. Magali twists it, this way and that, and the colors move with the light—jade, sea green, aqua and black swirling into each other like ocean currents viewed from above. It's wonderful.

And now Magali is crying, great heaving sobs she can't contain, and Jinn is holding her close to him with relief. He says softly and happily, *I knew you'd like it.*

—

After that, Magali is happy. She is happy even though she feels guilty for it, but she has been starved of light for so long that she clutches this happiness and refuses to let go. She may not deserve this, but she needs it. Jinn and she spend every evening together, and in his company, she feels some of herself return. Jinn was right. He knew Wisa, and he knows Magali. She can be all of herself with him.

Her happiness infects Grandpa. He is still older than she ever remembered him looking, but he smiles now too. Slowly and more rarely than before, but it is there. They say Wisa's name again. Jinn comes over for tea, and they talk about her. Jinn and Magali tell Grandpa about the mango tree and the night of climbing. They laugh about how Wisa followed Ava once, slipping milows down her dress. Grandpa tells them about the time Wisa snuck into Old Silu's house and stole her prized figs.

But Jinn is wise. He knows it is not enough for the three of them to form a shelter of their own. The festival is three years away now, and like it or not, the luddite colony is their refuge. They live in a society. *You need to meet the others*, he tells Magali. *Sia, Ori, the rest of them. They need to see you for themselves. You have to put their minds at ease.*

They don't want to see me.

How would you know? You haven't spoken to anyone in a year.

Magali is resistant to the idea. But Jinn goes to Grandpa, who then sits her down and explains, over elderflower tea, why she should do it. It is important for the colony to remember her as she was.

Part of her wants to remind Grandpa of the terrible things the colony said last year. She wants to say, *I don't want to be the old Magali. I want to be the person Wisa made me.*

But she knows they are right. So she goes for fenni nights with Jinn and is startled by how everyone receives her. People used to cross the alleyway to avoid her. Now when she smiles at them, they smile back.

Of course people weren't avoiding you! Jinn says, as if it's the most obvious thing in the world. *You were just terrifying for a while. Sia used to shiver and shake every time you looked at her.*

Magali doesn't know if she believes him. Still, the luddite colony holds its love and its suspicion in equal measure, as simultaneous truths that don't contradict each other. So when she smiles, old friends open their arms to welcome her back. Jinn introduces her like a rare bird just returned from tropical lands.

Look who's here! he shouts. *I told you she wasn't gone.*

Her peers laugh; they talk to her like the last year hasn't happened. No one mentions Wisa, but Magali doesn't expect them to. She didn't even expect this much.

Some people still avoid her. Ava walks away when she approaches; Freyn always follows. But the others make fun of them for it. *Ava's been seeing madness everywhere*, Sia says, winking at Magali. *It's a wonder she's not crazy herself.*

And as her peers change, so do the adults. Magali opens her cottage door to find neighbors on the doorstep, plying her and Grandpa with food. *It's my secret recipe*, Dazane says, bringing over roast loomirs and trying to fit the dish through the door. *Welcome back, dear. Don't tell anyone the recipe or I'll have to bury you.*

All Magali can see for miles is love. She doesn't understand how it happened, but it is there. She doesn't know if her own grief blinded her to it, if the colony has changed its narrative again or if it was only a few people who thought her mad last year, and the rest kept their opinions to themselves. She can't tell. She doesn't care. This is good enough.

It is good enough even when Ava hisses to her, *You can't fool me.* It is good enough even when Jinn's mother catches her outside their cottage and digs her nails into her wrist. *You're not mad, yes?* she asks.

Magali is alarmed. Lira looks terrible, her skin clammy and fish-like, her eyes darting from side to side. The question comes out of nowhere;

Magali is here to collect a sprig of red cabbage and see if she can catch a glimpse of Jinn. She is still holding the cabbage.

Lira chuckles, and the sound crawls up Magali's spine. *Don't be upset, don't be upset*, she says. *Only have to ask. It runs in your family.*

No, Magali says cautiously. *Not mad.*

Don't be upset, Lira says again. *You're making my son mad, you know. What kind of a mother would I be if I didn't ask? I have to ask, don't I?*

The wounds from Lira's nails stay for days afterward.

Jinn finds out. Magali doesn't know how, but here he is, bounding up their steps to apologize. There is an urgency to him, as if he's afraid Magali won't be there if he tarries for too long. As if she will have shut him out again.

It is my great-grandmother, he says. *I think she told my mum the same stories and they sit in her. She is easily scared but she doesn't mean harm. Honestly. She won't do it again.*

He says this earnestly, looking her in the eye. He wears his heart so openly, her own twists. How can anyone this soft and good survive?

Magali?

She takes his hand in hers. *Forget it*, she says, and she puts all the love she can into those two words. She doesn't say, *I wasn't upset; I am only worried about your mother.* But he seems to hear it anyway, for he bows his head and covers her hand with his.

Thank you, he whispers.

It is difficult to say how time stitches things, in what pattern. You look up one day and think, oh, I have everything I wanted, and you don't know how it happened. Or you look across to the person you hold dear and whom you now share most of your time with, and try to remember a time when they were foreign to you, when you grew in different soils and toward different skies. It is often unimaginable.

This is how it is with her and Jinn. It is not the amount of time they spend together, although they *do* spend most of their days together. It is as if Wisa's leaving tied a thread between them that binds them forever. No one sees Magali as clearly as Jinn can. And she loves him in the same way—with a sharpness that observes a person as a whole, good and bad, and loves all of it.

She doesn't tell him that, of course.

It feels strange to say it in words. Jinn has been a friend so long, and occasionally an enemy, that to ask him *do you think we're lovers?* is mortifying. Especially after the night they shared in the forest, and then her decision to ignore him for a year. She doesn't deserve him. The friendship is enough, Magali tells herself. I am content.

But, of course, she isn't and so she spends a lot of time dropping hints. She asks if it is true he and Ava were once promised to each other. If Sia and him were lovers during the year that Magali was considered mad by the colony. Or is there someone else he loves? He can tell her. She'll help him—that is what friends are for.

It is childish. She knows this, but she cannot help herself. It is as if the words arrive on their own. Jinn spends a lot of time laughing easily and ignoring these statements. He's developed a new calmness around her, an ease of self that is attractive and irritating. Magali wants him to be as agitated as her. It annoys her when he isn't. Wisa would know what to do, Magali thinks and her pain is there, although not as sharp. She wonders where her sister is. She hopes she is okay.

You know, she says to Jinn one day when they're sitting on the tree that skims along the river, *I thought you'd be the one to leave. Out of the three of us. Because you—oh, it's stupid, but because you disappeared when we were young.*

When I told you I didn't know my great-grandmother's stories?

It seems like such a small thing now. Magali feels foolish for mentioning it. She doesn't confirm or deny it, just dips her big toe into the water and makes lazy circles with it.

I never left, Jinn says. *I was right here. You stopped talking to* me.

You were different, Magali says.

She sneaks a sidelong glance at him. He looks contemplative, as if he cannot deny this. Then he closes his eyes and lies down on the branch. The sun catches his eyelashes, and Magali fights the urge to run her fingertip along them. If Wisa were here, she'd definitely laugh at her sister.

I don't think I'll ever leave, Jinn says lightly, his eyes still closed. *I suspect I love you.*

He never says it again. But once is enough for Magali, as is the hard, answering joy in her.

And so another two years pass. The colony falls back into its seasonal rhythms, even as the island falls apart around them. Jinn spends most evenings at Magali's house; she knows Grandpa is glad of the company. Grandpa calls them gemels: two trees grown so entwined that they've grafted onto each other. He says it softly, with a secret smile he doesn't try to hide, and Magali's happiness is hushed and hard. It's real.

They go back to the cave only once. They look at the pattern with changed eyes.

What do you think she was looking for? Jinn asks.

I don't know, Magali says. *But I hope she finds it.*

Myung's Diaries

No. CM

Kilam birds are teal, with crimson tails more than twice their length. When they dance, they take to the skies above cliffs, and the rough winds contort these tails into astonishing shapes.

The bird chroniclers draw these dances in charcoal, in powerful brushstrokes and light lines. Alone on these cliffs, they have grown attached to their subjects. Involved. Ask them and they tell you that mankind is not separate from nature but a part; birds imitate us as we imitate them; the past can be found anywhere.

For kilam birds do not only dance to mate. Flocks of them dance in thunderstorms, where thunder cracks the sky and lightning shows us new ways of seeing. In the sketches, the birds' wings are bent in intensity, their eyes feverishly human. When the storm ends, the kilam birds descend to the beach and remain there for days; they are shaken. Life returns to normal only slowly and it is some time before the birds are wheeling in the clouds again.

For some birds, however, life has never been normal. These are the kilam birds who dance without storms. They dance until they are exhausted, then they drop to the ground, rest and dance again. Day and night, they do this. Some of them forget to eat. Others plummet from the sky into the ocean and drown. On mooned nights, you can see bird bodies contorting into shapes not meant for their species, straining for a glimpse of a foreign life.

When these birds finally return to land, they are changed. They never fly again. They wander amid rocks to hunt shadows. They sleep on shadows of branches, peck at the shadow of a fruit, stab at the waves to catch the shadows of crabs that float on the surface. In time, they starve and their bodies are consumed by the land.

They are, for all intents and purposes, mad.

II

Wisa spends these three years trying to go mad.

Not mad the way Esites talk about it, where you rock back and forth and whisper about ideas you have. Truly mad, where you shed the shackles of anything that holds you to a time and a place. Where you change how you see, so that you can glimpse bits of the black sea not meant for human eyes. Centuries later, bird chroniclers will find this type of madness in certain kilam birds. They will watch them fling themselves off cliffs and nearly drown themselves in the sea in an attempt to see what is not meant for their species. *What drives them?* the chroniclers ask in their notes. We have no answers. We watch Wisa do it now.

She travels everywhere. She keeps to the wilderness; she avoids people. For a brief while, she follows the bazaar alchemists, wondering if they have any tricks to teach her. But they truly are con artists. Next, she goes to the craftsmen in the red sands; she hears they're taking new apprentices. Maybe craft is her way to make this world. But after a few months of learning with them, she realizes craft is a pale imitation of what she needs. So she asks the island for help.

Tell me how to find the alchemists.

But Wisa is still too much of a *girl* to understand what the trees can tell her. She needs to shed her skin. So she wanders, eating the roots and fruits Grandpa taught her were safe to eat, listening carefully.

Esi is changing. The change has shifted from the community level, and is moving now to the level of the land.

The best way to describe it is in the folktales of the Esites themselves. The people in the whalebone mountains have a story about their early existence. They believe the mountains were formed by a tribe of cosmic whales that wandered the black sea looking for a place to rest. When they found the island of Esi, they arranged themselves in a line, shrugged off their thick blue-black skins and fell asleep. And there they remain to this date. The mountain tribes have a saying: *Beware the whales for they are not dead, only sleeping.* They believe there will be an "awakening"—the day a great whale will open its eyes and the small humans will find themselves staring at it.

The myth of the purple forest also speaks of an awakening, although the people call it "mara," which means "moment of death." It is when you are staring into the dense foliage of the forest, leaf and insects and dripping water. You are alone, yet you are poised and terrified, for you feel—

—a leomir, already mid-air, inches from you, claws unsheathed and fangs gleaming. You look up and meet eyes. That gaze, only a split second but charged, is mara.

In fact, all of Esi has a name or myth for it. Communities along the coast call it "signi," the moment when the sea climbs to the sky in a wall of water. Those in the red sands speak of a day the dead roots will awaken and churn up the earth. In each of these stories, there is a moment where you and the land lock eyes, a moment of recognition.

Across Esi now, this moment is building.

Esites complain of feeling cold under a blazing sun. They say the ground sometimes loses its firmness; it rolls and rollicks as water. Travelers swear the trees are bending their heads to look at them curiously; others claim they went to sleep in one patch of land and awoke in another. Drifters are losing days, others are gaining some. It is as if the island has opened across channels in dimensions more plural than a human can know and it is bringing with it debris and behaviors uncanny and alive.

The festival is two years away.

Across this landscape, Wisa looks for her world. Her feet crack and bleed, but she keeps walking. The longer she walks, the fatter the world in her head grows, until it is begging to burst into reality. But she doesn't know how to pull it from her and make it true.

She finds her answer in a stone structure. She comes across it by accident, nestled at the edge of the red sands. There is no mango tree in this structure. Instead, a trumpet vine grows at the tip of its arched walls, spilling red flowers like forked tongues. It is the first plant she's seen in weeks. The structure is sweet and shaded, and Wisa cries, for it is a beauty only luddites could appreciate and hers were far away.

But it makes her think of young Grandpa and his mad brother, Isom. Of Isom's eyes and the way he stared across time at her.

Your daughter is here.

Wisa tugs at her eyelids. Over and over, Grandpa sat in the forest and drew the shape of madness, trying to pin it to the page. But choosing to draw it chased the spirit away; it would not be held. Perhaps Isom, looking across time, knew something her Grandpa did not. Perhaps it has always been obvious, what she has to do.

To be mad is to be open.

We have seen this moment before. When Magali climbed the mango tree and asked to go mad, when the ruins transformed for her, she faced this moment as well. A moment where you can either retreat from the chasm and find yourself again, or fall forward into the unknown. Magali retreated. Wisa falls.

Where Wisa goes, we cannot follow.

This journey presents itself to us as rotten fruit; memories slide off our palms in pulp. This is hers alone. All we have are flashes of imagery and a song of dissolution. Wisa, pressing yellow berries into her mouth. Wisa, smashing her hand over and over again with a volcanic rock. A stew of rye, blackened by fungus. The striated chewiness of the tart mushrooms. Colors—behind your eyes, in your nails, in the tips of branches bending to paint you. The burst and flare of fireants eating you. The pricking of a needle as you go through your memories one by one, orphan, skywalker, daughter, sister, alchemizing them into the perfect understanding of yourself as a smooth, flat mirror—and then smashing it to cut yourself with the shards. Writhing bodies all around you, other

Esites in different places and times, trying to reach where you are going. Pluck ideas from their hands. Try different mushrooms. Search out coral molluscs. The spikes of a poisonous river fish, stuck all over your body. A weatherworn and skeptical woman watching you, her clothes not from this island. You reach for her but she does not reach back. The slow, swimming dissolution of reality, like sugar melting and then crystallizing, the gaps between the crystals flowing in three, four, five dimensions. Another woman, also not from this island, younger and possibly timeless, and she is reaching for you, worried and agitated—*Myung*, you think and you don't know where the word comes from—but she cannot get a hold. For every splinter of light, you see shadow, and as you comprehend the landscape of space, so you glimpse—only glimpse, the smallest crack—the landscape of time.

In this landscape, Wisa meets the alchemists. She travels back in time to the early days of Esi, so far back now we don't know how to count it, and meets those who began the festival of madness. She sits with them as they boil metal into gold. She reads their texts and wanders through their majestic stone structures, watching as they reach for an understanding of the black sea. She reaches with them. The trees on this Esi are young; they tower only twenty feet above her. When she touches them, they whisper but it is not the same torrent she hears in her time. The whispers are few; they are light, like laughter.

The alchemists welcome her with open arms. They call her *sister*. Here, she learns how to make her world.

III

It is evening. Magali walks from Boba market, carrying a parcel wrapped in leaf. It is the third anniversary of Wisa's leaving. One year until the festival of madness.

The parcel contains blue oysters, not the dried powder but fresh ones. Grandpa always has trouble sleeping on this day, so Magali tries to get these for him. It is not easy; you have to hunt out the more questionable sellers of Boba market to find them.

This time, she has had to wade through a crowd unlike anything she's seen. The docks were thronged, agitated. Travelers swarmed from ships, hoping to glimpse Esi's festival of madness. They brought crates of books; they packed supplies to last a lifetime.

The drifters talk of travelers who slip into the forests and hide, hoping that the Esites will forget about them. Then, when the festival rolls around and Esites force all non-natives onto boats and ships, these travelers will be left behind; they will be witness to a festival of madness.

Imagine, they whisper deliriously to themselves, *being able to write about Esi's festival.*

They are always found, though. That was what a sailor told her, his vial of soil tiny against his broad chest. He was an Esite, from the ice plains most probably; his vial was filled with a maroon moss commonly found there.

Do you have any news, sister? he asked. *Do you know how we've changed?*

He had been out at sea for years. He had missed Esi, you could see it. But Magali told him no. *Find a drifter,* she said. *Or a fisherman. Do not ask a luddite.*

He nodded respectfully. He was about to disappear into the crowd, when she thought of a question and held his arm to stop him.

Has anyone . . . She dropped her voice *. . . an Esite, have they left the island before the festival starts? Just sailed far away, returned only years after the turn of the century?*

He nodded, like he knew what she was asking.

There are stories, he said. *But it does no good. They go mad anyway.*

Now Magali cuts through the fields, toward home. Along the way, she rummages for a long stick and carries it with her, its tip trailing in the dirt. When she reaches a mango tree, she hits it, collecting the green mangoes that splatter to the ground. We pick up what is left. We eat as we walk behind her, the raw flesh tart against our tongues. We have been in this story for lifetimes.

Magali's mangoes remain uneaten. At the fringes of the colony, she places the fattest one on Old Silu's memory stone; she carries the other two home. The house is dark. Grandpa sits at their long table, looking at the garden as it loses light. Magali sets the mangoes down and goes through the rooms, lighting candles. Her room has only one ghodra; Wisa's has been rolled up and put away. Magali closes the door.

In the kitchen, she cuts the mangoes into long strips, throws them into a pot. She plucks curry leaves and grinds spices, adding them. She unwraps the leaves and lifts the small blue oysters, shimmering and slimy on her palm. She cuts them up small, slides them into the curry. A thick slice of a mango is placed by the kitchen door, for the lizard Gul and her many offspring.

Jinn knocks on the doorframe; he comes with his own haul of long white vegetables known as pehta. Grandpa and he break these the traditional way—by lifting them high and smashing them on the edge of the table. They collect the uneven pieces on a leaf. Magali brings the curry, and Grandpa puts forward a small collection of gye flowers: yellow flowers that taste red hot and burn your tongue. They lay a leaf for Wisa, and they make sure she has an extra serving of the gye flowers. They are her favorite.

Later, Magali doesn't sleep. She goes outside, past the garden and into the fields. She lies in the grass. Somewhere near her is the crack that leads to the golden cave. It wouldn't take her long to find it. She thinks of Wisa, crouching and looking left, then right, before dropping into the crack. She imagines them fighting on the floor of the cave.

The grass rustles, then parts. Magali lifts her head. It must be Jinn, coming to see if she wants company. It could be Grandpa; perhaps the blue oysters didn't work and he couldn't sleep either.

It is neither.

Wisa stares at her sister in fear. A shawl covers her shoulders and head; it emphasizes her wide eyes. She is unrecognizable. The Wisa who left the colony was petite but uncontainable. She could sit still for hours but when she moved, it was a blur, like water gushing.

This woman is disjointed. Perhaps it is her left hand that gives you this impression; it is mangled and moves in ways that catch the eye. But no, it is more than that. She looks like she has been put together badly; you may not see the cracks, but you can feel them.

Slowly Magali sits up. She asks: *Are you really here?*

Wisa steps back.

She is, Magali realizes. She is really here. For a moment, she doesn't know what to do. Then she stumbles to her feet and gathers her sister into her arms; she holds her tightly. She says: *I'm going to kill you for leaving.* She says: *Didn't you eat for three years?* She says anything that comes to mind, just keeps talking; she's trying to keep her sister safe in words.

Say something, she whispers, *so I know you're not a ghost. Speak so I know you're not dead.*

Into the hollow of her ear, Wisa says softly: *I choose you.*

They don't go home. They stay in the fields, not speaking. They lie in each other's arms, noses pressed to shoulders, breath warm on skin. They sleep, they laze. Magali says nothing about Wisa's mangled hand.

At dawn, when the insects are thick around them and the sky is a bruised pink, Wisa says: *I have to show you something.*

She sits up, purring. The grass to the left of them rustles, and Wisa pounces. When she is upright again, her hands are cupped closed. She stretches them out to Magali and then, with a deep breath, opens them.

Perched in the bowl of her palms is a little black bat. It is slightly smaller than her thumb, its nose wet and twitching. It stretches its pale wings as it yawns, and when it looks at Magali, its eyes are so limitlessly black, she sees the black sea in them.

This is Wisa's child. She calls it Quir.

The Festival of Madness

I

Across the colony, luddites are beginning to remember.

Ava dreams of a craftsman standing on the wall of a stone structure. He is summoning the sea floor within the stone ruins. As the sea floor rises, so do terrifying creatures, which Ava cannot describe; she only remembers them in smoke and shadow.

Ior dreams he is a beetle stuck to the bark of a tree. He swears he lives a thousand years as that beetle, trapped in amber, traveling through Esi as the tree walks and talks, as rivers flow around it and hills change shape. For weeks after that dream, he cannot speak properly. It is as if a thousand years of not using his voice has erased it.

Lira dreams of a whale, teeth jagged and large. She sees Wisa, swallowed by the whale. She sees her son, his heart cut out, weeping. She wakes up hysterical.

Look now, to the forest. To a cluster of jamuns, heavy on the stem. From the corner of our eye, we spy a little black bat. It is inching toward the fruit. It stops. Looks at us. We see ourselves reflected in its eyes—Laleh, Myung, Blajine and all the Kilta ghosts. A proliferation of selves and stories, sprawling across the black sea. It stretches toward us, curious, as far as it can go . . .

Quiiirr, a voice calls. Bushes rustle.

Quir refocuses on the jamuns, scampering down the branch and tugging at the cluster's stem. Its nose wriggles with the effort. It tries to capture the whole cluster and so it fails, its claws gouging through the fruits' flesh as it loses balance and tumbles toward the ground, sticky with juice, forlorn and not even trying to fly. It falls straight into Wisa's palms.

Nine months until the festival of madness.

II

They won't let Wisa into the colony.

Magali fights to change their minds. She calls a meeting, uncaring how it looks so close to the festival. *Wisa is one of us*, she says. *When have we ever turned our backs on our own?*

But the colony is unyielding. No number of fenni nights can erase the wild gleam in Wisa's eyes, her mangled hand, her unhinged smile. Murmurs move through the crowd. Madness on their doorstep. A creature, sniffing the air. Hunting for a way into their hearts.

You can join her if you like, Ava spits, *but she cannot come here.*

The vote is unanimous. Jinn clutches Magali's arm; he is asking her to stand down. Magali shakes him off. Hypocrites, the whole lot. Luddites go mad too; they must if everyone on Esi does. What use is it to stuff their ears with cotton? Do they think locked doors keep insanity out?

I evoke my family, she says loudly. Lira has buried her face in her hands; her friends are shaking their heads. *I evoke our role as memory keepers, and everything we have given to this community. Wisa is a Kilta. She deserves the protection offered to a Kilta.*

Eyes, moving as one, to the figure to the left of Magali. Grandpa. He steps forward, their wise man.

She cannot come, he says. *Avoid speaking to her. Those who worry about their dreams or who feel changes to their bodies, come see me. We have medicines for it.*

The meeting is over. People drift off in clusters, gossiping about their fears. Magali is left in shock.

The fight in the Kilta house can be heard throughout the colony. Magali screams, begs, pleads. How is this her Grandpa, unbending and inflexible?

We promised to love her—

I will always love her, Grandpa says. He has sat at the kitchen table as Magali paced, upturned chairs, threw pots. *This is a fact. But she chose a path, Magali, and we cannot follow her down it. She is not our Wisa anymore.*

He cannot believe that. *Meet her*, Magali begs. *Please, just see her. You'll see that she's the same . . .*

Enough. Grandpa holds up his hand, the gesture imbibed with an authority he has never used over her. This is Kua, the memory keeper, the Fool, the shaman. *Do you think this is easy for me? But I have one child left, and I must protect her. You forget I have lived so much longer than you. I have seen more than I want to see, more than I can forget. You simply do. not. know.*

Wisa doesn't mind that the colony won't let her in. She is happy. She spends hours cooing to her lizard Gul, who is an old matriarch now and has taken three days to forgive Wisa for (a) leaving, (b) returning without gifts, and (c) bringing back an overly excited bat. She makes her home in a jacaranda tree whose branches are low and conversation pleasant. She plucks pink flowers for Magali, to show her their beauty. She selects the strongest seeds and encourages Magali to watch them, for hours, for days, months maybe, as long as they take to sprout. She eats erratically—whenever she holds out her hand, food seems nearby. When she spots luddite children spying on her, she smiles; it is mangled, smashed, deranged. The children flee.

She doesn't blame Grandpa. She knew he would choose this way. Kiltas are good, remember? Goodness is akin to principle, and principle doesn't bend even for those you love.

But here she is wrong—only a little wrong—for Grandpa comes to see her.

He comes at night; perhaps he hopes she will not realize. But an owl pecks her awake, and she is elated! Terrified. The first time Grandpa had seen her in Boba, she was strange but whole and he had scooped her up and loved her like it wasn't a choice, no decision to make there, just the rightness of the world once his blanket was around her shoulders and she was coming home. And now she is strange and mangled, but worse, she has taken everything he has given her—gentleness, the quiet respect for their smallness in the black sea, for sanity—and thrown it away; she has broken his heart.

Panicked, she tries to disappear into the foliage. But the jacaranda bends its branches, giving her no place to hide. Bad, bad tree. Then Grandpa is here.

If the Grandpa she saw in the stone structure was young, then the Grandpa she remembers from her days in the colony is timeless. Now time has leaked off him to reveal paper-thin skin and a body that is more bone than muscle. For the first time, he looks old.

She climbs down the tree then, slowly. Look, Grandpa, she says with her movements, how careful I am. How good, how true, how whole. Please love me.

But when she is on the forest floor, she realizes she has already broken him. She is another loss in a lifetime of them. Another dead family member he cannot resurrect.

I am here, she thinks. Slowly, she closes the gap between them, holding her hands up tentatively, as you would for a wild animal—see? I mean no harm. Grandpa's eyes flit to the left, and, too late, she remembers her mangled hand. She hides it quickly behind her back.

What have you done? he whispers.

Nothing bad, she wants to say. I only took what the universe offered, Grandpa; I swear. Fruit grows on the highest branches of any tree. Does it not deserve to be plucked?

She is in front of him now; she can smell sandalwood and jasmine from their soap. He is close enough to hug. She smiles, and he touches the corner of this smile with his thumb.

My jaan, he says. *My beautiful jaan.*

Wisa knows he means, *You are dead to me.* He will not be back.

―

And so, in the end, it is only Magali and Jinn who make their way into the forest day after day to be with Wisa.

They are here now, as Wisa brings back a Quir soaked in jamun juice and puts it in a copper bowl. She fills the bowl with water, and Quir purrs happily. Jinn crawls over to the bowl, and Wisa joins her sister at the roots of the jacaranda tree. They clasp hands.

For a moment, they sit and listen to Esi. Bulbous jackfruits grow out of barks. Creepers wind their way around rock and branch. From the harbor, the wind carries sprinkles of sand and conversation. All speech has an echo to it now: thick and liquid golden, sometimes susurrus crimson, dripping echoes that are audible only to a few.

Soon now, Wisa whispers to Magali. *The festival will be soon.*

In front of them, Quir enjoys its song bath. It changes into—*cruck*—a goldfish and then—*cruck*—a strip of seaweed and then back into a goldfish to better enjoy the water. This is true joy. Incandescent delight. Is there anything as wonderful as a song bath? We don't think so. We couldn't imagine it. Next to it, Jinn hits the copper bowl with a stick and the bowl vibrates. Quir collapses in delight.

Both Magali and Jinn love Quir. They play with it for hours, patting their laps and saying *here, Quir, here.* At the beginning of this story, no one could have imagined this: a coy, loving and irascible bat that delights in song baths, cuddles, and dark purple jamuns, although it does not need to eat. Quir gambols in their love, delighted by its two new friends. Two!

Still watching Quir, Magali squeezes her sister's hand.

How did you make it? she asks.

I don't remember myself, Wisa says. *It was strange, that time. Like I was in myself and out of myself, in many places and in one place. I remember making a pot out of a tortoise shell, boiling elements. Following memories that weren't mine. It didn't come from me, Quir. It couldn't have. It came* through *me maybe, but it is not of my making.*

Wisa, that doesn't make sense.

Wisa smiles. *I know.*

But she does not have the language for it. Already her time with the alchemists is running away from her. It is flowing out to somewhere she cannot follow. All she remembers is Quir, crawling out of a tortoise shell, its eyes luminous and black. It is the most beautiful thing she has ever seen. She will love it forever.

Do you want to see what it can do? she asks Magali.

Magali doesn't know why Wisa looks both excited and ashamed when she asks this, but she nods.

Jinn takes Quir out of the copper bowl, and the three of them crouch around it. An air of solemnity and ceremony hangs around this scene. We lean forward, eager. Our bat is puffing its chest, letting out little cries. It wants to please.

Quir, Wisa asks softly, *can you make a snail?*

Easy, oh, easy. *Cruck* and Quir is a snail.

A loya flower?

Flowers are tougher. You never want to be *too* perfect; you have to capture their softness and decay. But Quir is good at this, very good. *Cruck*. A flower lies in the grass, its magenta petals open. Magali glances at Wisa and her sister nods. And so Magali touches it, feeling its softness and fragility.

Quir, Jinn whispers, *you marvel.*

Wisa says: *A tree?*

Quir hesitates. Which tree? It picks the closest—the jacaranda—and transforms.

It is a tree: roots, branches, leaves, purple flowers heavy in its canopy. It is also only the size of your palm.

Bigger, Wisa says.

The tree grows an inch.

Bigger, Wisa insists.

Quir pushes; it strains. It expands a little more.

Wisa's face is low, her eyes shining. You see it, the eagerness of a girl to have a world she was promised, a place she could crawl into and call a refuge. *When you are born*, she used to say, *I will live in you. You will give me everything I want. And I will love you.*

But now her world is here, and it is only the size of her palm.

Magali has never seen Wisa like this: hungry. Intent.

Bigger, Quir, Wisa whispers. *I know you can do it.*

Jinn looks at Magali in alarm; he reaches out to touch Wisa and stop this, but he pulls his hand back at the last second. There is a pause, and then the tree sprouts a few top leaves. Then it collapses, a root changing into a bat's claw, its trunk growing furry, and Quir is back, looking at them with guilty eyes.

Wisa says, as if confessing: *It cannot grow big.*

Quir is distressed. Jinn gathers the little bat to his chest; he coos at it. *You did great*, he says. *Marvelous. I've never seen anything like it; you're the best bat in the black sea.*

Magali takes her sister's hand. Wisa is looking at her with large eyes, the same way she looked on the ghodra that night Magali and she swore to be sisters.

It's a good bat, Wisa says softly. But she says it like it is a question.

Magali gathers her into a hug. *It's the best bat*, she says and Quir lets out little cries of pleasure.

III

Drifters don't visit the colony anymore. They circle around the settlement, plunging instead into the forest; they are pulled by other interests. Swiftly, like locusts eating through vegetation, they swarm across the island to devour stories.

Stories are surfacing about the last festival of madness. Rumors, lies, truth—who can tell? They say the last festival of madness reached such fevered heights that the island cracked. A deep gorge opened down its middle. Oh, the Esites fixed it with craft, but now the warbler no longer sings but cries and each tree grows at least one crimson leaf. And the first festival of madness—the very first! Oh, you would have shivered had you been there. It was just us, hacking down trees and ripping apart animals, making a game of their feathers and bones. And when our senses returned on the seventh day, how we wept to see what we had become.

The luddite children, the little ones, sneak out into the bazaars to glean snatches of these stories. They do it as dares; they are testing themselves. *I'm not scared*, little Sinal tells Jinn; she's no more than nine. She still runs when Wisa smiles at her.

At home, Kua brews medicine to help people sleep. The dreams are getting worse. People are waking up with memories they swear are not theirs. They say they live lifetimes in the space of a night, the memories still fresh behind their eyelids when they wake.

I can feel the longing right there, Zia says, clutching her heart. *I can feel his pain. I never knew this man, Kua—why can I feel his pain?*

Six months to the festival of madness.

Birds are wheeling in the sky, agitated. Flocks of them are migrating, as if fleeing a storm. The sky around them is pale blue, white clouds fluffed up; you couldn't find calmer weather.

This sky is reflected in a pond, disrupted only by the bodies of the Kilta sisters. They're floating on their backs, their legs spreadeagle. It is so peaceful, Magali can almost pretend like Wisa never left. Like the festival is not a few months away. In this vision, her sister's hand is whole, and she doesn't look at Magali like she is seeing three of her.

In this vision, Magali never saw a glimpse of Wisa in her garden, starved and screaming.

Magali feels suddenly out of control. Life is slipping away from her and it is changing into shapes she will not be able to recognize. She could lose Wisa again. Wake up one day and find the darkness has swallowed her.

I dreamed of a genie, Wisa says, her voice drifting from somewhere to Magali's left. *It was so big the sky couldn't contain it. It had to stoop. I wanted to make Quir like that.*

Her sadness worries Magali even more.

You have a world, she says, swimming toward her sister. *Here, with us—Jinn and me.*

Wisa doesn't speak, only smiles. She holds her nose and submerges herself slowly, so that Magali is left standing in the mud. Alone. Then Magali feels hands grabbing her ankles and she is upturned into the water with a splash. The two girls break the surface for air, and splash each other with glee, much to the annoyance of all the fish.

Later, Magali hugs her sister. *Don't you dare leave again*, she says and Wisa nods.

As Kua walks toward the forest, he looks at the birds. Of all the strange occurrences—dreams, visions, *bhavlas*—this affects him the most: nature changing to follow patterns he cannot fathom.

The wilderness has always been unpredictable, Isom reminds him now, *whether you could see it or not.*

Isom has become more defined as the festival grows closer. He wanders around Kua's kitchen, making himself tea and advising Kua about ripe brinjals. He is still a figment of Kua's imagination—isn't he? As far as Kua can tell, Magali cannot see him, so he cannot be a real ghost. But then Magali was taught not to talk about her double sight from a young age, so maybe she can and does not say. It is funny how the lessons you teach your children to protect them end up becoming a wall that separates you.

Now Isom walks with Kua to where they can find the woody mushrooms. Each time Kua ventures into the forest, he wonders if Wisa knows of his arrival. If she will come, peeking around tree trunks, shy. He is fearful of it; he longs for it. He knows better than to reconcile the two feelings.

Kua runs his thumb over a mushroom's gills; he inhales the scent of mud and fungi. At least this has not changed. This he can hold on to.

When he looks up, he sees a little black bat.

The bat is staring at him. Its eyes are unlike any bat's he has seen, luminous and endless. It is not shy. It is sizing up Kua, trying to decide which part of him is the best to land on. Deciding it is the ear, Quir launches forward and settles on it, rummaging through Kua's hair.

Kua knows who this is. Magali has spoken about Quir at home. *Just see it, Grandpa,* she had begged. *You don't understand . . . I don't know how to explain until you see it. Wisa's made a miracle.*

Now Quir—*cruck*—changes into a squirrel and scampers down Kua's arm, onto his open palm. It cocks its head, as if to say, *hello! I have heard much about you.* Kua is amazed. Quir changes from a squirrel into a bat, then a lizard, then a bat again; it is showing off. It struts on Kua's palm, proud.

Isom looks over Kua's shoulder. He doesn't seem surprised by this creature, as if he knew it would turn up; he just wasn't sure when. The hallucination puts his hand on Kua's arm and Kua feels suddenly overwhelmed. The world has upturned; he cannot find any footing.

The little black bat is patting his wrist soothingly; it changes into the sui songbird, which is Kua's favorite bird; it sings a little, hopping. Kua can see Wisa in it. She is there in its playfulness and joy, in its wide ability to love and heal.

Isom leans his forehead against the back of Kua's head. Kua's heart clenches, for in Quir's luminous eyes he sees what he never considered. Madness can be beautiful.

Isom says softly, *It's not your fault.*

Three months to the festival of madness.

Ava is missing. Freyn swears she was sitting next to him and laughing, when she leaned to the side and disappeared. The luddites don't believe him. They cannot afford to. They comb through the forest for days, beating gold pots and calling her name. The drifters watch them, amused.

Jinn finds it suddenly urgent to be near Magali. He makes excuses to come by her house, to go with her to the forest and see Wisa. His mother is unraveling; she keeps within the house and talks, softly, to shadows; she calls out for him frantically. Jinn should stay home; he knows this, but he cannot help himself. Each time he sees Magali, sweaty and smiling, some fear in him is assuaged and it is easier to breathe again. She is here. She hasn't disappeared. He holds her hand every chance he can; sometimes, when she is walking ahead of him or is absorbed in a task, he brushes his fingers across her shoulder or arm. Touch is everything. Touch is how you hold the world together when it insists on melting.

Don't be scared, Wisa tells him when they are bathing Quir. *Magali won't go anywhere.*

But how can Wisa know? Even her madness has its limits. A human mind is only a mind, after all. And Esi has become something else—grander than their imaginings, more terrifying than their dreams.

Is this madness? Magali whispers in his ear, flushed under his touch, alight with the softness of pleasure. She is full of gentle happiness. Jinn wraps his arms around her and presses his nose into her neck. Over her shoulder, he watches a moa pick its way through the jungle, its enormous bird feet pressing into the mud, its small head hidden by leaves. Its body is the size of a long boat.

Moas went extinct hundreds of years ago.

Jinn closes his eyes and holds Magali closer.

Elsewhere in the wilderness, Quir hovers mid-air, watching the forest fill with a proliferation of birds and beasts. In a patch of sea-holly crushed by a paw print, there is a glinting object. Curious, Quir flies closer.

It is a stone, shaped as a smooth egg. We've seen one like this before—Jinn found it in the river and gave it to Magali as a peace offering. When you hold it up to the sun, it is as if you are staring into a trapped sea. The stone lies beside Magali's ghodra now. At night, she runs a finger across its smooth surface, marveling at its depths.

This stone egg is different. It is forged from six pieces of ice pink and yellowish white; it is blood red along its seams. It is heavy on your palm, but not in a way that can weigh you down. If you peer into it, you sense the same vastness as the sea egg. As if you are not looking at stone at all, but vast tracts of fabric spooled tightly into a ball.

As if you are holding the seed of a universe.

There are stories washed away by the black sea; they leave no trace. You could not fit them all into this retelling. You couldn't even begin to speak them for you don't have a strong enough tongue or enough languages. Some stories must simply be left to lie, to disappear, to be shortened into fragments that then scatter across the island. There are stones like these all over Esi. Drifters collect them because they are pretty, because there is nothing easier to trade than a beautiful rock that entices. They call them the strange fruits of an even stranger forest.

Quir inches closer and sniffs the stone. Then, curious, it swallows it.

―

They find Ava's body in the river; it is bloated and half-eaten by the fish. What she was doing in this part of the river, they could not tell you. Whether she was dead before the fish tasted her, they could not say either. What they especially cannot explain is how Ava, young and with thick black hair that was her pride and joy, now has white hair and wrinkles around her eyes.

Two weeks to the festival of madness.

―

Wisa is curled at the roots of a jackfruit tree tickling Quir's belly. It is giggling, delighted. Gently, Wisa touches its nose and it opens its mouth wide, wide, as if it cannot hold its happiness.

Quir, Wisa says softly, *make a tree.*

She wants to cup the small thing in her hand, feel the canopy brush her skin. She wants to imagine she can have the forest for herself to hold, that she is a giant with feet that can stamp out seas.

Cruck. Quir becomes a nightdome, a tree found only in the black plains. It sprouts dark purple leaves and white flowers, its mother-of-pearl bark shimmering.

It towers over Wisa. It breaks through the forest canopy.

Silence. It is as if the island is holding its breath. Wisa stares at Quir in quiet awe. Then, *cruck,* Quir is a little bat again, looking at her with pleased eyes.

Six days to the festival of madness.

The luddites are moving indoors. Vegetables are being harvested, meat pickled, rice and fruit piled into earthen pots and distributed among households. Here and there, families take in their favorite plants—the blossoming bougainvillea, the white jasmine, the hibiscus. Everyone is put to work, the children as well, and the difficult labor from sunrise to sunset keeps their minds clear.

The island changes. Those who wake up in the mornings say it is as if they are still dreaming—as if everything is seen through glass, thick and cracked, so that reflections are distorted and the colors all wrong. Displaced spirits wander the whalebone mountains; Esites now share their land with mammoth animals that went extinct millions of years ago, with ghosts of families and cleanly dressed alchemists pulling threads of time out of their gleaming pots. Conversations become difficult to hold. Logic breaks like candied sugar, sweetening the madness. People pluck at their skin, longing to split through it; they walk away from their homes and lives, looking to shed them. The travelers have been herded onto boats; they bob out at sea. Esi is only filled with Esites now.

Four days to the festival.

In the whalebone mountains, drifters are talking to the Puidra craftsmen, the keepers of the birds. Slowly, drunk on fermented palm wine and rotting berries, the craftsmen begin to call in the clouds, casting a long shadow over Esi. In the colony, luddites pull out stores of raw cotton and beeswax, fashioning ear corks; they reinforce their windows and roofs with mud, sealing any cracks through which sound can travel. Lira sits in the corner of her home, whispering to the wall. When Jinn asks, she says: *Your father is here. But shush, don't tell anyone.*

Wisa feels a tingling at the back of her teeth, a building just behind her heart.

It's Quir, she says at the edge of the colony, half hidden in the trees and clutching Magali's wrist. She hasn't seen her sister in days. *Something's happening. You'll come, won't you?*

Of course, Magali whispers urgently. *Jinn and I. Now go. Go before someone sees you.*

Two days to Esi's festival.

Esi is opening up. It is a pomegranate, tearing to reveal millions of ruby worlds within it. Children wander five, ten, eleven steps away from their home and find themselves in another land; they cannot find their way back. Women glimpse slices of Esi's history in between the trees. Visitors from strange times wander into settlements and say hello.

Quir cannot sit still anymore. It flies from tree to tree, frantic. It cries to the clouds. When Wisa tries to soothe it, it snaps at her. If she touches it—*cruck!*—it bursts into whatever she is thinking, quickly, furiously. It cannot control itself. Wisa retreats and watches anxiously.

Out of the shadows, the mad craftsmen emerge. These are alchemists, from this time and others. They gravitate toward the stone structure, where alternate black seas are struggling out of the earth. The drifters got it wrong; the craftsmen don't make the worlds. They have come to watch them.

The drifters themselves are growing frantic: here are the answers to questions they've asked for centuries, all handed to them on a platter.

They carve it into trees; they make it into songs. We *will* remember, they tell each other. We will *keep* this.

In stone caves, alchemists from millennia ago are doing the same thing. They are filling a pattern etched into the stone with gold. They are making a root system of memory, so they may remember what a festival of madness looks like. But time will flow away from both alchemists and drifters. As has happened for thousands of years, everyone will forget.

Along the island's waterways, down its roads and along its mud paths, Esites are traveling. They are leaving their homes as a pressure builds at the back of their heads.

And then, it is here.

The clouds spit forked tongues of black lightning; mist obscures the island. Esi transforms. It is as if there is a fruit in each Esite, growing riper and riper over the decades, dancing on the tip of rot, and now it has burst, its juice fermented and sickeningly sweet. Every desire an Esite has grows gargantuan proportions. Yearning tugs out their insides to soak the land in their blood. They want. They want with no idea of what is on the other side of that word, want for the sake of want, and reality with its simple outlines and known dimensions is nothing more than a cage.

And the island obliges. It throws open all its doors so that time streams mingle and mix, so that you are carried away on currents beyond you, so that you glimpse, fleetingly, before your mind collapses under the enormity of what you are viewing, the forest of time.

Magali is living a thousand versions of herself at once; Magali at five, screaming for her mother; at two, learning how to walk; at forty, her ink brush poised above paper; Magali with parents who never died; Magali leaving the luddite colony to become a sailor; Magali dead, wandering a barren landscape as a ghost; a million Magalis writhing under the surface of her skin, piercing her mind, commanding her limbs. She is lifted, buried, drowned, simultaneously more than herself and oh so much less, and she wants to tear the world with her teeth to make space for it all.

A single crystalline word emerges through the haze.

Wisa.

She must get to Wisa. Wisa, lost, clutching her wrist. Wisa saying, *You'll come, won't you?* Wisa looking up at Quir, who is a nightshade, mouth open in amazement. So Magali stumbles from the luddite colony and toward the forest, clutching her sister's name with all her might. Wisa.

The forest is overflowing. People, ghosts, all of the island's animals and birds—they are being pulled here by something as potent as Wisa's name is for Magali, their own North Star. Magali is too far gone to recognize the signs, but we can. This is a storm, and all of Esi is moving toward its eye.

Look now to the clearing from where it radiates, our focal point. We have been here before; we have watched Magali trade a pouch of silta pearls with a drifter for answers she didn't like. Rainbow coats lie on the ground by the dozens, drifters clutching each other in terror, elation, birds digging claws into flesh as they screech.

Everyone is watching Quir.

Wisa's child is ricocheting around the clearing, flung by the force of its magic. It is—*cruck!*—turning into creatures so fast, it is losing its shape. A mob has gathered around it. No one is shouting wishes, but Quir is caught in a multitude of possibilities: thoughts, desires, pieces of time. *Cruck*, a white leomir, roaring and running—*cruck*—a man with a stick—*cruck!* two children, running around and laughing before—*cruck*—

Wisa is here, crawling toward her child. She is pleading. But her child flies away from her, unable to be held. *Cruck!* A moa with its little one. *Cruck*, a redfern tree, its roots plunging in and out of the earth, barreling through the mob, smashing bodies into each other. Magali is crushed against a trunk, pain shooting up her side. *Cruck!* A woman plunging a knife into a lover's body—*cruck!*—a creature half-goat, half-lion—*cruck!*—

Wisa. Magali must get to her sister.

But Wisa has made it to the center of the clearing; she has stumbled to her feet, ducking as Quir shoots past her. *Quir*, she shouts and oh, we hear the elation in her voice; this is everything she dreamed and more—*cruck!*—Quir is the golden genie, bald head bending as he reaches for Wisa, as his hand curls around her—*Make me my world!*

Cruck!

Quir is a simurgh.

Magali screams with the awe of it. No one has seen a simurgh for thousands of years, except in fables. Now its talons clutch the boughs of a tree and bends them with its weight, such that it seems it will tear the tree into two. It raises its wings, sweeping them along the canopy, bathing the crowd in shadow. Then it bends its head and looks its creator in the eye.

We hold our breath.

With a piercing cry, Quir takes to the sky. It flies up, into the mist cloaking Esi from the black sea, until it is swallowed whole. It is gone. All that is visible of Quir now is this melody, nowhere and everywhere at once. Then this too stops.

Beneath the clouds, a shadow begins to spread.

We cannot look away. Like gold melting in an alchemist's pan, like the soft pooling of water, the shadow grows—a hurricane, its epicenter perched above the clearing. It spreads until it reaches the limits of the island, then it begins to change.

The shadow is taking on heft; its shape and dimensions are evolving, color leeching in. Esites watch in terror and awe. Magali forgets Wisa; the only object of importance is this shadow, the fermented focus of their wonder. Parts of the shadow elongate toward the ground, solidifying into stone. Others twist and split into roots, then branches, plopping into leaves. Far from the clearing, those who cling to their boats in the glass lakes watch the shadow turn into the smooth sheen of undisturbed water.

When the transformation ends, we are staring at a mirrored version of Esi.

For one incandescent moment, time stops. Rivers of past, present and future cease to flow. Ancient animals look up at the upside-down island: at the emerald forests, the whalebone hills, the deserts. At leaves, fluttering in the same wind. Water, gushing above and below, their sounds mingling to become deafening. At themselves, startled.

Every creature on Esi, every ghost and memory, is captured in this reflection. Magali sees her mouth round into an O of surprise, watches as her doppelganger's face changes. When she lifts her hand, her twin does the same. They clasp. Her reflection's grip is warm and sweaty.

Then—*cruck*—the island disappears. Quir is back, a little black bat, curled in Wisa's palm. She cradles it and weeps.

Kua is here, in the crowd, having given up his luddite practices to be with his granddaughters. He is fighting through the squash of bodies to get to Wisa. When Quir changes into the island, we watch him look up like everyone else. We see his horror.

Then Quir changes into a black bat. Somewhere in that moment of transition, when Quir is feeble and translucent, Kua glimpses—it is difficult to describe what. Call it a tear within Quir's body. Imagine air parting, ever so slightly, into a cut that inches downward to grow larger. Look closer, and it seems as if Quir is stitching a cobweb that simultaneously tears and holds together the elements.

Then Quir solidifies and the cobweb disappears into its belly. Only Kua saw it for those few seconds and he does not know what he was looking at.

How can he? Who has been taught to recognize time?

IV

For seven days and nights, Quir flies across Esi, touched by Esites to transform into their wishes.

For seven days, Magali, Jinn and Wisa find a seaside cave and have a festival of their own—one of triumph and love, of stories closing and selves realized. They are mad these seven days, but it is a madness that feeds off their love and revels in their belonging. They become all of themselves, past and future, dead and impossible, human and otherwise; they surrender. They stay in the wet, salty rock and transform, tumbling into hysteria. In flashes, Magali thinks of Grandpa, of the first time he took them to the stone structure to show them the careful wisdom of plants, and she hopes she can explain this to him one day, how they became the forest, how they pushed the limits of possibility. Perhaps he will be proud.

Those seven days feel like years. Time loses its structure; it melts into the vastness of Esi's forest of time, into the many time streams that flow through the island and that Esites wander into. Some return; others don't. On the sixth day, time begins reforming. The sun moves; the moon appears. Doors between time streams close; the pomegranate rejoins until it is a single crimson fruit.

On the seventh day, Esites begin to walk home. Puidra craftsmen climb the mountain to dispel the already paling clouds. In the stone structures, worlds begin to lighten and melt; by tomorrow morning, they will be gone. Hordes of craftsmen sweep across the landscape, fixing Esi's bleeding and broken body. At the harbors, ports ready themselves to welcome back travelers.

Wisa wakes up in a daze. Fragments of these seven days are embedded in her memory, like glass shards, but most of it is blurry. Already it seems impossible that so much happened in such little time. She feels older. Her memory is leaking, out, out, a tide receding. Across the island, drifters are stumbling to their feet with the same sensation. They sing snatches of songs they don't remember composing; they ache with a bittersweetness of what is lost to them. The trees on which they scribbled memories are already healing over.

Wisa walks onto the shore, into the sea air. Magali and Jinn are still in the cave, curled together in sleep. Wisa doesn't wake them. She walks along the sand and cuts through the fields.

Where is Quir?

Wisa's worry is irrational; Quir can take care of itself. But there is a stillness to the forest today; she notices it the moment she crosses its boundaries. It unnerves her. The trees have stopped whispering. The animals are gone. Wisa spots a small monkey peering at her, and it disappears quickly into the leaves. Not gone then. Hiding.

Wisa keeps walking. At times, an insect will fly close to her ear, or a bird will chirp in the canopy. These sounds give her comfort. But then they fade and the stillness returns.

When Wisa does finally hear a clamor, it does not belong in a forest. It is the sound of a crowd. The murmurs are high-pitched, scared. Wisa begins to run.

The mob is thick. The people don't want to be here, but they cannot leave; they are rooted to the spot in horror and fascination. Freyn is here, Lira and Grandpa. Wisa makes herself smaller; she avoids him. Eel-like, she slips forward, between bodies and legs, to the front of the crowd.

They are clustered at the roots of a tree. Someone murmurs—*festival*—another—*how can it?*—and suddenly time feels different here, the memories stronger. In the rest of Esi, the festival is leaking away, all traces erased but here . . . something is holding the memory.

Then Wisa sees it.

A giant simurgh is perched on the branches of the tree. Its wings drape onto the forest floor. It is tossing its head, its crown wobbling. It is agitated by the people surrounding it. It is wounded.

Quir? Wisa whispers.

She walks forward, toward the bird. She can feel people whispering, but they do not follow her. She stands alone.

The simurgh bends its long neck. Intelligent black eyes look into hers.

Wisa holds out her hand. This is Quir; she would know it anywhere. She clicks softly, calling it. The neck bends lower, the bird wary. She reaches her hand out farther and, slowly, the simurgh puts its beak in her palm. She strokes it.

Quir is terrified.

Quir, Wisa says softly, trying to keep the growing horror out of her voice, *can you turn into a bat for me?*

The simurgh cries out. The mob screams, stumbles back. The bird tries to retreat. But Wisa wraps her arms around its beak and steps forward to follow it; she holds on. She strokes its feathers until it loosens.

Please, Quir, she whispers.

The simurgh closes its eyes. Slowly, ponderously, it descends from the tree. One foot hits the ground with a thump. The second follows. It begins to change.

As Wisa wished, Quir turns into a black bat. It becomes *her* black bat, with its wet nose and luminous eyes. Except, it used to be the size of her thumb. Now it towers over her, stooping so that its head is below the branches.

In her child's eyes, Wisa can see pain, confusion and fear. Quir cannot become small anymore.

"Don't Let the Mad Sisters Get Me"

Memories live in drawings, but they also live in words.

Specifically in fairy tales. Or in sea phrases repeated across the black sea, even though sailors don't know where they come from.

Centuries after Wisa and Magali experience a festival of madness, after they become a luddite folktale, Myung will travel the black sea. She will feed herself on explorations; she will grow shrewd on what the many islands tell her. She will hear about Esi, but she will not notice it, not yet. What she *will* notice is the sea myth of the mad sisters of Esi. It is said that on bewitched nights, if you have been out too long on the waves, if you have forgotten your talisman and lost your anchor to land, then the mad sisters of Esi rise up out of the black sea, whispering until your head is full of their voices and you slip into the darkness to join them.

And so a sea phrase was born. When the black sea becomes petrifying and you don't know if you will live through the night, sailors clutch their talismans and beg to the sea god. *Please, Alban, please—don't let the mad sisters get me.*

But no one remembers the story behind it. Not even the cartographers or the oldest sailors. The mad sisters have always existed, they say. There is no story.

But there is always a story.

The Girl and the Cracked Sky

The luddites have a folktale about a girl who was so greedy, she wanted to make a world. She wandered among the ancient trees of their island, begging for their wisdom. She begged all the creatures to tell her how to make her world.

You cannot, said the wise bulbul, *for it would crack the sky.*

But the girl wept and said: *I do not care, for this is my dream and it already is as vast as the sky.*

You cannot, said the old water trout, *for it would drink up the rivers.*

But the girl wept and said: *I do not care, for this is my dream and it is already a sea inside me.*

On and on the girl went, asking the wise creatures of the forest. Over and over, the creatures said: *You cannot*. And over and over, the girl said: *I do not care.*

Now the girl had a sister who loved her dearly. The sister saw how the girl tossed and turned at night, kept restless by dreams of her world. She saw how she stared into the sky, as if hoping her world would pull itself out of the clouds and swoop down to her. *Mai*, the girl would say to her sister, *do you not think it lives up there somewhere? That it is waiting for me?*

Her sister ached when she saw the girl like this. She thought and thought until she remembered a story their mother had told her about a chestnut seed hiding in the fronds of the tallest fishtail palm. If boiled and drunk, the seed was magical, capable of inducing madness. It would give its drinker anything they wished for.

So the sister left to look for the tallest fishtail palm, and when she found it, she climbed to the very top. She hunted through the stinging fronds until she could pluck a thick round seed, like polished wood. The sister took this seed to the girl and told her to boil and drink it.

But boil only a little, she warned the girl, *for Mother said it was of potent magic. We will do it together. Let me rest for a while for I am tired. Then when I wake up, we shall find your world.*

The girl was overjoyed. She made a bed of leaves for her sister so she could rest immediately. So tired was the sister, she fell into a deep sleep. The girl sat by her feet and waited for her to wake up.

For days and days, the sister slept. At first the girl was patient but when her sister did not awake, she gathered firewood to make a fire. *It is best to be prepared*, she said to no one.

When the sister still did not awake, the girl went home and brought a small pot to boil the seed. *So we can start the moment she opens her eyes*, the girl told no one.

When the sister still slept, the girl dropped the seed into the pot to hear the sound it would make, then she built a fire and poured water into the pot to see how it would boil.

When the potion had boiled and the sister sighed peacefully in her sleep, the girl said to no one: *My sister would not mind if I drink this. After all, it is not her world or her dream. And she walked so far and hunted so long for the seed, she would want me to have my wish as soon as possible.*

And before no one could reply, the girl drank the potion in great, greedy gulps.

But she had forgotten what her sister had said: that she must use only a *little* of the seed. The girl had boiled the whole seed and drunk the whole potion. When the sister woke up, she found the girl writhing on the floor. Her world was a massive creature that was growing and growing—swallowing the rivers and pressing itself into the sky, cracking it. As the sister cried out, the creature swallowed the girl and then leaped into the depths of the black sea, never to be seen again.

Heartbroken and bereft, the sister wandered through the island's ancient forests, crying for the girl. She found the pot with the potion and discovered a single drop left. She drank it. Then she leaped into the depths of the black sea too, and transformed into a silver bullet fish, swimming and swimming to be reunited with her sister.

A sailor is listening to this story below deck. A storm is approaching, and a traveler is telling stories to distract the crew from what is coming. The traveler himself heard this story from a fisherman, who heard it from another traveler, who read it in a historian's account of a travelogue—and so on, back and back and back, never ending. The sailor has never been to Esi—he can't recall if there is even an island in the black sea called this—but somehow the story sits deep within him. He can imagine the sisters as close as the storm. He can feel the smooth chestnut seed. Taste the potion burning down his throat.

His mother never wanted him to become a sailor. She said there were spirits in the universe. Now, as the asteroids fly by faster, our sailor curls into a prawn and rocks back and forth. He imagines the sisters swimming around the ship, terrifying creatures casting dark shadows on the hull. When the magnetic storm grows, he cries out. When it hits the ship's deck, sailors running helter-skelter and pulling ropes to stay alive, he weeps. *Please, Ma*, he begs. *Don't let the mad sisters get me.*

And so it is that a piece of Esi's history no one remembers became a bedtime story told to luddite children to warn them about greed and madness. Then it became a folktale, until some traveler or sailor or merchant picked it up and the story traveled across islands and the black sea to settle in the mind of a sailor in the middle of a storm, so that it could emerge, sharp and salty and sure, as a sea phrase. Don't let the mad sisters get you.

And this is how Myung finds it. Although she doesn't know how the sea phrase came to be, she cannot help but feel that there is a history here—vast, wide and urgent—a rope thrown to a drowning sailor, and if she could only clamber back along its length, she would reach that bit of history she needs; she could pick it up and slot it in her; she would be complete.

Fabrics of Time

I

All memories of the festival have faded, except one.

It is eight days since the festival of madness ended. Quir has changed itself into a river snake. Its body curls across the island, its tail on one end and its head on the other. It believes this shape will make it less visible. It is trying to hide.

But there is no ignoring the thick, scaly body that shimmers in the faint light. Parents put their hands to their mouth and whisper. Children try and clamber over it. Esites have forgotten the festival of madness . . . but they also remember. They cannot tell *what* they remember—it is too foggy, dancing at the edge of their consciousness. But each time they look at the reptilian body, it grows sharper. They *feel* it.

Every day, Quir grows bigger. It rests its head on a small beach near the luddite colony and tries to hide in the foliage of the palm trees. The craftsmen have called the clouds back; they cloak the island in mist. Travelers remain bobbing on the outskirts of the island, unsure of why they haven't returned.

On the island, the Esites are scared.

Lira tries to keep Jinn at home. She tells him of her dream, of a great whale and Wisa being swallowed, of Jinn on his knees, his heart pumping blood in the sand. But Jinn will not listen. He gravitates toward Magali as if the madness never receded, as if he cannot imagine life without her, and Lira curses the day Kua ever brought Wisa home.

But when Jinn gets to Kua's house, he cannot go in. The garden is swarming with drifters, a blur of multicolored coats that blinds the eye. He can see Kua among them, holding his hands up, shouting to be heard. He can see Magali. She is quivering, alternating between fear and rage—or perhaps she does not alternate; perhaps what she is furious about is what she is scared of. Ava, poor dead Ava, used to say Magali had spirit blood, that she could probably see a lot of what was forbidden to luddites. In this moment, Jinn believes it. Magali looks as if she is willing to reach in and pull out the guts of the world, as if she will shape it into anything, absolutely anything she likes, just to get what she wants. Want the moon, children? Magali will get it for you.

His love for her overwhelms him. He pushes through the drifters toward her.

In the forest, Wisa has climbed as high as she can on the eucalyptus tree. She has not come down for four days. She drinks whatever water pools on its leaves. She eats nuts stashed in tree cavities. On the forest floor, she can see the mob grow bigger. They are howling at her, spitting with rage. They are scared.

Alchemist! someone shouts. Everyone has forgotten this was an insult once, during the first festival of madness; now they remember. *Alchemist!* they howl.

A mother shouts, *what have you done?*

Wisa doesn't know. She hides in the leaves, Gul scampering up and down her arms in worry. She wants Magali and Jinn. She wants to run to the beach where Quir is. Her baby is so scared; it has been singing to her for days. She wants to comfort it. Whatever happened, it is not Quir's fault.

Kill her! someone yells.

The mob takes up the chorus. *Kill her!* It builds into a crescendo, and then dies. Wisa is relieved—until she realizes they have not abandoned the idea; they're merely discussing it. The first few cries were impassioned, but now the mob talks about the possibility in the quiet tone of conversation. *Should we kill her? Should we kill the creature and her?* This is worse than the impassioned calls. There's a coldness to it, which reminds Wisa she is made of meat and bones. She tries to melt into the tree; she does not want to die.

She cannot tell when the crowd disperses—has it been days or weeks? But at some point, drifters move among the mob, herding it with their authority, and people begin to leave.

It has been settled, the drifters shout. *Move along. We've settled it—they'll be gone.*

The drifters give Kua a choice. He's the Fool; he knows the festival of madness better than any of them. *Fix this*, the drifters say, *or else we can't promise what will happen.*

Drifters are not subtle. He knows they mean they will kill Wisa and the creature. Or they will let the mob do it for them. Either way, his child will be no more. Unless he finds a solution, a way for her to get out of this alive.

Kua does what any parent would do. He picks the option that keeps his child breathing.

Exile them, he tells the drifters. *Let her and the creature disappear into the black sea never to be seen again. But let them live. They've done nothing wrong; they've lived by this island's principles—by your principles. Let them live.*

Magali cannot accept it. After the drifters leave, she screams at him. Magali has not yet learned that there are things in life she cannot change. That she is small, a speck floating in the black sea, and sometimes going with the tide is not a choice but an inevitability. Kua's heart is breaking. He has lost his son and his daughter-in-law, and now he has exiled the child he took in and called his own. He watches Magali run out the door to find Wisa, and he knows he will lose her too.

Now he sits on Wisa's ghodra, broken. Blajine crouches beside him, agonized. She knows what it is like to be weighed down by the enormity of decisions, to bear burdens no single person should bear. Kua cannot see her. He can only see Isom, sitting across from him. His brother looks kind, as he was in the days before he went mad. He holds Kua's face in his hands. He wipes Kua's tears with his thumbs. He says what he has been saying for decades, except the words never fit into all the other times he had said it. Now they do, for this is the moment to which they belong.

It's not your fault.

Magali runs into the forest and climbs Wisa's tree. Wisa meets her half-way, and they cling to each other. Wisa is crying. She knows what awaits her and she is scared.

Magali is furious. *We'll fix this,* she says. *We'll hide you; we'll think of something. Don't cry. Don't worry.*

Then Jinn is at the roots of the tree and climbing. He sits at the end of the branch, holding his throat to keep his emotion contained. Over Wisa's shoulder, Magali looks at him. She cradles her sister closer, fingers entwined in her hair. She whispers: *We'll fix this.*

But there is nothing to fix. After Wisa stops crying, she settles into a strange peace. She brushes the hair off Magali's forehead.

I will go with Quir, she says.

No, Magali says. *I won't listen. There are so many ways out of this. We can hide you in the island. We can disguise you. We can put you on a ship—you don't have to go with Quir—and we can find somewhere in the black sea for you to stop and rest. Then we'll find a way to change the drifters' minds. Or—no, don't look at me like that. If we can't, then we'll make a new home on some other island. Wisa, please, don't . . .*

What about Quir? Wisa asks softly.

Magali doesn't have an answer. Who knows how big Quir will grow? How it will survive? She doesn't understand their beloved little bat, or what will happen to it. It is best to leave it to its own devices. Surrender it to the laws of the black sea.

Grandpa loved me when no one else would, Wisa says. *Now Quir needs the same love. How can I leave when no one else will love it?*

How can you leave me? Magali cries.

Wisa is silent. She doesn't know how to fit them into words, all the moments that went into this decision. She wants to tell Magali that Grandpa had bought her a julma and it was the sweetest one she had ever eaten. That no one had asked her to stay before. That when she lived in the colony, she thought that Grandpa and Magali had a strain of robust morals stitched in them. She imagined a great white heron did it for all Kiltas when they were born. That their first words were: *I'll never harm. I'll always love. I will always choose good.* She wants to show Magali how she used to tap her chest to check if she, Wisa, was also good all over. That she left the colony to know if she was and to make her world. And once she made it, she loved it. And now she will go with Quir because it is the right decision; it is what Grandpa would do. And maybe no Kilta ever dreamed of making a world that broke Esi, but now she knows she is good all over. She is. She's a Kilta.

It needs me, Wisa says. She tries to hug Magali, but her sister pulls away.
You said you wouldn't leave, Magali says. *You promised.*

II

Later that night, Wisa climbs down from the tree. Magali and Jinn are sleeping by the roots, curled together in a way they do not allow themselves during the day. Gul is sleeping on a branch; Wisa kisses her head softly.

Then she is running. She runs swiftly through the forest, bare feet silent on grass, and it is like we are seeing her at the beginning of this story again, when we didn't know what would happen. She runs into the colony, moving as quietly as a shadow, flowing down its alleyways with that precision of a mapmaker. There are places you never forget, no matter how long you have been away or if you are mad. Wisa cannot forget her way back home.

At their garden, Wisa pauses. The door to their cottage is open; she can see the faint light of a candle, positioned so that it can be seen through the crack. She walks past the vegetables and the bushes where Miqhai slept. She pauses at where Magali came up to her when she was showing Gul how well she could balance on one leg. *Can you climb as well as you talk?* And here is where Grandpa set her down and adjusted the blanket around her shoulders. This was her first evening in the luddite colony. She hadn't met Magali yet. She thought she was only here for dinner. *Scared?* Grandpa had asked and Wisa had shaken her head. He smiled, picked her up, and they walked into her new life.

Grandpa is sitting by the table now. The candle has been placed far away from him, so he is half in shadow. He is staring at the wood, his hands clasped in front of him. When Wisa comes in, he looks up.

Two cups have been set before him.

He gets up to take the pot off the fire and pour them mint tea. His hand trembles and, easy now, like she has lived here all her life, will go on living here forever, Wisa steadies it with her own.

Grandpa doesn't say, *I hoped you would come.* Nor does he say, *I am sorry.* He sits in front of those cups and sips, eyes staring into nothing, like if he said everything he wanted to say, he would never stop.

Wisa sits opposite him, and sips too.

She feels . . . content. Scared, but also pleased with this moment. Of being with Grandpa one last time. She knows he has forgiven her for leaving; she has known that for a while, actually. He didn't leave that day in the forest because he hated her. He just could not bear to see her like this. But she is still Wisa. With her mangled hand and broken smile. She still loves everything she loved before.

Why didn't you tell me? she asks. *About Isom?*

Grandpa puts his forehead in his hands and rubs it lightly. Ever since he saw Wisa at that festival, her creature changing around her, he has wanted to be with his child. He longed to find her, but first the drifters were here and then he had to choose to give her up to save her life. After that, he did not know how to face her. He put the candle out tonight in the hope that she would come. But he did not expect it. He had no right to. *Your daughter is here.* And when she arrived, walking through the kitchen doorway like she had never left, it was as if the shadows had formed Isom, his brother back from the dead, until she sat and smiled and Kua's heart broke all over again.

How do you know? he asks, not because the story is a secret but because he wants to hear her talk a little while longer.

I saw you, she says, *in a stone structure. You couldn't see me but Isom . . .*

Your daughter is here.

Here's the thing about doubt: it is necessary but useless. Doubt asks that you don't choose any of the options before you—refuse to let your child be exiled and watch her be lynched instead, exile your child to an uncertain future and a possible death anyway, say you'll exile your child and hide her, under the risk she'll be found and now her and Magali are being gutted before your eyes—but you have to choose because the options do not always live together and not choosing is also a choice. You must decide with the little you know, not knowing if the choice will be right or wrong. Isom said *your daughter is here* and Kua heard the mad babbling of a brother he had already lost. Only she *was* there. And he could not have known that time didn't flow in one direction; he had to be *here* to know that, at this table, having watched a strange fabric knit itself in the center of a beast he must now kill, expel or keep safe. Doubt is a piece of the option you didn't choose, the infinite potential in the solid and singular reality, and the only way to live is to make it your friend.

Jaan, Grandpa says because tenderness is all he has left.

Wisa smiles.

I know, she says. *I love you too.*

III

Magali wakes up as dawn breaks. Someone is shaking her awake. On the edges of sleep, she thinks it is Wisa, but the face doesn't match and the clothes are not right—

And then Magali is up, jolted awake, because where is Wisa? It takes her a moment to realize there is no one beside her but Jinn. In sleep, he no longer wears the tense look he has when he is awake, as if holding the world's pain at bay. But even like this, he is attuned to her movements, and he opens his eyes as Magali looks toward the canopy to find her sister missing. Then they are running, hand in hand, toward the beach.

Wisa is lying on the sand.

Purple-pink mist moves above her. It reminds her of a sky at sunset, colors that shouldn't mix becoming one. She has stayed on this beach all night, waiting to see her last dawn on Esi. But, of course, she will not see the dawn—the purple clouds still surround the island, hiding Esi from the black sea. So she watches the crabs instead, making maps around Quir's reptilian head.

Throughout the night, Quir has been changing. Its transformations are slow now, no longer a swift *cruck*. It withdraws its vast body from Esi, coiling piece by piece on this beach. It is changing color.

Wisa waits. She considers memorizing what she is looking at. The color of the sea. Coral rocks. This starfish. But memory is faulty, she knows. Almost everything is imagined. She wonders how she will remember Magali in later years, if she lives that long. She doesn't know what will happen once she leaves with Quir—how it will change or whether she will live. She is scared.

When Magali and Jinn break out of the tree line, scrambling over rocks and shouting her name, Wisa knows it was not the sunrise she was waiting for but them. She turns toward them, holds her arms out, and

Magali slams into her body, clinging to her until it hurts. Her sister is babbling. Wisa feels only soft triumph: *My sister is here.*

Jinn goes to Quir. Their little black bat, little no longer. He strokes it. It sings mournfully and tries to nuzzle him. Jinn is desperate to hold it, to comfort it like he did the first time Quir showed them what it could do, but Quir is too large now and won't fit in Jinn's arms around it. He rests his forehead against its rippling body.

You're the best bat, he says softly.

There is nothing left to do but wait. They sit side by side, watching Quir change. Wisa wishes she could see into her sister's mind. She wants to tell her she said goodbye to Grandpa, but this will only make Magali sadder. She wants to say, I will be okay, but she cannot; the words won't leave her throat.

Jinn takes Wisa's hand. *Thank you for making me mad*, he says.

She smiles. To make someone mad! What a success. She feels wonderful again. Ah, to be loved and missed. *Take care of Magali*, she whispers. She brought them together—what a magnificent, stupendous crowning glory! Her best yet.

Jinn doesn't smile. Magali loops her arm through his.

Quir has become a whale. Its body stretches out along the beach; its back rises to break above the trees. Those in the whalebone hills see it and say their whale prince has returned to claim its dead flock. Those in the luddite colony hear the ground shake and whisper that Esi is finally punishing them. The three of them stare at their child in awe. They are sitting in front of its eye. It blinks and they are caught in it—Magali-Wisa-Jinn.

Family.

Wisa stands. She walks toward Quir's mouth as it opens. The inside is cavernous and dark. Gossamer fabrics flutter from the mouth's roof to drape along its insides. We recognize it—it is the cobweb Kua saw forming. Only now the fabric is larger, and it has multiplied.

Decades later, Laleh and Myung will look up in their chambers and see these great fabrics fluttering above them, each as large as Esi. They will call them *time cobwebs*.

Wisa stares into the abyss. You have done this before, she thinks. You have survived on your own. But it is not true anymore, is it? Now she knows how to belong to a whole, and it makes the loneliness scarier.

Behind her, Magali is staring into the same abyss. The Wisa she saw in the garden came from this whale; she is sure of it. Whatever happens to her, it happens to her here.

Do it now, Wisa tells herself. Before it gets too hard.

―

When Wisa steps into the mouth, Quir sighs, its gratefulness washing over her. It makes the next step easier, and the one after that.

She doesn't hear Magali behind her. She doesn't realize her sister is entwining her fingers with hers until the grip is unmistakable. She looks at their hands, and then at her sister.

She realizes what is happening.

No, she says.

Magali ignores her. She is staring into Quir's mouth, her shoulders braced. Then she is walking forward, past Wisa and into the lead, Wisa's hand rising to follow her.

No, Wisa says again, startled. She looks at Jinn, but he won't meet her eyes.

IV

Travel back to last night.

Wisa is sleeping in the tree. Magali is entwined with Jinn at the roots. She rests her head on his shoulder, not knowing where the tears come from or why the pain is so deep. Nothing has happened as yet, she tells herself. Wisa is here. Nothing has happened.

Jinn says: *If she goes, you will want to go too.*

Magali does not answer. She likes his arms around her; she could stay like this forever. She thinks of Wisa sleeping, her shoulder blades moving, imagining what it would be like to be alone.

She'll be scared, she whispers. *She'll do it anyway but* . . .

Magali . . .

You won't come, Magali whispers. *I know. You can't. I won't ask you to.*

Jinn rests his cheek on her head. *You could die*, he says.

They're gemels. Two trees entwined until they have grafted onto each other. Magali tries to remember his warmth, his smell. She knows then she has already made her decision.

I love you, she says.

It is the first time she has said it. Nothing in Jinn's body changes; he keeps holding her, still and sure, a rock she can always cling to. But she knows, somewhere inside, this has cracked him.

—

No.

Wisa is pulling her sister back but Magali is pulling her forward and now they are both inside Quir.

Go back, Wisa says, struggling with her sister. *Don't be silly. Jinn, help me. Go—back—*

It is useless. Magali has had years of hard labor; her body is sculpted and strong. Wisa cannot move her. Jinn has averted his gaze, his fists balled by his sides.

Listen. Wisa holds her sister's face, frantic. *You don't have to do this. Go back. I'll be fine. I'll be more than fine—I'll be happy. I'll find a way to come back and then I'll meet your grandchildren and we can complain about how stupid children are—*

Magali is laughing and crying but she isn't moving.

Listen, and Wisa's words are melting in her tears because she isn't just fighting Magali, she is fighting herself, this horrible and selfish joy that has risen up in her—my sister is here; she is coming—*think of Grandpa. It will crack him, kill him; he doesn't deserve this. Go back. Look at Jinn; you can't leave him. Magali, please—*

Magali pins Wisa's hands to her sides. She is not crying anymore; she is the Magali of old. Want the moon, children? Come, Magali will take you.

I choose you, she says.

Magali—

I choose you. Do you choose me?

But Wisa is not looking at her sister. Behind Magali the fabrics are changing.

V

The fabric behind Magali is shimmering in a gentle light. The colors are reforming into images.

Magali, caught with her in the belly of a whale.

Magali laughing as Wisa tells her a story.

Magali starving.

Magali lying on a black surface, time cobwebs fluttering above her, too listless to move.

Then the colors ripple, and the images change. It is Magali again, but with Jinn. She is out in the black sea, traveling from island to island. She is collecting songs. She talks animatedly to bartenders and academics; she keeps copious notes. Jinn is always there, at the edge of the frame, drawing maps with her, brainstorming. They are building something. Wisa sees children—three, no, four of them—clambering over Magali, demanding her attention, calling her *Mama*.

Two strands of time, each forking from this moment. Each depending on the choice she makes.

VI

Wisa gathers her sister into her arms and hugs her with all the love she has. They cling to each other as if they are the only solid features in this black sea.

I choose you, Wisa whispers. *I choose you. Remember that.*

Then she pulls away, and pushes her sister, hard. Surprised, Magali stumbles back.

It should have made no difference. They are standing so far into the whale's mouth, what is one step? But Quir is Wisa's child; it is a wish-giving creature. And so Magali finds her feet sinking into sand. She stumbles onto her knees, and when she looks up, she is outside the whale, Jinn is reaching for her and Wisa is disappearing into Quir's closing mouth.

VII

This is the last time Wisa sees Magali. Her sister is kicking in Jinn's arms, shouting, wrenching herself loose. The image grows smaller and smaller as the whale's mouth closes. Then it disappears altogether.

Now there is only darkness.

Musk and wetness.

The fluttering of gleaming fabrics.

The whale of babel thumps its tail twice, shaking the island. Then, with a cry, it launches itself into the sky.

Magali's Quest

Magali changes.

She is twenty-four years old when Wisa walks into the mouth of a whale and disappears into the black sea. At twenty-five, she disappears too. She packs a satchel of dried meat and a selection of medicinal plants she's taken from Grandpa's workshop. She dresses in robes bought from a drifter; they're thick and oily, like the sailors wear. She tells no one but Jinn.

I can't stay, she whispers. *I have to find her. I'll come back when I do.*

But Jinn comes with her. On the morning she leaves her luddite life behind, she finds him standing on the outskirts of the colony, his own satchel packed. He holds out his hand for hers, and they entwine fingers.

It is not easy to get onto a ship. People are not favorable to Esites who want to be sailors. *You lot don't have sea legs,* a captain tells them. *You love the land too much.* Captains who *are* Esites appraise them with squinted eyes, and then spit on the deck. *You're luddites,* they say. *You won't last a week.*

So Magali and Jinn sneak onto a ship. They hide themselves in barrels, and then talk fast when a ship's boy discovers them and tells the captain. The captain wants to throw them overboard, which is the penalty for stowaways. But Grandpa saves them. Sailors tip out Magali's satchel to find Grandpa's medicinal plants, and then they won't touch her. *She's land-sent,** they tell the captain. *She can help us.*

And so Magali becomes their medicine woman; she brews potions from memory, calling upon images of Grandpa moving carefully through his workshop, mixing plants and talking in soft and soothing tones. Jinn works with the crew, his body changing with the labor. At night, they lie in their hammocks and breathe in the smell of each other.

Dock after dock, they ask about Wisa and Quir. Has anyone seen a cosmic whale? No? Perhaps a young girl then, with a mangled hand and a broken smile? No? Was there anything they saw in the black sea that looked unusual, like it didn't belong?

They are laughed away in most places. Their questions are too vague; they are ridiculous. Magali doesn't know how to make them more specific. How do you put what they have lived through into language? Once in a while, someone will say, *Oh, I've seen that,* and then Magali and Jinn will jump ships. They'll leave their crew behind and find the first captain willing to take them to the place the person described. But there's never anything there. Either Wisa and Quir have moved on or the person was lying.

On new islands that are still wild and unsettled, Magali leaves Jinn behind on the ship. She wanders across unfamiliar terrain until she is sure she is alone. Then she howls. She crouches and screams with frustration, wolf-like and bereft. How is it possible to lose a creature as large as Quir? Surely someone has seen it? *Someone* must know.

But if there is such a person, Magali never meets them. More years pass. Those who own seaside dhabas along the black sea's trade routes know Magali and Jinn well now. They know the pattern. Each time the couple's ship docks, these two come into the dhaba. They walk among the sailors and ask their questions. Always the same ones, about a whale and a girl. The owner shakes his head as he cleans a glass. Then, once they've asked every person and got the same answer from all of them—*what in*

---

* Land-sent (noun): A spirit or holy person sent by the land to keep sailors safe during their voyage through the black sea. The term is commonly used by sailors to describe medicine women or explorers with a keen eye for what animals and plants may kill sailors on new islands.

the black sea are you talking about?—they come to the bar. They sit down and order a drink. Fenni, usually, which means they are Esites; no one else drinks the stuff. And then they eat, in silence.

Can't be a great life.

But familiarity breeds friendship in these parts, and so the owners are warm toward the couple. They keep two glasses of fenni ready when they see the pair come through the dhaba curtains. They like Jinn more—he is easier to talk to, and kind. He even laughs. The woman, however... Something has gone wrong with her. Something is souring.

Magali grows quieter. When she dreams, it is always the same nightmare. Wisa, starved and gaunt. Lying in a pool of endless black. Long, glittering fabrics flutter above her. Her eyes are half-closed; her breaths are shallow. With one last burst of inhuman effort, she clambers to her hands and knees. Then with all the rage and fear she possesses, she screams.

She is always screaming Magali's name.

We'll find her, Jinn says when Magali wakes up shivering. *She'll be somewhere in the black sea. We'll find her.*

But Magali no longer believes him.

There are moments of happiness. Years even. You can't live a life without them; they come, even in the depths of despair. Jinn and she have a child—a girl, chubby-fisted and as stubborn as Magali. Then a boy, and then another girl. *Let's settle down,* Jinn says. *Choose an island, make it our home.*

But Magali can't stop searching. If she did, she would die. So her children come onto the ships with them. They learn nautical symbols before they can speak. Every sailor is their uncle or aunt; they delight in the tough food of seaside dhabas. Jinn dotes over them, and Magali doesn't regret losing him to the task of child-rearing. He is made for it. She . . . not so much. She loves her children, of course. Very much. But she is not always sure she likes them.

Then one day, she sees Wisa.

It is brief. Magali is alone on a new island, studying a colony of clam shells. Finding Wisa is her purpose and North Star, but Magali has not forgotten the vision she had on Esi's harbor. She is a memory keeper by training and nature. Now she bends to examine these clam shells, which pass on memories through song.

Clam shells on this island have a brief life, a month at most. Yet this colony has lived for thousands of years, longer, thanks to the songs they sing to each other. These songs remind the colony how to survive; they warn new clam shells about which rock pools are poisonous and what predators to watch out for. As the colony learns, the song changes.

Magali is writing down the physical properties of a clam shell when she hears it.

It is music. It is not the same as the song of clam shells; it is not even really a song. The closest sound she has heard to it comes from an old memory, so old now, she barely remembers it. But as the song builds, she realizes: this is what Quir sounded like on the beach. Not *exactly* like this. This song is deeper, richer, existing in dimensions lost to Magali.

Then Wisa is in front of her.

Her sister is dressed in the same clothes she wore when she left Esi, the clothes Magali saw her in all those years ago in the garden. But she is not starved. She is not screaming. She looks healthy and flushed, like she has just witnessed something miraculous and it is pulling her heart out of her chest. Her expression is caught in wonder, and it doesn't fade when she sees Magali.

For a moment, the sisters stare at each other. Magali is at the edge of a hysteria so acute, it steals the breath from her. She doesn't know if she has finally gone mad. She doesn't care.

You're a dream, aren't you? she says, laughing and crying. *You're part of my dream?*

Or you're part of mine, Wisa says awe-struck, reaching for her.

Then her sister is gone.

Magali stays by those clam shells for hours. She doesn't trust herself to move. She hopes Wisa will come back, but mostly she doesn't want to leave the place that gave her such a perfect moment of happiness. The clam shells around her sing, so softly she can barely hear them. In the end, Jinn comes to find her. She lets him take her back to the ship. Only after she has held him for a while, wordless, as Jinn grows more and more worried about her silence, only then does she tell him what she saw.

It really was Wisa. She is sure of it.

Drifters who say they know how double sight works have always been lying. It is a tricky gift. It operates with a logic we cannot piece together. Magali doesn't know why her double sight gave her this glimpse of her sister. Why it opened the doors between their worlds *now*. She suspects it has something to do with Quir and song, but it is a half-formed suspicion. She cannot understand it, but she does not care.

Now, Wisa visits. She comes when Magali is alone. Jinn and her children have settled on the nice island of Gultan; Magali lives with them for part of the year, and for the other part, she travels. She visits islands to study their songs; she looks, always, for Wisa.

When Magali is crouched by a spiked creature or making notes in her ship's cabin, Wisa arrives. She appears unexpectedly, as is always the case with double sight. They talk as if they have never been apart. Wisa never describes where she is, but she tells Magali she is happy. Magali tells her about Jinn, about song and memory-making.

They spend these moments carefully. They give each other their full concentration; they center themselves with touch. Who knows how long this will last? But month after month, Wisa comes. Magali allows herself to believe this may stay.

It lasts for two years. Two years is all they get. The last time Magali sees Wisa, Magali is in her cabin collating notes. For once, she senses Wisa's arrival. There is a chill in the air, a trickle of cold that tickles the nape of her neck. It gives her goose bumps. She feels the approach of an ending, that faint sorrow and emptiness you get when something is complete. When she looks up, Wisa is in the corner of her cabin.

Her sister looks different. Nothing has changed in her appearance, and yet she carries herself with . . . confusion. Defeat almost. Magali knows then that this is the last time she will see her. She is certain of it. Even though it has only been moments since she arrived, the edges of Wisa are growing blurrier. As if she cannot stay in Magali's universe anymore.

Later, Magali will understand that this was because Quir was growing bigger, into a universe of its own. Time was separating, as was space. New laws were being shaped across the boundary of the whale's body. But she knows none of this now. All she knows is that she is going to lose her sister again. Wisa opens her arms, and Magali crawls into them.

How are you? she asks, cupping Wisa's face in her hands. It is a question she dared not ask, but she must now. It may be her last chance to know.

Wisa looks away. She is getting fainter, and Magali wants to smash the whole universe to make space for her pain.

I forget myself, Wisa whispers. *It is so large here, dark, I don't . . . I don't know how to see myself anymore. To say how I live. I feel like I'm disappearing.*

Magali tries to hold on to her fading sister, to the piece of time slipping back out. *I'll remember you,* she says and now she is crying. *I promise, I'll remember you.*

She keeps her promise.

She pulls out a blank sheet of paper, the kind cartographers use to draw maps, and places it on her table. She holds the edges down with rocks she has collected from different islands. She picks up her brush, made from fine squirrel hairs, like Grandpa's, and dips it into the ink pot.

She knows now that she will never find Wisa. The black sea is too large; her sister has disappeared into one of its wormholes. All she can hope is that Wisa is looking for a way home. But to succeed, Wisa will need a guiding light.

So Magali will build her one. She will build what she imagined on Esi: a museum of song, sung throughout the black sea so that Wisa may hear it wherever she is and remember herself. So that she can follow the song back to Magali.

Her brush hovers over the paper.

It is the first thing they teach you in a luddite colony, in a way—how to remember.

They do it through plants. Grandpa takes the children to the stone structure, with the roof torn off and the rain coming down in sheets, so you stand there when you are four or five years old, water pressing your clothes to your skin and the earth smelling of leaf and promise. It is cold in that stone, but even as you huddle together and squeal at the giant grass tickling your neck, Grandpa talks.

Plants have the most sophisticated growth of any living creature, he tells you in his soft, rolling voice. *They speak to each other through alchemy, through fungi and insects and birds, through heat signatures. In a sprawling forest, they connect through root systems, teaching new plants how to grow, changing their own shape and height to support a thriving ecosystem.*

Look, he tells you, and you do. You see plants bursting out of the stone, cascades of creepers, the utas growing horizontally to a wall and dripping red flowers, the ancient mango that climbs toward the sky, breaking out beyond the four walls as its roots travel to the floor along stone seams, transforming a side of this building into a root grid. You see split mangoes on the ground, their yellow flesh nurturing seedlings, the leaves of a weed opening in a lighter green like a blush, and you hear it suddenly, where there has been only rain and quiet—bird calls and insect hums, the crackle of heat signatures, the growing of a branch, the whole world working together to make this jungle.

And the remembering is there. In the growing and the staying still, in the talking and the silence, this largesse not pinned to any one plant but kept safe and carried forward by a network of moving pieces.

This is what Magali thinks about when she places her brush to the blank page, when she begins the floor plans of what will be the greatest project of her life: the museum of collective memory. There are many kinds of remembering. There is remembering the day, remembering others and then there is remembering yourself, the parts that entwine to make you.

Remembering has power; it is how the forest lives.

Breathe

We pause here.

We sit down. We rest. We've spent lifetimes in this story—it is not so easy to leave.

Stay.

Breathe.

There is no rush.

We stay until we can remember again a strange island bobbing on the edge of the black sea, housing all the Kilta ghosts.

Ojda.

Only when this name comes to us to do we get up and wander out of this story, into the present.

Fairy Tales of Wisa

I

Mad Magali has finished her story.

It took her ten years to complete the floor plans of the museum of collective memory, another twenty to build it. *All things fade*, Jinn had said to her once. He'd meant it kindly, but she never forgave him. She had said to her sister *I'll remember you* and she meant it. In a world where stories fade or become something else—a fairy tale, a myth, a sea phrase—remembering is a sacred act, requiring the largest of marvels.

And so she moved her family to Ojda, bound them in life and death to memory-keeping. Now she lives on as a ghost, keeping the story of her sister within herself, pure and untarnished.

Slowly, Laleh comes back to herself. The collective consciousness she shared—that elusive "we"—is ebbing away. She can feel Rostum's shoulders pressing into her; she can sense the warm presence of the ghost behind her. Slowly, she becomes aware of the limits of her body.

She is once again an "I."

The ghosts of the Kilta family sit in silence. They sit with the story they have waited centuries to hear; it may take them another century to absorb it. So much of what made a Kilta a Kilta felt unknowable once upon a time. "Live on Ojda forever," it was said. Why? The Kiltas would shrug. "Don't let visitors come here." Why? Another shrug. They never questioned these maxims because they didn't know they *could* be questioned, that there was an answer to the strange workings of a strange family.

But now they had their answer, and they looked at their lives from a new angle. So many people had changed themselves in service of a single woman's desire. Children had given up dreams of traveling the black sea and focused on loving Ojda. Parents had disowned their own blood if they chose to leave the island. People had formed narratives of themselves based on family moorings. Now they look at the start of it all and they wonder—was it worth it? Those who left the island and blamed themselves for years examine their useless guilt. Those who stayed examine their useless loyalty.

Everything is more powerful when you don't understand it. When something is story-less, its mysteriousness makes it easier to accept. But when something has a story, it shrinks down to the same level at which you view the rest of your life—and suddenly it is open to evaluation.

In the plains of Ojda, Kiltas are getting to their feet in agitation. They don't think what they were put through was worth it. Others are holding hands, tears dripping down their cheeks; they feel Magali's pain; they would have done the same.

At the front of the crowd, Myung is sobbing.

Her crying is desperate; her nose runs and she is holding her mouth to muffle the noise, but it isn't working. This crying is beyond her. She rocks slightly with the force of it. She is thinking of the cartographer.

For decades, Myung had searched for the story of Wisa. She saw it as a way to find her sister. To understand herself. On her journey, she visited a cartographer. She wanted to see a map of Esi. But the cartographer told her there was no single map. When Myung heard that, she believed she had reached another dead end. And so, she broke down. Alarmed, the cartographer made her tea, and Myung told her about the story she was searching for.

But the cartographer only shook her head.

People are always curious about the beginning of things, she had said. *It's silly. Things simply are. I never liked mirabilia diachronism. A bunch of stiff academics trying to see into the innards of a fairy tale. Why would you peel a fairy tale back to find out what it once was? Why know the history? It's a fairy tale now and it will be something else later, a new story, or perhaps a sea phrase, or a map, or a drawing. Your job is not to know what it once was or what it will become. Your job is to simply enjoy it. Listen to me, Myung Ting.* The cartographer enveloped Myung's hands in hers and patted them. *Beginnings are only matters of choice. So are ends. And any archive of you will be complete at any moment of time you choose to look at it, for you are here and you are living.*

Now Myung cries because the cartographer was right. Myung knows the story of Wisa; she's understood the beginning of the whale of babel, and she feels no different.

Laleh's sorrow is not for herself. It is for the whale. Myung used to say that the whale loved Laleh more than it loved her, but Laleh knew this was not true. It was simply that Myung never listened. The whale was speaking to them all the time—in gentle, sonorous sounds, happy songs, little whispers. The whale loves them both equally, with everything it has, because this is how their whale has been taught to love: with all of itself. Even though it is so big that Laleh struggles to comprehend it, even though she's never seen its eye or its shape, she has always felt close to it. To her, the whale is her companion.

Quir. This is its name. When was the last time someone called it by its name? Does Great Wisa—only Wisa now—call it Quir? And where is Wisa? Laleh and she are the only people the whale has left.

Laleh drifts away from the crowd. She doesn't want to be in this dream anymore. There are so many people here, acting out their desires in complicated ways. She is exhausted. She wants to be with her baby. She wants to comfort it.

As soon as she thinks it, the whale's song grows louder. In the World of the One Tree, Laleh opens her eyes. She is not awake . . . not precisely. She is still on Ojda. She can see the ghosts mill about her; she can hear the babble of conversation. But she is also in the whale of babel. Now she sits up in the whale and crawls along the branch. Climbs down the tree. Moves toward a door.

Throughout this dream, Ojda has been her primary reality and the whale has been a faint vision. Now the positions reverse. Her surroundings in the whale sharpen, growing more solid. Ojda fades, until it is only a vague impression.

Laleh *is* waking up. Her mind moves from the haziness of sleep into awareness. She can feel Ojda disappearing. Perhaps it would have disappeared altogether had Laleh not turned to look at her sister one more time . . .

And seen Blajine.

Blajine is looking directly *at* her. Not through her. Not beyond her. At her. The keeper is frowning, as if trying to place this new person. She looks at Myung and then at Laleh, and makes the connection.

And so Ojda doesn't disappear. It lingers, and Laleh lingers in the dream with it. The ghosts are turning now to Mad Magali. She has stood up and walked around the dead fire. She is staring at Myung. Laleh's sister is still sobbing. But years of disappointment and pain have shriveled Mad Magali's heart into a plum seed. It does not blossom in pity now.

Traveler, she says, raising her voice so that she can be heard over Myung's crying, *you said to us that you came from the whale of babel. You said you knew Wisa. I have told you the story you asked for. I have cut myself open and said it, even though it cost me to do so. Now it is your turn. Tell me about my sister. Where is she? How is she? And how is it that she came to make you?*

But Myung only wraps her arms around her knees and rocks. She says, *I don't know.*

II

Mad Magali is furious.

The traveler has been lying. How can she know nothing about Wisa? How can she have lived in the whale and not met Magali's sister? Myung trembles; she says, *I thought you would know. I thought you would tell me.* Jinn is here, putting his arm around Magali but she is shrugging him off; she relived that story, for what? To lose her sister all over again?

I told you she was lying, she tells Jinn. *I told you!*

Maybe she just doesn't remember, Rostum says, worming his way between Magali and the traveler.

The ghosts break into an argument. How can she not remember? Who forgets how they were born? It is spiraling into a Kilta argument, with no end in sight.

In the pandemonium, Blajine helps Myung to her feet. She takes her to the cottage and tucks her into the bed made of old fairy tales. She makes tea, which Myung doesn't drink because she is already asleep, exhausted by her tears. Blajine places the cup at the foot of the bed and steps outside.

It is quiet. Either the ghosts have dispersed or she cannot hear them. Either way, she welcomes the peace. She sits outside the cottage, staring at Ojda's strange landscape. Never the same view. She thinks of the woman she glimpsed just before the fight broke out. She doesn't look like a Kilta. Rather, her features are similar to Myung's. Blajine wonders if she is Myung's sister. She wonders how the woman got here. But then she gives up wondering: too much has happened in the past few days; she is too small to absorb it.

Ojda, Blajine says. A few rocks ten feet away from her quiver in fear. *Enough now. We're family. I know it hasn't been easy between us; I know I haven't always been the kindest. But you've tried to kill me, so I think I was being fair. Anyway, enough. We're family and that is all there is to it; we put up with each other like this, just as we are. No hunting for my shin bone or trying to gouge out my heart while I sleep. I am like this: four limbs, old knees, unexciting and grumpy. You'll have to take it. And if you do, I promise to take care of you until I can't. I love you, in my own way. And you love me too, even if you don't know it.*

Ojda is silent. The wind plays gently with Blajine's hair; rocks roll closer and nuzzle her knees. She strokes one. *I can't believe you let a traveler trick you*, she chides it and it bursts into a flower forty feet tall in embarrassment and panic. Blajine pokes it; it deflates, abashed.

Blajine sits there for a long while. In that time, Ojda doesn't change once; it stays still, as if afraid the slightest movement will scare her away. Blajine pats it. She enjoys the peace.

When she goes back, Myung is awake. The traveler is drinking tea and reading from the pages wrapped around the bed post; it is one of Blajine's favorite fairy tales.

Where did you find these? Myung whispers.

Blajine climbs into bed with her and slips under the covers. She looks at the extract Myung is reading.

> ". . . But you don't understand," cries the knight. "This is not who I am! I was cursed by the lightning fork to become naked, thin and small. And now I'm stuck on a perpetual search as knight, magician, witch, alchemist—so many skins—to find my real skin."
>
> "Well then!" Wisa says. "What were you before?"
>
> "I don't know," says the knight miserably. "I've tried and tried to remember, but I simply can't tell . . ."

It's from "Wisa and the Lost Knight," Blajine says. *From the book* Fairy Tales of Wisa. *I've wrapped others around my bed, look.*

She points to her favorite clipping, stuck to the top of the headboard. *This one is from "Wisa and the Whale's Tail."*

"But why are you crying?" whispers her yakuth. It nuzzles her face with its soft head; it curls around her. "Don't cry, little Wisa," it says. "We saved the chamber; the djinns are happy."

But Wisa continues weeping. Her tears drop from her chin and bounce off the marble floor as pearls.

"I am weeping because I cannot find the whale's tail," she says. "I am weeping, for without the whale's tail I shan't know how this tale will end."

"Must it end?" asks the djinn. "Can it not remain?"

"It must," Wisa says firmly. "For I am not made for one story, and neither are you . . ."

Myung puts down her tea and crawls along the bed, reading extracts. Blajine goes to a stack near the window, covered with a cloth. These are her mother's possessions. It is a Kilta tradition, when someone dies, to bury their belongings on Ojda but Blajine could not bring herself to give these up. Now she opens a wooden chest and pulls out a book.

The book is large, leather-bound with a gold-embossed title. *Fairy Tales of Wisa: Kilwi Classics Edition.* The pages are yellow with age, stained with fingers that have flipped through them, stuffed with drawings made by the Kilta children.

One of us brought it back, Blajine says. *It is a family treasure. We hide it because Mad Magali doesn't approve; she doesn't like anything that uses Wisa's name. But every Kilta grows up on these as bedtime stories.*

Myung turns a page, and runs her hand over a jagged edge, where a story has been torn out.

I did it when my mother died, Blajine says. *I missed her so much, and she used to read these to me. So I tore my favorite ones out and stuck them on the bed. So I could read them when I woke up. So I could feel like she was always here.*

Myung understands. She wishes she had taken something of Laleh's before she left the whale. She wishes, in fact, that she hadn't left at all.

Magali is mad at me, she whispers and Blajine shrugs.

She's mad at everyone, Blajine says. Then she adds: *You can stay here, if you like. On Ojda. I wouldn't mind.*

She doesn't look at Myung as she says it.

Thank you, Myung says, and she means it. She settles lower into the bed and puts her head on Blajine's shoulder.

Read me the best one.

They go through fourteen stories, taking turns to read them aloud. Then Blajine begins to cook dinner, and Myung sits on the floor of the cottage, peeling vegetables.

Is Wisa like this? Blajine asks. The stories are still traveling through her mind. They are so vivid, it feels like Wisa is with them in the room.

I don't know, Myung says honestly. *We have creation stories about her, but I think Laleh made those up. Or maybe she knew something I didn't. I don't know. I never saw Wisa. I always longed to. I think she's still in the whale somewhere, but it's so large we've never met her. We always thought she was looking for us.*

Blajine thinks about the girl disappearing into the whale's open mouth. What happened after that? How did she make Laleh and Myung? But this part of the story seems lost.

Are you upset? Blajine asks. *That you don't know how you came to be?*

Myung is not sure. *If my sister were here,* she says, *she would find out.*

III

In the whale of babel, Laleh wanders through different chambers.

She has not left the dream; it is still there, playing in the corner of her eye; she can see Blajine and Myung crouched over their meal, Mad Magali arguing with Jinn. But Laleh doesn't focus on it. Her attention is on the whale now.

She has no destination in mind; she simply walks to feel the whale, to remind it she is here. *Quir*, she whispers and her whale shakes. It has not heard its name in so long. *Quir*, she says again, smiling. It is difficult to reconcile the chambers with the little black bat she saw in the story. It is difficult to imagine the shift from something she can cuddle to something she cannot comprehend. But the whale's song anchors her. In it, she hears the memories it keeps close. She feels its love.

Don't cry, darling, she says. *It is you and me now. As long as it is you and me, we will be all right.*

Ahead of her, something moves.

Laleh stops. She is still straddling two worlds, so she is not sure of what she saw. She inches closer, toward the time cobwebs that flutter in each chamber of the whale. She looks carefully.

There is a person before her. Her head is bowed, her hair obscuring her face. She is petting a snowy white yakuth that is resting its chin on her lap. The yakuth's eyes are half-closed; it is dozing. The woman strokes it absent-mindedly. Her hand is mangled, as if someone smashed it over and over with a rock. Then she lifts her face and her hair falls back.

This, then, is the moment Laleh has been waiting for. Even before Myung longed to see people, even before she left the whale and Laleh dreamed her way onto Ojda, even before she lived lifetimes in this dream, this is the moment Laleh has longed for.

A chance to meet her maker.

It is Wisa.

What of Fairy Tales That Sing?
FOREWORD TO A KILWI CLASSICS EDITION OF FAIRY TALES OF WISA

Syla Munsir

Philosopher of the Caspian Ocean

Fairy Tales of Wisa

The Kilwi Classics Edition

[Front flap]

T his never-before-seen collection of *Fairy Tales of Wisa* will shock you! Come, travel the worlds of the whale of babel as Wisa wanders through its belly on a series of enthralling adventures, battling dragons and befriending simurghs.

Featuring four new stories just discovered, plus, a foreword by the famous Syla Munsir chronicling the discovery of the *Fairy Tales*, this gorgeously illustrated compendium promises you an adventure of a lifetime.

Foreword

The first story of *Fairy Tales of Wisa* appeared on a crumbling island, written on the bark of a tree. The villagers cut it out and read it to each other, soon making a festival out of it. For one night each season, they'd gather around a bonfire and enact the story. In the smoke, Wisa would appear, alive, and fight adventures in their midst.

A traveler came to a festival and fell in love with this imaginary Wisa. He wrote down his own version of the story and circulated it on the black sea. This tale was paler; Wisa had talking friends and worried about mundane affairs, like how to wear her night-time hair. The story didn't find an audience and disappeared from circulation.

But then a young cartographer discovered another island with a pamphlet buried in the sand. This Wisa was the Wisa from the first story: wild and eccentric, capable of battling any creature. She had a yakuth as a companion, and in this story, she helped a knight find his missing skin. Fascinated and having heard of the original island, the cartographer went on a voyage. He found fairy tales across lands as diverse as fish, each featuring the same enigmatic personality, Wisa, battling monsters in a whale with many chambers in its belly. He traveled on this quest for sixty years. When he died, his daughter took over the journey. Finally, a hundred and twenty years after the cartographer first began his travels, a hundred and eighty-five since the traveler attended the festival, and two hundred and six years since the island found the story written on the tree, a complete collection of *Fairy Tales of Wisa* was published.

For a long time, we believed it was nothing more than a beloved children's story. But the kids tumbling into the Vortex of Noma said the whale was real; they spoke of chambers not in the fairy tales. Academics latched on to this, and the scholars of mirabilia diachronism began hunting the black sea for the origins of the whale; archaeologists went looking for it. And so our literature on the whale was born.[*] We dreamed of a new universe growing in this one, birthing new ways of living.

I am a philosopher of the Caspian Ocean, not an academic. My fascination does not lie with the truth of the whale or Wisa, but with what these stories reveal about us. Twenty-two years ago, when I first visited the Vortex of Noma, when we hadn't acknowledged the whale was real, I wrote an essay on these fairy tales:

> Imagine, for a moment, that the whale of babel is real. That there is a woman called Wisa with night-time hair singing nonsensical lyrics around a fire as she dances a ritual of madness, looking at us slyly from beneath hooded eyes. Imagine that the fairy tale we've loved for so long, a whale full of water trees and disappearing chambers, is real in some place or time, and a knight in woven rainbow armor really does wander through the belly of the beast alone, stringing up adventures like pearls on a thread.
>
> Your child will have no trouble imagining it.
>
> Is there a reason that only children tumble into the Vortex of Noma and return? Is there something we are born with, soft and malleable, that hardens as we age? For children are falling into the vortex and returning with snippets of far-flung islands clutched in their hands. We are left on shores and flimsy boats to string together the fish-silver curiosities they collect. Understanding eludes us. Wisdom turns in to smoke. I cannot shake the feeling that gibberish is nothing but words ordered on a logic that's beyond us, and I press my ears to my toddler's lips as she gurgles the secrets of the universe.

---

[*] The most famous of this is Mina Zoya's *Choosing Fabrics: Imagining the Whale of Babel*, but you may recognize others as well, such as *Navigating the Whale of Babel* by Uki Jull and *Babel Beginnings: Understanding the Whale's Architecture* by Kim Diq.

Why do fairy tales fascinate us? Why do they stay by our side long after we hear them and become our little pieces of pleasure? Fairy tales don't listen to the bounds of our world; they take place "once upon a time," outside of our reality. They have their own logic. But they also hold infinite possibilities. Where does Wisa's mythical beast come from? Why does it grow worlds? What is her quest and who made her rainbow coat? These are small questions, but they hold large fascinations. They promise more—more than we can see, touch, hear, feel. More than we can know. And it is delicious.

I believe that when we read we are searching for a smooth and polished mirror so that we may better see our reflections. This is the fascination all narratives hold over us: we are looking for ourselves.

But I believe it is not just mirrors that we seek—it is magic mirrors. We don't only want reflections of ourselves; we want to know if there is the possibility of change in our future, whether there is more to this reality than we can touch and smell, more to ourselves. We seek potential, our wilderness. This is why fairy tales are more beloved than most. These are stories that let us stare at ourselves, the essential parts of our humanness, before we step through into a new world; before we become something more.

I hope this collection gives you as much joy as it's given me. I hope it sparks your sense of wonder. These tales are magic mirrors—they offer glimpses into a world we can only dream of, a world that is rich and somehow emblematic of us. Take a breath. Put your hand on the glass. Step through.

WHALE OF BABEL, AGAIN

The Long-Awaited Meeting

Half in the whale of babel and half in my dream, I stare at her.

Wisa.

Great Wisa.

The two names sit beside each other. The Great Wisa from my stories and early memories of the whale, and the Wisa I learned about in Magali Kilta's story. They layer onto each other, but they don't merge. They cannot.

I look at the woman in wonder. It *is* her. There is her mangled hand and her broken smile. She is wearing a long coat that shimmers with the colors of the rainbow. This is not the rainbow-colored coat of the drifters, which was thick and had clearly dyed bands of color. This shimmering is closer to the rainbow glaze of the time cobwebs.

I view Wisa from behind one of these fabrics now. It washes her out, making her seem almost spirit-like. She is the same height as me, which disappoints me. I expected Great Wisa to tower over the palms in the World of Bird and Leaf; I expected her to crush chambers with her toe. Then I am ashamed of my disappointment. We are made in Great Wisa's likeness, so does it not make sense that she would be the same shape as me?

Oh, Myung, if only you could see this.

My dream is still there. Like the two names of Wisa and Great Wisa, coexisting simultaneously but not merging, I straddle two realities. When I look at Wisa, the whale of babel sharpens around me. I can see the cobwebs more clearly; I notice the black streak on the face of the yakuth curled around my creator. But the dream is still there too. I can feel Myung as a presence on my shoulder. She is in bed, reading *Fairy Tales of Wisa*. Sounds from Ojda filter through to me: birds squawking; Hormuz pontificating about the multiplied effects of Magali's story on the edified status and continued existence of ghost hood; Mad Magali, wandering across Ojda's plains now, shouting at the universe for her sister.

Her sister is here.

I don't know what to do. I feel paralyzed by the weight of my own longing, by everything I have lived so far. I have longed to meet Great Wisa since I can first remember. But now I don't know how to approach her. What would I say? I always imagined Myung would be with me, and she would make the task easier. Myung would simply run up to Wisa and hug her. Or ask her questions about how she made us. Why she made us. She would say: *Are Laleh's creation stories true?*

Myung, I miss you.

Wisa is scratching her yakuth behind the ears. It rises up, its long silver tail rippling in the air. She climbs onto it. I realize what is happening a second too late; she is whispering in the yakuth's ear, and then they are off, out of this chamber, away from me.

Wait!

I run. I call on the whale of babel with the strength of my will and it gives me a baby simurgh to ride; the bird catches me in its talons, and I climb onto its back as it flies; I am astonished at my stupidity and angry at my cowardice. I always act late. I always think, think, think until everything disappears. If I lose the chance to meet my creator because of this, I will never forgive myself.

But the simurgh flies after the yakuth with a speed that gladdens me. Wisa slips through a door and we follow. She slips through another and I chase her there too. We are moving through chambers too quickly for me to notice them, but even with my single-minded focus, I realize I have never moved through doors like this. Wisa seems to simply conjure them up, darting in and out of chambers like a needle and thread. She does not find a door as much as it rushes toward her to swallow her up.

Wisa, I shout. *Great Wisa!*

But she does not hear me. Her mind is so full of large thoughts that I am but a speck in her grand imaginings. Some part of me cannot reconcile this with the Wisa I saw in Magali's story, but the other part of me doesn't care. This is the way it is; it is how it has always been.

Great Wisa, I shout. *Please!*

And then she is gone. She slips through a door and my simurgh moves to follow, but it is not quick enough. The door vanishes and we crash through another one instead, a new door hiding right behind the first one, and now I am in a chamber of crystal shards that light up like moon slices, and I cannot find my way back to her. Once again, I am alone.

We have a story about the time cobwebs. I made it up when Myung and I were in a world so dark we couldn't see each other. Myung was scared. She didn't know how she could find a door in this chamber or how we would ever leave. I was scared too. But Myung's fear steadied mine, and I looked up at the only other fixtures with us.

Even in the darkness, you could see the time cobwebs.

And so I told her a story about them.

> When Great Wisa created the sisters, they found joy in all things. They knew no despair. But when Wisa tried to leave them to wander in new chambers, they grew fearful.
>
> "Do not leave," the sisters begged, "for we would be lost without you. How are we to walk through these chambers? How are we to find doors? Great Wisa, this whale is vast and we are too small. Without you, how are we to live?"
>
> And so Great Wisa drew from her heart a shimmering cloth. She hung these fabrics across the chambers and in them, she poured her love and her wisdom.
>
> She said: "If you are lost, my sisters, look to these fabrics, for in them are my gifts. If you ever fear falling, remember that these cloths will catch you. If you are lost, then you must sing and our beloved whale will sing back to you."

I loved this story even as I said it. Here, Great Wisa tells you it is okay to be scared.

Now I sit in the World of the Sliced Moons, the crystal shards rotating around me, and I am scared. I was so close to meeting Wisa, to asking her my questions, to doing what Myung and I have longed for—but I missed my chance. I fear I will never get another one. I fear my dream of Ojda will fade and I won't see my sister again. And I will live with pain and hollowness in my heart, and because it is in my heart, I will have failed the whale as well.

But I think of this story now and I feel better. I look up at the fabrics and, even in my moment of despair, I am at peace. Great Wisa is with me. Her wisdom is in these cobwebs. And I will always carry Myung in my heart.

I don't know why I think of it, but an image pops into my mind. It is from Magali's story. It is a little black bat, Quir, climbing out of a pot and shaking the gold off itself. It is looking up at me with big black eyes. And Wisa's voice carries to me, across time and space.

It grants your wishes.

An idea is forming. Before my whale was the whale of babel, it was Quir and it was made to give people what they asked for.

Now that I know this, it is obvious that it has always been true. How else could Myung find a way out of the whale when it is so vast and she so small? Why else would doors hide when Myung needed them to? Or appear when I asked for them? And why has it always been so easy to forage in the whale? I've seen enough of the black sea now to know this is not the way of that universe. People starve. They accidentally eat what could kill them. They spend whole sleeps growing food, so that they may survive during difficult seasons. Everything I have eaten in the whale has been good, pure and fortifying. It has been what I wanted, when I wanted it.

I only had to think of it.

I close my eyes.

Quir, I whisper. *Please. Take me to Wisa.*

The whale's song changes; it grows lighter, plaintive. It is begging me, I realize. It is saying: *Please. Do not ask for this.*

But I need this. *Just once*, I promise. *Let me meet her only once.*

And so slowly, reluctantly, a door opens at my feet. I am peering into a world I recognize—the World of Bird and Leaf.

I step in.

I reappear two feet from the ground, and tumble onto grass. I do not know why the whale has brought me here, back to the chamber where it all started. I stand up, trying to guess where in the chamber I am—

Wisa is in front of me.

Up close, she is not like the woman I saw in Magali's memory. She is older. Her hair is gray and her face is scarred with wrinkles. It is so shocking to see signs of aging in the whale (I've seen it in the black sea, but never in the whale) that I take a step back. She is staring at me with equal astonishment.

Each time I thought about meeting Great Wisa, I imagined a reunion sweeter than the sweetest fruit. I imagined her benevolence and pride. She would look at Myung and me with tears in her eyes and say: *You have taken care of my whale well, my sisters. You have been good keepers.*

But this Wisa does not know me.

Then her expression changes. Recognition? Realization? Or maybe she has just got over her shock. She grabs my wrist.

Listen, she says urgently. *There is still time. Tell it it can't. Tell it—*

Then, as if blown away on a breeze, she is gone.

I crouch and put my head between my knees. I do not know what is happening. I want Myung. I want her curiosity and her ability to see even the most baffling of things, even the most crushing, as simply another opportunity for adventure. I feel so many things at once, I am overwhelmed. I am devastated that I have dreamed of meeting Wisa for so long and this is how it went. I miss Myung. But above all, I am angry with the whale of babel. For keeping me in the dark. For letting me jump through doors without telling me what is on the other side. For hiding from me all the things I realize now it must be hiding.

For nothing makes sense, and that only happens when there are secrets.

The whale cries out.

It is a shrill cry; it judders through me. It is saying sorry, over and over. I don't want to forgive it. My hurt is large, and I want someone to blame. But I know I feel the same anger with the whale as I do with Myung—absolute, but also with an awareness that it will end, that it cannot transcend the love.

The whale's song changes. It is trying to make it better. It will tell me all, it promises. The ground beneath me shakes, and the World of Bird and Leaf changes.

The river flowing around the circumference of the chamber rises up, the water streams and solidifies into silver fur. The lake at the end of the river is reforming into a dragon's head, its nostrils as large as caves and its horns the size of hills.

It is a yakuth. No, it is Wisa's yakuth. I recognize the black streak across its face. It is curving its torso now, bringing itself to the ground. It rests its chin in front of me.

Trembling, I place my hand on its fur.

The yakuth closes its eyes. Then it exhales, and two puffs of brilliant white smoke envelop me.

And I remember.

The Story of Ourselves: Part One

For you to understand, we have to tell you everything.

We are born in a shallow pot, in liquid gold. Even in our small shape, we contain multitudes in us; we know it. When you speak, you talk of yourself as a singular, an "I." We could never be an "I." We are "we," even if all you could see was a little black bat.

Our first memory is of you. We clamber out of the pot, shaking, and you wrap us in cloth. You warm us with your hands. We don't know you and so we do not love you—not as yet. But we remember your hands. We remember the tears in your eyes.

You take us home. Everything that happens on the island of Esi is so brief to us, no more than a blink of an eye. What is two years compared to the billion centuries we will live? But you show us your family. They love us, like you do. And then we love you too. Fiercely. We treasure everything in that blink of an eye.

Most of all, we treasure you.

Later, you will ask: when did you decide to do what you did? You haven't asked it as yet, but you will. We know you. So we will tell you now.

This is the moment.

We have become the whale of babel. We are floating somewhere in the black sea. You are in a chamber. You are tapping your feet and rolling your shoulders. *Quuiiiirrrr*, you call, half-laughing. The chamber trembles. Your yakuth shivers, trying to keep time to a beat that is too fast and sharp for its sinuous body.

The music is low. Soft. Only you can hear it. Around you, the chamber leans closer, curious—you smile and wink, shaking your head in time with the drums.

Now the trumpet comes in and you are dancing, long languid strides, your arms in the air. *Quir, darling*, you call, *louuuuder, please.* The music swells, brash, excited. You move your feet faster, your footwork elaborate; the chamber peers closer—oh, Wisa, you have always been lovely. You are smiling now, beckoning, and ozums pop from the ground; murids grow from asteroids. Even mountains bend their great snow-white heads to watch this little woman dance on the air. You snap your fingers; you shout, *Listen!* And the music is growing now, growing audible to the chamber itself, and moons begin to leave their posts; your yakuth swivels in frenzied circles—*Quir, darling*, you say, *it is not the details; it is never the details. Let's go maaaad.* And we don't know what you mean but it doesn't matter for the music drops again, rhythm drumming its way into the fabric of our being, the fabrics of time fluttering above you, but you don't give them a single glance. You are in the middle of a mob, creatures wiggling through doors to get to you, ozums going delirious with joy, yakuths bursting out of the air, and you whisper, *are you ready?*

And there, among the throng of worlds swirling around you, is another person. The only other person by your side for decades, young and ageless. A figment of your imagination.

Your sister smiles and the chamber bursts.

Color. Music. A flood. Creatures popping into new shapes, worlds shifting, and you at the center of it, kicking your legs and waving your arms and screaming, elated, ridiculous, mad—*sun!*—as an ozum swells to become a supernova—*giant!*—as a mountain stands up on its shaky legs—on and on, the music tumbling into a jangle of notes, your sister's hands in yours as you kick and jump and tangle in a frenzy, laughing. If we could hold time, this is what we would hold. This incandescence of a joy that is wholly your own. That becomes ours.

This is the moment we decide.

But you understand time in a linear fashion, and so we will start at the beginning.

We begin with you inside a whale. You are on your knees, weeping. We weep with you, an aching song that travels through our belly and curves up our sides. We tremble. You keep your face in your hands and don't look at where we are going. Grief eats at you. On a beach on Esi, you leave your sister behind as she screams. You try to forget her.

We swim. Some part of you expects us to change—there is no need for us to be a whale—but we don't. We just swim, powerfully and steadily, as far from the source of your grief as we can take you. We swim over fairy tales and into dreams, through cracks of time, just swim, until you get off your knees one day, wipe your eyes and look around.

We have grown. You can no longer see the mouth you walked in from, nor the slope of our body as it moves toward the tail. You walk. It is damp and warm, your hair sticking to your nape. In pockets, the air is light and here you find moss on your whale's insides, seedlings curling out from it, buds pushing through. It reminds you of monsoon—*putuk*. After a while, you notice the light. Shafts falling at different angles, sourceless.

When you stumble upon a door, it is no more than a gash in the roof of the whale. Large enough to fit your body. You look up. The surface of the door is burnished and gleaming. You jump for it and the ground lets you go. You float. You grab the corner of the gash and wiggle through, the edges lapping at your body like water.

The space you enter is dark. It takes a moment for your eyes to adjust but by then you are already panicking—there is no world here, only emptiness. You can't see where this begins or ends. The floor is floating away, the door growing smaller. You swim toward it, desperate, but now the door is only a pinpoint, the size of the tip of your nose. Has it shrunk or have you grown?

Your eyes adjust and your breath catches. Around you are fabrics, made of a sheer rainbow glaze. They criss-cross each other, no beginning or end.

Each fabric is at least as long as Esi.

You are petrified. You are so small.

For a long time, you drift.

Sometimes you swim, crawling through those doors when you find them. Sight, you learn, is a trick. We grow in chambers, yes, but we are not made for your vision. You cannot tell dimensions except for sudden shafts of light and then you wish you couldn't see at all, for each room can hold a thousand of your island, a million, a billion. Space flows in ways you cannot understand. You are drifting through folding and unfolding origami.

Once, only once, you travel to Esi.

It is brief, a liquid image that won't stay. It happens with no warning. You are floating in the darkness of our chambers and when you blink, you are in the luddite colony, in your garden. It is night. You have spent so long in darkness that even the moonlight is too bright; you shrink from it. You don't know how you got here. The flowers feel fragile in your fingers; the grass pokes at you. Then you look up, and Magali is staring at you. She's young, only sixteen. She's horrified. You howl, *Maga*—

She's gone. The garden is gone too. You are back in the pitch black.

You drift.

You go through a door.

You drift.

Another door.

Then you stop moving. Around you, the blackness breathes. You've swum through eight hundred and seventy-two doors. You have counted. Enough. You want to die.

But you don't. Instead, your sister appears. One moment she is not there, the next she is standing above you. She is wearing the same clothes as she wore on the beach in Esi—her hair is wild; she is covered in sand and sweat. You assume she is your hallucination.

You are grateful to see another person, even if she isn't real.

Get up, she says.

Are you Death? you whisper.

No.

You curl into a ball. She jabs you in the ribs. You moan. Suddenly, you want to pour all choice into this imaginary sister. If she wants you to act, she must make you. If she wants you to be wise, she must be that wisdom for you. It is a unique pact we make with those we love: *when I cannot be wise or brave, be those things for me.*

You're being self-pitying, she says.

I want to die.

Don't be silly. You've been here before.

When? you whisper. *When have I been inside a child I made, floating in a space so large I cannot see, describe or understand it? When have I been so alone that loneliness feels like a spirit by itself, coming from me and yet stalking me? When have I wept just to hear a song other than my breathing. When?*

Wisa Kilta, I won't indulge this. You have been here before.

She means on Esi, before you came to the luddite colony. The island was so large you didn't understand it, couldn't describe it, couldn't fully see it. You floated on the fringes of a civilization, fitting in nowhere, leaning on the strange impulses that drove you. You were eaten by loneliness so soft it wormed into your bones. So pervasive you could not ignore it. You found a way to survive.

It irritates you that she is right. You bury your head in your arms.

Quir, you command, *let me die.*

Your imaginary sister is pulling you up by the armpits, holding you upright even as you become a dead weight. You know you are being ridiculous, but you cannot help it. You will not make this easy. You flop and flail, relax your neck so that your head lolls. Some part of you really wants to die. Some part of you is grateful for this, for your sister holding you up, for not having to think or act, for being able to surrender to the arms of someone who loves you. You like that this shadow-Magali—Magali-ilk, you call her—staggers under your weight.

Look at me, Magali-ilk says.

You raise your head reluctantly.

When you were here before, she says, *when you were alone and scared and had no one in the world but yourself, what did you do?*

This answer is easy: you dreamed of creating a world where you belonged. And then you created it.

Magali-ilk lets you go. You don't flop; you are holding yourself up. You look at the blackness again. It has grown cracks, space flowing in and out of these lines in unknown dimensions. It is empty. It is *empty*.

Which means it can be filled.

Much like a blank canvas.

When you look back at Magali-ilk, she is gone.

But the idea she gave you remains. Your little black bat—little no longer—is a wish-giving creature. It is eager to please. If these chambers have nothing in them, why not *make* something in them? Why not build worlds?

―

We tell you now: these are your glory decades. This is when you become the Wisa we remember, with magic in your step. Nothing can stop you. Nothing is out of reach. We learn from you, beloved. Everything we do or did, we learned from you.

You don't know how to begin creating worlds but you experiment. You try asking for them. You try visualizing them (this one works well). You even try song, and you are surprised to find it works the best—you can sing things into existence by imagining them and pushing that vision into any sound that feels right. You don't realize, of course, that we are singing with you. That we make whatever you want or ask for, and song is the easiest way to tell us what you need.

You start with food. It is a practicality we never thought of, but you are conjuring up your favorite sugarplums and although their taste is a bit off, they fill you. You have been starving, slowly. You've stumbled across pools of black water that you can drink, but the soft and mushy objects in them, which wriggle like prawns, haven't been enough to nourish you. Once you've eaten everything you can imagine—once you've made yourself sick—you begin to make worlds.

Oh, the worlds you create. Onyx cliffs. Curled cloud seas. Trees carrying moons in their gnarled fingers, hornbills swallowing suns, crustaceans blooming into nebulas. You jump through doors and transform chambers. It doesn't matter then how big they are; you fill them with your imagination. This is what you longed for in a way, on Esi. Freedom. Expanse. The ability to burst as large as possible. You shape dragons that grow from big to small each time they walk, stitch a sky from algae that dance apart and dance together, place giant pearls in the sky that grow, slowly, into lattices.

Then you calm down and begin organizing chambers along themes, so that you can identify them. We help you. Elsewhere, in far more chambers than you can ever visit, we copy you. Pitch black changes into a thick, milky mist. And from that mist, worlds emerge. They are made of what we absorbed on Esi—shapes, memories, people's desires. They morph into each other organically, and form new shapes. Worlds unlike, perhaps, anything you have seen.

You're lonely.

You conjure yourself up a creature with a dragon head and a long eel-like tail. You call it yakuth. It becomes your companion, but it is not enough. You want people. You want your family. All worlds are empty beyond a point if you have no one to share them with.

You've forgotten us already. We're too large now; we've become the concepts of "chamber," "world" and "black space" in your head. You no longer see us as a "little black bat." As Quir.

But we are here. We have always been here. We lead you to a chamber we have made, designed with the plants of Esi, each in varying sizes. We fill it with the scents of your beloved island. We sing. And you hear us.

You weep. *Quir*, you say, *my child*.

Darling, dearest, beloved—our cosmos is made for you.

We are looking at:

You, in an empty and unpainted chamber. There is no music. You hold out your arms and dance, slowly, your steps wide and your arcs graceful. You twirl. You bend backward into a dip; the air catches you. You cry. Tears drip off your chin, liquid swirls that uncurl into rabbits and white storks, flying away. You cry because your heart has grown larger than your body and it wants to bloom like the sea constellation you will paint above you. You cry because there is wonder here and you are full.

Then you keep crying, even when you double in half and press your palm to your lips, clutching your cheeks until they turn white and your fingers leave red marks that stay for days after.

The glory years end when you see Myung.

You spot her through a time fabric. She is in a world you have never seen before, a chamber with an upside-down island and a civilization of blue monkeys. She does not see you. You reach for her, astonished, but then the fabric flutters and she is gone.

If we could have spared you the vision, we would have. But time doesn't work straight in our belly, no matter how much you insist on seeing it as linear. So we cannot control what you glimpse or what you long for—

And so you go mad.

You become obsessed with finding her. It is no longer enough for you to make worlds and tend to them. You want this girl.

You move through chambers now with a purpose: you are looking for patterns and clues. Where does the girl come from? Are there more like her? You are so desperate for company that you cling to these questions like a lifeline. You retreat from us. We sing and we sing, but you don't come back.

We are not enough.

If your sister were here—your real sister, not Magali-ilk—she would tell you that you are a mote in a whale far larger than you can comprehend. That you have moved through this creature's belly by forces you cannot see. That you find doors only because the doors find *you*, traveling across space and time so that you may stumble upon them and pass through. Otherwise you would have been lost in a single chamber forever, so large are they and so small are you.

You know this, she would tell you gently, tucking your hair behind your ears. *Quir has always liked to be seen. Wisa, it is like you—it needs love.*

Then she would grow serious. She would say: *What does this tell us about this whale? Think, Wisa. Look carefully, as you would on Esi. It tells us that there are more chambers than you know or can know; this whale now exists outside of your imagination. It tells us that you can make sea constellations that sing a map of your whereabouts or send yakuths in herds to find the girl. But you will fail because your efforts will be too weak to cross the spaces they must cross. Wisa, my jaan, you are smaller than you like to believe. You're so small, nothing in this universe fits in your hands. Have you forgotten what it was like before, when there was only blackness and no paint, when you drifted? Have you forgotten your terror?*

You will look at your hands in shame, for, of course, you have not forgotten the terror. It gives you nightmares, dreams where everything you've painted disappears and then you slowly start to shrink, smaller and smaller, until you disappear too. When you wake up, you hug your yakuth close.

Your real sister has more to say. She would take your hands and tell you, *look at me.* Then she would wait until you do. Once you are staring at her, wide and trusting, when you have placed your fate in her hands, she would tell you:

Give up this quest for the girl. Walk away. The longer you search, the more you will realize your own insignificance. You'll learn that the painting is a way to keep yourself together, to ignore how little you control. If you walk away now, you'll find happiness in these things. But the longer you stick with this quest, the more those things will fade. And you will fall apart.

You would nod. You would listen. We believe it, we do.

But your sister is not here.

―

More time passes.

You do not find Myung. You give up the quest slightly; even if you don't admit it to yourself, you are losing hope.

But as hope leaves, so does everything else. You stop swimming. You drift again. When a door passes you, you stare at it listlessly, unsure if you want to go through. You think of your sister entwining her hands with yours on the beach of Esi as you both stared into our cold, dark mouth. You, pushing your sister away as she tried to follow.

No, you had said.

Now you wish you had said yes. You hate yourself for this desire, but you would give anything to have your sister beside you. Beloved, we know this is why you stand up one day and make a coat of shimmering rainbow for yourself. Why you make a staff like the one Grandpa used to carry through the forest. You are trying to save yourself. You know if you don't, this loneliness will kill you.

I am Wisa Kilta, you say. You say it again, louder. *I am Wisa Kilta!*

Your voice echoes back to you.

Then you do the worst thing possible.

You begin to explore these chambers.

You have a universe at your feet; you have understood this now. You have also understood that the girl you were on Esi (but you're not that girl anymore) would find joy in discovering this universe. In categorizing and speaking to it. And so that is what you try to do: explore us as you would a new and strange landscape.

But we are not a landscape. We are a cosmos. A small one, but we are growing bigger with every moment. We are not made for your eyes. The more carefully you look, the more scared you become. It is as if you have played with us for years and years but only now do you notice our claws. You stay close to your yakuth. You tremble.

It hurts us, your fear. We are not trying to scare you. But our vastness is terrifying, for it is the mirror that reminds you of your fragility. You feel the tininess of your lungs, the brittleness of your bones. Your body has no more substance than dust. It is so easy to vanish.

We almost lose you then. You have fallen apart so completely, there's only the barest thread of you left. You hold on to that thread, and you whisper, desperate: *Quir*.

We answer. We push through space and time, through boundaries we didn't know could be crossed, to give you what you need.

We sing.

Our song is tart and sweet, powerful and relentless. It sweeps through chambers with fervor, melting everything into a current thick with color. You are swept up in it. You are lost and found. This is our gift to you, our rope thrown to a drowning sailor, our beloved.

For in that flood, you see them.

Grandpa. Magali. Jinn. Your grandpa is dancing in foolish looseness, an absent-minded smile on his face. He is old, but he is still Kua; he's dancing to music other than what you are hearing, the twang of a luddite strula. And Magali is grinning at you with love, her hair streaked with the odd white hair, wrinkles sprouting from the corners of her eyes. She is holding Jinn's hand, whom she must have married by now, and these—oh, please, let it be—these are her children, small and light, clambering over you, asking questions you cannot hear, pulling your nose and checking your hair for shellfish. They giggle with a joy beyond you. They are so perfect, it hurts.

Then the song ends. Only the fabrics remain untouched; everything else is a thick sea of paint. Opposite you is your sister.

Not the hallucination of your sister. Your sister. She is older, dressed in sailor robes, her hair stiff with salt. She is so beautiful—still strong, even in her frailty, like the black sea never stood a chance with her. She can see you.

You're part of my dream, aren't you? she says, laughing and crying.

Or you're part of mine, you whisper, reaching for her.

Then the sea moves and she is gone.

We are looking at:

You. Your nose is in line with our face, your eyes enormous. This is a time from Esi; we have just been born; the edges of the moment are blurry and indistinct. We are crying, although we don't know why.

Perhaps we tried to become something and couldn't. Perhaps we saw where we wanted to go but didn't know how to get there.

You rub our head with your thumb; you make shushing noises. *Don't cry, little Quir*, you say. *If you cry, I cry.*

We cry harder, just to test the theory. It's true: you weep. You cradle us to your chest, cupping your hands around us and in the slatted darkness, we feel safe, warm. *It's you and me now, darling*, you say softly. *It's you and me.*

We assume it is a promise.

It is as if the song breached a boundary between us and the black sea—now you flow into your sister's surroundings, a gift from her double sight.

Oh, these visits are everything. You learn that your sister is a traveler. You would not have imagined it: you thought your sister is a tree, made to grow roots and keep them. But this is not how it turned out. Magali lives on ships, builds fragments of her life on quays and uproots them to keep moving. Jinn is with her, although you do not see him; when you visit, Magali is alone.

I used to see you in nightmares, she tells you. *You used to scream for me, over and over, and I could do nothing.*

Your sister is collecting the black sea's song. She travels across it, capturing the music she hears in notes and glass vials. Later, she tries to draw the melody. We have seen this image in Kua: his head bent, hand tracing a pattern beneath the surface, searching for a shape. Magali is studying the songs' shapes and depth. She wants to understand their reach.

What a strange impulse it is, to sing. To throw your voice as far away from you as it will go. To make a home for a feeling.

It's incredible, she says, showing you her notes. *The joule sings to ask the earth to churn for it, but the sleeping squids, they sing to conjure up dreams and these dreams hold the questions that the Caspian philosophers are beginning to study. There is so much in song, so much we haven't understood. How good is it at holding memory? Can it stay still in time?*

You like seeing her like this—alight, alive. These visits heal you. You go back to tending your worlds; you forget about Myung. You dance and teach your yakuth to dance too. You are happy. We believe it, we do.

I'm coming to find you, Magali says.

You smile; you kiss her knuckles tenderly. You know it will not happen; that quest will take more time than either of you has. But it's okay. This is enough.

Sometimes, you think about the girl you saw in the time cobweb.

You're not looking for her anymore. But you wonder how she exists. You have traveled through so many chambers by this point, and there has been no sign of human life. You have not seen a single other person except this girl. How?

You ponder this question for years, and slowly, the answer begins to form. You don't say anything to us. Not yet. But we catch you staring at doors for longer than is necessary. Watching the fabrics more closely. Vague impressions coalesce in your mind—you *know* this girl; you're sure of it—but the answer is just out of reach.

You look at Magali-ilk.

Magali-ilk turns up in the moments you need her. When you search for Myung or when you are exploring, she is by your side. Now, when you look at her, she doesn't look very much like Magali. Oh, she is the sister you remember on the beach, but you have seen the *real* Magali now and she has changed in ways you could not imagine.

Still, there is something sweet about this hallucination. You love her; we know you do. Perhaps she is an anchor to a simpler time, where the black sea followed rules you understood. Perhaps you simply love her, the hallucination herself. After all, who else has been by your side?

You hold her hand and ask: *Are you lying to me?*

She doesn't answer. She lies down next to you and watches the fabrics flutter, for she is a part of your mind and she knows you already know the answer.

For one day, you will wake up with the story of the girl in you. You will have figured it out. And you will crawl to Magali-ilk, your heart hammering and your palms sweaty. You will take her face in your hands. For, of course, she is your hallucination, but she is not *only* your hallucination.

Quir, you will say.

Her face won't change. But in this light, you will imagine that her eyes look limpid and large. Like a little black bat's.

You will be crying.

Oh, my darling, you will say. *Oh, my beloved. I know who the girl is. You mustn't. You can't.*

The Story of Ourselves: Part Two

The first time we realize you die, we see it. You are playing a game with Magali-ilk, laughing, running, and then in the same chamber, you are there, older, frailer. When you smile, your face crinkles. When you lift your hand to pet your snow-white yakuth, still as young as the day you imagined him, we see the structure of your bones, stare at your veins winding down your arm like rivers.

We don't know what is happening. We scramble through space and time. We look at you again, carefully—weeping in the first room, reveling in your first yakuth flight, hunting desperately for Myung, and it's true . . . you're changing. Slowly, ever so slowly, time for you is running out.

We cannot believe it.

We do not believe it. Time is endless. Everything here lasts forever, changes only when they want to, if they like. You are here now. You live in us, not on Esi or the black sea; you don't follow their laws anymore. You follow ours. Don't you?

But you are dying.

We cannot look away from it any longer. In black sea time, you should have died already; you are a sea turtle, with centuries under your skin.

Still, you haven't escaped death entirely. It comes for you, only slowly. *Run!* we want to shout. *Look, there it is, Wisa—flee.*

But you don't notice anything. You move through chambers, playing with your yakuth, talking to your sister—the imaginary one and, when double sight lets you, the real one. You haven't realized the story of Myung and Laleh, not as yet. You are content. This is your universe now; you have made a home.

We try to save you. Gossamer fabrics flutter slowly to life. They reach for you. Pieces drift gently onto your shoulders; they try to stick. They attempt to stitch themselves into cocoons that will keep you preserved. But they only rot off, obeying a language of living we do not understand. Why can we not keep you? Why won't you stay?

You learn you are dying at the same time you realize who Myung is. The knowledge is entwined; each one is born from the other. You hold Magali-ilk's face in your hands. The sister we made from your memories so you wouldn't be lonely.

Oh, my darling, you say, and you are talking to us. *Oh, my beloved. I know who the girl is. You mustn't. You can't.*

Dying doesn't scare you. Perhaps you have expected it. Perhaps you know no other way. All things must end, you tell us, but it is a small wisdom given to small humans. We can do better. We can change this.

You grow agitated. *Quir,* you say. *You must let me go.*

The chambers echo your voice back to you; it rings among the fabrics.

Quir! you shout. *Let me go.*

We don't answer. You were made in a sea different from this one; you were shaped by small possibilities. We can offer you a bigger, wider world. We can show you what you cannot imagine. And once you see it, how could you walk away? You would love it. We believe it, we do.

We will keep you. We are determined. We have learned to reach for what we want. You taught us this.

You take matters into your own hands. You look for the girl. Maybe if you find her, you can get her to change our mind. Maybe it will work.

But when you do find a girl, in the World of Bird and Leaf, it is not the one you saw but *another* one. You see Laleh.

You are startled—you didn't expect this. But you overcome your surprise and grab her wrist.

Listen, you say. *There is still time. Tell it it can't. Tell it—*

But the chamber swallows her up, and you don't know if she's heard you.

You grow older. You change.

It is difficult to describe. Suppleness gives way to rigidity, but not only in your limbs. We have seen it before, on Esi: in the settlements you took us through, and then later in the luddite colony. As people grow older, the giving of adulthood disappears—or changes. Changes, perhaps. Their eyes become stonier, their opinions more defined with an edge of sharpness to them. They look at society and drift away from it. Sometimes peacefully, an old man who falls asleep at every gathering around the fire, snoring gently among cup clinks and conversation. Sometimes acerbically, a woman who states what she thinks with vitriol that goes beyond the moment, throwing her full conviction behind her words; you don't know why it means so much to her.

Your changes are different but the same. There is no society here, nothing to drift away from but yourself. You grow slower. You take your time. You notice the time cobwebs falling on your shoulders and you let them lie; they make you feel stronger. You know they will rot away soon.

Like all humans, you ossify. You become more and more certain you must die. Magali-ilk tries to talk you out of it, but you lose your temper. This is your way; this is how it should be. Our Wisa, the Wisa on Esi, delighted in changing her mind. Now you are different. Your conviction is a sifted conviction, a belief formed from years of living. It means something. It is dear to you, your hard-won wisdom. You will not give it up for anything.

Quir, you whisper.

You are lying on your yakuth as it sleeps. Below you, water spreads as far as the eye can see; somewhere in this chamber, there is your island of weaving crabs. We don't answer. Your dying has felt agonizing; even though we know what is coming, what we will do, this is still painful to live through.

Quir, you say and you smile. Your face crinkles; you are eaten in a map of wrinkles; your hair is snow white, like your yakuth's. You are so frail. We fear the next gust of wind will break you, the next door swallow you whole. Our Wisa.

Quir, you insist and so Magali-ilk shakes out her sandy hair and transforms, spirit-like, into a black bat. She crawls onto your palm, looks at you carefully. We are listening.

I'm sorry, you say softly. *I know this is hard. I am leaving and you are not, so I have the easier task of the two. But don't be sad, my darling. We never truly leave the ones we love. Grandpa is here always. Magali is here. I carry them with me. When I go, you will have these worlds; you will have our pieces of time. It will be enough. It becomes enough. And if you grow sad and you cannot find me, quieten your chambers. Find some beautiful music. Dance. Dance like you mean it, Quir; dance like there isn't enough wonder in all the black sea to capture the delight in your heart. And you'll see, darling—you'll see I'm always with you.*

Gently, you stroke the little bat's head.

Darling, you can go on without me, you whisper. *Let me die.*

You die.

Your yakuth wraps your body in its fur and carries you through worlds. It flies where we tell it to go. We take you to the chamber we modeled after your home. When you are reborn, we want it to be in a place that is as close to Esi as possible.

You will ask us: how did you think of it? You haven't asked as yet, but you will. We know you. So we will tell you now.

You gave us the idea.

You were sitting at the top of a mountain; you were telling a cluster of yakuths the story of yourself. They were enthralled. The little ones pushed closer to you, drinking in your words. You were delighted by the attention. You had reached the part of your story where we are born. Where you ask us to become a nightdome and we take your breath away.

(We love this part.)

But that day you wandered from the script. You said: *I didn't expect Quir to become this. A whale of such magnificence was beyond my imagination. I don't know how it happened; perhaps it was because of the stone egg.*

We remember that egg. Ice pink and curdled white, blood red seams. Smooth to the touch. It tasted striated when we ate it, full of texture and depth. There are others like it on Esi, relics of a time you cannot remember but that we glimpse occasionally. Alchemists and boiling metals. Fabrics, pale and gossamer.

Magali had a stone egg like it, you said. Your voice was wistful; you were no longer thinking about the story. *I loved it from the first moment she showed it to me. It reminded me of Quir, of the black sea swirling in its eyes. I imagine if you nicked the stone and unspooled it, you could find yourself holding a universe.*

And this is it. One sentence: that is what we pluck. Universes compressed into stone eggs. Of you being bone and blood, and in that the seed of what makes you. The beginnings of another Wisa. That's all we need—a little bit of you to remake you.

So that is what we do. Your yakuth lays you down gently on a rock. Then it flies off to grow as large as the chamber, wrapping itself around the circumference, before melting into a river and falling asleep. We spin a new Wisa out of the bones of the last; we stitch you with the gossamer fabrics of time so that you will be ageless, so that we never have to watch you die. So that you never leave us.

But we have learned from your last life, from your loneliness. And so we make you two.

―

We watch you now. You run through our chambers with no trace of tiredness in your limbs, no thought of death. We watch as you pick new names: Laleh and Myung. Although you will always be Wisa to us, we are glad. New names give you freedom, a chance to become someone else.

You don't remember who you were before. This is not what we had intended but time works in ways beyond us. We are sad at first, but then we realize this is best. Many times you have told us you are a bird, made for the wind to slip off your wings. But you don't know yourself as well as you think, for you are, in fact, a tree and your roots are entangled in Esi. You longed to be part of a forest.

Now you are free of that burden. You can be anyone you want: knight, princess, witch, explorer.

But even as we watch you find yourself, become sisters, step through your first door, even as we delight, we know it won't last. For there will come a day when Myung will look at her reflection, and a new urge will be born.

Grandpa had a phrase in the colony: *The tree lives in the forest but the forest also lives in the tree.* No matter how many chambers you visit, you are still a tree. Your forest won't die. You never stop searching for your family.

And so now we watch you wandering through chambers with a renewed purpose. The air is cold between your two selves. We see you try and understand Wisa's presence in your life. Great Wisa, you call her. We ache. One of you, Laleh, will try and find a way to keep Myung in the whale. But Myung—we will lose her. We feel it, deep within us. She will go through chambers looking for more people. She will ask the many beasts of our belly: *Do you know Great Wisa?*

They don't know what to say. For you are Wisa, here and now, and they would like to know you.

The End of a Dream

On Ojda, I would play a game: I would stare directly into the painted sun. When I looked away, eyes smarting and little pinpricks of light bursting inside my eyelids, I found I could not stop staring at this sun. It was imprinted on my retina, a little oasis of mustard in the flowing darkness. I now carried it with me.

Certain pieces of knowledge are like that. They arrive and everything is imprinted by them. They are enormously large and yet impossibly small, catastrophic and not that important really. A fiery giant burning in space, and the little ball in the sky you can pinch between your finger and thumb. It colors everything.

The smoke blown from the yakuth's nostrils has disappeared. I can see the World of Bird and Leaf again. I lift my hand, as if seeing it properly for the first time. It is a smooth hand, the skin supple and strong. Made of tissue and cells, but also striations of fabric that catch the light. I am created of time. If I cut my palm now, the skin will heal. It is how Myung has healed in her adventures across the black sea. Very little can kill me.

Perhaps nothing can.

I am a child of a universe.

My mind travels to the past and I see it in a new light—how creatures knew me, why Myung felt made for me, the connection to the black sea and the Kilta family that brought the dreams. Somewhere in me is Wisa.

Memories that are Wisa's, and feelings too. A remembrance of what it is like to *be* Wisa. I am not all Wisa, of course: some parts of her were given to Myung, and we are both part Quir and the time cobwebs. But Wisa is there, in my body.

I can become her.

Great Wisa. Me. I step into the name easily. And the grandeur and the loneliness of it strikes me. There is no one else. It is just the whale and me.

Darling.

The whale's song is so soft I can barely hear it. It is hiding from me. It doesn't want to see what I think of it; it doesn't want to hear how I will leave. It protects itself. I reach for it and then stop. Not now. Not yet.

I wander back into Ojda.

As I focus on the dream, Ojda sharpens and expands to fill my vision. Now it is the World of Bird and Leaf that sits docile in the corner of my eye. My feet are on Ojda's harsh soil; I can feel the heat of its sun and the whispers of its memories. The cottage is in front of me, and I can hear Blajine and Myung inside. But I turn away, toward the river. There is someone else I must meet first.

Magali is sitting by the riverbank, staring at the water. Ojda's landscape is nothing like Esi's—it is arid, the colors darker and the shapes stranger—but for a moment it is as if I have wandered into the past again and I am staring at my sister on the riverbank in Esi. We are going to catch milows. I am going to teach her how to speak to the fish. Jinn is on his way.

Magali looks up as I approach, and the illusion fades; she is older than I ever knew her on Esi.

Not now, she says. *All of you cursed children, begone.*

The hardness in her eyes pains me. Where is my Magali? Where is my sister who could call the moon to her, who bore everything with a half-smile and lightness in her stride?

I said go away, child!

But I only sit next to her. I take her hands, because touch is important for this; she needs to feel me. I run my thumb across her veins and the frail bones of her wrist, and I tell her everything. The whole story, from the moment Quir closed its mouth. I leave nothing out. Not the fear, or the madness, or the desperation to die. Not the joy her presence gave me for two years. Not the peace I felt in the end. I made a life for myself; I learned how.

And when I am finished, I smile. It is Laleh's smile but underneath it, there is the memory of how Wisa looked before the madness, when I first came to the colony.

Magali is pulling her hands away.

No, she says bitterly. *No.*

I can see her incredulity, watch her thoughts play out. Laleh has Wisa's features, yes, maybe her nose, but she has none of . . . what *makes* Wisa. There's no spark, no crackling energy that electrifies you when you are in her presence, no off-key statement that is frowned upon and yet makes you smile because you can taste the freedom she conjures up. This is not the reunion Magali expected. This is Wisa? Her sister? Immortal, ageless?

Not all Wisa, I say. *Some parts of hers are Myung's. And I remember briefly, in snatches, and then the memory fades. But she is here. I am here.*

You're not the right person, Magali says. Her bitterness spreads. She draws herself up to full height.

But I am the right person, just not the same person. It is what happens when you wait for someone to come back to you or you make a map to go somewhere you once loved: they change. Nothing is ever as you left it.

Magali, I whisper, touching her cheek.

She says: *I won't listen to any more of these lies.*

She disappears. I want to follow her, but I know it won't help. I ache for her. Centuries of waiting and Magali cannot greet me because it is not as she imagined it. Centuries of holding on to a ghost of herself, only to learn it was never going to be like it once was.

Maybe if I find Jinn . . . Part of him knows already. He sensed it when I spoke to him on Ojda. *Wisa used to say things like this,* he had said. He knew before all of us. Jinn will understand.

But there is no time. This dream is ending. It is as if Magali needed to be told my story for the circle to close, for a map of a sprawling collective forest to be complete, and now that it is done, I am waking up.

There is one last place I must go.

I travel to the cottage and enter it.

Myung is in bed, asleep. Blajine is sitting next to her, thumbing through the pages of *Fairy Tales of Wisa*. She looks up when I step over the threshold; she stares at me solemnly.

You are Laleh, she says.

Laleh. I chose the name for its cadence; I chose it because I loved the way Myung said it. Now it means as much to hear Blajine say it. No one has spoken it for so long. My name settles on me and I feel strong. I was about to say, *Laleh and Wisa*, but now I don't. I am a bird, the wind slipping off my wings. I can wear a new name. Laleh is true. Laleh is enough.

I climb onto the bed and sit by their feet. There is so much to say but no time. The dream is fading. The World of Bird and Leaf is expanding slowly from the corner of my eye. This cottage is growing hazier.

Take care of her, I say. *Please.*

Blajine nods. *Will you come again?* she asks but I don't have the answer to that.

Myung's eyes are fluttering open. *Who are you talking to?* she murmurs sleepily. *There is no one there.*

She loves you, Blajine says to me. *You know that, don't you? She left but she's been trying to come back. She's been trying for decades.*

I rest my hand on Myung's foot. My wonderful sister—princess, witch, knight. *I know.*

Myung sits up. *Is she here?* she asks. *Is Laleh here?*

Blajine nods.

Myung cries out. She throws herself at the end of the bed, but she lands too far to the left of me. Now she is looking up, into what she thinks is my face, but I am to her side and she is staring at nothing. Myung still cannot see me. I won't get my reunion.

The dream is splotching at the edges now. Myung and Blajine are fading. And I feel regret. It is small, but present. *Let me stay*, I whisper. *Let me be here for the mundane things: the cooking and the fights and the next time Ojda bursts into a flower forty feet tall.* But the dream is propelled by its own force; there is no stopping its dissolution. My regret lingers for only a moment. Then it washes away. I have spent lifetimes in this dream; it has been rich and it has been beautiful.

It has been enough.

. . . Tell me how to find you, Myung is saying. She is speaking fast, her words tripping over each other. *Tell me where you are and I'll come, please, Laleh. I am so sorry. Please . . .*

I stroke her foot. *Tell her I forgive her*, I say to Blajine. *She needs to know that. Tell her . . .*

I don't know if Blajine hears the rest of my sentence. The dream is almost gone; I am staring at its echo. The feeling is still diamond hard in my fingers, but the vision is mist. In the World of Bird and Leaf, Wisa's great yakuth, my yakuth, has shrunk to the size I first created it, and it is curling its body around me. It looks at me questioningly. At the edge of waking, I smile at it. Myung and Blajine are only wisps now. Myung reaches for me, and I can hear Blajine—good, dear Blajine—say in a voice that is distorted and tipping on the edge of babel:

It's okay. I can see her and she says to tell you that it is okay. She understands. You weren't meant for only one story.

―

Then the dream is gone.

I wake up. I bury my face in my yakuth's fur. The whale is quiet. I can hear the faintest trace of its song, but it is holding back. It is locked in the pain of losing me.

Darling, I say.

I run my fingers through my yakuth's fur as it swirls around me. There is a beat pulsing in my blood; music I once knew and loved. Know. And love. I see Magali-ilk from the corner of my eye, but I shake my head. I don't need her anymore. She disappears.

I wriggle my toe. I lift my heel. I tap my foot on the forest floor. The whale glances at me; I can feel its attention. I tap my foot lightly at first, and then harder. I listen to the sound I make; I am tapping in rhythm. The whale peers closer. Slowly, cautiously, unable to believe what it is seeing, it crawls out of its hiding place. A simurgh flies down to watch me. Another joins it.

Darling, I say, throwing my voice out, *you know this song*.

And my whale, my Quir—it does. Its song changes. It sings louder. Strains of music begin to drift to me. Drums first, in time with my tapping, deepening in complexity. Then trumpets. Then the clarinet. I feel joy rise up in me, my shoulders moving. Despite myself, despite it all, I am laughing.

Quir, I say. *Let's dance.*

EPILOGUE

Myung's Map

A keeper. Dressed in seafaring robes worn down by a mad island, plant fiber and stardust encrusted in the seams. She strides across a multicolored landscape, draped in and out of shadows from the stone blocks that float above her.

How many years has it been since Myung arrived on Ojda? A hundred years—five hundred in black sea time. Some of these were spent with Blajine. You couldn't say all of those years were peaceful, but they were happy. When Blajine died, Myung buried her in the song bowl and Ojda grew a scowling statue in her honor. The ghosts of the Kiltas gathered around and sang. Then they cried, including the just-born ghost of Blajine, who bawled the loudest because she liked the theatrics. Then she drifted off to find Dastur Uncle and ask him if the story of that palm tree island is true.

(It is. He has the scars to prove it.)

Myung doesn't leave. She wanders around Ojda, aimless. She keeps the museum singing; she tells Blajine this is because she is a Kilta and she is proud of the name. She puffs out her chest when she says it. But everyone knows it is because she hopes Laleh will hear the song and find her way back to her.

Myung spends her time talking to the family ghosts, learning about the forest she didn't know she belonged to. When she laughs with

Rostum Uncle or sings with Ayesha Aunty or tries to make sense of the elaborate stories Jinn tells her—he's very fond of climbing and expects her to be too—she is overcome with guilt. Somewhere in the black sea, a girl is wandering alone in a many-chambered whale. Maybe she has a simurgh for company, maybe a yakuth. Maybe she's never left the last chamber Myung saw her in because she couldn't bring herself to walk through the door. Each time Laleh will pass a burnished surface or look up at the gleaming bodies of the pearlfish, she'll see only herself.

One night, Myung dreams of an old woman she does not know. The woman is as gnarled as an ancient tree; she is wearing a rainbow-colored coat. She whacks Myung on the shoulder with a stick.

What are you loitering here for? she shouts. *What you want is out there—go get it!*

Myung's shoulder hurts for days afterward. But the whack jolts her and an old friend squeezes out from where it had been hiding. Myung can hear it scurrying about. A spirit that has been sleeping for a long time is now finally waking up.

Myung hunts out her *Myung's Diaries* and rereads them. The kilam birds. The alchemists who made time. The changing maps of Esi. She walks through the museum of collective memory and studies the academic articles she read to come here. She hunts for clues. She pulls out her map to Ojda, made from sea stories and rumors, a place they say couldn't be found. She thinks about mirabilia diachronism; she rereads *Fairy Tales of Wisa*. She lingers on the foreword. Now when she wanders across Ojda, she talks to herself. She begins a new diary, No. CMXLII (unpublished, of course), and transcribes her journey here, opening with the whale of babel and including the tale of the mad sisters. The Kiltas don't disturb her; they know what the beginning of an idea looks like.

When Myung climbs to the highest point of Ojda and sings, she can hear the faintest—faintest—trace of someone singing back.

And so she trudges to the sea of changing mists and unearths a quill. She tugs and spools reams of paper. Tottering under the weight, she walks to the cottage—no more than a hundred steps away for any Kilta and Myung is a Kilta now—and begins her latest quest.

It is a map. It is not a map like the museum of collective memory, nor is it a map of stories like *Fairy Tales of Wisa*. We couldn't describe what kind of map it is; we don't have the language for it. It is a map of surrendering, of things outside yourself, of following impulses you cannot understand and cleaving—open, open—to the whole black sea, no matter what wonder or pain or love it brings. It is a map with madness as its wind rose and it is Myung's way home.

Blajine watches her work with swelling pride. She's chuffed. *I told her how to make that*, she tells no one. *I said: sister is a special word; it's a careful relationship. You have to be mad to love like that.*

Acknowledgments

All my thanks to:

Alap Parikh, beloved partner in art, love and life. Thank you for being my home.

Shirin Mehta, mother and dear friend, who read this book many (many) times with such empathy, and whose intelligence and love helped it become its best self.

Charley Miles, soul sister, for many things, but specifically for pulling me out of more abysses than I can count.

Helen Marshall, for her incredible heart and support, but mostly for showing me what art can become.

Samit Basu, for his guidance, friendship and sheer clarity of perspective, straight to the heart of this profession.

Cameron McClure, for being the best champion you could ask for. Thank you for approaching the art and the business with such wisdom, kindness and grace, and for guiding this book to its best home.

Navah Wolfe and the entire DAW Books family, for embracing this unhinged novel exactly as is. *Mad Sisters* and I are lucky to have you.

The HarperCollins India team, who threw their weight behind this ridiculous novel and ushered it through every hoop so that it could soar:

Poulomi Chatterjee, Swati Daftuar, Kartik Chauhan, Sohela Singh, Tanima Saha, Ramnika Sehrawat.

Upamanyu Bhattacharyya, for this gorgeous, award-winning cover illustration.

Lavanya Lakshminarayan, Nikita Deshpande, and Prayaag Akbar for lending this novel their time and their incredible minds.

My early readers, Lucy Elizabeth Foster, Vince Haig, Gautam Bhatia and others already mentioned, for their invaluable advice and encouragement. Thank you also to Rahul Soni, for his gentle kindness, care and telling me not to give up when this book was on draft three.

The Sangam House family, particularly Arshia Sattar, for offering me safe harbour twice in the storm of life. Thank you also to Giles Hazelgrove, whose generous note at the end of a rejection email fuelled me for many months, and to my 2021 residency family (Akhil Katyal, Priya Sarukkai Chabria and Sita Reddy) for listening to a piece of this novel with such kindness.

Dad, Tanya and Tushad, for their constant, cosmic love and their belief.

EPHEMERA

The Creation of Ojda

Parts 1 to 3

Once upon a time, there lived a woman on a small island in the black sea. This woman was full of stories. They swam between her ears like a million tadpoles, wriggling down her nose in their attempts to escape. So each night she would build a big fire on the beach and place her children around it. She would tell them stories. And the stories would fall from her lips, warmed by the fire, to transform into creatures: pelicans, dragonflies, pomfrets. And in these shapes they would wander off, now free.

But the stories would not stop. The more she told, the more were born in her head until it felt like she was a shell carrying the roar of the ocean. Her lips began to ache. Her voice began to fade. The stories grew violent. They fought for her attention, to be spoken so that they might grow wings or fins or spindly legs and travel the black sea. But she could not speak them all.

So she went to her husband, who massaged her scalp and made soothing noises. One by one, he gave her all the herbal remedies he knew, including the crushed shell of the Milky Way crab. Nothing helped. So he listened to her stories, sitting by her feet as the room filled with creatures, bringing her water when her throat was parched and food when her stomach rumbled. For six days, she spoke, and for six days, he listened. Then on the morning of the seventh day, he said:

"Wife, I do not think these are stories. Why, I recognize that whale swimming above our island, its underbelly covered with a scar, and I am certain I have seen that woodpecker at our window. I think these are memories."

The woman was puzzled. Why would the universe's memories come to her? Why did they need to grow wings or fins or spindly legs? Her husband swore to find out. He made a canoe out of smooth beach wood and kissed his children's foreheads. "Take care of your mother," he said. "Love the story animals, even if they frighten you. Fish well."

And with that, he set out. He steered his boat to the heart of a dying star, which everyone knew was the prophet of the black sea. We cannot say it was an easy journey. His canoe was strong and his heart true, but these alone do not ensure a successful voyage. Cosmic waves tried to swallow him, monsters sought a bite of his hard flesh and rogue comets plunged down to sink him. But each time he proved too small for the black sea, the stories would find him. Shoals of silver fish, flocks of pelicans, an angry otter—all animals birthed on his ordinary island—swam with him, saving him from the cold sleep. And so he learned awe for his wife's gift; he grew to love these creatures.

When at last he arrived on the shores of the dying star, alas! He was struck dumb. The star was so majestic, his voice grew fearful of making an appearance; it leaped out of his throat and hid. In vain, he searched and searched. He began to despair.

Then the sea shook. Above him, a dark shape moved among nebulas. He shielded his eyes and squinted, then clapped his hands over his ears. A high-pitched and mournful cry filled the air. It was the whale with a scar on its belly. It did nothing, only swam past, but its cries reminded him of an ancient and lonely creature. Of his wife, growing softly mad.

And so he searched harder, scouring the bottom of the boat until, at last, he found his voice and spoke.

The star answered his prayers. It promised that the stories would no longer fight to come alive in his wife's words. But in return for this gift, he, his wife and all their children to come must promise to love the stories. Treat them as their own. The fisherman wept with gratitude. He promised.

When he reached his island, he found his children waiting by the shore. They ran to his boat; they spoke before he could. Their mother was unwell. She no longer tossed and turned, murmuring stories in her sleep. Now she vomited crystals.

And when the husband looked again at his tiny island, he found it altered. The sand was brighter, the trees paler. Everything was covered in tiny, tiny crystals made of a single sharp and unmistakable color—bone white.

Swiftly, thinking quickly, the fisherman made a plan. He gathered as many crystals as he could in his fishing net and flung it out to sea. His children ran forward to help him, pulling old nets from storage and, one by one, they flung them out to sea.

For years, they did this. The woman and her family collected crystals in fishing nets and hauled them out to sea. There, they released them, watching the strange constellations they made as they drifted away. These were their years: gather, haul, unloose. Crystals piled up on palm trees. They made the beach longer and the shore shallower. They congregated in boats, turned up in the salt, drifted down into hair. Gather. Haul. Unloose.

It was years before the island became recognizable again, and a few more months after for the crystals to disappear completely. Now empty of stories, the woman sat by the beach and watched the waves. She wondered about the birds and animals that fell from her lips. She grieved.

It was a sudden grief—swift and crippling. It seeped into her bones and creaked among her joints. It beat in the same rhythm as her pulse. But it was not only her grief. Her husband would sit for days in the boat, unable to cast his net. When he did, he cut loose any fish entangled in it. The children ate what they could forage; they kept themselves alive. Their parents were lost.

One night, the woman said softly, "Husband, we are cursed."

Her husband wept, for he knew it to be true. *Love the stories*, the star had asked them. But they had sent them away, let them loose into the blackness of the sea, hoped for a life without the memories of what came before. And now they were being haunted. He confessed all to his wife, who listened in the quiet of candlelight. "I meant no harm," he whispered. "I only wanted you to be free." But the woman knew that no freedom could be found by breaking the promise. The stories had chosen her; she must honor that choice. She patted her husband's hand kindly. She knew what to do.

At first light, the woman bundled her children and their belongings into the largest boat they owned. Her husband strapped supplies to the back of the boat and climbed into the helm. Together, they set off to find the crystals.

Who knows for how long they traveled? We only know the end of the story, the day the daughter rubbed her eyes and said, *look, Mama*. And her mother saw it. In the distance, a bone-white island glittering with the glamour of cold stars, waiting for its keepers to come find it. When the women stepped onto land, her grief lifted and her husband once again knew himself. The children laughed and ran about until their mother called to them. They pulled out flowers and fruit from the boat and crushed them into colored pastes. Together, the family painted the bone-white island the many shades of a paradise.

Never again would a Kilta leave the shores of this island. They were home.

Part 4

At night, while her family slept, the woman crept onto Ojda's beach. She had a secret; she knew why the universe's memories had chosen her. She spoke this knowledge into a single nugget of gold and buried it, saying nothing to her family. This memory was meant for only one person, a sister she had lost long ago. And thus, this nugget remains, waiting for the sister to claim it.

The Tola Dictionary of the Inexplicable

15th Edition, Tola Publishers, 87459. Retrieved from the Museum of Collective Memory, Corridor ---•|, Object XXID

Double Sight

The standard definition of *double sight* says it is "the ability to see your family in visions or as ghosts" but this isn't quite correct. It is more individual than that, more real. The easiest way to explain it is by example.

Say there are two sisters, separated by many islands, named Squid and Ray. Ray has double sight. She may be walking across the beach one day, when she looks up and sees her sister, Squid. Her sister is here, in front of her; they can talk, speak, walk. Squid is *present*. Then Ray bends to pick up a shell, looks around and finds her sister has disappeared again—just like that.

But the beauty of double sight is that Squid wasn't a ghost or a vision. She was really present. She was there in body, and she cannot remember what she was doing on her own island during her time with her sister. None of her friends can remember seeing her. It is as if she disappeared and reappeared *beside* her sister, like she slipped through a loophole in time. And yet, if a fisherwoman were to approach Squid and Ray as they walked along the beach, she would see only Ray; Squid would be invisible to her.

No one knows what gives a person double sight—it feels like tricks of sight, a weird blurring between reality and unreality. It is notoriously difficult to prove you have it, because the person with the double sight is never the one traveling; they're always the destination. It tends to foster disbelief. Would you believe someone who said they could see their great-great-grandmother, that, in fact, their great-great-grandmother was standing *right* next to them and talking to them, but that this great-great-grandmother was obviously invisible to you? You would think they were mad.

And yet double sight exists. Relatives remember activities they did with their gifted family members, and there are accounts of people seeing into the future or the past because of these tangled webs of relations.

This phenomenon has only ever been recorded in the natives of Esi.

The Tola Dictionary of the Inexplicable

15th Edition, Tola Publishers, 87459. Retrieved from the Museum of Collective Memory, Corridor---•|, Object XXID

Dreams of the Caspian Squids

The Caspian Ocean is a small patch of black sea just off the island of Limqart. It is home to a civilization of cosmic squids, all of them asleep. They spread out among asteroids, stars glinting behind them, their tentacles linked. They undulate in a gentle, unseen current. As they dream, they change color, depending on what they're dreaming about.

A philosopher of the Caspian Ocean spends her time watching these colors. She thinks. The wisdom of a Caspian philosopher is greatly prized. Some of the universe's biggest questions have been answered while staring at these hypnotic colors, while tracing the varied and complex hopes of a squid civilization.

Famous philosophers: Syla Munsir, Roku, Nadia Jole, Bipin Fore

New Ways of Seeing: Tracing the Shift in Academia Through Nine Mysteries

Hutta, Ero, Tola Publishers, 88615. Retrieved from the Museum of Collective Memory, Corridor •-•- | \ / •, Object XII

Chapter 3. The Tola Fable

At some point in academic history, we began to walk away from the idea that logic was the ruling principle of our universe. Too much was inexplicable. For a long time, we believed we could find a theory to link it all—including contradictions and anomalies—but we soon came to the realization that the problem wasn't the universe. It was us. Our minds were too small and our logic too riddled with bias. "Black sea" we called our universe and yet we still believed we could chart its depths. But time and time again, we ran up against the limits of our tools. Records and books do not hold the whole of human history. Ask the bird chroniclers on the island of Kilam. We cannot understand "the other" by trying to view it through the lens we made.

And so we surrendered, embraced "I don't know." And once we began plumbing the depth of the Vortex of Noma, we realized the universe was telling us things all the time. We just weren't listening.

So we revised how we did things. We looked at sea stories, myths and dreams. We discovered that people have been dreaming about the festival of madness for centuries now.

In Osca, a woman fell asleep on the beach and woke up to an elaborate mural drawn in the sand: three people on a whalebone hill, summoning interstellar clouds. She had no memory of drawing it. Old archivers of the Library of Leonin say their manuscripts whisper of the Esite festival of madness. In Uta, a girl found a twelfth-century-old parchment in the belly of a blue-green fish, outlining seventy-six miracles witnessed during Esi's festival of madness. It is not clear what these miracles are. They read as gibberish.

But the most beautiful dream is the Tola fable.

If you have access to Gazim's poetry, I recommend you read this fable in his words. I don't have the talent to reproduce his splendor, but here is a factual and somewhat academically dry account of what happened:

A child in Tola inhaled a batch of pallé pollen and fell into a deep sleep. She slept for seven days. When she awoke, she could only describe what she saw in the grammar and imagery of a fable. She dreamed she was walking on a land with crimson sand and whalebone hills. Palm trees bent double in the wind and silver vines entwined to form shelters. And everywhere on this island were animals: swans, mongooses, iguanas, purple-bellied birds and river snakes, scurrying and whispering to each other in a language the girl did not understand. They did not look at her, only whispered, whispered, whispered in a wave so deafening that the girl was surprised it could be made by such small creatures.

But it was not just the animals. It was the trees. They murmured between themselves by passing words along leaves and along growing roots—roots that didn't stop at the edge of the island but grew out into the water and down to the seabed, so that the fish, eels and sharks swam frantically and spewed bubbles of the trees' words.

And the girl found herself on a beach, clear of trees and clear of animals—except one. In front of her was an enormous whale, almost the length of the island, blinking in the sand. It was crying. Then, with a deep moan that shook the island, the whale bumped on the shore to launch itself into the sky, where it swam away.

Academics have dedicated their careers to studying the Tola fable. It is widely accepted that the child dreamed of Esi; the topographical features match. The animals are likely representations of Esites, which is in line with how a fable works. I have read academic papers that have tried to locate the time of the fable—what time period was the child dreaming of? No one has any clear answers, but Kuli Myna comes close in her paper "Shadows and Light in the Tola Fable." She argues that, based on descriptions in the dream, the island was probably experiencing a dispersion of heavy cloud cover and the subsiding of lightning. This would mean the child dreamed of the end of the festival of madness.

Could the whale be the one creature we have not been able to find: the whale of babel?

The Tail of Tales: Deciphering Time in the Whale of Babel

Daqui, Ima, first published in the *Journal of Enduring Mysteries*, Vol. 209, Issue 2. Retrieved from the Museum of Collective Memory, Corridor |••| | /, Object CMXCIX.

To understand time in the whale of babel, we must slip into a child's mind. My nephew turned three years old last month, which is when he discovered a secret word: *why*. It is a miracle word. It requires minimal effort (from him) for maximum results (from me). He says one syllable, and I talk for hours, searching the limits of my knowledge so that I may answer his tiny question. When I am done, he simply asks "why?" again, and we begin the process anew.

This paper is thanks to an evening spent babysitting for my sister, a faded copy of *Fairy Tales of Wisa*, and my nephew's endless *whys*.

Time in the whale of babel is unpredictable, as evidenced by multiple accounts of children returning from the Vortex of Noma and by the *Fairy Tales* themselves. In *Chosen Fabrics: Imagining the Whale of Babel*, Mina Zoya posits that because time exists as a fabric in the whale, it operates independently from space, splitting what we know as spacetime. "The rules of such a cosmos cannot be imagined by us," she writes, "because our imaginations have been shaped by an alternate reality. In a place where you can touch time, linearity would mean nothing. Perhaps time itself would mean nothing."

Yet time *does* mean something in the whale: it has a presence and acts as a shaping force. It merely takes on different forms according to its frame of reference. Puzzling out these forms is a challenge. But if we look closely, patterns emerge.

The first pattern is what I call fabric time, or objective time. This is the time you witness if you consider the whale from a distance, as a fixed, self-contained cosmos. In this type of time, past, present, and future are happening simultaneously. Time does not "become"—it already is.

The strongest evidence for this is "Wisa and the Mirror's Mirror," a fairy tale in which she chases an unknown entity across chambers, only to discover the entity is herself. It is not specified whether this new Wisa is from the past or the future; she is simply described as "coming from another time." Some scholars have argued that this Wisa is from an alternate dimension, and that time in the whale doesn't move along a fixed, sliding scale (i.e. backwards and forwards, into the past or future) but in all directions (i.e. into multiple dimensions). Yet this Wisa is not a stranger; she is not shaped differently from the old Wisa, and the story implies she is Wisa herself rather than a clone or an aberration. Wisa seems to recognize her and they chat as if speaking to reflections ("'How I have longed for a mirror,' Wisa says, 'and to see myself clearly.'"). The new Wisa *is* the old Wisa, just from another point in her life, and the story calls it "another time" because it makes no distinction between past, present and future. It's all just Time.

My nephew remains unconvinced by this. According to him, "If big Wisa and little Wisa are in the whale, together, why don't they see each other always?" The simple answer is the size of the whale is so vast, these run-ins are rare, if not impossible. Remember that chambers are the size of solar systems, occasionally a galaxy; a hundred, two hundred, even thousand Wisas could be in the same chamber and never notice.

But if time in the whale of babel simply "is," how is it that the whale creates new chambers? In "Wisa and the Laws of the Chambers," it is said that "New chambers appear all the time, for the bounty of the whale is infinite." If past, present and future are happening at once, how is this possible? Surely a cosmos where the future already exists would be static? Yet we know that new chambers do form, for Wisa visits a chamber that is still forming; we get to watch it curdle into existence. So the future *exists*, but it is *also* becoming. It is simultaneously present *and* not there.

How?

We can hazard a guess. Imagine fabric time as a circle. Within this circle, all the events of the past, present and future play out. Let's call this circle Q. Our mistake is imagining Q as a flat area, such as a stage or a floor. Instead, think of it as honey; thick, viscous, holding all events in a three-dimensional space, some small and hidden, others large and obvious. As the whale expands, these miniscule, hidden events grow larger and become more apparent.

We have precedents for this in our own universe. A female fetus in the womb is already born with the oocytes she will carry in her lifetime, which means the egg that made you was incubated and created in your grandmother's womb. You existed, even if you were not apparent. Or think of Russian dolls, the smallest doll nestled deep in the belly of the largest, hidden but present. It is the same in the whale of babel. The future is real and tangible within the sphere of Q: it has happened and is happening and will happen; it only grows in apparentness as the whale expands.

We rarely encounter these twists of time in *Fairy Tales of Wisa* because Wisa is like us: she processes time linearly. She references the past, and believes in cause and effect, as well as beginning and endings. As she says in "Wisa and the Whale's Tail":

> 'I am weeping, for without the whale's tail, I shan't know how this tale will end.'
>
> 'Must it end?' asks the djinn. 'Can it not remain?'
>
> 'It must,' says Wisa firmly, 'For I am not made for one story, and neither are you.'

This is the second pattern of time in the whale, what I call Wisa time or relative time.

Which leaves us with the whale itself. As the theater in which these different types of time perform, surely the whale experiences fabric time? And if it does, does that make it omniscient? Yes and no. It is true that the whale experiences fabric time, and can see into the past, present and future. Yet, *where* the whale decides to look determines what it notices—and what it misses. In "Wisa and the Witch Doctor," for example, we see Wisa communicating with the whale for the first time through song and dance, where it becomes apparent the whale has no idea about the calamities befalling the chamber. It was simply not paying attention.

To answer my nephew's "But why?" it's because there is too much information in the whale and in the fabrics for it to process at one time. It is the same with our brains and our environments: there are a billion events happening around us but, to effectively process them, our consciousness must pick what to focus on. Being omniscient is not all it's cracked up to be.

New Ways of Seeing: Tracing the Shift in Academia Through Nine Mysteries

Hutta, Ero, Tola Publishers, 88615. Retrieved from the Museum of Collective Memory, Corridor •-•-| \ / •, Object XII.

Chapter 4. The Kibr Nightmare

If you've lived for more than a decade in the black sea, then you will be familiar with the widely circulated mystery of the Tola Fable. Yet few know that the fable has a counterpart, a dark reflection buried carefully by centuries of academia: the Kibr Nightmare.

When researchers travelled to Tola to interview the child who dreamed the fable, they discovered she had an elder brother who spoke of a vision of his own. This vision was not induced by pallé pollen but was brought upon by a sleep "deeper than death." The nightmare described events that were more grounded than the Tola Fable, and more gruesome. Scholar Vita Jaal, who has published the only complete record of the nightmare, described it as "visceral and undeniable, wholly absorbing in its recollection."

Why, then, did academia try to bury it? And what has led to its resurgence today?

To understand the academic shunning of the Kibr Nightmare, we must look at it in detail. The nightmare is remarkable for its realistic imagery. It doesn't cloak itself in metaphors or fairytale-like imaginings; the brother, Kibr, speaks as if he were truly there. Below is an extract from Jaal's comprehensive retelling:

Kibr spoke of an island with crafts he cannot explain. Houses blooming and dying. Skin that knit itself together when cut open. Birds made of leather and wood. Towering stone structures that pierced the sky, eternal; gold dripping from every hand like common metal. He described a mountain range made of bone, its many channels crammed with manuscripts. Men and women with overflowing hair, crouched over pans in their stone structures, whispering as they bubble concoctions, petrified animals rotating above them. And this—a dais, in the center of their tallest tower. On it, a single floating hair. No, not a hair. A strand: gossamer and shimmering. Hypnotic.

Time didn't work straight in his nightmare, he said. Everything moved up, down, sideways; he could not always follow, he could not keep up. Scenes changed, bursting from each other like creatures crawling from the belly of the last. Two strands, three, growing from the bark of a tree, covering a patch like a spiderweb. A woman, distraught, babbling in the bazaar as a crowd gathered around her: *I only stopped for a rest, put my hand on the tree to catch my breath and I felt it, cold and shivery, and then I lost my time, lost it and couldn't find it. I've been wandering for centuries,* she was weeping, hysterical, *wandering and begging, and we've brought it onto ourselves, we've done this, and we cannot escape it.* There was dread, building like a steady drumbeat to the nightmare. (Kibr hit his chest. *Thump. Thump. Thump.*) Alchemists shook their heads in disbelief, but now a tree was shaking too, shaking the mud off its roots as it pulled it free to take one step forward, then another, its branches writhing. Forests began to move. Rivers rose up and plucked people into their embrace, holding fast until their lungs filled with water. *Halt it*, the people commanded the alchemists, and they returned to their stone structures and their pans, but time was now knocking on their minds, pieces of lives they didn't know rattling around like pebbles, distracting them, gnawing at them. They fumbled with their instruments, dropped their vessels, *don't panic*, they said as their own eyes grew wide and horrified, like an animal's when it sees the sacrificial knife. Birds began eating their young. People pressed blades against their necks, thighs, stomachs, anything soft that would split open and free the selves writhing under their skin. Bodies acted without permission, flinging themselves off buildings, bashing skulls against rocks, strangling loved ones, crawling to the bottom of a lake. The most powerful alchemists, those already half mad and thus last to surrender to the chaos, tried to burn the strands but they could not be destroyed. So, they threw their magic against the stone structures instead, set fire to their mountain libraries, but the desire took them too in the end, the forest of time was too much, and now people were hacking at the trees, ripping apart animals and people, laughing as they scattered bones. Branches burst out of hearts, birds hatched out of hands, eyeballs pressed into soft clay mud as trees lay splintered in two. There was so much blood, Kibr said, so much—

And then he wept and wept, until we made him a sleeping draught so he could forget.

Jaal goes on to speculate that the vision may be speaking of Esi's festival of madness, much like the Tola Fable, but that this was an earlier festival, perhaps even the first. Most scholars, however, dismiss the retelling as fabricated, a story invented by a brother jealous of the attention his sister was getting. They cite three main reasons for their disbelief. First, the nightmare was not brought about by an external substance, such as pallé pollen, but simply occurred. Second, the length of the vision was not extraordinary. Kibr only slept for a night; his sister, on the other hand, slept for seven days. Third, the details seem simultaneously too real *and* too exaggerated. As Buyi points out, "It is unlikely that a boy would be able to describe the events of a vision that traumatized him with such poetic eloquence, not unless he'd spent many hours composing that vision—or was 'helped' by the imagination of the 'scholar' who was 'recording' him." (Jaal has refuted these accusations in a sixty-page paper that mainly focuses on Buyi's lack of personal hygiene.)

The shunning of the Kibr Nightmare offers an interesting insight on academic thinking at the time. We'd begun to accept that the universe was wider than we imagined, ordered on a logic we didn't understand, but we still had a firm notion of what that logic should *feel* like. It should be docile, otherworldly, *removed* in some way. The Vortex of Noma, *Fairy Tales of Wisa*, sea stories, fables—these were wrapped in a patina that connected us to the most mysterious of times, our childhood. It helped us empathize with their inexplicability. Speak of anything harsher, however, even if it was accessed through the medium of a dream, and we were keen to dismiss it as *too* true, *too* real: the workings of a mundane, adult mind. Indeed, Buyi points out that Kibr was nearing twenty years old at the time of the vision.

Yet evidence has now emerged that the Kibr nightmare may be true; an old seastory corroborates it. "Our Island of Gold and Blood" is a sailor's tale about a paradise filled with gold; any sailor that lands on its shores leaves with a fortune. Yet, one night, the island wakes up. Trees begin to hunt; animals melt out of the air to eat people; natives go mad, babbling about things the sailors cannot see, hacking at anyone in their path with knives, nails, teeth. Most of the sailors die, but a few manage to escape the island. They spread word of what had happened, warning others to stay away.

But of course people do not; the paradise is too tempting to resist. Ultimately, a survivor of the massacre returns to find the paradise restored and the natives at peace. They promise her that what she witnessed has been "leashed and buried under the soil, tamed to sleep." When she asks why it has not been killed, they tell her it cannot be killed but that she has their oath that when it emerges again, the island will be kept free of visitors. She leaves with her glittering fortune, her silence bought.[*]

---

[*] For a detailed comparison between the Kibr Nightmare and the seastory, see Paal Kunti, *Crimson Tides: What Horror Stories Tell Us About the Black Sea*.

The linking of the Kibr Nightmare to "Our Island of Gold and Blood" has been instrumental in unearthing and addressing academia's biases. Only now have we begun to investigate the significance of the Kibr Nightmare, and what it might tell us about the enduring mysteries of our cosmos. For if it does speak of Esi's first or early festival, it may offer us a clue to an element that has eluded us: the fabric of time.

Hocus-Pocus: Summoning the Black Sea's Forgotten Magic

Losa, Priya, Leonin Library Press, 891117. Retrieved from the Museum of Collective Memory, Corridor ---|•|/, Object III.

Esi's legacy of madness is not just whales or museums. It runs deeper and gentler. It is in us. Which one of us has not looked over our shoulder for instincts we cannot explain? Who has not sought things that cannot be grasped? Who has not lost their head, or thrown caution to the wind, or jumped off heights that could kill us? Scrubbed off versions of ourselves so we may be born anew, so we may be once again unfamiliar? We reach, over and over, for that which is outside of understanding. It is why we travel to the Vortex of Noma and peer into its depths. Why we read stories on the whale. Why we tap our tragus and wander the corridors of the museum of collective memory, searching for those parts of ourselves that are vast and invisible and yet always present. We have our own small version of madness, and we cradle it close. It is what makes life worth living.

About the Author

Tashan Mehta's *Mad Sisters of Esi* was published by HarperCollins India in 2023 and won the AutHer Awards for Best Novel, as well as the Subjective Chaos Kind of Award for Best Fantasy. Her debut novel, *The Liar's Weave*, was published in 2017 and shortlisted for the Prabha Khaitan Woman's Voice Award. Her short fiction has been anthologized in *Magical Women*, the *Gollancz Anthology of South Asian Science Fiction: Volume II* and *Solarpunk Creatures*. She was fellow at the 2015 and 2021 Sangam House International Writers' Residency, India, and writer-in-residence at Anglia Ruskin University, UK, and has mentored at numerous writing residencies. She resides in Goa.